i

Jace's Elusive Woman

Louise Furley

JACE'S ELUSIVE WOMAN

Louise Furley
Copyright 2021
All Rights Reserved

ISBN: 978-1-7378341-4-4 (Paperback)
ISBN: 978-1-7378341-3-7 (eBook)

Cover art by *Pixel Mischief Design*

Jace's Elusive Woman

Chapter One

*T*he mix of aging businesses strung along the coast of the northeast town near Chicago had seen better days. Other than sporadic whistles from barges floating in with the salty breeze wafting off the ocean a few blocks away, it was quiet in the streets of Cale's Harbor.

Finally starting to feel safe in her acquired identity, passing a paltry green grocer, she was almost to her car parked to the side of a boarded up bar.

As had become her habit of self-preservation, first glancing over her right shoulder then her left, the young woman tucked swirls of escaped tendrils back up under the cap, tugged the bill low over her brow and kept moving.

Almost to her car, she was just beyond the shoddy bar and in front of an alley when a disturbance down the far end of the alley caught her attention.

Her step halted and the slim fingers about to straighten the overlarge sunglasses hesitated.

Towards late afternoon, the buildings that flanked the alley blocked most of the sun making the corridor dankly dim. She pushed the sunglasses up over the cap and moved a few steps inside the alley.

The piercing contrast of the bright blue, cloudless sky made it difficult to see into the gloom. Adjusting her vision to the muted light, it took a few seconds before she could discern what the commotion was.

Down the alley, a group of men were embroiled in a vicious fight. Grunts and cries from the kicks and the punches thrown echoed off the abrasive brick walls and tumbled down the grubby asphalt.

She clapped her hand over her mouth to stifle her scream as five of the men ran off scattering through a back parking lot, two others started to take chase but stopped and returned to join two that stayed.

The four men stood looking down at a man lying prone on the blacktop, watching his life flow out in a scarlet pool around his head then stream slowly in small rivers over the rough tar to the wall.

Something on the ground in front of the woman caught her eye. It was a wallet. One of the bruisers must have dropped it. Reflexively, she bent and picked it up.

At that moment one of the men noticed her. The man yelled down the alley at her, "Hey!"

Her head jerked up at the shout. Clutching the wallet, she shot out of the alley and ran to her car. Her sunglasses flew off when she wrenched the door open and slid in behind the wheel.

Her heart slamming in her chest, she frantically tried to stick the key in the ignition but her hands were shaking so badly she dropped the keys on the floor.

Keeping her bobbing eyes peeled over the dashboard at the alley, she felt all over the floor desperately trying to find the keys.

"Oh my God!" the words ripped out of her- the men were charging through the dumpster riddled darkness straight at her. Scooping up the keys she fumbled them into the ignition, turned it on and threw it in gear.

The men were only feet from her when she jammed her foot on the gas pedal and tore off.

Glancing in her rear view mirror, panic drummed through her veins seeing the four men rush over and pile in a car parked only a few yards from where she'd been.

Boots pounding down the asphalt, the men scrambled into the black car with the numbers 442 in gold along with two parallel gold stripes painted down both sides.

The four men as big and powerful as professional wrestlers squeezed into the car, so thick with muscles they sat almost shoulder to shoulder.

The driver slammed the keys in the ignition, switched it on and the car hauled ass down the street after the old green car the woman was fleeing in. He said with cold patience, "Keep her in your sights, boys."

The young man riding shotgun said cheerfully, "She turned right at the stop sign, Jace. She's driving an old piece of shit, shouldn't be any problem catching her."

From the backseat, a man observed, "Looks like a 2010 or 11 Ford Tempo."

The 442 roared down the street in pursuit of the green Tempo.

"You idiot, Donnie," one of the men in the backseat said without rancor, "how the hell did you drop your wallet?"

In the front passenger seat, Donnie Bowie pushed his shaggy mane out of his face with long nubby knuckled fingers. A sheepish grin on his lightly tanned face.

Brushing the back of his hand across his upturned nose, Donnie crossed one lanky leg over the other resting his ankle on his knee. "Geez, Caddell," he half turned to look at the huge dark-skinned man in the back seat that was rubbing broad fingertips over his shaved head. "We were in a fucking fight for shit's sake. How the fuck do I know?"

His brown eyes flit to the driver. "Sorry, Jace. I didn't notice it fall out." When the four men had observed the woman pick up the wallet they all checked their pockets. Cursing with his hand on his empty back pocket, Donnie admitted it must be his.

Intent on following the green car, the driver, Jace Nico, didn't respond. The green car made another turn; Jace gassed it and maneuvered around several cars to get right behind the green one.

Stomping harder on the pedal, he tried to pull up alongside the Tempo when it suddenly turned right and he shot right past.

"Fucking A!" Donnie yelped throwing his hands out to hold onto something as Jace wrenched the steering wheel causing the car to skid in a circle. Holding the wheel tight, he spun the 442 fishtailing down the road after the girl.

"There, she's hitting that side street, Jace." The other man in the backseat pointed his hand through to the front seat.

"Got it, Victor." Just touching the brakes slightly, Jace yanked the wheel and skidded around the corner. "Where is she?" he asked when he could no longer see the green car.

With his hand braced on the dashboard, Donnie searched out the window, said, "Don't see her, bro."

A smirk in his voice, Caddell asked, "Are you chasing her, Jace, because she saw us, took Donnie's wallet, or because you want to see if she's as beautiful as that brief glimpse we got foretold?"

Not replying, Jace slowed until he was creeping along.

As the car rolled slowly, Jace muttered, "The bitch is hiding. Donnie, Victor, keep looking to the right, Cad you got left." Just as he passed a gas station he saw the barest inch of the green car's bumper sticking out from behind the building.

"Got ya," Jace ground through clenched teeth. He snapped the wheel and headed straight for her.

Immediately the Tempo spun around the gas station forcing Jace to have to go around behind the building in a circle to get to her.

He was still making a turn when she peeled away down a side street.

"Whoa, Jace, the girl is good!" Donnie crowed, impressed.

Grunting in response, Jace raced after her. In a flash he was right behind her again.

"Go on, Jace, get her," Victor goaded from the back as Jace downshifted and cranked the wheel as he followed her down yet another street.

Wired from the chase, Victor pawed his fingers down the length of his black Fu Manchu moustache that ended at his chin, then he clawed them through his black mane slicked back off his forehead.

"You got a damned four-barrel, five-speed, dual exhaust, Olds 455 V8 with freakin' t380 horsepower, you can't catch an itty bitty piece of crap 130-hp, V-6?" Victor chuckled meanly, his dark eyes rolled. "I never thought I'd see the day Jace Nico was bested by a woman. And a small, young one by the looks of her."

Next to him, Caddell Munro laughed, pristine white teeth gleaming against his dusky dark skin. "Yeah, we thought you were the best driver out of any of us considering the racing you've done. But, hell, maybe you should let young Donnie drive, he can probably catch her!"

The men all laughed at Jace.

He said nothing, just gripped the wheel so hard his knuckles were white.

They had caught up with her again and he was trying to nose her with the front of his car to pull over. She refused. Instead, she unexpectedly drove up on the sidewalk again effectively causing Jace to shoot past her.

He hit the brakes and jerked the wheel doing a complete doughnut spin and charged after her.

Looking over at him, Donnie said, "You're grinning, dude."

Shaking his head, Jace said, "No, I'm gritting my teeth thinking about what I'll do to the bitch when I catch her."

The threat hanging in the air, the three passengers grabbed ahold of anything they could as Jace pursued the girl at top speed until he reached her again.

This time he got the front of his car a few feet ahead of hers and kept slightly turning the wheel forcing her to move over again and again, more and more until he snapped the wheel and she had to turn or she would have run smack into a building.

The little green Tempo blasted down the alley he had forced her to turn into.

Jace yanked the wheel of his 442 so hard and fast the car bore almost up on two wheels making a tight U turn then turned into the alley behind her.

Slowing then pausing the car, a grim smile pulled Jace's harshly handsome face up.

"Why aren't we going after her?" Donnie asked, confused.

Knowing Jace better than Donnie, the two men in the backseat remained silent. They watched the green car racing at top speed suddenly slow, until it came to a complete stop.

Donnie cawed gleefully, "There's no way out of this alley, huh? She's fucking trapped!"

Cornered, the girl was desperately trying to turn the car around in the narrow alley when Jace floored the Olds. He aimed the car straight at her.

She'd gotten the Tempo sideways when Jace jammed on the brakes, wrenched the wheel and the 442 skidded sideways all the way down the alley, tires squealing, dirt and trash flying up all behind the car until it came to a screeching halt a few feet from the Tempo.

Dust and smoke billowed all around both cars in a brown cloudburst.

Appearing that Jace was going to crash right into her, the young woman had her hands up over her head preparing for the hit.

Now with her car helplessly blocked, the noxious pungent stench of burnt rubber filling the air, Jace jumped out and stormed over to the Tempo with a gun in his hand.

Putting the gun to her window, he pointed it at her and ordered, "Unlock the door."

She didn't move.

Jace knocked the barrel of the gun lightly against the window and commanded just loud enough for her to hear through the glass, "*Open the fucking door.*"

Very slowly she brought her hands down.

Jace tried to see her face but the hat was pulled down over it. She'd lost the sunglasses in her mad getaway. He could see a huge pair of eyes staring in dreaded fright at the gun.

He tapped the window again, once, said with a chill in his deep voice, "Won't say it again, woman."

Very slowly she pulled up on the door handle and pushed the door open half an inch. Jace snatched the door and flung it open so hard it bounced back on its hinges.

He reached in and grabbed her upper arm and hauled her bodily out of the Tempo. He didn't say a word as he dragged her to his car.

When he reached the 442, he put a hand on top of the girl's head and he shoved her in. Then he climbed in beside her, pushing her over with his body until she was crammed between him and Donnie on the old fashioned long seat.

Victor got out of the back seat and ambled over and hopped in the Tempo.

No one spoke over the girl's frantic breathing as Jace headed back out to the main street.

He drove only a few miles before he turned, maneuvering the car down a winding one-lane road to a small weathered marina. Victor followed in the Tempo.

Just as Jace parked the car, a white truck pulled up and stopped a few feet from him.

The girl was shaking so hard in obvious terror, squished between the two men they both could feel her vibrating against them.

Donnie glanced over at Jace's stone face.

Getting out, Jace said to Donnie, "Keep her in the car." Closing the driver's door, he trod to the white truck.

Caddell exited from the back of the 442 and headed to a locked gate, punched in a combination then swung the gate open.

"So," Donnie turned smiling to the young woman, "you are smokin' gorgeous, what's your name?"

Instead of answering him, she threw out her hand and pointed to something outside his window.

A boat full of bikini clad women was tooling by with music blaring, squeals and laughter floated across the water.

Donnie's eyes popped wide as pancakes, his mouth hung open as he watched the boat going by. He never heard the driver's door open or saw her slide out and run.

7

Fleeing down the parking lot in jeans and a blouse she ran to a row of craggy, shack-like buildings. Hurrying to hide behind them she didn't dare stop to look over her shoulder.

Just as she rounded the first building Jace stepped out right in front of her and said calmly, "Really?"

Trying to keep from crashing into the big strapping man, arms flailing, her scream was bloodcurdling.

Jace quickly clamped a hand over her mouth.

There were not a lot of people around at that time of day at the tiny rustic marina but he didn't need her drawing any attention.

She turned to run but he grabbed her around the waist. She swung at him, hitting as hard as she could, but she only cried out in pain like she'd hit a tank.

"Okay, enough of this." Jace bent and threw her over his shoulder and marched back to the dock.

She froze for a second then violently kicked her feet and pummeled his back with her fists screaming, "Let me go!"

Her hits seeming to have no effect on him, he just traipsed back across the parking lot and onto the dock.

His friends gathered, watching him carrying the girl kicking and hitting, never losing her hat, her screams muffled against Jace's powerful broad back.

The guys grinned like baboons but they kept their peace as he tromped past them.

At the end of the dock, Jace lowered the woman into a speedboat to Victor who held onto her in the rocking vessel until Jace jumped in.

Half terrified, half angry, she tried to wrench out of Victor's hold, spouting, "What do you think you're doin'? You cannae snatch me off the street like this!"

Ignoring her protests, Jace gripped her arm and pulled her over to a cushioned bench seat. He put his hands on her shoulders and pushed her to sit down then he sat down beside her.

Crowding her against the corner of the boat, he made it impossible for her to even stand up much less get out of the boat.

She started to protest again but Caddell and Donnie climbed in and sat down.

Jace called out over the slight ocean breeze, "Hit it."

Victor revved up the boat and it roared away from the marina.

Donnie sat across from the girl staring hard through his windblown scraggly hair at her plump breasts bouncing from the boat cutting over waves.

The trapped girl's face glowing crimson, she pulled the cap down low over her eyes, crossed her arms high over her chest and looked over the side of the boat away from all of the men.

Seeing her embarrassed face, her frightened eyes not daring to look at any of them, Jace said in a deep growl, "Donnie, go get the rope ready."

When the younger man's eyes didn't budge from the girl's chest, Jace ordered louder, "*Donnie-*"

Donnie tore his gaze from the girl to look at him. Jace jerked his head sharply toward the front of the boat.

"Okay." His eyes still on the girl, Donnie stood up on his long legs and went to do as Jace said.

In a few minutes they approached a large ship. Invisible to the passengers meandering on the top deck, they pulled in low and close to the hull.

After tying the speedboat to the ship, Donnie and Caddell grabbed a ladder attached to the side of the ship and started climbing up. Caddell opened a steel door and they disappeared into the side of the ship.

"Okay honey, up." Jace stood and pulled the woman to her feet then he drew her over to the ladder.

Stepping away from the edge of the rocking boat, she cried, "What? You're insane, I'm nae going-"

Giving her no choice, Jace grasped her around her waist, easily lifted her up over the side of the boat and set her feet on a rung of the ladder. "Grab on, honey, or you're gonna fall."

With a little squeal she awkwardly grabbed a rung then clung to the ladder and didn't move.

"You're getting on the ship, woman, climbing up on your own or over my shoulder. I'm good with either way." Jace's hard smile met Victor's amused one.

She hesitated, then realizing she wasn't getting past the two brawny men, she gingerly put a foot on the next rung and climbed up that one step.

Her body shaking so hard, the ship suddenly dipped from a swell, one of her hands slid off the ladder and she swung backwards with a scream.

Jace leaped onto the ladder behind her. His feet on the rung below, he wrapped an arm around her waist and grabbed onto the rung above the one she still had a hand on.

Pressing against her back to hold her on the ladder, he let go of her waist and caught her loose hand guiding it back to her other one. He could feel her gasping body shaking against his torso.

His mouth near her ear, Jace rumbled, "Okay, I'm right here behind you, I won't let you fall. Just go slowly." He waited while she took tremulous deep breaths.

The ladder wasn't made for small women or children, the rungs were spaced far apart. She started to move, climbing excruciatingly slowly. Holding her breath, she made her way up the ladder. He stayed behind her each step, barely touching her body.

When she was almost to the top, Caddell reached down, caught her under her arms and effortlessly hauled her up and set her down on the deck.

When her feet touched the ground, she stumbled, dizzy from holding her breath. Caddell threw out a huge basketball sized hand and grabbed her upper arm holding her steady.

Jace jumped off the ladder swinging the iron door closed with a clank behind him.

Caddell informed him, "Donnie went to help winch up the speedboat into the ship."

Wrenching her arm from Caddell's grip, the woman blurted to Jace, "What do you think you're-"

Jace wrapped his fingers in a vice grip around her arm and started marching her down a narrow metal encased hallway. The banging and clanging of the engine room they moved past was almost deafening.

She dug her feet into the rubber-matted floor and tried to pull from his grasp.

His voice laced with ice, staring emotionless into her terrified green eyes, Jace growled, "You keep fighting me and I will put you over my shoulder again and give my friends another view of that fine ass of yours. It won't bother me any, you're light enough I could carry you all day. Now, let's go."

He held her upper arm tightly, pulling her close to his body and almost up on her toes, roughly half carrying half walking her.

She wouldn't have been able to keep up with his long-legged strides even if she had wanted to without him hauling her along with him.

They went up a few steps to another deck then down a long mostly carpeted hall until he stopped outside a cabin. Still holding her, he fished in his pocket for his keys.

Frantically trying to tug her arm from his iron grip, she said in a panic, "Listen, mister, this is- is kidnapping, you cannae just grab me off the street like this-"

He pulled his keys out, unlocked the door and pushed her inside. Following her in, he closed and locked the door behind him.

She stood paralyzed; staring wide-eyed at him with her arms protectively wrapped around her body.

Chapter Two

*D*ropping the keys on a table, Jace reached out like lightning and snagged her cap off her head, tossed it in a corner then crossed his arms over his black t-shirt.

Thickly muscled biceps flexed and his bulging chest swelled under the cotton, he watched her hair tumble over her shoulders and down her back curling into a V almost to her waist.

His eyes travelled the length of her long curly hair, his pupils engaging at the distinctive color. With an effort he pulled his stunned gaze from her hair, moving it impassively to her face then it crawled down her slender yet hourglass figure like stroking fingers.

Legs akimbo in snug black jeans and heavy boots, he said coldly, "Okay, take 'em off."

Her arms wound tightly around her body, she asked puzzled, "Take off what?"

His eyes narrowed at her, but she looked sincerely bewildered. "Your clothes, honey. Take them off."

Her affronted gasp choked in her throat, she backed a few steps away from him. Looking way up at the tough masculine stranger who towered over her, she sputtered incredulous, "What? I am nae taking off my clothes."

Arms still crossed like thick ropes over his chest, he said with a shrug, "Suit yourself, but if I remove them they will be in shreds. Considering you have nothing else to wear I would think you would want to preserve them. So, either you do it in one second- or I will."

She took several more steps back. In shock at being chased then grabbed off the street and stuffed in a car, then dragged onto a ship. Confusion mapping her face, she asked, "Why would I be taking my clothes off?"

Jace slapped his big hands on his narrow hips at her obtuseness. He said coolly, "Because, honey, we're going to fuck."

Her brows jumped in astonishment, her hands fell to her hips. "What? Are you crazy? No we are not, why would we?"

He couldn't believe she wasn't getting her situation. "Listen, honey, because you lost and I won. Because I chased and caught you, you are my spoils of the conquest. Besides the obvious fact that you're one very hot female and I would want you anyway, but the whole hunter chasing prey thing just put me over the top. So, off with them, honey."

Her forehead furrowed in confused anger, she crossed her arms. "Stop calling me honey."

His brows arched, amused at her indignant stance and boldness considering her precarious position. "I don't know your name, I have to call you something. But I generally like to know the name of the woman under me that I'm fucking, so, what is your name?"

Frowning mutinously, she said nothing.

"Let's see," Jace said, tapping his fingers on his chin, looking her up and down.

"You have no purse. Victor said there was absolutely nothing in your car except Donnie's wallet, which that alone is highly suspicious, so," he smiled, "your ID must be on you." He made to reach out for her but she jumped and ran to the door.

Fumbling crazily with the lock, she squealed when he wrapped one granite arm around her arms pinning them against her side and pulled her back. He boldly patted the pockets on her jeans with his other hand.

Clamping her mouth shut, she struggled futilely against his superior strength.

Still holding her slim back tight against his hard chest, Jace smugly pulled out the driver's license and read, "Lissa Mallory."

Flipping it over, he looked at the back, asked, "Is that short for Melissa or Alissa or something?"

Forgetting her fear of him for a second she scowled her annoyance, stating tartly, "No, it's just Lissa. Now, please, give me back my license and let me go." She jerked her body to get free but she couldn't budge an inch out of his hold.

Jace squinted at her. "Is that hair color for real?" He looked down at the plastic picture in his hand then back to her. "It's a deep, rich Bulgarian rose the likes I've only seen in paint stores, with streaks of highlights that are glowing insanely under these lights."

He stuck his hand in the waves. Transfixed, he rubbed the dark tresses between his fingers, then watched a shiny lock curl around his finger.

Not answering him, she jerked her head trying to yank her hair from his hand.

Smirking, he let the lock go, watching it fall softly down the front of her to coil around a breast. Staring at the hair curled around her breast the smirk disappeared.

He muttered through suddenly dry lips, "No problem. I'll find out in a minute if it's real or not." He stuck her license in his pocket.

"Hey," she squawked, trying to push out of his grasp, "give me that back."

"You won't be needing it." He picked her up in his arms like she was a feather, carried her to the bed and set her down on it. She immediately tried to scramble away from him but he caught ahold of the belt on her jeans and pulled her back then climbed on top of her.

Twisting around, he reached down and pulled off both her sneakers dropping them on the floor then moved to lie atop her.

Using his weight to pin her down, he said, "Now, honey, sorry, *Lissa*, I found chasing you, and catching you, incredibly hot and pissing infuriating at the same time. You made me look bad for a moment in front of my friends. So, I will relieve my anger and my lust at the same time. We'll figure out if you're with Warrington later."

"Who?" she blurted, thrashing frantically under him, trying to buck him off her to no avail. Squirming to get away, she cried, "Get off of me, let me out of here! Stop-"

Jace cut off her yells by covering her mouth with his. She struggled more furiously, hitting and trying to kick him.

Catching both her wrists, he gripped them in one hand and pushed them up over her head, then put his other hand on her neck, clutching under her jaw to hold her head still. The kiss at first was to silence her and show her who was boss.

But her lips as small as they were, were full and soft and she tasted unbelievable. He had to have more. She was dammed enticing even though she held herself rigid not responding to him.

He pushed her lips apart with his and invaded her mouth with his tongue, tasting every velvet inch of her on the way to seeking out her tongue.

Jace shocked himself. Already aroused, the mind-blowing meshing of their mouths made his head spin. Taking a breath, he blinked to clear the sudden encompassing lust fog from his eyes and looked down at her.

His throat constricted and his heartbeat doubled.

She looked like a woman being made love to. Her beautiful heart shaped face was blushed a pretty pink, green eyes sparkling, her lips were swelling to a deep red.

Already turned on from the chase and then the kiss, with the flush he was forcing on her she was growing even more desirable before his eyes. His body heated way up, and hardened ten more notches.

Lissa took the opportunity of his taking a breath to scream.

Jace quickly lowered his head again and kissed her, stifling her cries. Still using his weight to pin her down and holding her wrists over her head, he let go of her neck and started to tug her blouse out of her jeans.

Tearing her mouth away from his, she cried with breathless anger, "Is this the only way a coward of a man can get a woman? By force?"

That stopped him dead. Braced on an elbow and still gripping her wrists, he set a hand on the other side of her and studied her. There were tears of fear in her big green eyes but her jaw was stiff with anger.

Stung at her words, he said, "You are a brilliantly cutting little bitch, aren't you?"

Sniffing, Lissa turned her head away from him and said with shaky bravado, "You have a foul mouth."

Jace couldn't believe her gutsiness. Here she was trapped under him, he held her wrists captive, and while he kept her in this vulnerable position his other hand was up under her shirt.

Feeling the warmth of her concave belly against his palm, he laughed. "You're kind of haughty and testy considering the situation you're in."

His head cocked with interest. "I'm detecting a faint accent, like sometimes you roll your r's and drop your g's. I've tried to place it, but," curiosity wrinkled his brow, "what is it? Irish?"

Demanding with grunting huffs, "Get off of me," struggling against him strained her throat, her voice rasped from the bottom of her lungs.

Smiling, he said, "I'll figure it out eventually, but now," his lids sultry half-mast, he lowered his head covering her objections with his mouth and moved his hand out from under her shirt to pry at her belt buckle.

"Mister-" Twisting her face from his, she cried out, "You- you-can't force me! Aren't you afraid of- of pregnancy, or jail- or –or disease…"

In response, he leaned his heavy body over her to the nightstand, opened a drawer and took out a condom. "No worries, honey."

Her eyes widened at the package. "What is this, standard operating procedure? You grab women off the street and bring them here and rape them?"

His hand hesitated at her pants for a second then he shoved his knee between her legs pushing them apart while dropping his mouth back on hers.

Grinding his mouth against hers, Jace pushed her lips open, searching her mouth with his ravishing tongue while he unbuckled her belt and started to tug open the button on her jeans.

With all her might Lissa jerked her head away, panting, "Stop, please, why are you doin' this?"

Pulling his mouth from hers with a sigh, panting with heated lust, he rolled back on his elbow again to peruse the woman struggling beneath him.

"I told you, because I'm boiling, so pissed and so aroused, the whole thing is an incredible aphrodisiac. I'm so turned on, baby, I can feel my pulse beating in my palms. It's like an intense adrenalin ride.

"Now, quit trying to distract me, it's going to happen, honey, I mean Lissa, so make it easy on yourself and surrender, enjoy it with me." He clutched her jaw to hold her head still.

Lowering his head again to kiss her, he slid his hand back down to her jeans. Tears rolling down her cheeks smearing onto his rough face gave him pause. He lifted his head, his hand stalled at her pants.

Choking back sobs, she cried, the words rasped out chiding him, "You are nae a real man, you can only get a woman by force."

Sighing, Jace leaned back on his elbow and let go of her hands.

"Girl, I don't have a problem getting women. Actually I thought you might be in for this as much as me. Only a woman with brass balls could drive the way you did. And with the dangerous chance you took taking Donnie's wallet, I assumed you were up for some hot sex sport."

Frowning at her shocked expression, he said, "As a rule, women don't generally turn me down."

Watching her wipe at her tears and swallowing hard to keep from crying, he held her chin with the curl of a finger and his thumb to force her to look at him. "Don't you find me attractive, little Lissa?"

Blinking back tears, her frightened gaze scanned his strongly handsome, tanned face. She looked up at his hair.

Wavy, sun-kissed, almost white blond on top but very dark underneath, his sideburns and beard stubble were dark as was the hair on his brawny arms. His eyes so dark blue and heated they looked all black pupil.

The shoulders that were over her could span a doorway, and the chest pressing against her curves was like buffed marble. He was wearing black jeans, snug jeans that outlined very lean hips, and his thick, hard erection.

Rolling slightly, he pressed his shaft against her thigh and watched her eyes cringe at the size of him.

Pretending nonchalance, which didn't fool him a bit, sniffing, she looked away and said, "I donnae care for blonds. Or tattoos."

Surprised, he moved back to the side of her and propped up on his elbow. Keeping one leg over hers, he crossed his arm over her stomach and set his hand on the bed beside her. He asked, "Why not? Start with the tats, what's wrong with them?"

Grabbing handfuls of her heavy hair she pushed them out of the way and shrugged. "They're for thugs and punks, rock stars and inmate wannabees."

Jace had tats on his upper arms. Miffed, he said, "I got mine in the service. It delineated that we were brothers at arms." He didn't mention that the rest of them were added during drunken rampages while he and his mates were on leaves.

When she didn't say anything, he asked, "What's wrong with blonds?"

She moved her gaze from his tattooed arms to his head and shrugged again. "They just look kind of, well, effeminate, weak, soft." She should have bitten her tongue considering her predicament at the moment; she was practically taunting him to attack her.

He leaned back further, dark brows arched high. "Really?" Grasping her wrists again, he rolled back on top of her and pushed between her legs, spreading them apart.

18

Bracing on his burly forearms on either side of her and staking her hands to the bed, he pressed his rock hard erection against her core.

His deep voice dangerously low and husky, he said, "Tell me, Lissa Mallory, what about me do you find weak, soft or effeminate?"

She closed her lips, staying silent. When he started moving erotically, thrusting his iron rod over her soft woman's cleft, she cried, "Please, please let me go."

Jace didn't move for a minute listening to her sniffing and gulping, her chest hitched with short cutting breaths.

Holding her hands down on the mattress, he watched her fighting to hold back her tears. Dark lashes curled over the biggest most crystalline green eyes he'd ever seen.

Then he did let go, moved off her and sat up. He looked down at her.

Her hands were still to either side of her head where he'd held them. She protectively pulled her legs together to the side and drew her knees up. The green eyes awash with unshed tears looked up fearfully at him.

Jace had never seen a woman so vulnerable, or so beautiful...or so unbelievably hot. Or so terrified of him. He dashed an arm across his forehead, let out a deep exhale. "Sit up, Lissa."

Surprised, she looked warily at him.

His big hands were folded innocuously in his lap, his dark eyes slid from her head to her feet and back but he didn't move at her. She slowly pushed to sit cross-legged on the bed, facing him.

Jace said quietly, "Okay. You win. For now. I've never forced a woman before, and I'm not going to today. But, I'm not promising anything about tomorrow."

In one smooth movement he rolled off the bed and left the room without another word, locking the door behind him.

Chapter Three

*J*ace strode down the hall forking long strong fingers through his thick hair. Lifting a shoulder, he used his shirt to wipe the perspiration beading over his eyes.

The adrenalin still pumped through his veins forcing him to walk swiftly, he needed to burn off the consuming lust fogging his brain.

By the time he reached the study his body had calmed, erection diminished slightly. Running his fingers through his hair again, he pushed away the picture of the gorgeous girl lying helpless on his bed, rosy lips tremulous, big green frightened eyes shimmering like ponds with tears.

He took a deep breath before entering the room.

The windowless room, lowly lit with a few fluorescent ceiling panels was like a den. It had a bookcase crammed slightly messy with jumbles of books against one wall, a TV in another, several cushioned chairs, a few small tables and the large table in the middle was surrounded by six chairs.

Ker Dove sat at the table.

Hunched over a computer, the Asian man glanced up briefly at Jace. "Hey," he mumbled looking back down at the screen.

Then he did a double take. Looking back up at his friend, Ker sat back in his chair with his hands behind his head, elbows out like wings. "Hmmm, your hair is a tangled mess, face ruddy with high color and I can feel the heat radiating off you from here."

His gaze scanned Jace's body. "Your muscles are beating against your shirt, and," his eyes dropped to his jeans, "ah, you have a-"

Jace held up a hand. "Okay, enough, Ker." Tugging at the legs of his jeans to loosen them, he pulled out a chair at the table, sank down, stuck his long legs out and crossed his ankles.

He tried to neaten the thick waves on his head, the motion was futile, giving up, he sat back and crossed his arms.

A small frown drew black brows down over Ker's dark eyes, his critical lips thinned behind the pointed goatee. The top half of his long black hair was in a ponytail, the rest flowed around his shoulders and a few inches down his back.

Caucasian features blending with Asian gave Ker a frightfully menacing and mysterious appearance. Brushing a finger across his neat moustache, he said, "Jace, that girl Victor said you took, you did not force-"

Jace directed an annoyed scowl at his friend. "Of course not. How could you even," his face flushed guiltily thinking about what he had done to her, what he might have done if her desperate sobs hadn't made him pause. He shook his head with irritation, "Never mind."

Ker's black eyes narrowed absorbing Jace's disheveled appearance. Dark color still warmed Jace's cheeks, a cross scowl marred his face.

"Uh huh. But you sure as hell wanted to. Or tried to." A tiny smirk pulled up one corner of Ker's hard carved yet full mouth. "I take it you tried, she refused, and," his gaze swept down the front of Jace's still swollen jeans, "you aren't too happy about it."

"Shut up, Ker, okay?" Bending his neck, Jace dropped his head back and closed his eyes. He winced at Ker's cool chuckle.

Leaning forward with his elbows on the desk, Ker's voice hardened, "Why the hell did you take her, Jace? What are you going to do with her now?"

His eyes opened, Jace stared at the ceiling. "I had to take her, bro. Besides having Donnie's wallet, she saw us. She thinks we killed that guy, and she would definitely go to the police.

"You know we can't have that attention brought on us. Plus, there's a chance she could be with Warrington's men. We might be able to get information out of her." He scratched one of his sideburns with a finger. "At the very least, if she is with Warrington she can't get to him now and tell him about us."

Ker snorted, crossed his arms, hunched over and laid his forearms on the desk. "That's pretty farfetched, Jace. By what Victor told me, it's unlikely she's with Warrington. And, so what if she went to the police? There's no evidence, no photos of us, it's doubtful she caught the tags." His lips pulled in at Jace's shrug.

Continuing, Ker said, "Even if she did, the plates on the 442 were not ours and can't be traced back to us. Granted your taste in cars can be attention drawing, but in the state Victor said she was in when you caught her it's doubtful she could have described the car other than it was black with gold lettering. Her full attention would have been on losing you in the frantic, racing chase. And now we're anonymously on a ship."

When Jace made no comment, Ker added, "You know Donnie's picture was real but his ID was false, it wouldn't be traced back to him either."

Jace replied, "Still, she had Donnie's pic. In the cops' hands he could have been identified at some point. Photo rec and all, people are easily identified these days using the DMV face recognition search."

A black brow rose in sly retort, Ker said, "If she were 60, grey-haired and overweight would you have taken her?"

Considering the question, Jace smiled slightly. "Only if she had the same sexy little accent and cute freckles on her nose." In one movement Jace pulled his legs in, leaned forward and set his forearms on the table. He muttered, "And a supremely exceptional rack. Ask Donnie, I had to pry his eyeballs off her."

"Jace, you took her because you wanted her."

Brows drawn down between the dark blue eyes, his lips, ample yet manly chiseled, were set in a firm line. Clearly pissed off, Jace denied Ker's supposition.

"Let it go, Ker. I had to take her for the safety and success of the mission. As well as," he twined his fingers together, "for her protection too. If she isn't with Warrington, and if any of them had still been around and saw her-"

He said quickly as Ker opened his mouth, "Don't say it's not possible, it's actually pretty probable they were still in the vicinity. They would undoubtedly return after we left to take the body and clean up the scene."

Jace moved his arms so his elbows were on the table and set his chin on his hands. "Therefore, it was absolutely necessary to take her with us. You know what would have happened to her if they'd gotten a hold of her."

"Hmmm." Ker reached for the mug that was beside the computer and took a swallow. "Okay, whatever. Now that you have a smoking hot babe locked in your cabin," the brief smirk touched his lips again, "with a sexy accent." Losing the smirk, his expression slid to serious. "What are your intentions for her?"

"I, uh...haven't thought it all through yet."

"So," Ker drawled, "why are you here then? How come you're not with her?"

Jace stretched his neck from side to side to get the kinks out, avoiding answering the question.

Sitting back with a slick smile on his normally inscrutable face, Ker said, "Oh, I get it. She's so hot you can't be alone with her, without climbing all over her even though she clearly does not want you."

Jace replied with a sheepish grin, "That's part of it. The other part is she's pretty angry. I may have been a little over, uh, zealous when I thought she would be willing to, you know..."

"Uh huh," Ker's mouth twitched.

Jace sighed. "And she's also really, really scared. I thought it would be better to give her some time alone to calm down. When the boat moves out she's going to really freak."

"I see." His elbows on the table, Ker tapped his fingertips together in a steeple. "So, after you kidnap a young defenseless woman off the street that just saw our brawling guys standing around a murdered man, literally drag her onto your boat filled with strange men, forcefully put the moves on her and then lock her in your bedroom and start sailing away," he took a breath before continuing.

"You decided she would feel better sitting there totally alone, having no idea what's going to happen to her, with her imagination running wild. She probably thinks we're going to gangbang her, then kill her and toss her body overboard. Jace, any abducted woman's mind would go straight there."

Jace let his words sink in. His gaze flit from Ker to the table. He set his palms on the table for a second, sighed heavily then pushed to his feet. "Yeah," he muttered. Wiping his sweaty hands on his jeans he started for the door.

"I've got to make a few stops before I go back to...her." His shoulders drew up at Ker's rare snicker as he left the room. Laughter and cheerfulness were not in the brooding Asian's grim repertoire.

Jace made his way below deck, his boots quiet in the carpeted hall. Passing several rooms, he stopped and knocked on one.

Chatter inside stopped abruptly. Footsteps neared the door then it swung open.

"Hey, Jacey, honey," a statuesque, full-bodied woman with blonde hair in frozen hair-sprayed swirls over her shoulder greeted him. A long, neon pink spiked fingernail tapped his arm. "What brings you here, babe? Me, I hope?"

Her tongue slid over big matching neon pink lips. Lusty brown eyes dropped to his crotch then made their way slowly back up, in clear invitation.

"Uh, no, Dona. I think I need," he scanned the room, there were several other women lounging inside. His gaze went from each one until it settled on a woman still over average height, but shorter and thinner than the others.

He said to her, "Glennie, I need a favor."

Surprised, the woman unwound her crossed legs and stood up. Arrow straight, platinum hair swept her shoulders like a

24

whiskbroom. Beneath a fringe of whisk bangs, cheerful hazel eyes smiled at him. "Sure, Jace, what can I do for you?"

She was the currently popular stick thin build with no bust or hips, older than the rest at 37 and relentlessly kind, Glennie was sort of the mother hen of the other women.

Looking uncomfortable, Jace hesitated, rubbing his chest with big square fingers.

Still in front of him, the statuesque Dona Sutherland eagerly watched his every move as if she was imagining him stroking her like he was doing to himself.

He stepped further into the room, nodded at the other women inside. Mumbling, "Ivy, Vicki, Eve, Tori," he moved nearer to Glennie Greer.

"Well, um, we have an unexpected guest. She's," how was he to explain that he abducted a woman off the street. "I can't explain why she's here, only that, you must disregard anything she says. She will make wild claims that she's been…uh…kidnapped and forced here against her will."

Gasps rang around the room.

Dona moved up behind him. Interest peaked in her deep, sexy purr, "Oh, do tell, Jacey. You can abduct me anytime."

He turned slightly, not wanting her behind him where he couldn't see her. Ignoring her comment, he explained, "Yes, ah, we are taking her to Scotland with us to…turn her over to…Scotland Yard, on ah, a warrant."

More gasps travelled the room.

Clothes and shoes were strewn everywhere, a half a dozen different perfumes vied for the lead in the cloying air. Ruffled plaid curtains were pulled back from the big window displaying the shimmering blue water beyond.

"Naturally," Jace continued making up his story as he went along, "she does not want to go so she's going to say all sorts of crazy things to get someone to help her escape. I'm asking you all not to tell her our final destination. However, the reason I'm here is…" his face reddened.

He raked a hand through his hair. "That in the meantime since we're going to be at sea for a while, well, she has no other clothes than what's on her back. No...uh, toiletries and stuff, you know, girl things." He could feel the heat rolling up the back of his neck.

"Oh," Glennie said kindly, "you need to borrow some clothes and feminine items from us to give to her. That's no problem. I take it she's fairly small since you singled me out." Her friendly hazel eyes noted the other women present.

They were all tall, voluptuous, heavily made up and blonde.

Except for Ivy, the only brunette who was as the others, tall and curvy but on the heavier side, her skin hued with cinnamon and slight hint of berry red.

Her weave bobbed under just at her shoulders. Always friendly, dark amber crescent eyes and her smiling nod told Jace Ivy would help too.

Jace sat his hands on his hips. "Yeah, she's quite slender, and um," this was damned awkward. "Kind of on the petite side, but you know, uh," he cupped his hands out in front of his chest indicating her full breasts. Red crept up his neck at the giggles in the room.

Sticking his hands back in his pockets, he said quickly, "Whatever you can loan would help."

"No problem." Glennie smiled kindly. "I have some clothes and underwear I was bringing to my stepsister. She's much younger and a lot smaller than me. I'll grab those as well as whatever else we can dig up."

His hands clasped behind his back, legs braced stiffly, Jace nodded his appreciation. "Thanks, ladies, whatever you can loan will be great."

Back in the room, Lissa waited a few beats after the creep left then got up and made her way cautiously to the door, prepared in case he came right back in.

Hand trembling with trepidation, she placed her fingers on the knob and carefully turned it. But it didn't turn; it was locked, from the outside.

"What?" she cried out. Frustration temporarily replacing fear, she pounded the door several times with her fist.

Bewilderment furrowing her brow, she set her palm on the door and murmured in a fearful whisper, "Why would he lock me in?" Dashing at her eyes, she said defiantly, "I will not give into tears, I refuse to let that *man* scare me."

She tucked her blouse back into her pants and buckled the belt, her cheeks flaming remembering the sex-crazed beast on top of her undoing her clothes.

Without him in the room drawing her full attention, Lissa took the time to check it out. It was plainly masculine. There was his bed of course. She felt her cheeks burn again just looking at it.

Blinking rapidly, she quickly turned away from it and looked around.

There was a nightstand beside the bed and a few feet away another bed but smaller, a double. It was covered with books, papers, some tools, a computer and folded clothes that should be in a drawer.

Across the room was a dresser. Next to it, half the size was another dresser, with evil looking sharp edges, it looked very old. A hot plate and saucepan were on it.

A few male things, a brush and comb, a carved wooden jewelry box sat on top of the bigger dresser with a mirror attached to the dresser.

On the opposite side of the room was a desk littered with papers, more books and tools, cords, plugs. At the desk was a chair with a shirt draped over it, another chair was tucked in the corner.

Near the window was a big rocking chair covered with a thick blue cushion, and beside the door was a short divan the beast was using to hold the rest of his clothes that he was apparently too lazy to hang up.

A streak of setting sun glimpsed through a slit in the dark blue curtains covering a window caught her eye. She made her way to the window, pushed the curtain halves open an inch.

The room brightened slightly from the light streaming through the water-spotted glass. The door opening suddenly made her twirl around. He was back.

Jace came in carrying a bundle of something with a packet on top. Striding into the room, he said, "The glass is tempered, strong enough to withstand a hurricane, please don't injure yourself trying to break it to make your escape."

His mouth quirked in slight amusement at the guilty look on her face.

Her eyes widened as if she thought he could read her mind then quickly dropped her gaze to the floor. He took a few steps towards her, her eyes jumped up to his, she backed away, tripped and fell backwards, crashing hard into the sharp corner of the smaller dresser.

"Oh!" she yelped. Wincing, she stumbled forward.

Cursing, "Shit," seeing red spread through the back of her white blouse Jace dropped the bundle he carried on the small bed and moved quickly to her.

His dark masculine brows darted down at her cringe away from him. He said roughly, "I'm not going to hurt you, turn around."

She just stared at him with those huge, frightened green orbs.

His mouth twisting in irritation, he grasped her arm and pushed her to turn her back to him.

A gasp escaped from Lissa as he yanked the back of her blouse up out of her jeans. She tried to turn back to fight him but he held her in place.

His voice softened, he repeated quietly, "I am not going to hurt you. I want to see what you did to your back." That rankled him, he wasn't used to explaining himself to anyone, especially a woman.

28

Gently pushing his hand under her blouse, Jace stifled his surprised moan that touching the silky skin of her lower back brought. *Hell, that's the first time that's ever happened.* He felt like a teenager. Just touching her bare back was making him hard.

Focusing on his task, he pushed her blouse up further, and wrapped a hand around one of her arms to hold her as she tried to get away from his intrusive hands.

Seeing the injury, he muttered, "Damn, Lissa."

"What? Let go of me, what are you doing?"

Moving his hand to her shoulder to keep her in place, Jace reached to the nightstand beside his bed and yanked out several tissues from the box siting there. He quickly lifted her blouse back up and pressed the tissues against her back.

Gasping sharply in pain, she cried, "Mister, stop- what are you doing-"

"Hush for a second," he ordered, "and don't move." Using his other hand he fished his cell out of his pocket. Swiping his finger to unlock it, he pressed a button and put the phone up to his ear.

Only one ring and a voice came through the phone. "Hey, One, what can I do for you?"

Jace said tersely, "Drew, come to my room, and bring a first aid kit." Nodding with the phone pressed against his ear, he said, "I'll explain when you get here." He clicked it off and shoved the cell back in his pocket.

Still pressing the tissues on her back, Jace moved his hand to wind his fingers around her upper arm to hold her still.

"Listen, honey, it's okay. You cut yourself pretty badly when you hit the dresser. Doc is coming, he'll fix you right up." Feeling her sway he held her arm more tightly. "You okay?"

Looking a tad green, she nodded wordlessly.

In a few short minutes there was a knock at the door.

Jace pulled Lissa with him to the door, unlocked and opened it.

A man dressed in a dark trousers and a black pullover sweater stood in the doorway. Around his early forties, full brown hair with wisps of grey at his temples, glasses shoved on top of his head, strong nose with big cheeks. He was built as powerfully as Jace but huskier. When Jace stepped aside with a nod, he entered the room carrying a case in his hand.

Jace closed the door behind him. "Thanks Drew."

One of the doctor's eyebrows arched at Jace.

Jace was holding Lissa in front of him with one hand clutching her arm and the other still up the back of her blouse.

"Oh, uh…" uncomfortably, Jace introduced them. "This is Doctor Drew Manor. Doc, this is Lissa Mallory, she's," he cut off; he'd explain her situation to the doctor later.

"Anyway, she knocked into that dresser," he nodded over at the offending piece of sharp furniture, "and she hurt herself. Here," he turned Lissa around and lifted the back of her shirt up.

"Mister, *please*," her voice squeaked, mortified at her blouse being pulled up in front of two strange men.

Doc's kind voice was low and pleasant, nonthreatening, he gently touched her arm. "It's all right, honey, Miss Mallory, I am a real doctor." He leaned over and set his case on a table. Opening the lid of the case, he said, "Let me see what you've done."

Her shoulders relaxed slightly from his soothing voice.

He instructed, "Jace, you can let her go now, I have this. Here, honey, lean over and set your hands on this desk here, okay?" He removed a pair of new plastic gloves from the case and pulled them on.

Jace reluctantly released her, took the bloody tissues and tossed them in the trashcan under the desk. Turning back around to watch, he cursed under his breath, "*Shit.*"

Manor had gently pressed Lissa so she was slightly bent over with her hands propping her up on the desk. He pushed her blouse up to her neck and opened his kit.

Jace quickly swiveled his attention away looking towards the window but it was too late.

Bent over the desk, Lissa's lissome back bared, exposing a lacey pink bra and the curve of her tiny waist into a perfect rounded ass in snug jeans. From the side, her breasts hung almost tumbling out of the bra in the position she was in.

Jace pictured himself behind her. Both naked, his arm wrapped around her waist, his hand clutching a supple tit while he thrust-he gulped the feeling down, tried to push the image out of his mind even as the blood rushed to his crotch.

Doc was quietly saying soothing words to Lissa as he cleaned up the wound. Disposing of the cloth he used he then slathered antibiotic over the cut and taped adhesive over it.

When he was done he smoothed her blouse back down. His voice kind, he told her, "You can turn around, honey, I'm finished. The wound is a bit deep but shouldn't scar."

Her face as red as a beet, Lissa turned, pushing her heavy autumn colored hair out of her face. Her head down, she peered over at Jace.

He was standing with his hands in his pockets staring out the window, which was peculiar because the curtains were still mostly closed.

She tucked her blouse back into her jeans.

"Nicely done, Jace," Doc teased. "You've only had her a minute and already you've broken her." He chuckled at the black scowl Jace, turning around sent across the room at him.

Doc had already been filled in by the guys how Lissa had been brought on board.

"I didn't-"

"I know, I know," Doc cut him off. He took a bottle of aspirin out of the med kit and shook two out in his hand.

Seeing him do that, Jace went into the bathroom and came out with a glass of water, he handed it out for Lissa to take.

She stared at it without moving, clearly not trusting anything from him.

The doctor poured the aspirin into her hand, took the glass from Jace and gave it to her. "Go ahead, honey, you're in a little shock right now. You gave yourself a good whack and very soon you're going to be feeling a lot of pain."

He handed the aspirin bottle to Jace. "Here. She's going to need more later." He closed then picked up the medical kit and opened the door.

31

Pausing in the doorway, he said to Lissa, "I'll come by tomorrow and change the bandage for you." To Jace with a grin, "Try not to damage her further, goodnight all." He stepped out the door.

Lissa started to follow him with her hand out as if about to grab his shirt. Her voice taut with nerves, she said, "No, wait, to-tomorrow, I won't be here tomo-"

Jace stepped in front of her and shut the door. Sliding his keys out of his pocket he locked it.

Chapter Four

Seeing her body tense as Lissa moved away from him, Jace trod over to his desk, pulled out the chair and sat down so she would feel less threatened by him.

She set the glass down on a table then stood like a statue. Her body stayed still but her eyes watched him warily.

He gestured to the other chair. "Go on, sit down. I'll stay right here, I promise." He forced an amicable smile on his face.

She stood for a bunch of long moments watching him. He leaned back in his chair, casually crossed his long legs at the ankles and crossed his big arms over his bulky chest.

When it didn't appear that he was going to spring up and attack her, Lissa cautiously moved to one of the chairs and nervously sat down, her legs were like jelly. Clearly struggling to keep her voice from quaking, she asked, "Are- are you goin' tae kill me?"

His face utterly impassive revealing nothing to her, he quietly replied, "No."

She waited but he said nothing else. "Well, uh, what do you plan tae do with me?" Her face blanched when a coil of pure lust heated his eyes. Wrapping her arms around herself she stood back up. Her legs quaking, she backed away from him until she was against the wall.

Jace rose to his feet. He could practically feel her fear it was so palpable, her body was shaking like a damned tuning fork. The rigidity in her body and her trembling legs confused him. He just got through telling her he wasn't going to kill her, what the hell was wrong with the woman?

Glancing in the mirror, he saw the way his carnal gaze shouted what he wanted to do to her. Hiding his desire for a beautiful woman was an uncommon act for Jace. With an effort he lowered his lids, striving to extinguish the heat in his eyes.

Lifting her chin, expressing false fortitude, she commanded, "Stay away from me," bringing as much fearless authority as she could to her quivering voice.

He held his hands up, walked further away from her to the smaller bed and cleared a spot then sat down. "Go ahead, Lissa, sit down. I swear I'm not going to touch you." He clasped his hands benignly together in his lap.

Her legs couldn't hold her steady anymore so she dropped on a chair. "I, uh…asked you…" she gulped down her panic and tried to clear the fear from her expression.

To Jace she looked like she was going to be damned if she'd let him see how much he frightened her.

Firming her small yet full lips, she raised her slightly pointed chin again. "I asked you, what are your plans for me?"

How gutsy this small woman was, he thought. She worked hard to mask her accent. Why would she do that, he wondered. He pulled up a leg, setting an ankle on a knee and explained vaguely, "The plan, at the moment is, we're going to travel to Maine to resupply and then we will go on to our next destination."

She coughed the nerves out of her throat. "Where's that?"

"Um," Jace didn't want to tell her just yet where they were going. She'd probably freak right out and he didn't want a hysterical woman on his hands. "I'll tell you when we get near."

Her cinnamon brows knitted in puzzlement. "I don't understand, why am I going with you? Where will I stay? Who else is on board? What will-"

He laughed holding up a hand. "Okay, okay, one question at a time. First I'll tell you who is on board with us. I have five team-uh, friends. We have been hired to…do a job."

At her frown, he quickly said, "Lawful, a lawful job. We're going to help build some factories and a plaza, like a mall. There are almost 50 other men on this ship going with us and there are some women on board too that will be working in different capacities..." he broke off, still not wanting to tell her he was taking her out of the country.

"Why are you takin' me with you?" The trepidation crept into her voice accentuating her slight accent. Her chin pushed up to show him she didn't fear him. Except her entire body screamed *stay away from me-*

Easily reading her body language, Jace bent his elbows and set his palms on the bed behind him to brace himself up. "I am taking you with me, us, because you saw us. You think we killed a man. Let me tell you right out, we did not kill him. We were merely-" he broke off, he couldn't tell her what they were doing with the dead guy.

"Uh, anyway, our identities need to be...unknown...for the time being and I can't take the chance of you running to the cops."

She jumped up, the curly hair fanning her back. "It's all right, you let me go and I promise I won't go tae the police. I swear I won't tell anyone!" Her pale face awash with frantic pleading, she pressed her palms together prayer-like.

"Sorry. Can't." He lowered his head, dark blue eyes looked up at her through a fringe of very long lashes.

"Please, I won't-"

His lips pulled in, he shook his head. "No."

Seeing his adamant expression, her face crumpled, she plopped back down in her chair. "What then, what will you do with me?"

Lissa watched him carefully for any sign of menace. He looked at her calmly, but the lust was still there, she saw it flare every time his gaze swept over her.

Jace sat forward. She flinched at his movement.

He frowned at the flinch. Women did not flinch from him. His lip curled, of course he had made her afraid of him, it was his fault. "I'm not going to do anything with you. After we get further out to sea you will be free to roam about. I got you some clothes."

He nodded at the bundle on the bed. "We have an excellent cook with us, my team- uh, friends are cool, they won't hassle you. I don't know much about the others on board, but they should be all right. If anyone bothers you, you tell me, immediately. Got that?"

She stared blankly at him.

"I asked you a question, Lissa, answer me." His voice turned hard, a man used to his authority.

Blinking hard, she replied shortly, "Yes."

Jace stood up. "I need to go on the bridge, we'll be leaving soon."

Shyly, in a quiet voice she tried to strengthen with a determined edge, Lissa asked, "Will you be lettin' me off when you dock in Maine then?" She tried to meet his level gaze without looking away.

Not answering her question, he strode to the door and set his hand on the knob. "By the way, don't bother telling the other occupants that I've abducted you, I've already told them you're a fugitive that we're taking to jail. They won't believe anything you tell them, or help you."

He opened the door, turned and smiled mildly at her. "Oh, yeah, your other question, as to where you'll stay for the duration. You will be staying right here, with me."

Her eyes popped, the emerald green of them sparked in alarm. Brows hitting a high arch of protest, she exclaimed, "What? No, I-"

His smile stayed, "You can sleep in the little bed, there's no way I'd fit in it. I'll clear my crap off it when I come back. Unless of course you want to sleep with me, I wouldn't kick you out."

Before she could respond he stepped out closing the door behind him. The click of the door locking echoed in the room.

When he returned an hour later she was where she was the last time he had gone out and returned, standing at the window.

Jace mused, *it's probably common with prisoners to be staring at freedom and trying to figure out a way to get to it.*

She didn't turn this time when he came in. It gave him a moment to check out the room, see if she'd been snooping around.

His gaze bounced around at the dressers, desk, closet, his bed was still made but rumpled from their earlier escapade on it- he blinked away, his body already stirred remembering the way she had felt under him, all soft, rounded and delicate.

Ahh, he looked at the other bed, his stuff was still sprawled all over it.

Jace went to the bed, picked up the folded clothes and carried them to the dresser where he stuffed them in a drawer. Back to the bed he piled up the books then brought them to his desk, returned for the laptop and put that on the desk as well.

Gathering up the other miscellaneous junk he just dumped everything on the desk. Later he would organize things and find places to put them.

As he passed near the window he plucked a jacket off the rocking chair and hung it in the closet, then took out sheets and a blanket and started the task of making up the smaller bed.

The entire time he worked she never moved.

Tucking in the sheets, he stuffed a pillow in a case and tossed it on the bed. Saying, "Hey," he waited, she didn't move.

"Lissa." Nothing. "Are you dead?" He tried joking, nothing.

He could already tell, this stubborn girl was going to drive him insane. Most women never stop yammering, this one was so mute he wanted to pinch her just to hear her sweet lilting voice.

"Damned stubborn, irritating," grumbling to himself he worked his way over to her. She jumped when he touched her arm.

"Lissa," his voice had an edge. Used to being in command and people instantly following his orders, he didn't cotton to being ignored.

She yanked her arm away from his fingers, never taking her eyes off the window.

His mouth pulled in testily, *little wench*, he snatched her arm and pushed her to face him. Green eyes filled with fear, and anger, glittered at him.

The anger overtook the fear, she tried to wrest her arm from his grasp. "Let go of me, you- you- creep!"

Boy, Jace thought to himself biting back a grin, *she was even hotter with a spit of fire in her eyes.* "Creep?" he parroted, amused, he'd never been called that before. "That's the best you got?"

She didn't answer him.

Heat flooded his body as soon as he'd touched her, he let go of her. She immediately showed him her back and started walking away.

He growled, *"Don't-* turn away from me or I will-"

She spun around, planted her hands on her slender but amazingly curvy hips and snapped, "Or you'll what?"

Her spine straightening took him aback. The corners of his mouth turned up in a cocky smile. "That's better. It's polite to face a person when they're talking to you." He smothered another grin at her affronted expression.

"Why you condescending, arrogant-" her fingers digging into her hips, she leaned towards him. Her lips flapped searching for names to call him, cheeks flooding with red. At a lost for more insulting words, her eyes narrowed letting only a slit of green out, and it was a furious green.

He goaded her further, damn she was turning him on with that cute little temper. "There we go, showing a little life finally. You're kind of spunky when you get your back up. That sexy little accent gets thicker too. Your O's get funny, like you say ar*roo*gant instead of arrogant."

Aghast, she sputtered, "Oh, you- you- you-"

Laughing at her, Jace said, "Okay honey, take it easy. I was just trying to chase away some of that panic and fear you're feeling."

Crossing her arms, she glared querulously at him and pouted, "I see. Grabbin' at me, pushin' me around, yellin' at me, that's a great way tae calm a person down. Where'd you get your psych degree- Tyrants R Us? University of Bullies?" The curly burnished hair waved over her arm, she impatiently tossed it back over her shoulders with an irritated sharp shake of her head.

Jace laughed out loud. Chuckling, he wiped at an eye, "Okay, you win. Again. This round."

Not amused, Lissa swung around with her back to him again.

His eyes twitched with annoyance. "Lissa, I told you not to turn your back on me." He waited, she didn't turn around. Then he saw her spine bend suddenly, her hand went to her lower back.

"What is it?" He moved quickly to her, gently turned her around.

Pain creased her face, her eyes brimmed with tears.

"Your back, you moved too quickly, here," taking her arm he sat her down on a chair. "Lean over, let me see," he tugged at her blouse.

"No!" She tried to twist away from him then cried out in pain.

Ignoring her struggles to keep away from him, Jace pulled her blouse up anyway to check her bandage. "It's not bleeding so you didn't open it back up. I'll get you a couple more aspirin."

Jace let her blouse drop and was surprised when she didn't immediately modestly tuck it in as she had done each time previously. She was obviously in a great deal of pain.

He hurried to retrieve two more aspirin and the glass of water and handed it to her.

This time she meekly took them with shaking hands. Her eyes were lowered, her lips strained tight.

"Listen, honey, uh Lissa," Jace said kindly, "you need to lie down and give your back a rest." He gestured to the bed he'd just made up.

"For the rest of today and probably the next two days I have to stay on the bridge while we exit the harbor. I'll bunk down there so you don't need to worry that I'll be jumping you, you can sleep in peace. I will though, stop by periodically to check on you and bring you food."

Lissa stood up and without a word turned her back to him again. She wrapped her arms tightly around her body as if to hold against the pain and steady her wobbly legs.

"Fine," his breath exploded angrily. He stalked to the door, grabbed it open and slammed it behind him.

After locking it from the outside, he leaned against it. He could hear her crying. His stomach clenched.

Oh God, what have I done?

Chapter Five

*O*ver the next two days Jace checked on her every few hours. He showed her how to use the inter-ship phone to call him if she needed him.

Lissa watched him silently. When he came into the room she was always sitting by the window. He tried to talk to her but she stayed silent, never turning around when he came in or spoke to her.

He left her food, which he frowned at every time he picked up the tray; she only ever took a few nibbles.

Doc Drew checked on her several times to see how her wound was healing and to visit with her. He knew she was frightened, lonely, and bored mindless.

He'd had words with Jace about her abduction and locking her in his room, but Jace had tramped down his mouth and refused to discuss it.

On the third day, Jace unlocked the door and strode inside. She was sitting by the window.

He said, "Uh, Lissa, how about I show you around the ship, you can meet the guys. You basically met some of them in the truck but we weren't all on a first name basis then." Smiling slightly he watched her shoulders lose some of their tension.

Lissa turned slowly to see if he was only teasing her, getting her hopes up and then cruelly dashing them. The door behind him was wide open.

Her mouth softened, the line between her brows disappeared. She stood up, her eagerness clear at finally being able to leave the room.

Jace said, "All I ask, Lissa, is that you answer me when I ask you a question, and look at me when I talk to you."

Her gaze rolled slowly up to meet his, but she didn't say anything.

"Lissa."

"Okay."

The word was so soft he almost couldn't hear it. But it was good enough for him. For now. "Come here," he said holding his hand out.

At her shrinking back from him it was obvious she didn't want to touch him but she also didn't want him to change his mind.

She moved slowly to Jace. He gently set his hand on the small of her back well below the bandage. Ignoring her attempt to move away from his palm he led her down the hall.

They were both wearing jeans. He had on a black thermal and boots. She wore a borrowed white blouse with a lacey collar and white sneakers.

Gesturing with his hand at the doors they passed, he said mildly, "These are some of the rooms of the other people on board. The women are all staying in one large dorm-like room. I'll show you where in a minute."

"Oh, good," she said with that sweet lilt in her voice. "I'll be stayin' with them then?"

His fingers tightened on her back. "No, Lissa. I told you, you're staying with me." He saw her mouth thin and pull in, brows dipped low shielding the look in her eyes.

She asked, "I don't understand, why wouldn't I be with the other women? It only seems natural that-"

"No. Discussion is over." He didn't mean to snap but there it was. Her steps faltered, he held her firmly around the waist until she walked smoothly again with her gaze straight ahead then he dropped his hand.

They walked in silence for a bit. Then he said coolly, "These are where the men are staying, there're 4 to 6 to a room." Countless doors lined the carpeted corridor.

As they traversed the hall, it widened to a brief lobby of sorts before opening into a big roomy space. Filled with several sofas and easy chairs, tables, lamps, book cases against a wall, TV, entertainment center, it was like a giant living room.

He explained, "This is the great room where most everyone hangs out while we're at sea."

There were two women lounging on a couch chatting. Both appearing in their late twenties looked up at their approach. His palm cupping her lower back again, Jace led Lissa over to them.

A blonde with big breasts spilling out of her tight dress eyed Jace's hand at Lissa's waist. Lifting her extraordinarily thick and long false eyelashes, dark brown eyes skimmed up Lissa's figure to her face, she didn't even attempt to hide her scorn.

"Is this the little criminal you've brought on board, Jacey?" Her gaze flitted to Jace where her expression turned sensual. Wide lips slicked heavily with shiny pink lipstick drew up in a bold seductive smile.

Feeling Lissa tensing, Jace said quickly, "This is Lissa Mallory. Lissa, this is Dona Sutherland," he nodded at the blowsy blonde with the dark spray tan.

"And this is Ivy Innes," he motioned to the young woman with mahogany skin and shoulder length weave.

Dona Sutherland did not deign to look at Lissa again.

Ivy gave Lissa a big toothy smile. Crescent-shaped dark amber eyes kind, her voice friendly, she said, "Welcome aboard, Lissa, I hope you enjoy the voyage. Jace came by the other day to borrow some clothes for-" she broke off at Jace's imperceptible shake of his head.

"Uh, well, honey, if you need anything please don't hesitate to ask, okay?" She smiled warmly at Lissa, her eyes jumped awkwardly to Jace.

Crossing her legs in the super tight skirt, Dona set her palms on the couch and leaned forward pressing her arms against her breasts displaying them for Jace's perusal. She was not happy when he barely glanced in her direction.

Sneering at his attention staying on what she deemed the little whore felon next to him, a nasty snark spilled out of those bright pink lips to Lissa, "I hear you're going to the pen when the ship gets to-"

"That's enough, Dona," Jace snapped at the blowsy blonde with a dour warning. "Come on, Lissa, let's see the rest of the ship." He smiled at Ivy, and glared at Dona while he gently nudged Lissa to continue walking.

Lissa turned back, smiled politely over her shoulder. Enunciating slow and carefully, almost eliminating her subtle accent, she said, "Nice to meet you ladies, I hope to see you around."

As they headed for the exit, Dona called out, "Jacey honey, if you feel like...talking...later, come get me!"

Jace's hand tightened on Lissa's back.

Dona continued louder, "We can suck down a drink and whatever else you want sucked sweetheart-"

Jace moved Lissa out the door without responding to Dona. He glanced down at Lissa, he couldn't read her expression.

Sweeping lashes covered her eyes and her lips were slightly pulled in. He felt abnormally uncomfortable with Dona's blatant sexual invitation in front of Lissa, especially while he had his hand in a possessive way on her waist.

This is exactly why he doesn't do relationships. A man gets caught between women and it always ends badly for him. Dona has been throwing herself at him since the minute she had boarded the ship a few weeks ago.

He'd had a fleeting thought previously of just doing her for an easy fuck. Now he was really glad he hadn't. Besides, it probably would have been work after all since he felt no interest whatsoever in the blown up girl. She'd been around the block. A lot, and clearly rode hard. Probably need a net to keep from falling in.

His fingers tingled against Lissa's back feeling her warmth through the thin cloth of her blouse. It took effort to keep his hand from sliding lower to cup her sweet rounded tush.

Her rosy hair tickled the back of his hand as it swayed with the beat of her hips. He should take his hands off her, give his body a chance to cool down, instead he squeezed her gently, she just felt too good to let go.

They trekked along a walkway, he pointed at an open door. "That's a study."

Lissa peeped in as they kept moving. She saw tables and chairs, a stuffed bookcase, another TV. It looked like a miniature version of the great room although it appeared geared more for work than just to hang out. They headed up a short staircase to another level.

"This," he opened a door, urged her to go in, he followed her, "is the dining room."

She looked around.

The room was filled with plastic, white round tables, and chairs with peach tinted seats that matched the walls. Up at the front to the left was a soda, coffee, and ice cream station, with condiments, cutlery, trays, napkins etc. Colorful cheery paintings of food decorated the peach and sparkly silver wallpaper.

The galley anchored the top of the room. A man in a white apron was bustling around in it. Another young man moved busily back and forth.

"Come on," Jace brought her to the kitchen.

A long aluminum counter like in a cafeteria stretched between them and the cook.

"Lissa," he pulled her forward introducing her, "this is Benny Moore, the best chef in the land." He grinned at the portly man.

Benny's plump cheeks moved up in a friendly grin, his face shiny with perspiration, he nodded at Lissa. "Hi there, sweet thing, nice to meet you."

Using the opportunity to step out of Jace's grasp, Lissa moved a half a foot discreetly in front of him. Her pretty, shy smile completely disarmed the cheerful cook. Her elusive accent increasing, she said in a hushed voice, "Um, I am pleased tae meet you, suhr."

Her hands folded demurely in front of her, the top buttons of the lacy collar of her blouse opened just enough to show the top swell of her curves.

Behind her, drawn like a magnet, Jace's eyes slid down the body hugging jeans outlining her onion-shaped bottom and very slender but shapely legs.

His grin ear to ear, Benny said, "Honey, it's Benny, or Ben, none of that sir stuff from our beautiful little stowaway."

The smile fled. "Oh, no, I'm *nae* a-"

"This here is Colby Wynn, sweetie," Benny dropped a hand on the young blond man's shoulder who joined them.

"He's my apprentice, Colby's a really quick learner. Dave, Jon and Dillon are prepping in the back." Colby gave Lissa a shy grin.

It was easy for Lissa to smile back at the fairly short and thin, cute, blue-eyed apprentice, he appeared to be Lissa's age or even younger.

Observing his prisoner captivating the two men, Jace dropped his hand on the small of her back possessively and said to Benny, "Okay, we gotta move on. We'll be back for dinner."

Dipping his head near Lissa's ear, he inhaled the scent of her hair and said quietly, "Let's go." Throwing a backwards wave at the cooks, Jace ushered Lissa out of the kitchen.

He showed her a few other rooms then took a short set of stairs up to the top deck.

"We're going to the bridge. There are two decks and the engine room below. I don't think you want to see the engine room. It's loud with motors and clanging and on the dirty side with oil and stuff all around."

His hand stroked up her back to the middle, he opened the door to the bridge and went in first drawing her behind him. "You will probably recognize some of them, they were with me when I...took you."

He felt her stiffen and shift away. "It's all right, honey," he reassured her, pulling her back near his side. "They won't hurt you, I swear. In fact, they will always protect you, trust me."

"From you?"

Frowning, he kept walking, slowly; she had gone all rigid against him. Jace figured all five team members would be up there, they usually preferred not to have to interact with the others on board if they didn't have to.

Two men stood at the helm, another was near the door. Two others were sitting down, those two rose as Jace entered. He drew Lissa inside a few feet. "Guys, this is Lissa Mallory."

Gesturing to a long lean beanpole with a mop of scraggly hair flopping in his eyes, he said, "This is Donnie Bowie, he sat next to you in the car. It was his wallet you took."

Jace could have bitten his tongue. Why the hell did he say that? It could set an antagonizing first impression that would last.

Donnie's wide-eyed goggle blatantly went straight up Lissa's figure, from her sneakered feet up over the tiny waist and up where they stalled on her breasts molding full and firm against the borrowed blouse.

"Eyes up, boy." Jace directed.

Donnie's eyes flickered. He blinked, looked at Jace's frown then slid his embarrassed ogle to the floor. "Yeah," he mumbled, taking a step back, said a belated, "welcome."

Next, Jace introduced a man with combed back dark hair, and dark eyes, with a Fu Manchu type mustache that gave him an edgy dangerous look. "This is Victor Tanjione."

Victor nodded briefly but said nothing.

Jace pointed to the next man, "And this is Julio Verera."

Short dark brown hair and round brown eyes, Julio smiled lightly and said, "*Buenos dias, señorita bella.*" He stepped back and next to a dark skinned man the size of an enormous bear who gave Lissa a broad grin.

Her eyes widened in fearful recognition at him. He was the one who had plucked her off the ladder like she was nothing but a butterfly and set her on the deck of the ship.

47

Jace said, "Caddell Munro, we call him Cad, which ask any of the ladies and they'll tell you how true that is-"

"Not!" Cad beat him to it.

He was so huge and tall, Lissa unconsciously stepped back knocking into Jace.

All of the men were well above average height, heavily muscled with powerful builds. But this one was like a small mountain, he was thick all over with cordons of muscles across his shoulders, over his chest and down his arms.

Jace was extremely muscular too but his powerful chest narrowed to lean hips, whereas Cad was solidly thick all over.

His hand already on Lissa's back, Jace moved it to her shoulder to brace her while she looked up, way up at the dark man with his shaved head and gold earrings in his ears.

"Don't be afraid of this guy, Lissa, he's just like a big grizzly, tough on the outside all marshmallow inside."

"I'd say he's grizzly on the inside too," Victor commented with a taunting smile. "You haven't heard him snore."

The big Black man let out a guffaw so loud Lissa shrunk against Jace, which was fine with him. He dropped his arms, linking his hands over her stomach and hugged her protectively against his chest.

"Seriously, his roar, and his looks are worse than his bite," Jace said.

Cad was used to people being afraid of him at first except for the boldest and wildest of women. He clasped his huge hands like baseball gloves behind his back.

His voice hushed and friendly, as nonthreatening as possible, he said with a warm smile, "Hya honey, welcome aboard. You need anything at all, anyone hassles you at all, you come straight to ol' Cad here, okay little one?"

Lissa nodded, blinking up at him. "Um, nice tae meet you, Mr. Munro."

"That's Cad, honey, okay?" He grinned showing her bright white, strong teeth. His smile was blinding, she smiled naturally back at him.

His head cocked, brow furrowed, Cad said, "Can't place that accent, it's so slight, like French or Irish maybe? What-"

Seeing her biting her lip like she didn't want to answer the question, Jace cut him off, "All right, moving on." He tilted his head to the man standing back just a little from the rest.

"Lastly, this is Ker Dove."

Jace could feel Lissa leaning back against him again, she was obviously terrified of Ker. It was expected. Like Cad and Victor, Ker had a dangerous presence, but where Cad was genial, Ker was like fearsome black ice.

Ker's almond shaped, unreadable dark eyes depicted him as Asian with an obvious Caucasian gene in the background. He stood casually but it was clear his body was honed, ready for action.

It was his eyes that were eerie. Frightening, harsh obsidian, they seemed as if to swallow a person up, and look right through them at the same time as if they didn't exist, or, if he wanted to, kill you if provoked with no questions asked.

The top part of his long black hair was swept back in a ponytail, the bottom spread over his back collar a few inches over his shoulders.

He had a black pirate's type goatee, a short and neat triangle. His sharp diamond-shaped face was hard, inscrutable and unsmiling. He wore a long-sleeved starched white shirt, black slacks and black boots.

Ker's eyes were on Jace's arms possessively wrapped around Lissa. She appeared uncomfortable but unable to move from his strong embrace. Expressionless, he looked at Jace who was smiling at him, then to Lissa whose abject fear radiated from her green orbs.

He nodded wordlessly to her then stepped back. His gaze moved back to Jace's, one brow quirked unnoticeable to anyone else except Jace who got his intent.

The others didn't much care what Jace did, but Ker and Jace had fought already about Lissa being on board. Ker was against holding her captive, but although he would argue with Jace, he never disregarded his decisions.

"Okay, we'll leave you guys to carry on with what you're doing, we can meet at 1600 hours in the study." Jace let go of Lissa but scooped up her hand and walked her to the door. Her hand was ice cold, her steps stiff.

Exiting a room full of hot-blooded men, knowing all eyes would be on her extraordinary ass as they were leaving, Jace moved her in front of him.

Outside the bridge, Jace took her hands in his large ones and rubbed them. "You can relax now. I'll take you back to my room."

Catching the nervous shift in her eyes, he said, "You can take a shower and change, maybe catch a nap. I have things to do, I'll leave you alone." The flicker of relief on her face annoyed him.

He unlocked the door to his cabin holding it open for her to enter. "Like I said, Lissa, I'm leaving you alone," he frowned when her relief flicked again. "I'll be back at 1730, uh, that's-"

"Five thirty," she said moving away from him.

"Yeah. Anyway, I'm going to lock the door-" he broke off at the look on her face. "What?"

Her eyes darted to the window then back to him. The relief of him leaving her alone was suddenly woven with fear. "We're so far out at sea now, what if, I mean, the ship could sink, you said the window is unbreakable."

Jace told her with strong assurance, "This is a powerful boat, honey, nothing's going to happen." At her anxious glance back at the window, he said quickly, "If anything does, I will be here to get you."

He grasped her upper arms forcing her to look at him. "Trust me, Lissa."

She studied his assured expression, then said snorting over her fear, she said with sarcasm, "You telling me tae trust you is a joke."

A confused query shadowed his eyes. Squinting at her, he said, "Huh? What do you mean?" His fingers tightened around her arms.

Lissa glared at his hold on her but he ignored it.

Leaning away as far as she could with him still holding her, she said baldly, "After chasin' me down, you snatched me off the street at gunpoint and are keepin' me here against my will. You told me you told everyone else on the boat that I am a fugitive you're taking tae jail." Her accent wormed in and out like small waves.

"You accosted me, and there's something fishy about this voyage. You're secretive about the destination, and the whole job thing." She shook her head.

"Not buying it." She twisted out of his grasp and crossed her arms. "Why on earth would I trust anything you have tae say?"

He stood with his mouth open, then snapped it shut with a half grin. *Boy, she bounced from terrified to crackling in a heartbeat. Spunky.* "Well, yeah, if you put it that way, I can see you being a little cautious."

"A little cautious? Are you kiddin' me, then? I'd feel safer alone on an island with a serial killer. Which," she narrowed an eye at him, "you could possibly be."

Her words jolted him. "Hey, come on now, Lissa," he said with irritation, "have I hurt you?"

At her askance expression he frowned. "Okay, I might have been a little fervent in my...uh...actions with you when I brought you on board but...but uh...I didn't rape you, or touch you really inappropriately once I realized you weren't willing as I thought you were. I-"

"Really? You felt all over me trying tae get my license. You pinned me tae your bed while you climbed all over me pulling at my clothes and threatenin' me. What part of that do you consider not inappropriate?" Her fear had turned to derisive accusation. She planted her hands on her hips and tilted her chin up at him.

Jace crossed his arms, a scowl tightened his strong jaw. He didn't mind a little fire in her, but she was making him feel like a lecherous rapist, when really, he hadn't... "I gotta go. I'll leave you to calm down."

Treading to the door, he opened it, stepped out and closed it quickly at the furious expression gathering on her creamy face.

Double-timing it he went back to the bridge. Yanking open the door, the men turned their surprised faces to him. Knowing he looked angry, his face red from her words, he glared back at them.

Julio said with a leer, "Hey, One Shot, we didn't expect you back so soon."

"Yeah," Donnie grinned lasciviously. "We figured you'd be-" he made a pulling motion with his fists next to his hips as he thrust them back and forth.

"Knock it off, Don," Jace barked at the younger man. "I am only keeping her here so she doesn't expose our operation. She is not here as my plaything." He commanded sternly, "Or anyone else's. Got it?"

They all, except Ker, laughed in his pissed off face.

Victor's voice slid out sexy and deep, "Babe has a helluva walk, Jace. Has a seriously sensual yet intriguing shy swing to that *sick* ass-"

"Victor, shut the hell up," Jace growled, his hand curling into a tight fist on the table.

"Yeah, sure, One, we believe you, you ain't wanting a piece of that hot-shit sweet honey." Cad's wide grin mocked his friend.

"She's off limits," Jace growled, "to everyone, me included. Now let's talk about the mission."

He turned back to Victor who was smirking at him. "You get anywhere with your cyber surveillance of Warrington's computer?"

Chapter Six

*J*ace opened the door to his room very slowly; he didn't want to get clobbered in the head with a lamp or something.

He peered inside the dimly lit room, then stepped inside and closed the door.

She was curled up on the small bed. Apparently she'd showered, her damp hair curled into ringlets spread over the pillow like rippling dark water with moonbeams streaking across the strands.

Jace crept quietly over and looked down at her. Sleeping Beauty, corny as the thought was, came to his mind. Rich dark mahogany hair flowing over creamy soft skin, long lashes curled against rosy cheeks, sprinkled lightly with fair freckles that skittered faintly over her dainty nose.

She slept so tranquilly with her small, full lips together in a pink puff, a contrast to the angry, green-eyed blasting woman he'd left a few hours ago.

A chill ran up his spine, he couldn't ever remember just standing and watching a woman sleep before. Usually it was hit and split before the sun thought about rising. He didn't usually stand around staring at and contemplating his sexual trysts like he was now.

Which was insane anyway because he hadn't even had sex with her, and yet he couldn't drag his mesmerized gaze away from the sound asleep lovely, and terribly vulnerable female.

The thought of having sex with her hit him like a red flare.

Jace moved away before he did something he'd be ashamed of later. He was feeling like a no from her right now wouldn't be enough to stop him. It wouldn't be hard to overpower her, it would be easy enough to pin her down and shove-

Taking a deep breath, he expelled it on his way to the bathroom. A cold shower would cool him off and bring his sexual tension down a notch.

He came out of the bathroom with a towel around his waist and another one he rubbed over his head drying his hair.

A small sound eeked-

Pulling the towel off his head he saw Lissa standing near the front door. She was dressed in clean jeans and blouse borrowed from Glennie. He noticed she filled it out a lot more than the flat-chested Glennie.

"Hey," Jace drawled with slight amusement, "you have a good nap?" Draping the towel around his neck he pretended he didn't see her hand on the doorknob.

With her back to the door, Lissa put both hands behind her on the knob, dismay at him standing there so imposing and half naked, replaced the guilt on her face.

Her gaze lit on the towel partially covering his thick chest, then to the other one that only went just past his thighs. He was a big man, a pink hue slid up her neck and over her cheeks before she looked away.

She tried to turn the knob behind her but it wouldn't budge, so she turned around and using both hands struggled to twist it.

"Sorry," Jace said, not really sounding sorry, "it's locked."

She swept around. "You said when we were at sea I could leave."

Walking towards her with the towel looking like it was about to untie and drop any second, his face was impassive, but his brows drew down low over his dark blue eyes.

Jace didn't bother telling her to sit down; she hadn't yet done anything he told her to do so far anyway. "We're gonna talk."

He sat down on the corner of his bed and watched some of the pink drain away leaving her skin pale. She leaned against the door, suspicion written all over her face.

"You can now go out and about, freely, however, I'd really rather you didn't leave this room without me, or one of my men with you. And when you're alone inside I'd prefer you keep the door locked.

"There are two locks; both can be locked with keys. You will be able to lock one of them from the inside pushing in the button, I have keys to both locks." He nodded at the door but she didn't look at it, kept her eyes square on him.

"I don't know the elements of the other men on board, and now that I've thought about it, knowing my breed," his lip pulled in wryly, "we can't always be trusted."

He caught her derisive look sweeping him up and down and got her point. "Anyway, as I was saying-"

"Apparently you're not used tae wearin' a skirt, mister, or you'd know tae keep your legs together," she sniffed with sarcasm.

"What?" He glanced down at his towel. His legs were wide like most men's are when sitting, the towel was taut, and short on his thighs. Feeling a unique prick of embarrassment, he stood up. "Yeah, well, I've never heard the ladies complain about what they see."

"Hmm." One brow arched drily at him suggesting she had no interest in what was under his towel.

Her snort irking him, he strode to his dresser, yanked open a drawer and pulled out clean underwear and black jeans. With his back to her he said, "I'm getting dressed now, feel free to watch."

Boldly allowing the towel to drop, he grinned inside at the gasp he heard. Her footsteps hurried to the window.

He pulled on the jeans and underwear and was buttoning his shirt when he trod in bare feet silently over to her. "You ready to go get something to eat?"

She jumped when he spoke.

Her palms were on the sill, Jace felt like leaning against her back and covering her hands with his.

He was so close, she hadn't heard him approach, his breath stirred wisps of hair around her head. She turned slowly, he was inches from her.

The citrusy smell of the shampoo still clinging to his wet hair lingered around him. Lissa tried to back away from him but there was nowhere to go. Setting her shaky hands behind her on the windowsill again, she stared uneasily at his chest.

Having a woman so fearful of him was an odd new feeling. Jace didn't think he cared too much for it. He stared down at the top of her head exasperated that she wouldn't look up at him.

"I asked you if you were ready to go eat." The words came out harsher than he'd meant them to.

When she failed to answer him his hackles rose. He chucked some fingers under her chin and pushed it up until he could see the green eyes afraid of him but trying to mask the fear with anger.

Lids hooded as he looked down at her, Jace grumbled, "You need to answer me when I ask you a question. It pisses me off when I have to drag words out of you."

His fingers tightened on her chin, holding it up and immobile, he bent and set his mouth, slightly open on her closed lips.

His fingers tightened more when she tried to pull away. He sucked gently with his lips over hers, tugging them softly before sliding away. Jace saw her pupils dilate whether in fear, anger or passion, he couldn't tell.

It was definitely passion that he felt. "I asked you," he said again with exaggerated patience, his voice slightly husky, "are you ready to go eat?"

His stomach twisted when he saw the sudden glimmer of tears she tried to hold back by blinking rapidly. She breathed out a soft, "Yes."

He still held her for a second, his fingers itched to stroke up the side of her face, steal around the back of her head and pull her against his mouth into a seriously torrid kiss.

Abruptly releasing her, he turned from her and said, "Let's go."

"Um," now that he wasn't near her, her bravado kicked in. Lissa asked blandly, "Was that unwanted kiss you just forced on me another *not* inappropriate move?"

Other than his jaw tightening, it didn't appear Jace heard her, he just went out the door and waited outside the cabin for her to join him.

After walking silently together for a minute, Lissa asked, "Is this your boat? Are you like the captain or something?"

A pleasant smile softening his harsh planes, Jace shook his head. "No. Our, um company owns this ship. I'm I guess the closest thing to a captain on board though. I am in charge."

They traveled the rest of the way to the dining room without speaking.

Inside, they joined his friends, Ker, Victor, Cad and Donnie for dinner. Jace pulled out a chair for Lissa and helped her sit before getting his own.

Cad gave her a big friendly smile. "Hi honey, you getting your sea legs?"

Her hands in her lap she replied politely, "Yes, *taing*, uh thank you for asking." She looked up at the big man, his kindness stretched across his dark face, and smiled back at him.

Her gaze moved to Ker. The skin around her mouth flexed at the purely blank look he gave her, his black hooded eyes like cold empty holes.

Her shoulders twitched in a tiny shiver, she pulled her eyes away lowering them to the table. She didn't see the frown Jace shot Ker, who in return looked blandly at his friend with a brief shrug of one broad shoulder.

"Miss...um, what's your name again?" Donnie's chipper voice broke through the tension at the table.

"Lissa," she and Jace said at the same time. Their eyes connected before she quickly looked away.

"Well, Lissa, do you play pickle ball?" Donnie asked. His hands on his scraggly hair, his gaze skimmed her body before she glanced at him.

Smiling weakly at the young man who was pushing his light brown curly mop around his head but not necessarily neatening it any, she said, "No, I don't know what it is."

A plate of meatloaf and mashed potatoes drowned in gravy in front of him, Donnie took a big forkful and stuffed it in his mouth. It didn't stop him from talking, "That's okay, Lissa, I'll teach you. A bunch of us are playing after dinner. I'll take you down to the rec area."

Lissa opened her mouth to decline but he'd already turned to Victor to ask if he was going too.

Jace stood up. "Come with me, Lissa, we'll get our food. Donnie will be on his thirds by time we're done." He pulled out her chair and led her to the front where they got salad and meatloaf.

When they joined the others, the men talked about football while Lissa ate her food silently.

The room was packed. People chattered, many eyed Lissa with curiosity. No one approached them. Their round table was a curved wall of big brawny men and one petite female girded amongst them.

After dinner, Donnie hopped up. He announced with excitement, "Okay, let's go, we don't want to be last to play!"

He led the group to the rec room, all except Ker who disappeared along the way to join Julio at the bridge.

The group could hear yelling and cheering, cursing and laughing before they reached the place.

Donnie grabbed Lissa's hand and dragged her to one of the four court areas set up. They weren't regulation size but the boat limited the space they had.

In less than fifteen minutes, forgetting she was being held prisoner, Lissa was laughing and panting, running back and forth trying to hit the speeding bouncing little white ball.

The other women were there, some played, some sat on the sidelines drinking and talking.

Jace played at a different court. In between striking the ball, his glance constantly flit over to see how Lissa was doing.

The strain around her eyes and mouth was gone, her hair tied up in a ponytail swung and danced as she ran breathlessly and giggled.

A funny feeling nipped at Jace's chest watching her have fun. Relaxed, her smile was dazzling. Now he understood when people said a person's laugh was infectious, hers had that lilting sound that was gone too quickly to savor. He studied her.

One of her front teeth was slightly crooked, it made her look even sexier, he felt a pull in his groin. Glancing at Donnie, he saw the boy couldn't take his eyes off of her either.

Looking around, Jace could see he and Donnie weren't the only ones, male and females alike shot glances at his stunning captive.

Dona, sitting with a cocktail in her hand, the blowsy blonde didn't care it was obvious that she was talking about Lissa. A snarl on her freshly painted wide lips, she gestured towards Lissa with the pinky of the hand that held her drink.

Lissa spun around in confusion when some of the men called Jace by his last name, Nico. Occasionally she saw his close friends earn a frown when they called him One, or One Shot.

During a break while she thirstily drank a soda with Ivy, she said, "Ivy, everyone calls Jace by different names, either Jace or Nico, and sometimes One Shot. What's goin' on?"

Ivy's attention pulled from the huge Caddell Walker, across the room, his big laugh boomed everywhere. "Isn't he dreamy?" Ivy sighed.

She took a sip of her bottle of beer then turned back to Lissa. "Oh, you asked me a question. Sorry, but that hunk 'o dark chocolate meat doesn't know it yet but we will be mating soon."

Her eyes still on Cad, she grinned at Lissa's embarrassed expression. "I take it you don't get out much, not a lot of girlfriends?"

A wall seemed to come down over Lissa's face but she kept a smile plastered with effort. "Not really. You were sayin' about-"

"Oh yes, Jace. It seems his close circle of friends, Ker, Julio, Cad, Victor, Donnie, even the cook and the doc call him Jace, and sometimes they call him One Shot. Since he's in charge, the others on board call him Nico, his last name."

She turned to look at Lissa. "You say Nico funny, like instead of saying it Neeko you say it like Nehko." Ivy angled her head at Lissa in curiosity. "You have this accent, what-"

"What does One *Shoot* mean?"

Ivy laughed at the way Lissa's accent made it sound. "It's pronounced shot, not shoot." She explained, "Anyway, the rumor is, they are or were, all part of some elite military secret opts kind of team and had nicknames applied to them to keep their names from getting out while on a mission.

"Supposedly they earned their nicknames. One Shot, someone said means that, uh," she eyed Lissa warily. The girl was after all being forced to stay alone in Jace's room with him, and obviously against her will.

"What?" Lissa prodded.

"Um, it means he can kill in one shot, one move...like with his bare hands." Ivy cringed, Jace would be furious with her if he found out she'd told Lissa that. Oh well, she'd already blabbed, she loved gossip as much as anyone else.

Shifting her eyes, she didn't see Lissa's cheeks pale. "The others, ah, Cad," she smiled, her gaze traced him lustfully, "is called Viper. Victor is KM for Killing Machine, and go figure, Ker is called Assassin. I don't know about Julio and Donnie. I think they're relatively new to the team."

She lowered her voice, "Listen, please do not tell Jace I told you, he wouldn't like it, you know what I mean?"

"Sure." Lissa mumbled. It's not like she and Jace were little chatterbugs around each other. Watching Jace talking with his friends, she didn't know how to take this new information. Jace was over 6'4, as were the others of the so-called team except for Julio who was 6 feet even.

They were all powerfully built men although Donnie was more of a beanpole. Jace had the broadest shoulders she'd ever seen, and the leanest hips, a perfect muscular V.

His hair was unusual with the top of his head light blond, the rest, underneath, his sideburns, beard stubble, his arms even his chest hair which she has partially seen to know for sure, were all dark.

As if he could feel her gaze on him, his eyes lifted and he looked straight at her with a half crooked smile. She turned her back quickly and chatted some more with Ivy.

The break over, Julio ran over to Lissa and told her she would be his partner in the next game.

Soon she was so into the game she forgot all about the disturbing information Ivy had let slip.

At one point, Jace and Lissa played double opponents. She laughed when she hit and he missed her shot.

On his returns, she had quickly picked up on making dink shots, a soft shot made with the paddle open, and hit so that it just clears the net and drops into the non-volley zone.

"Oh yeah? You think you got me, honey?" Grinning, Jace power-housed his shot back at her and was surprised when she returned it.

"Huh," she sniffed, "that's your best shot? You should be at a daycare playin' with the babais, more your speed," she taunted, mirth tugging the sides of her mouth.

It was odd that she had for the moment forgotten she'd been abducted and was being held against her will on a boat in the middle of the ocean.

"Why you-" Her taunting put a goofy gleam in Jace's eye spurring him to play harder. Eventually his team beat hers. He stepped over the net, took her hand to shake it.

"Wait, aren't the losers supposed to go around the net and shake the winner's hand?" Lissa asked, laughing as Jace's large hand captured hers, completely enveloping it.

"I can afford to be magnanimous since I did win and soundly trounced you." Jace shook her hand with a grin.

61

"Oh my," she said slyly, "what a big vocabulary we have."

That brought a burst of laughter from Jace.

They played one more game not together on different courts.

When his game was over, Jace declared he'd had enough and went to get her. "I'll take you back to the room." He caught Lissa's mouth turning down, he'd told her, didn't ask her.

She said nothing, just allowed him to cup her elbow. He said goodnight to people on the way out.

Opening the door to his room, Jace walked her in. "I have some things to do, I'll, uh, see you later." Again she said nothing.

Locking the door from the outside, he left.

By the time he returned much later, she was sound asleep in the smaller double bed.

The other nights he'd slept on the bridge or in Ker's room. He wanted to let her get a little comfortable on board before he invaded her space by sleeping in the same room with her.

To not wake her, he undressed quietly and slid into his bed.

Chapter Seven

*W*hen Lissa awakened the next day, she peeped over at the other bed. It was empty.

She had half woken as he came in some time last night. He slept, half-assed made his bed and was gone before she woke again.

Crawling out of her bed, she showered and got dressed. She unlatched the lock on the inside and turned the knob on the door and was amazed Jace hadn't locked her in from the outside.

Unsure of what to do, or where to go, she left the room and wandered down the hall to the great room.

There she found the other women hanging around talking. A few had books or readers in their hands.

"Hey, Lissa," Glennie called over from the couch she shared with Dona Sutherland and Ivy Innes. "Come and sit with us!"

Lissa shyly made her way over aware everyone was staring at her, and most undoubtedly had been gossiping about her. Feeling awkward in borrowed clothes, she sat in one of the chairs near the couch.

Glennie gestured to the other women lounging in chairs around the room, "The tall blonde there is Vicki Ross, that tall blonde is Eve Esson," the two model looking girls smiled vaguely at Lissa.

Glennie motioned to the other side. "That tall blonde is Tori Fergus," she laughed, "and that tall but not blonde, is Ivy Innes. You've met her of course."

Lissa's legs shifted uncomfortably, she crossed then uncrossed them. "I feel like the runt of the litter," she said self-decrepitating, her smile rueful. "At least I have a sister brunette." She grinned at Ivy.

"Sure," Ivy plucked at her weave. "I wish my hair was that unusual, beautiful bright color, your highlights are intense. Can I ask, is your rosy color real? If not, who's your hair dresser?"

Lissa laughed happy to be a part of the group, "No, I donnae have the patience for salons, just get it cut when I remember tae."

"You poor thing," Dona twittered drily from the couch. "It's probably outside your price range to get a good dye job, huh?"

"Anyway," throwing a frown at Dona, Ivy said to Lissa, "you sure looked like you were having fun last night." Her weave curled at the ends in a long bob at her shoulders. She smiled pleasantly at Lissa.

"Huh," Dona grunted from the couch. "I bet she had more fun later. You did okay I'd say for a foreigner, capturing our tall, well hung, and handsome leader." The sneered comment about being a foreigner was directed at Lissa's accent.

Lissa didn't catch it. "Oh," she shrugged delicately. "I didn't do anythin' after the game, just slept like a baby." She smiled politely.

"Oh come off it-"

Glennie cut Dona off, "Dona, leave her-"

Dona held a hand up to Glennie. "Whatever, girl. I want to know what we've all talked about." She smiled a knowing leer at Lissa. "Jace packs those jeans like crazy, looks like he's hung like a horse, is he?"

Before Lissa could respond, Dona went on, "You know he's a player, a ladies man, unfortunately he hasn't given any of us on the boat the time of day. Yet. Not that we haven't tried, right Vicki?" She laughed across the room at another blonde with big boobs that didn't look any more natural than Dona's.

Her attention back to Lissa, Dona asked, "So, how is he in bed? That buffed body, the secretive eyes and titillating aura of danger, I bet he does it wild and rough, you must be sore as shi-"

Lissa's palms slapped right on her own red cheeks. "What? No, no, we haven't, he hasn't-"

"Get real, liar, that alpha male stud isn't going to be alone in a room with a woman at night, and not go for it. So," she leaned forward to Lissa, "spill it girl, is he everything and more in the sack? Forceful and aggressive, huh? Did he tie you up? Spank that ass? Go down on-"

"Dona!" Glennie shrieked seeing the mortification streaking Lissa's face.

Climbing quickly to her feet, Lissa blathered, "I've ah, uh, got tae go, need tae be-" she stammered hurrying out of the room with Dona's shrill laughter ringing in her ears.

She fled down the hall, kept running, didn't know where she was going when blam- she ran square into someone and fell straight back landing flat on her butt.

"Oh shit, here," a man bent over, took her hand and pulled her to her feet. Nicely built with dark sandy hair and blue eyes, he said, "Hey, I'm sorry, are you all right?"

Lissa pushed her heavy locks out of her eyes, caught her breath and looked up at the handsome man. "Uh, yes, I'm all right. I'm sorry, I wasn't lookin' where I was goin'."

"My name is Brett, and you are damned beautiful." He stared at her, then grinned. "Hey, you're that girl, there's a bunch of rumors about you. No one can decide if you're a stowaway or Nico's squeeze, or some say that he's taking you to jail-"

"My name is Lissa, and I am none of the above," she jerked her hand from his. "Again sorry," she started walking back down the hall when he reached out and grabbed her wrist.

"Wait," he hauled her close to him, strapping an arm around her back. "How 'bout we go somewhere, private, and, get to know each other a little better? That's a sexy accent you got going on there, babe." He pushed a lock of her hair off her shoulder then stroked her face.

"I don't think so, I need tae go- uh, *to* go somewhere, please let go of me." Lissa tried to sound assertive without being rude. She kept pulling away but he held her fast.

"Babe, I don't think you have anything better to do then hang with me, now come on. Jace Nico's a player, that means he's done you and has already moved on." His face hardened at her resistance, the blue eyes getting angry.

Keeping his arm wrapped around her waist, he used his free hand to dig his fingers into her arm and started pushing her down another hallway.

"Listen, whatever your name is, stop, let go of me right now! I am not goin' anywhere with you!" Lissa's voice rose in her fear that this man would overpower her and drag her off somewhere and-

Using brute strength, he grabbed her around the waist, bent his knees and went to throw her over his shoulder- Shrieking, she slapped at his hands trying to push him away- her flailing hands didn't hurt him but he was quickly growing pissed.

"Quit fighting me, girl, if you're jailbait you're up for grabs, and I'm taking my share."

She threw herself vehemently to the side to break free but he still held her wrist, snapping her back to him he raised a hand to strike her-

"What the hell- Rawley, let go of her, *now*." Victor Tanjione came stomping rapidly down the hall towards them.

"Mind your own business, Tanjione, you can have your shot with her when I'm done. Come on," he said to Lissa wrapping his arm tightly around her tugging her with him.

"I told you to get your fucking hands off her," Victor's voice a low snarl like the warning from a vicious animal. He stepped in front of them, his arm lashed out like a ramrod, his hand banded around Brett's throat.

Victor's fingers like thick steel nails dug in so deep around his neck, gasping for air, Brett released Lissa to pry off Victor's death grip.

Brett choked and gagged, his face bulged, turning red. He couldn't speak, yet Victor didn't subside. He shot over his shoulder to Lissa, "Are you all right?"

Lissa fell back against the wall, her eyes like terrified saucers at the sudden violence. She nodded unsure if Victor would turn his fury on her when he was done with Brett.

Victor suddenly released Brett, who buckled to his knees with his hands around his throat gasping and coughing.

Victor ordered, "Get up, Rawley, get the hell out of here." He waited as Brett inhaled deeply with coarse wheezes trying to catch his breath.

Taking a step towards him, Victor commanded again, "Get the fuck out of here now or I'll-"

Brett scrambled to his feet and without a backward glance moved in half-staggers down the hall.

Victor turned to Lissa who stared in wide-eyed terror at him.

"You sure you're okay?" Victor's voice was calm and gentle. With kind concern in his warm dark eyes, he smiled at her.

"Uh, yes, yes, I- I thank you. I didn't-" Lissa pressed one hand against the wall, the other over her rocketing heart. To her, the handsome man with the Fu Manchu moustache, black hair and heavy crested black eyes looked stylishly dangerous, like a dapper yet highly ferocious motorcycle gangster.

"That guy's an asshole, sniffs like a dog in heat after all the women but that's the first I've seen him become physically abusive. Where are you going? I'll walk you." Victor's hands hung at his side, he could see Lissa was extremely upset and he didn't want to make it worse by touching her.

When she stayed flat against the wall watching him with apprehension, Victor said kindly, "I'm not going to harm you, Lissa. I would feel better though if I walked you safely to wherever you're going, okay?"

He was trying to get her to go willingly with him, but it didn't matter, no way in hell was he leaving her there alone.

She whispered to the Jekyll and Hyde man, "Um, I was goin' tae the kitchen." Her head lowered, frightened eyes rose halfway up to him, so scarily violent one second, caring and tender the next. He was as big and powerfully built as Jace, and seemed just as dangerous.

"Come on, I'll walk you there," he said it calmly, holding out his arm for her to take. She hesitated, then slipped her hand through his arm.

They were halfway down the hall when Victor cleared his throat.

"Listen, I have to tell Jace what happened. I'm telling you this because I have a feeling you aren't going to say a word about it to anyone, especially to him. Jace and our team have no secrets. He's going to be pretty pissed as it is, and he wouldn't be happy hearing about it from someone else. Okay?"

He bowed his head to see her expression. Just as he thought, she appeared nervous all over again. "Don't worry, Jace won't be mad at you, this wasn't your fault, but he needs to know."

Once he saw her safely to the kitchen he left and went straightaway to find Jace.

Cook gave Lissa a cheerful greeting, "Hey little one, what brings you here?"

When Victor told him what happened, Jace got up immediately to go right after Brett but Victor and Cad held him back.

The men were all in the study reviewing a pile of papers on the table in the middle of the room, except for Donnie who was manning the helm.

Victor held a hand at Jace's chest. "It's covered, bro, he won't be bothering her again. You don't need to go and get Doc all busy fixing the damage you would do to Rawley. Let it go. We have work to do now."

The planes of his face sharpened, his mouth pulled in tight, Jace looked down at the hand on his chest, then up to Victor's calm expression. The air slid out of his lungs, he nodded. "For now. If I see him I'd break his fucking head in."

Victor dropped his hand and he and Cad backed away.

Ker handed Jace a sheaf of papers, and said, "We've all studied these, you need to read them."

Jace tipped a crooked smile at his friend accepting the distraction.

Julio had worked awhile with the men, but like Donnie, he didn't know Jace as deeply as Cad, Victor and Ker did. He didn't know enough to keep his mouth shut at the moment.

"Jace, man, how you going to rationalize keeping her here? You can get life for kidnapping you know." Julio's fingers typed a mile a minute over his laptop while he spoke.

Rifling through a stack of papers, Jace paused in mid-shuffle.

Victor and Cad kept doing what they were doing; they never questioned Jace's decisions, or orders.

Without looking up, Jace said, "She's a material witness, and she can identify us as killers, possibly screwing up the entire operation." He continued shuffling the papers skimming one after the other.

Julio kept going, "You said she didn't see anything. That she got there after we did and the informant was already dead. And, we're pretty sure she's not one of Warrington's people."

Staring at the clutch of papers in his hand, the vein over one temple started beating. Jace twigged his fingers through the front of his hair.

Already edgy because he wanted to go after Rawley and talk to him with his fists, and he wanted to see for himself if Lissa was okay, he rolled his broad shoulders. His eyes fixed on the papers that crumpled under the pressure of his hand, he said, "Then she's in protective custody. As I've said before, she might have been seen by them."

"Why not take her to the local police for-"

Cad clapped Julio on the shoulder. "Dude, your turn, go get us something to eat."

Julio started to protest but thought better of it when he caught Jace's intractable expression, the vein twitching faster.

The men worked for a couple of hours. Julio had gone and gotten them dinner bringing it back to the study.

When they were done for the day, and Jace had calmed down, he left and went to find Lissa.

Assuming Victor had taken her back to their room, he was surprised to find the cabin empty. Leaving the room, he traversed the rest of the ship checking every nonresidential room, every nook, every cranny, the longer he looked the more annoyed he became, and then the annoyance turned to worry.

When he searched virtually everywhere without finding her, he was starting to freak. They were in the middle of the damned ocean; she had to be on the ship. He even checked the engine room.

He was searching the dining room for the second time when he heard her laugh. At the same time he smelled something delicious, like something baking. Which was crazy because Cook was good at plain and simple but he said he couldn't bake for shit. They made do with ice cream for their sweet-tooths.

He followed his ears and his nose as Lissa's giggles and the luscious smell were coming from the same direction.

Jace headed around the back to the galley, the one place he hadn't checked, why would she be in the kitchen?

He walked in quietly and saw Lissa standing with Cook and Colby, and the other kitchen helpers drawn in by the fragrance of pastry baking.

Dillon Beck, Jon Smith and Dave Lewis circled her. They were all laughing.

Lissa had a white apron tied around her tiny waist, her curly hair tied back in a long braid, soft autumn wisps curled around her face.

Colby was imitating her slight accent, badly, it made them all laugh louder.

Wiping an eye, Dave said to Colby, "You're not rolling your r's dude, you're supposed to trill 'em, not spit 'em!" The laughter burst again.

Colby grinned. "But I *donnae* know how," he pretended to cry. The men roared hysterically at him.

Lissa giggled, letting her accent out in full. "Ah ken giive yoo ah laason laetta, Coolby."

"I see why you try to hide your accent, Lissa, with buffoons like these guys," Cook chuckled, the men all laughed again.

"What's, uh, going on here?" Jace asked when he got close.

Young, fair-haired Colby's laughter bubbled out of him. He told Jace, "It started when Cook had asked how windy was it outside, and Dillon said it was deader that Kelsey's nuts. And then Dave asked what does that mean, we were all saying a bunch of goofy stuff when Lissa explained to us why Kelsey's nuts were so dead-" the other men shrieked with laugher.

Jace stood bewildered.

Lissa had a hand over her mouth, she was laughing behind it, her eyes sparkled like green diamonds with fun.

At Jace's confused expression, Colby explained, "Apparently it came from a real guy named John Kelsey. A friend of car magnate, John Ford, he set up the Kelsey Wheel Company. The saying refers to the security of his nuts and bolts.

"It was originally advertised that 'nothing could be tighter than Kelsey's nuts,' that turned to meaning a person was stingy. Then it was 'nothing could be as safe as Kelsey's nuts,' then it went to the-" seeing Jace's not amused face, and his eyes narrowed to angry blue slits, Colby petered off then shut his mouth.

Jon offered cheerfully, "Then we all started trying to copy her accent, it's so cute."

"Dave was best," Colby said. They all started laughing again.

Jace's disgruntled frown was turning into a churlish scowl.

"Oh, Jace my boy, look what she did!" Cook cried gleefully pointing at the counter where a cherry and a lemon meringue pie were cooling.

Dillon had a pie server in his hand and his tongue sticking out of the side of his mouth about to slice into the cherry pie.

Jace's expression was a cross of anger and confusion.

Cook said, "And, she has chocolate, homemade mind you, chocolate chip cookies in the oven. They're just about ready-" a timer rang,

"Yes!" Cook crowed, opening the oven door, a heavenly smell wafted out. All the men's noses leaned toward the oven. Cook slipped a mitt on his hand and reached into the oven.

"What the hell are you doing here?" Jace roughly snapped at Lissa. His anger spilled out, worry had gnawed at his innards at first hearing about Rawley's attack on her, then as time had gone on and he couldn't find her, he had been on the verge of panic that she'd gone overboard.

Before she could answer, he snaked his hand out and grabbed her wrist. "We're going."

As he pulled on her, Cook stood up with a tray of steaming cookies, chocolate oozing out of them.

"Here Jace, if these are as good as her pies, they'll knock your socks off!" He shoved the tray in Jace's face.

Jace held up a hand, his face twisted in anger. "No, thanks, Benny, we have to-" a cookie had split and melted chocolate spilled out of it, the smell of rich chocolate rushed Jace's senses.

"Uh, maybe just one." Jace went to reach for a cookie but Cook said, "Wait! They're hot!" He slipped a spatula under a cookie, slid it off and held it out for Jace to take.

"Yikes," Jace let go of Lissa's hand to juggle the cookie. "You weren't kidding about hot!" He took a bite, his eyes rolled.

"Yeah? Just like I said, incredible, huh?" Cook held the tray scooping off cookies and handing them to the other drooling men. "Lissa has been here all day baking. She's a Godsend, Jace."

Benny leaned in so no one else could hear and scolded him, "Don't you bark at her, son, she's done nothing wrong. She'd been here all day baking, and the girl is a darling."

His mouth grimly set, Jace snatched another cookie, then picked up several more put them in a napkin and said harshly to Lissa, "Leave the apron."

He waited while she, ire filling her eyes at the way he spoke to her, untied her apron and handed it to Benny.

Pulling the band off the bottom of her braid, she separated the twined hair with her fingers, fluffed it and said sweetly to the cook, "Thanks, Benny, I had a fun time. Can I come back again?"

"Are you kidding me, girl? The men have been bugging me forever to get some sweet stuff in here." He winked. "And besides you they wanted some cookies too," he chuckled at his joke. "You come back any time, honey, tomorrow would be great!" Benny grinned hugely at her then bent and kissed her cheek.

Giving Benny a dirty look, which the cook merely sniffed at, Jace wound his fingers around Lissa's arm and ushered her out of the kitchen.

They didn't speak as he walked her back to their room.

When they got inside, Lissa tugged at her arm. "You can let go of me now, Mr. Nico, you don't need tae guard me, I promise I won't hijack the boat or anythin'."

Not letting go of her, he set his napkin of cookies on the dresser, and asked, "Why were you in the kitchen of all places?"

She glared at his hand on her arm but he didn't move it. With a heavy sigh, she said, "I sat with the girls for a while. They were so borin', all they talked about was makeup and shoes, and men and," her cheeks suddenly brightened.

"And what?" he asked, curious at the pink blossoming on her cheeks.

She shook her head, said flatly, "Nothin'." There was no way on earth she was going to tell him they had been talking about him, and her, and...his size, *God*, she turned red again.

His eyes flashed at her. He wanted to know what burst such color into her cheeks, but he let it go. He would interrogate Glennie later.

Releasing her, he yanked off his light jacket and tossed it on the short divan by the door already covered with clothes. Sitting on his bed, he said nonchalantly, "Fine. Anything else you want to tell me that happened today?"

Her brows lifted in disinterest. She looked down at her hands, they were dusted with flour. "No."

"Nothing?"

Not answering him, she headed for the bathroom to wash her hands.

When she came out he was leaning against the doorframe. Startled, she jumped. He took her arm, dragged her over to a chair and sat her down.

"Really, Nico, I would appreciate you just tell me what you want instead of draggin' and shovin' me all around." She rubbed her arm where he'd held her.

Standing in front of her, Jace crossed his arms and glared down at her. "Victor told me he interrupted something today. Want to tell me about it?"

Lissa glared right back at him. "No. Tis none of your business. Speakin' of business, don't you have work tae do with your boys?"

His body stiffening at her insolence was the only clue revealing his irritation. "Lissa, you are my business. This is my boat, my job, I can't have any trouble-"

She stood up cutting him off. Her lips pulled in tight, she blew them out. "I did not cause any trouble."

He put his hands on her shoulders and shoved her back down on the chair. "I will tell you when you can get up."

Stunned at his dominant behavior, her mouth opened, no words came out, it shut. Lissa jumped back up saying furiously, "How dare you, you can't tell me what I can do! Who do you think you are?"

Barely containing his rising ire, Jace put his large hands on her slender shoulders, carefully curling his fingers around them, then very slowly forced her to sit back down. "Tell me what happened today, don't make me ask again."

"Let go of me you brute! Nothin' happened. It was no big deal, I had everythin' under control." Incensed, Lissa struggled to escape his hold.

Increasing the pressure on her shoulders, Jace said coolly, "Really? You had everything under control? Like you do now?"

Seeing it coming, he twisted sideways so her kick missed his privates. If he wasn't so mad he would have laughed at her feeble efforts to get away from him.

"The way Victor tells it, Rawley had all but thrown you over his shoulder and was traipsing off to his cave with you, and you were powerless to do anything. The kick you just tried to give me I saw coming a mile away. You fight like a damned girl. From now on, you will stay here, in this fucking room unless I say otherwise."

Beside herself with helpless rage, Lissa wriggled and kicked with everything she had. Her voice shaking with impotent anger, she cried, "Donnae you forget, you brought me here, against my will. I hate tae be any trouble, you may drop me off at the nearest port, I will find my way home. At least the dock workers will have better language."

Jace leaned over putting his face in hers, his blue eyes dark and sparking fury, his voice grated like an iron fence across cement. "You will do what I say, Miss Mallory. You're right. I brought you here, that makes you mine to do with what I want. And what I want is no more trouble from you, therefore, you will not leave this room unless I say."

She opened her mouth to protest but he spoke right over her.

"And, you will tell me immediately if anything like that happens again, anyone touches you, hurts you. Do not make me hear it from someone else first, again." His tone dropped deep and low, moving inches closer to her face, he ground out, "Do I make myself clear?"

Lissa's eyes flit back and forth looking for an escape, but he kept his large hands dwarfing her shoulders. It was as if a bull was holding her down, she couldn't move. Her only weapon was to glare back at him.

His face darkened, the grading of his facial features calcifying as the fury spread through his body. Letting go of one shoulder he clutched her jaw, she refused to drop her eyes, and she refused to answer him.

Through gritted teeth he said harshly with menace, "I can beat you within an inch of your life, maybe then you'll cooperate." Jace felt satisfaction when he saw the fear light her green eyes.

He said soft and low, "You don't have a clue as to what a dangerous situation you are in."

She still refused to answer him.

He suddenly let go of her and stormed out the door, slamming it behind him.

Chapter Eight

*H*e needed a fucking drink.

Breathing hard, Jace stalked down the hall, his heart pounding out of his chest. Damn bitch, he was so mad he could- his steps slowed.

Raising both hands he smoothed his hair back, he wasn't mad, he realized, he had been afraid for Lissa's safety, and frustrated. What he wanted was to take her, push her down and slide between her legs until she cried out his name.

He pictured her beautiful body writhing in insane pleasure under the magic of his hands that were right now dying to touch her body, along with his mouth, everywhere. That was what he was really feeling.

Frustrated desire combined with fury over Brett's attack on her had him on the edge of exploding. If Victor hadn't been there…

In retro-panic Jace pushed his hair back off his forehead. Looking at Lissa, the fear of what Victor had described happening, along with his own hunger for her, Jace knew he had to leave the cabin before his control snapped.

He craved so badly to latch his mouth on her plump perfect lips, her anger only turned him on more. God, already hot as hell, when she was pissed she was glorious. And he wanted a piece of that. A huge piece.

Jace shook his head in derision, what a fool he was. It wasn't fear he wanted to see in her crystalline eyes, he wanted her to look at him with desire and…affection. He laughed, hell, to be honest with himself, he wanted much more than her affection. Damn, he regretted threatening her like a barbaric warlord just now.

Shaking his head again, he took long grousing strides down the hall. What was coming over him? He had never gotten this angry, or this hot, or this tyrannical over a woman before.

It didn't help that he had been stabbed by the unique feeling of the jealousy stick when he'd come upon her laughing it up with the men in the kitchen.

She never behaved that way with him. He grunted wryly, of course he was her kidnapper and jailor, what the hell could he expect? Actually, he remembered they'd had a good time playing pickle ball. Her eyes had been lit with gaiety when she teased him.

She had laughed without restraint, it was all he could do to keep playing and not pick her up and lay with her on the damned court-

He strode into the small makeshift bar area and went behind the counter to pour himself a drink. He wished he'd noticed Dona Sutherland was there before he had gone in the room.

The statuesque blonde swished her bottom off her padded stool, and with a drink in her hand, swaying her ample hips so hard she could set off all the bells in a pinball machine, sashayed right over to Jace.

He kept going, moving to sit with Ker, Victor, Julio and Cad already hunched over drinks at a table.

Dona got to him before he made it there.

She slung her glass-free arm over his shoulder and almost spilled her drink on him. Her eyes were bloodshot, lipstick smeared, her words slurred, "Jacey baby, were you goin'? Let's you and me go have some fun. We can find a private place easily enough."

In a catty little sneer, she asked, "Is that foreign delinquent slut still in your room?" Dona snuggled up to him even as he tried to pull her arm off him.

"Just throw her out, Jacey, she can find a place to sleep easy enough, any of the men here are more than willing to have her."

She said, "I know Brett is dying to bang her, she can stay with him while you and I get it on."

Feeling his fury over Brett roil up his chest like heartburn, Jace wrenched away from her, this time her drink did spill. "I'm not interested, Dona, take a hike."

He stalked away from her over to his friends and slumped down in a chair.

Dona stood unhappy for a moment, then she saw her empty glass and grinned sloppily. "I need a drink!" she announced to no one then tripped back to the bar where one of the other women, Vicki, made her another drink.

"Damn, Jace, you got them dropping in your lap." Cad laughed slapping Jace on the back. "You're letting the little one cramp your game, bro. It's clear she's getting your panties in a twist. You need to either do her and move on, or put her out and let one of us-"

"Shut the fuck up," Jace snarled. He got up, went to the far side of the bar, got two bourbon double-shots and a beer, came right back sat down and threw back the first double bourbon.

Slamming the glass on the table, he wiped his mouth with the back of his hand. He ignored Cad's taunting grin.

By the time he tossed back the second bourbon and chugged half the beer he was feeling less crabby.

The men were discussing their next move on their mission.

Jace said aside to Victor, "Just so you know, Lissa says she had everything under control today."

A burst of beer spewed out of Victor's mouth.

The others looked at him with brows cocked in amusement.

Wiping his mouth, Victor laughed. "Is that what she told you?" Taking a swig of his brew, gulping thirstily, he smiled shaking his head.

He told Jace, "She was fighting for all she was worth, bro, I give her that. But Brett Rawley was a half a second away from picking her up. He had a tight hold on her and was bending to toss her over his shoulder. If I hadn't come by right at that moment he would have been gone with her. She didn't stand a chance."

Victor decided against telling Jace that the guy was about to take a swing at the young woman. Filling himself up with bourbon, Jace would be too hard to hold back this time, he'd go right after Rawley.

"What the hell?" Cad banged a fist on the table making all the glasses and bottles jump. "What are you talking about?" He had helped Victor earlier check Jace's wrath but he had just entered the room and hadn't heard what had the man so riled.

Victor reached over and clinked his beer bottle with Cad's. "This morning on my way to the bridge, I see that fucker, Brett Rawley, has his hands all over the girl, Lissa, and he's dragging her down the hall to his room. She's fighting like crazy but she was like a leaf in a storm, had not a chance of getting away."

"Wasn't she screaming for help?" Julio asked watching Jace start boiling again.

Victor twitched one shoulder. "I think it was happening so fast and she was scared and shocked, I don't think she could."

"What- the- fuck!" Cad stood up hollering. "Where is that bastard, I'm gonna kill him!"

Victor grabbed Cad's shirt and yanked him back down, the big man crashed onto the chair. Victor said calmly, "I took care of it, he won't bother her again. Don't go stirring things all up again. Everyone, just drink up."

Finishing his beer and about to get up to get another, Jace said, "No worries, I told her she can't leave my room at all without me. I got it all under control." He strode off to get another beer.

The men at the table looked at each other then burst into laughter.

Victor said, "Yeah, he's got about as much control over that girl as she had of Rawley. Ha, like she'll do everything Jace says, ha- that's a joke. Hey," he leaned in with his palm out, "how soon before he's thundering about her again?"

Julio pulled money out of his pocket and threw down a ten-dollar bill. "I say by midnight tomorrow."

"Ha!" Victor said, "I got by dinner," he added his ten to Julio's.

Shaking his head, Cad smiled. "They won't make it to lunch." He tossed his ten on the pile.

They all turned to Ker who had not said a single word since Jace had joined them. He reached in his pocket and laid down his money. "Breakfast."

As soon as Jace left in the morning, Lissa showered, dressed, and slid out behind him. She made her way quickly to the kitchen.

Cook was surprised to see her. "Hey honey, it didn't look yesterday like Jace was going to let you come back here."

Lissa bustled right in dismissing any mention of Jace with a wave. "Oh, he likes tae bluster but he cannae tell me what tae do." She was wearing a short skirt and blouse. Pulling a clean folded apron off a table she tied it around her waist and asked, "Do you have confectioner's sugar?"

Cook started to warn her that Jace wasn't a man that liked his orders ignored, then he heard what she said about the sugar and totally forgot all about Jace. "You going to make frosting? Does that mean cake? Cupcakes?"

He followed the grinning woman when she went to gather the flour and eggs.

Jace stayed on the bridge most of the day with the other men discussing their plans. They would be making their first port stop in a couple of days. Confident that Lissa was ensconced in his room, he had told Julio to bring her lunch and dinner.

Julio was going to spend most of his day doing laundry and working on his computer in his room. Victor had given him some tasks to research.

There was a cooler on the bridge with sandwiches and cold drinks in it so Jace ate both lunch and dinner without having to leave. Yawning, he said to Ker, "We can finish this tomorrow."

He didn't wait for Ker's response since the man well known for his brooding silence, usually made no comment.

Out the bridge and down a few steps, Jace strode leisurely back to his room.

One of the other men, not part of his team but was also going to do the job Jace had been hired for, saw him pass by from the great room. He hurried out and stopped Jace.

"Hey, Nico," the man greeted him.

Jace greeted the brown haired, brown eyed, shorter man. "Hey Derrick, what's up?"

Derrick had fluffed and moussed his hair up on his head to give him more of an illusion of height. He had a Roman nose and a small pot belly. "I heard we're making port around Wednesday."

Jace nodded. "Yes, that's the plan."

The guy ducked his head a few times, shoved his hands in his pockets, then said in a quiet voice, "I uh, I have a girl near there, so, uh, how long will we be docked?"

"Just a day, maybe two, depending on how long it takes to get supplies and gas up. We won't know for sure until then. At least one day though for sure. Better call her now and get it set up." Jace winked with a grin and went on his way.

He was stopped two more times on his way to his room.

Opening the door, he expected to see Lissa sitting reading or sewing. She'd already sewn up tears in a couple of his shirts. She had mentioned to Doctor Drew the other day she wished she had a sewing basket to have something to do with her idle hands.

Jace had found one on board and gave it to Drew to bring to her. But now the room was empty, and dark.

Checking the bathroom and not finding her, he pulled out his cell and dialed.

"Yup?" Julio answered.

"Hey, J, was Lissa here when you brought her dinner?" There was dead silence on the other end of the phone. "Julio?"

"Uh, well, to be honest, One Shot, I got uh, busy and I kinda forgot about her until now."

Jace asked quietly, "What about lunch?"

"Um, gee Jace, like I was busy all day, I-"

Jace's harsh voice bit into the phone, "Did you see her at all today? Did you go to my room at all?"

"Well, uh, like I was saying, I was bus-"

Jace clicked off, shoved the phone in his pocket and stormed out the door. This time he went straight to the kitchen.

She wasn't there, but a cake with fluffy white frosting and a muffin tray of multi-colored cupcakes were on the counter.

"Benny!" Jace roared through the kitchen.

In seconds Benny's plump body came huffing from the back storeroom.

"Jace, dude, what's the matter? Why are you yelling?" Benny saw Jace standing next to the cake and guessed. "Oh. You didn't know she was coming here today."

Benny's white T-shirt had pink and green frosting stains on it, telling on Jace that he was duplicitous in helping decorate the sweets.

"Where is she?" Jace demanded. His hands curled in fists at his side, teeth clamped together. His jaw worked hard enough to crack marbles.

"Well, I don't really know. She left, I don't know, around 15 minutes or so ago. She didn't say where-" Benny was talking to open air.

Jace turned around, his long legs hoofed him out and he was gone.

"Boy," Benny shook his head. "I sure wouldn't want to be that little honey when he catches up with her."

Outraged that he had to go search the whole damned ship again, Jace's boots thumped loudly down the hallways. Unclenching his fists, he forced himself to cut down on his speed and smoothed the fury from his face, he didn't want to advertise his annoyance.

It was bad enough that girl had him running in circles everybody else on board didn't need to know it too. Already his friends teased him about her driving him nuts.

Used to being in charge and his commands followed without question, the fact that she refused to do as he told her just drove him around the bend.

Yesterday Julio had mentioned giving her a good hard paddling on her butt if she didn't do as he said.

Jace's lips turned up, *yeah, that was a great idea.* As soon as he gets his hands on her-

Chapter Nine

Over half the people on the boat were in the great room. A few were on top deck sun bathing, the rest were in the dining room eating or just hanging in their cabins.

Hoping he wouldn't have to check individual rooms, Jace went towards the study. Doubting she was there, he decided at the last minute to check it.

Ker and Victor happened to be coming down the hall a dozen or so yards behind him.

He could hear voices before he reached the study. "Hey," just as he entered the room, he started to ask if anyone had seen Lissa then his eyes about burst when he crossed the threshold.

She was there all right. She was sitting on Brett Rawley's lap with her hands bound together with rope, and a cloth tied over her mouth. Jerking and twisting, she was struggling to get away from Brett but he had his arms around her and was laughing at her efforts.

The short skirt she had on was bunched up her slender thighs, and the shirt she wore showed glimpses of midriff skin when she tried to swing her arms to get loose from Brett's restraints.

Brett latched one arm around her, holding her bound arms down and maneuvered his other arm so he could get his palm high up on her bare thigh.

She tried to pull her legs up and away from his hand, but hooting with salacious laughter Brett forced them down.

Standing just inside the room past the chair were Donnie and Julio wearing astounded expressions.

Shouting, *"What- the- fuck-"* in a heartbeat Jace bent and grabbed Lissa's arms wrenching her right out of Brett's hold and off his lap.

Wrapping his arm around her back to brace her, Jace pulled the gag down off her mouth.

Gasping for breath, her green eyes were bright with alarm.

Jace moved with her the few steps to the couch and helped her sit down, then turned to Brett who was sitting dumbfounded with his arms still out like he was waiting for Lissa to hop back on his lap.

Standing as a sentry between Lissa and Brett, Jace snarled at him, "What the hell is this all about?"

Furious that Jace had barged in and taken Lissa from him while Jace's friends stood there gawking stupidly like lost coyotes, Brett went for nonchalance. "Dude, you need to learn to share your toys."

"The hell? She is not a fucking toy, Rawley, and she's not being shared." Jace glanced at Lissa behind him.

Panting from fear and her struggling efforts, Lissa's hair, a mussed cloud around her head, some of it draped over one eye. Skin so pale in her fright it was translucent. The gag hung around her neck, her skirt was all scrunched up, her chest heaved from her panic, and her wrists were still bound.

"Why the fuck is she tied up?" Jace barked, sitting down next to her. He took her hands and untied the rope. As she rubbed her wrists, he tugged her skirt down covering her thighs.

Brett laughed like they were all great friends having a good ol' boys time. "Bitch wouldn't stop fighting me, wouldn't give it up. Doesn't know when she has a good thing goin' on with a hot guy, right?"

Seeing a bruise on Lissa's cheek, Jace's face darkened as his anger escalated. Cupping her chin to look at it, a frown pulled his mouth down. He brushed his fingertips under the wound. "What happened? Where'd you get this?"

Lissa's eyes glassy with tears darted to Brett then dropped to her hands in her lap not answering him.

Jace looked over at Brett, the man's face colored in guilt.

"You hit her?"

Brett held both hands up, with a curl of smirk he laughed. "Dude, what can I say? When I grabbed her in the hallway she screamed. I had to shut the bitch up. It was only hard enough to stun her, not knock her out. Nothing to make such a big deal out of."

Jace jumped up, grabbed Brett's collar and yanked him off the chair. "You fucking hit a defenseless woman, you piece of shit?" Letting go of his shirt Jace shoved him so he stumbled back.

"Okay Rawley, you fucking prick, now you can hit someone your own size." Jace pointed his thumb at his chin and commanded, "Hit me."

"Huh?" His mouth dropping open, Brett said, "Come on, man. She's just a pretty bitch. The word is she's on her way to the lock-up, who cares what I do to her?"

"Hit me," Jace demanded, his voice lethally calm. Hands at his side, eyes firing bullets aimed at Rawley.

"Naw, come on, dude." Brett inched away, nervously tucking his shirt in; he scratched over one ear as he headed towards the exit.

In a flash, Jace moved to stand in front of the door. "This is the only chance you're going to get, take it Rawley, now." His hands still hung at his side, not up in a fighting stance.

"This is ridiculous, I'm not gonna-" Brett suddenly shot out his fist to sucker punch Jace.

Faster than a flash of light, Jace threw up his forearm blocking the blow and slammed his other fist into the side of Brett's jaw.

Brett's head snapped hard to the right. Jace clubbed him again, then just went crazy. His fists pummeling, he hit him again and again until Brett wailed, staggering to his knees.

Jace clutched his shirt around the neck to hold him up and kept pounding him with his fist, blood flew everywhere.

Falling on his back, Brett threw a few defensive swings but Jace knelt over him still fiercely slugging him.

"Stop!" Lissa shrieked. Scrambling to her feet she tried to get between the sparring men.

Victor and Ker just entered the room. Quickly taking in the scene, Victor snared his arm around Lissa's waist and pulled her back out of the way.

She cried out, "No! Nico stop! Let go of me, Victor, he'll kill him, please stop him!"

Victor whispered in Lissa's ear, "Honey, if he wanted him dead he already would be." He held onto her keeping her out of the way, they didn't need her accidentally being the recipient of one of Jace's blows, as delicate as she was he could kill her.

He nudged her to sit back down on the couch out of the way and stood in front of her.

Kneeling over Brett, Jace snagged his collar again, lifting him off the ground he punched him square in the nose, blood gushed spraying in all directions.

Ker bent, clutched Jace's arms and pulled him up. "Okay, enough, One."

Jace stood panting with his fists clenched, blood dripping from his knuckles, boots straddling Rawley. He wiped his sleeve over his eyes to clear the sweat. Ker tugged him away from Rawley.

Groaning, Brett struggled to his hands and knees, sat back on his heels and wiped at his face.

He stuck a finger in his mouth. Blood streaming from all over his head, out of his nose, he cried furiously at Jace, "You broke my fucking tooth you asshole."

Jace took a step towards him, Ker held him but loose enough. If Brett kept whining he'd let Jace go and shut him up. The step Jace took was enough.

Cowering, Brett covered his head and clambered wobbly to his feet. Stumbling to the door, his forearm on the doorframe, fingers digging into the wood to keep from falling, he sagged against it.

Coughing and hacking, his head hanging, blood dripped on the floor. His light hair dark with sweat hung over his teary swollen eyes.

Jabbing a finger at Brett, voice like pitted iron, Jace told him, "You'll leave here alive today and on your own two feet, Rawley, because I'm letting you. Touch her again and you're a dead man." Jace's unemotional quiet tone was more bone-chilling than if he'd shouted in a rage.

His hands leaving trails of blood on the walls Brett staggered out. They heard him cursing and groaning stumbling down the hall.

"And you two," Jace shrugged out of Ker's grasp, swung around and gestured to Julio and Donnie who were still standing exactly as they were when Jace had first come in, mouths hanging open in astonishment.

Glaring at them, Jace went and sat down next to Lissa.

With her back against the corner of the couch that was plumb against two walls, Lissa pulled the gag off her head and threw it on the floor.

Jace picked the rag up, wiped his bloody hands on it and said to Julio and Donnie, "What the fuck were you two doing just standing there watching that bastard do that to her? What the hell is the matter with you?"

Protesting, "Jace, bro," Julio held his palms up, "we just got here like a half a second before you. We heard a scream, we were trying to find who was screaming and checked in here. We had just asked the guy what was going on, when you came in."

Donnie added sheepishly, "Man, bro, we didn't know if she was into it, you know, like BDSM?"

Turning his head in disgust from them, dropping the rag, Jace picked up Lissa's hands and lightly stroked her wrists looking at the damage to them. There were deep rope burns around them from her frantic struggles.

He told her, "You're going to go see Doc Drew."

Lissa shook her head slightly, she still hadn't raised her mortified eyes to his. She murmured, "I'm fine. Tis nothin'."

"You will not argue with me. Get up, Ker will take you there now." He glanced over at the tall, strapping Asian who as usual stood blankly expressionless.

Lissa didn't move.

"*Lissa*," Jace hissed.

"Bro," Victor said with a hint of humor. "You've got her fenced in. She can't get out unless she climbs over you."

His lips pushing out, Jace could see that he was sitting next to her with his long legs wide. She was curled up in the corner with a wall blocking her on one side and his leg in front of her, penning her in from the other side. It was like he was unconsciously guarding her.

His mutter quietly scathing, "More like fencing you guys out since you're so goddamned quick to protect her." He stood and helped Lissa up.

Looming over her, he caressed her face gently, holding the side of her jaw up so she had to look at him. When her green eyes met his blues, he said, "Ker will take you to Drew, then to our room. I will talk to you when I get there."

Lissa blinked. Although his touch was tender, vicious fury blazed in the deep blue orbs. He stood calmly but his body was so rigid he was almost vibrating.

Without comment, Lissa walked over to Ker. The guy frightened her, but at the moment Jace was like a raging Frankenstein's monster. Ker for once seemed the less threatening of the two.

Not touching her, Ker walked beside her on their way to the medic.

Lissa cut a side-glance at the tough yet elegant man. As always, he wore a long-sleeved starched white shirt, crisply ironed tight black pants and black boots with the toes narrowing like a cowboy boot.

The black hair, the top in a ponytail the rest loose around his shoulders fluttered in the air as he walked with a lithe, arrogant confidence.

Doc disinfected then wrapped bandages around her wrists and put antibiotic ointment over the cut on her cheek. It didn't need a bandage; it was more of a bruise than a deep cut.

Smoothing the ointment, he said, "I don't know, honey, most the people on this ship haven't darkened my doorway, other than the occasional hammer hit thumb or drunken fall, and here this is your second visit. What's up with that?"

"Oh, I'm just...clumsy," Lissa said weakly, mortified at her ordeal. Too many people had already witnessed her embarrassing assault and her ridiculously futile efforts to save herself.

Crossing his arms, Doc's brows lowered seriously. "Clumsy doesn't make rings around wrists, honey. You can tell me if," he glanced at Ker who stood impassively by the door, "someone is...abusing you?"

"Drew," Ker's deep voice came low and quiet from the doorway.

The doctor threw a glare at Ker and turned so his body shielded Lissa from Ker's view. "Seriously, Lissa, if there is something wrong here you need to tell me."

Her smile was warm and grateful. "Everythin' is okay, Doctor, really." She said to Ker, "I'm ready, Mr. Dove." No point in putting off the inevitable told-you-so and tongue lashing Jace was going to give her.

Ker put his hand lightly on Lissa's back to usher her out. He paused, turned to Doc and said, "You got questions, Drew, ask Jace."

When they hit the hallway, Ker dropped his hand and they walked in silence to Jace's room.

At the door, Lissa knotted her fingers together to keep them from shaking. As Ker turned to go, she said with a trembling lip, "Mr. Dove..."

He swiveled to face her, one black brow up in question.

"Mr. Dove, I, uh...could you..." what did she want him to do, protect her from the clearly enraged Jace?

A surprising kindness gentled his black diamond eyes. His hands clasped behind his back, looking down at her, Ker said softly, "He won't hurt you, Lissa. I promise you he won't." He brushed her cheek with a knuckle and said, "My name is Ker."

The tall, extraordinarily strongly built man turned on his heel and moved silently down the hall, his boots not even making the tiniest sound on the hardwood interspaced with carpet floor.

Not knowing he would be waiting around the corner until she went into the room just to make sure she did, Lissa stood and watched him until he was out of sight.

Taking a giant breath, she held it for a second then exhaled slowly, trying to let out her nerves with it. Her hand on the knob, she hoped the door was locked, it would be an excuse to flee.

But the knob turned easily in her hand.

Sucking in another big breath, she opened the door and stepped into the room.

Chapter Ten

*J*ace was hunched over his desk, a pen tucked over his ear, a pad of paper sat next to the computer he was tapping away at. She tiptoed through the room, maybe he was so involved he wouldn't see her.

Without looking up, he said, "I want you to sit your ass down in that chair." He motioned to a chair with his head.

That took the wind right out of her fearful sails. Her lips compressed in a tight line, she kept walking towards the bathroom, maybe she could lock the door and stay there until he fell asleep.

"I won't tell you again, Lissa, sit down." His voice was deceptively calm and hushed.

She flipped around with her hands on her hips, eyes reproachful, her chin in the air, she said with affronted dignity, "You can order all you want, Nico, but I'm not going' tae-"

Before she could blink Jace was out of his chair and standing in front of her. "So," he said laconically, his fingers relaxed on his hips, "did you have everything under control again a half hour ago, like you did yesterday?"

Her lips parted, she closed them. There was no denying the dire situation he had rescued her from today. A splash of anguish puckered her pretty face for a split second. Her eyes dropped in mortification at the whole situation.

On the way back to his cabin, Jace heard from Brett's friend Dillon, that Lissa had been heading back to their room from the kitchen, no doubt hoping she'd get there before Jace even knew she was gone. When suddenly Brett had popped out of nowhere, strung his arms around her and when she screamed he socked her.

Then he tied her hands like he'd just lassoed a calf, tossed her over his shoulder and carried her off to the study.

"Well, that's neither here nor there," she gave him a non-answer, "it doesn't give you the right tae tell me what tae do." In her agitation her accent fluctuated awkwardly.

Jace lowered his head so they were eyeball to eyeball. Oppressive lines deepening around his eyes, the rigidity of his jaw should have warned her.

Now the danger slid into his voice. "Don't you see, when you don't do as I tell you, you get into trouble, and like I said, I don't want trouble on my ship."

She twirled away trying to get to the bathroom. "It was not my fault. I didn't go lookin' for trouble. I was walkin' down the hall mindin' my own business when," drawing a belabored breath, she said, "we can talk about this later. I'm going tae-" her arm was jerked so hard she thought it would come right out of its socket.

Jace pulled her to face him. His face dark with fury, he snarled, "The trouble was your fault because I told you not to leave this room without me with you."

He tugged her arm when she turned away towards the bathroom and said wryly, "I've got news for you, honey, it would take me one kick to open the bathroom door. It wouldn't do you any good to try to hide in there."

With him looming over her looking so furious, his broad shoulders blocking her way, trying to mask her fear with annoyed bravado, she twisted out of his grasp and snapped, "I was not goin' tae hide, I am not afraid of you. I didn't ask tae be here and you will not tell me what I can and can't do."

Lissa crossed her arms for emphasis. "You can posture and reprimand me all you want, you can't make me do anything." She grimaced as she was trying hard to neutralize her accent.

Jace seized her arm again careful of the bandages on her wrists and dragged her back to the small divan. "Oh don't worry, honey,

I'm done with the reprimanding, it is obviously a waste of my breath."

She dug her heels in. "What are you doing? Let go of me!"

"We're done talking, sweetheart. I should have done this in the beginning. Julio was right to suggest it." He shoved the clothes off the settee to the floor with one swoop of his big hand and sat down.

"What are you saying? What are you- stop it!" Lissa squealed as he hooked an arm around her chest pulling her down. With his other hand at her lower back he pushed her so was lying across his lap on her stomach.

She immediately tried to roll off. "Nico! Have you gone insane? Let me up right now!" Her voice trilled out high on the edge of a scream.

Jace held her down with one hand on her back. "A child gets spanked when it disobeys, the same will work for a recalcitrant woman. It'll give you something to think about next time you have the inclination to disobey my orders."

"What! You can't, that's battery! Don't you dare!" Her words were muffled from her head hanging down and her face covered with hair. She kicked and tried to claw at him but she hadn't anywhere near the strength he had.

"Stop wiggling, it will only be worse for you," he ordered darkly, pressing his hand flat on her back to hold her still. The shirt she wore rode halfway up her back, he hesitated when he saw the mark from when she'd gotten cut backing into the dresser.

Keeping his hand away from her healing wound, he pushed her skirt up to her waist ignoring her screams; he had no intentions of actually hitting her.

Her butt writhed and bounced in her struggles to get away. Not planning on following through with the paddling, it was more of another threat to get her to listen to him. Taken by surprise, his eyes were captivated. His anger suddenly dissolved.

She was wearing a tiny wisp of lace panties that at this point was barely covering her tush, and with her writhing, *damn*, Jace set his hand on her bottom. She froze.

"God, Lissa," the words rasped out of him. Her blouse got bunched up under her shoulders exposing her entire back and the matching lace bra. His hand palming her, he lightly stroked her soft flesh. He was hard in one second flat.

"Nico, please," she struggled, bucking and straining to get away, whimpering scared, trapped.

His brain firing with little electric shocks, Jace couldn't think. He couldn't rip his eyes away from the perfect round globes under his now clenching caressing hand. In his mind he had already shed his pants and was stroking his shaft between each globe.

Pushing under the tiny panties, he slid his fingers into the crease between her cheeks and lower to her core.

Her fearful voice eased through the heat that was scorching his brain, bringing him to his senses. It was a herculean effort to take his hand away.

With eyes riveted on her partial nakedness, his body throbbed like an engine revving. Before he could think about it, he yanked her skirt down to cover her and pulled her shirt back down. He couldn't remember feeling this insane with lust even as a fledging teen.

Still lying across his lap, Lissa had stopped moving.

Scrubbing a hand up his face then on up to his head, Jace dug his nails across his scalp. His heart beating a blazing tempo, he realized he wasn't going to get control of his body, or his inflamed mind, with her sprawled across his legs and that incredible ass in his face.

The urge to lift that skirt again was almost too indomitable to fight. An apology was beating at his lips trying to get out, but his mouth was locked closed. It would negate the point he was trying to make. That he was in control. Of her.

He curled his fingers around her upper arms and lifted her up to sit on his lap. Jace couldn't look at her; she'd see the shame that burned there.

What the hell was he thinking? Threatening to spank her? He had sunk to domestic violence at this point. He'd just been so enraged that she refused to do as he said and continued to put herself right in the line of danger. He about had a heart attack seeing her bound and gagged ensnared in Brett's perverted clutches.

Just now when Jace had her over his legs, he knew he wasn't going to hit her, just show her he could, then he'd made the mistake of lifting her skirt. Hell, he was as big a pig as that asshole Rawley.

He'd rescued her to turn around and do the same thing to her. Hold her and grope her against her will. Although Rawley had planned to take it to the nth degree, Jace was still guilty of assault.

She sat motionless, her head down.

Jace could hear her making inaudible distress sounds. He wrapped his arms around her. She froze again, then turned her face up to see what other punishment he planned for her.

Still half dazed, he put his fingers around the back of her neck, his thumb around her jaw and brought his mouth down. Her lips were already parted, he kept them open with the power of his, kissing her with crazy passion that enveloped him so quickly like a struck match.

He just as quickly let her go and dropped both arms signaling her she could leave, if she wanted to.

Lissa slipped off his lap. Adjusting her blouse and skirt, she clenched her hands in tight fists, her face bright with furious livid red.

Jace saw it coming but kept his hands on his thighs, he deserved it as she drew her hand back and slapped him a stinging blow. At least she thought it was, however, with her small hand hitting his large hardened face he didn't feel it all that much.

Judging by the pain shooting across her face the strike had hurt her much more than him. He didn't let her know that, he wanted her to preserve some of her pride, some satisfaction that she took back some dignity, some control.

The corner of his lip pulled in slightly watching her without lifting his head. He'd never seen a woman so mad at him before. A shiver ran through his body.

She was exquisitely aglow in her righteous furor, so incredibly gorgeous and blood throbbing hot, he tugged at his jeans to loosen them. What a deviant chauvinist he had become. His mother would kill him if she'd seen his behavior. Any of it, since he'd first taken Lissa.

Standing as inflexible as a wooden beam with her hands rolled back into fists, she spouted at him, "You- you- you- just beat a man almost tae death and then did exactly what he was tryin' tae do tae me. You- you hypocrite, you- beast!"

It was impossible to raise his eyes to look up at her, but he did. His face was utterly expressionless, no regret, no shame, no apology, which apparently infuriated her even more.

She spun and ran into the bathroom, slamming the door.

Jace got up wearily, went to the desk and sat down on the chair in front of it. He set his arms on the desk, dropped his head in exhaustion and guilt, bewildered as to what to do now.

The thing was, since the second he saw her that day in the alley he'd wanted her. The car chase only fueled his desire. Without examining his feelings, he had rationalized a reason to take her, and with that action, his Neanderthal brain told him she was his.

He felt such an intense connection to her, it further confounded his caveman brain that she didn't feel the same about him.

When she came out, a soapy whiff of cherries and lilies filled the room, he kept his eyes on his computer.

She rustled around, folding down her sheet and arranging the pillow, meanwhile the fresh fragrance of her swirled around his head, taunting him right back to arousal.

He half turned his head not looking at her, said off handed, "You uh, done in there?" His skin crackled with electricity at the sound of her bare skin sliding on the sheets.

She murmured a very quiet, "Yes."

Waiting a beat, he shut off his computer; he wasn't looking at it anyway, got up and went to take a very long, very cold shower.

By the time he came out dressed in boxers and a T, she was asleep. He crossed the room silently and went to stand by her bed.

If she woke and saw him staring at her she'd probably scream in fright and call him a perv. But he couldn't help it. There weren't many moments when he felt free to stare at her, he'd look like a stalker or lovelorn loser if anyone saw him.

Standing in the semi-darkness, Jace watched her freshly scrubbed luminescent skin glow with health and vitality. Long dark lashes curled up on her pink cheeks. Light freckles like a sprinkling of cinnamon over rich cream dusted her cheeks and nose.

Awake, her large green eyes down to her slight and delicate nose, the little plush lips in the heart shaped face, made her look like one of those doll things with the big eyes and tiny full mouth. Yet, she was incredibly more graceful and finely molded. His brow twitched seeing the bruise under her eye.

He was surprised she could sleep at all after that happened to her today. Of course she'd spent a long day baking, she'd fought and struggled with Rawley, and then fought and struggled with Jace. A pang of contrition hit his gut.

She was probably exhausted, physically and mentally, still trying to grasp and adapt to what happened to her. The whole getting taken against her will, assaulted, and held prisoner on a ship now in the middle of the ocean.

The sheet had slipped down to her waist, she rolled from her side to lie on her back.

Jace followed the vibrant wet tresses waving across the pillow and a few curls spiraled down curving around her breasts lushly molded in the tight T.

His hand flexed to reach for the curls when he felt a tug in his boxers. Quickly he pulled the sheet up and covered her shoulders.

He stroked her face, then leaned over and kissed her cheek as light as a butterfly wing.

Before his lust came unleashed again, he trod to his own bed to lie down, knowing it would be a sleepless night for him.

Chapter Eleven

*J*ace rose early the next day before the sun was up. Looking over, he could tell Lissa was still asleep. Shoving back the covers his feet hit the floor.

He got up and went over to her. Indulging himself for a brief second, he stared at her. Then, he put out his hand and gently shook her shoulder.

Her lids fluttered before cracking open. She shifted away, clutching the sheet to her chin when she saw him standing over her.

His expression stoic at her flinch from him, Jace said coolly, "I will be on the bridge most of the day. I'll have someone check on you periodically." He nodded to the phone on the nightstand. "You can call inter-ship if you need me."

His hands loose on his lean hips, he said, "You will not leave this room." Ignoring the narrowing of her eyes and the lips curved down at his command, and that she would be stuck in the room all day, he turned from her and moved to the door.

Her voice stopped him. "Nico, why am I tae be sequestered here?" She sat up keeping the covers up to her chin.

Jace responded with a sigh, "I can't believe, after yesterday that you even have to ask that. It is for your protection."

Lissa slid her legs to drop her feet over the side of the bed. "I don't understand, why just me? There are other women on board. Why-"

As soon as he took several long legged steps to her, she shrunk back expecting a physical attack.

Shocked at her reaction, Jace raked a hand through his hair to slow him from speaking too harshly. Taking a breath, he said, "You seem to be the only female here that..." trailing off he didn't want to bring up Rawley again, or his own reprehensible behavior of last night.

He headed back to the door, hesitated then turned slightly and said, "I don't have to explain my actions to you." Her hurt expression implanted in his brain, he went out the door and locked it.

Having no desire to eat breakfast, Jace went straight to the bridge.

Ker glanced at him when he came in. "You don't need to be here, One, this is my watch. Victor is next." Then Ker took in Jace's haggard unshaven face, drawn eyes. "What's up?"

Normally, Jace kept his business to himself but this was his best friend, nonjudgmental unemotional Ker. Jace opened his mouth and spilled his guts about the aborted spanking.

Ker nodded as if he had already figured the fact that Jace looked and acted like shit had everything to do with the girl.

"Spanking?" Ker's dark brow arched. "Doesn't sound like you, or any of us to be manhandling women. Unless it's part of consensual sex games. Maybe you should steer clear of her until you get your head screwed on right."

Jace's nod expressed his pained conscience. "Julio had suggested it to keep her in line." Wincing, his face colored at the derisive look Ker shot him. "I wasn't going to actually do it."

"Oh. So you're taking lessons from Julio the Lothario now?" Ker said drily. "Good move. She ought to fall right into your lap now and obey every word from your commanding mouth. Every woman likes to be restrained and threatened and groped against her will."

The corner of his lip ticked up at Jace's morose scowl. Ker's black eyes canted towards Jace. "So, this kind of started first thing in the morning yesterday, before breakfast?"

That was a strange question, but Jace felt bad enough he wasn't really paying attention. Nodding, he replied, "Yeah. Apparently she split right after I did."

A spot of energy pushed some angry steam back into his voice, "Right after I specifically told her not to leave the room without me with her."

"Hmmm," Ker muttered, patting his pocket that he'd be putting his winning bet money in.

They stood side by side looking out over the ocean through the large bow window. Ker said, "She's got balls."

Jace jerked his head at his friend with a short grin. "I doubt it," he said deliberately misunderstanding him. "You've seen the way she looks. I'm pretty sure she's all woman."

At the helm, his strong capable hands on the wheel, although it was on auto-pilot, Ker cocked his head, sounding a shade snide, "Yet you don't know 100%, unless you've seen her entire naked body, which it sounds like you haven't, and aren't going to anytime soon." If Ker were the snickering kind he would be doing that now.

Jace scowled at the ocean. "Shut the fuck up, Ker."

The two men stood in camaraderie silence for an hour until Victor arrived to take his shift at the helm.

Jace said to Ker as Victor checked the tracking notes, gauges etc. before taking over, "So, can you go take her to breakfast? I don't think she wants to see my face." His head twitched at Victor's knowing snort.

Ker flicked a glance at Victor, said to Jace, "Of course. Lunch too?"

"Nah, have Julio do that. You have better things to do than play nursemaid all day." Jace's voice was thorny and uncomfortable with both the other men's gleeful eyes on him.

They were amused at his expense. They had both told him it was a bad idea to bring her on board. But they saw a consuming engrossment that took over his entire being every time he was with her. He was a dog that would bite, if Lissa was like the bone taken from him.

Smoothing the grin off his face, Ker muttered to Victor, "You owe me ten," and took off to see to his task.

Jace slouched in one of the captain's chairs.

Victor stood easily watching the surf slap occasionally at the hull. His tone light with a touch of humor, he asked Jace, "Trouble in paradise?" He chuckled at Jace's scowl and compressed mouth. "Fine, no personal chit-chat. Let's talk some more about the cyber surveillance of Warrington's computers."

That was a safe conversation. "Okay." Jace straightened up in the chair. "What'd you get?"

One forearm on the dash, the other in his pocket, Victor said, "His was harder to crack than most, he must have a genius on his payroll." Victor's smug look indicated therefore he himself was a super genius.

"Uh huh, I get it, you're damned smart. So," Jace prompted him to continue.

Victor grinned conceitedly at his friend, "I am, aren't I?" Moving past Jace's eye-roll, he said, "It was encrypted upon encrypted. He has used throwaway laptops with dead-end URL addresses. I had to find my way through a webbed global maze of tower bouncing."

Brushing his knuckles across his chest, he said smugly, "I traced it to him and used a new program to unlock his encryptions. I still need to follow the paper trail but at least I can move forward. I have Julio researching some stuff too." Smoothing his fingers over his Fu Manchu moustache, he glanced back out the big window.

The two discussed some of the information Victor had uncovered and the agenda for their mission for a couple of hours.

Donnie entered the bridge. "Hey," he greeted wandering to the helm. "There's land, we should be docking for fuel in 30 minutes give or take." He peered through his mop of scraggly hair out the bow window.

Jace said, "I need to get on deck with the cards. Donnie, grab Julio, you guys will anchor us up, Ker will pump it." As big a boat as it was it took skill to get it in the dock to refuel.

There was a group of stewards that did most of the grunt work outside the ship as well as inside. Jace left the bridge and strode to his room.

As usual, he was wondering what would await him, what Lissa's attitude would be.

Chapter Twelve

*G*ingerly Jace unlocked and opened the door. One hand tucked in his pocket he closed the door behind him.

Lissa sat in the roomy rocking chair beside the window with her legs curled to her side and was reading a book. The early evening sunlight streamed in firing the brilliant highlights in her rosy hair.

Jace stood for a second, pondering how to make peace with her. Other than the Stockholm syndrome deal happening, it was doubtful she was going to come around to where he wanted her. In his arms. His bed. Willingly.

As his boots scuffed across the carpet, she closed the book and looked at him. He could read nothing in her expression.

Sitting demurely with her hands folded over the book in her lap, her soft face was smooth and tranquil.

"Hey," Jace said, "we're going to stop briefly to refuel. You want to come on deck? There's finally something to see other than endless ocean."

Her eyes lit up. She dropped her feet to the floor, then hesitated, asked, "Really?"

Lissa's hesitation and slightly suspicious look like she thought he was tricking her, tore holes in his gut. He nodded seriously with a bit of a smile beckoning her to come. "Yes, of course. Come on."

Already pretty she glowed with a bedazzling smile. Wearing a light blue T and jean shorts, she slipped her sneakers on and said cheerfully, "I'm ready."

Not carrying a wallet when he was on the boat, Jace unlocked a small drawer in his desk, took out credit cards and tucked them in his jean's pocket. "Okay," he smiled at the excited young woman and held the door open for her to pass through.

In the hall, he stopped. Puzzled, she stopped too and waited.

Partly to show he wasn't going to argue and partly because he knew she'd be upset, he crossed his arms over his chest and braced his legs. Starting off awkwardly, he said, "Listen, Lissa, about going to shore…"

Her head tilted up to him with an eager smile. "Yes?"

"Yeah, well, a few, probably most people are going to take the opportunity to go ashore. I'm afraid that you," he cleared his throat, scratched at his neck, then stuffed his hands in his pockets.

"Yes?" she repeated, her brows starting to shift down.

"You can't go ashore. You have to stay on the ship." He watched for her reaction.

Lissa bit at her lip, looked about to cry but she stubbornly refused to give in to more weak tears of frustration.

"Lissa, uh, I'm sorry, you just can't get off."

"But Nico-"

"No."

She put her hand on the wall, the other behind her back. "Why can't I?"

"It just is. Do you want to at least go on the open deck or do you want to go back to the room?"

"Can't I go with you or one of your men to ensure I don't run to the police?"

"No."

The plush lips set hard, she shook her head then started walking forward towards the steps to the upper deck.

Letting his held breath out in a hush so she couldn't hear him, he followed her to the stairs.

When they reached the top deck it was filled with most of the people on board milling about waiting to step onto solid ground if only for a brief time.

The swampy salty smell of the ocean and the slap of the waves against the hull hadn't stopped, but the rocking of the boat had stilled some as it moved very slowly through the inlet to the dock.

Jace led Lissa over to where the pin-thin Glennie and taller, heftier Ivy were standing near the railing, their hair blowing in the breeze as they watched the shore grow bigger as it got closer.

He left Lissa with them and went back down to work with the others fueling the boat. On his way he stopped and spoke quietly with Cad.

"Cad, go stay near her, I can't have her getting on shore and disappearing or talking to anyone."

Smiling with his lips closed and cheeks rounded, Cad replied, "Sure, One, no prob."

"Thanks," Jace said and went on his way, boots clomping across the planked deck.

Cad joined the women hanging over the rail. He came up behind Ivy and leaned over pressing his big body into hers.

Ivy wasn't slim by any means and had that big junky trunk that Cad specialized in.

Giggling, there wasn't anyone else on the boat that big, Ivy recognized his thick body crushing her against the rail. She turned so he was now pressing the front of her, feeling every thick hard, muscle-bound bit of him.

"Hey, baby, why don't we take this downstairs?" Ivy murmured while licking his ear.

Cad enveloped her in his big bear hug and kissed her. "K," he agreed against her lips. Rolling a hand down to squeeze her belly, he liked meat on a woman's bones.

He started walking with her then suddenly stopped. "Oh, Ivy, we have to wait until the boat leaves shore."

Not happy about him not speeding to a room where they could continue what they'd started the other day, she asked, "Why?"

Snuggling against him, she stroked a finger across his lips. "Don't you want hot and ready Ivy, baby?"

Both his huge hands settled on the sides of her waist, he bent and kissed the tip of her nose, at the same time he cut a side-glance at Lissa. His duty was to watch her. "I do, sweet brown sugar, you know I do, but we have to wait." His tone indicated that was final.

A pout pushed Ivy's lips out. "Well then, maybe this rich dark meat is too much for you to handle. Maybe I need to leave you alone and go find myself a more willing- oof!"

Cad slammed her into his chest and kept one bear paw holding her there. He looked down at her and smiled. "Baby, I have an order to follow, you can wait until it's completed."

Ivy knew where her hot sexual bread was buttered. Sighing, she smiled seductively up at the huge guy, shook her weave back off her shoulders and settled herself in the corner of his arm.

"Okay, big man," she moaned, giving in. Secretly she loved a man that took charge, and take charge was Cad's middle name.

They had moved a few yards away from Lissa but she was still in Cad's sight as she wandered the deck checking out different views off the railings.

The couple bided their time making out with an occasional spray of seawater splashing them.

Glennie had gone to shore with the others and now an hour later everyone was filing back on board.

Wearing a midriff exposing shirt that barely covered her melon sized breasts, and tight short-shorts, Dona sauntered up clutching a plastic bag filled with newly purchased items.

Seeing everyone else was occupied, Dona made her way crookedly in the sky-high heels, ample butt bouncing in the short-shorts over to Lissa.

The boat was slowly pulling backwards from the dock.

Dona said off handedly to Lissa, "So, what's going on with you, girl?" She leaned one arm on the railing, her eyes were on the stairs leading from lower deck.

Jace and Ker Dove, two of the most powerfully built, mysterious and dangerous men Dona had ever seen, were deep in discussion heading up to top deck. She'd dreamed of doing them both at the same time.

Lissa responded politely, "Oh, not much really. What have you there?" She motioned to the bag Dona carried.

Opening the bag a little, Dona vaguely looked in at her purchases. "Oh, just a little somethin' somethin'. I can't pass up shopping even if it's a dinky little dock shop. I bought another cute jacket, a rain slicker actually, and a matching hat. So adorable, you know?" She reached in and pulled out the pink and green hat to show Lissa.

"Hmmm, how pretty." Lissa replied diplomatically. Neon pink and chartreuse amoeba-like designed vinyl was not her thing.

"Yeah," Dona sighed closing the bag and resting her arm back on the railing. Hiking up one stiletto on the lower railing made her bottom jut out displaying even more skin, the half-moons already showing under the uber-miniscule shorts. "It rains so much in Scotland you know, I need-"

"What?" Panic struck Lissa's face like a bolt of lightning. She practically shouted at Dona, "Where? Where is this boat goin'?" Her fingers wound around the railing like she was hanging on for dear life.

"Well, uh, I remember now Jace saying something about not telling you where we're going, but I already let the cat out of the bag. There's no reason why you shouldn't know."

"Dona!" Lissa shrieked. "Just tell me where we're headed!"

Giving the younger woman an eye-roll, Dona said, "Okay, okay, take a pill for Pete's sake. I guess after our last refuel, we're going all the way to Scotland."

The much taller blonde, snobbish nose wrinkling well over Lissa's head, not deigning to spare her a glance, said, "Of course the likes of you has never been to Europe," the haughty sniff loud enough ensuring Lissa got her diss.

"Scotland?" Lissa's voice dropped to a raw tight rasp. "No, please, no." Frantically, she looked around, spotting Jace she ran to him.

109

The grin he sported at her approach fell when he saw her stricken face. "What is it, Lissa? What's wrong, honey?"

Seeing the sparks about to fly, Ker kept moving to have a few words with Cad before he left with Ivy on his arm.

"Tell me we are nae goin' tae Scotland," Lissa begged, her fingers curled groping anxiously at Jace. The word *Scotland* splintered out in a broken whisper.

Jace's face pooled into a profane scowl. "Who told you-" he looked up to see Dona watching them.

Seeing his face flushed angrily, Dona angled her head away with her chin high in the air. Showing him what he's missing, she bent forward over the railing sticking her half exposed corpulent butt-cheeks out at him. She stuck her sculpted nose in the air and turned like she was interested in watching the shrinking shore.

"It doesn't matter. Nico!" Lissa cried. "Please, please, I cannae, I *cannot* go tae Scotland!" Clutching maniacally at his sleeves, her voice wrenched beyond desperate.

Thinking it was just because she didn't have a passport Jace said calmly, "It's okay, Lissa, I told you as long as you're with me, it will be all right."

"No!" she yelled, her face white as a sheet. "I can't go tae Scotland, I can't, you don't understand!"

Losing the smile, he asked coolly, "Are you wanted for a warrant or something there? Because if so, tell me, I can help you."

"Jace!" Dona scurried over, her high heels clicking across the wooden deck, butt cheeks and boobs bouncing. Ignoring Lissa's freak-out, she nudged the smaller woman aside while plucking at Jace's arm.

Huddling her bulbous boobs on his chest, she told him, "Listen, leave the little felonious tramp to her temper tantrum, why don't you and I go visit your cabin?"

His attention darted unwittingly to the blonde trying to rub her embellishments on him. He turned away from Lissa to fend off Dona. "Cut it out, Dona, I'm busy, go away. You-" Hearing someone yell, he spun around. Lissa was gone.

Someone was yelling because Lissa was climbing on top of the railing.

"Lissa!" Jace shouted taking off in a sprint.

She kept climbing until she had a foot on a lower rail and a foot on the top and both hands holding on to the top railing. The whipping wind slashed her hair back; her lower foot left the rail and was moving to the top railing.

"Lissa, stop!" Racing to her, his heart in his throat, just as she had both feet on the railing and was about to push off, Jace leapt, hooked his arms around her and flew in the air with her.

Just before hitting the planked deck, he twisted taking the brunt of the fall pulling her on top of him.

Jace lay on his back, his arms still wrapped like steel around her. Panting in his terror, his heart banged against his ribs.

Squirming, Lissa pushed at him, so overwrought she was wheezing. Her words infused with pain, she croaked through gasps of terror, "Let me go! I cannae go tae Scotland, *cuidich mi!*"

In one movement, Jace rolled to sit up pulling her to sit between his legs facing him.

Trying not to tear her shoulders off her, he didn't clutch them quite as savagely as he wanted to, but he did push them together so her arms almost met in front of her chest.

"Goddammit, Lissa, what the fuck is the matter with you? You can't jump off a fucking moving boat this big, you could have gotten killed!"

Seeing that Lissa was beside herself with panic and had just tried to jump off the moving ship, Ker and Cad hurried over.

Not knowing any more than Jace did, they used their bodies to block Lissa and Jace from the curious onlookers.

Victor and Julio rushed out of the bridge leaving Donnie at the helm. They linked with Ker and Cad, surrounding the distraught couple sitting on the deck.

"Oh my God," Dona's sneering drawl steeped in scorn. "What a drama queen." She toed Lissa's thigh with the pointy toe of her high heel. "You little attention whore, you need to-"

Suddenly Ker and Cad elbowed her back and behind them like they were a brick wall around Jace and Lissa.

"Well!" Dona spouted and stalked off in a hissy huff.

Jace was holding Lissa with strong solid hands. She was fighting desperately like her life depended on it to get away from him.

Julio asked anxiously, "Jace, what's going on? You guys okay?"

Lissa tried to scramble to her feet but Jace held her immobile.

Tears streaming down her face, she chanted in hysterical wheezing breaths, "Let me go, please, let me go, let me go, *leig le*! I cannae go tae there!" Intent on getting away, she kept struggling in raging hysteria.

Sliding his hand behind her neck to cradle her head, Jace said softly, "Lissa, calm down."

It didn't make any difference. Her wheezing breathing gasped like she was drowning, eyes wild, she hit out at him. Her voice scraped shrill in her throat, chest heaving, she screamed, "Let me go!"

"No, goddammit. Calm down." Jace wrapped his arms around her, pulling her in to huddle against his chest. Feeling her spastic shuddering in his arms he was at a loss to know what to do.

"You must be one hell of a swimmer," he muttered blithely. "The waves are rough and we're already a mile or so out."

Subdued by his strength, her voice fell dull and flat she mumbled. "I cannae swim."

"What?" Grabbing her upper arms, shaking her, he demanded, "What are you saying?"

Shrugging, she said as if it were no big deal, "I cannae swim. I thought the current might carry me tae shore. If it didn't, then..."

She couldn't see the flabbergast turn to horror when he understood that in her ignorance she thought the current would just gently float her to shore, and if it didn't, it didn't matter to her if she died.

It hit Jace that she fully planned on jumping, and if he hadn't seen her in that split second she would have jumped to her death. His arms tightened so hard around her, she gasped for breath.

The men circling them to keep out prying eyes were shocked hearing her intentions. They glanced around at each other but said not a word. This was Jace's scene to defuse.

"Please, Nico, please," Lissa cried, fighting again, straining at his big arms binding her. Tears flowing, her breathing so raggedly hard and constricted she sounded like she was having a full-fledged panic attack.

His legs encasing her, Jace just kept holding her tight to his chest, loose enough so she could breathe but tight enough she couldn't flee from him. He didn't bother repeating that she couldn't go, it was pointless, she was so distraught she wasn't hearing him.

Eventually fatigued, she stopped struggling, but the tears still fell. Her chest heaved in heavy deep sobs wracking her slender body. Her frantic terrified sobs were tearing him up inside, but Jace wasn't letting her go.

"Victor," Jace said to the black haired man who was watching Lissa, his face wreathed with distress at the young woman's despair.

His worried eyes on Lissa, Victor murmured, "Yeah, One?" He tensely ran his fingers down his moustache that curved around his mouth to his square chin.

Jace said quietly, "Can you and Julio clear us a bit of privacy?" A curious crowd was gathering.

"Of course." Like most of the team, they found a woman's hysteria troubling and felt helpless to do anything of any good use.

Victor was relieved to have something constructive to do to help. He and Julio set out to disperse anyone near them while Cad stood at the front of the couple with Ker guarding the rear.

When Lissa's agony drained, leaving her a shivering shell and she no longer fought him. Jace slipped his hands under her and stood up with her in his arms.

Face a sober mask, Cad led the way clearing a path.

113

Biceps bulging, Jace easily carried the subdued Lissa, her starkly bleak face hidden, pressed against his shoulder. Ker followed to keep the curious away. Her face pinched in confusion and concern, Ivy scurried after them.

When they reached Jace's room, Ker opened the door.

Jace carried Lissa inside. Ker closed it behind them, he and Cad quietly left.

Inside, Jace went and sat down on the rocking chair by the window, cuddling Lissa on his lap. It finally dawned on him, her accent she struggled to conceal, was Scottish.

He'd had an idea before but hadn't wanted to admit it to himself. Must have been why he subconsciously wasn't telling her where they were headed.

"Baby," he murmured, sliding his hand under the lustrous waves of hair gently pushing them off her shoulders. "Tell me, what it is, why are you afraid of Scotland?" His heart stung at the sudden anguished gasp from her, she tried to climb off his lap.

Holding her firmly, gently, his long legs pushed the chair to rock slowly in a lulling rhythm back and forth.

Knowing she couldn't get away until he released her, she settled down again, her head rested on his shoulder.

In her ear his voice a deep tenuous whisper, he asked her again, "Are you wanted by the police?"

She shook her head with a fragmented sob.

Fearing she would attempt to flee again, Jace tightened his arms when he said, "Lissa, you try to hide it, but I recognize your accent. It's Scottish."

First she froze, then trembled, but said nothing.

Jace continued rocking. Then he stopped the chair's movement. His arm a shelter around her, he combed his fingers through her hair, a soothing motion to help her relax.

Threaded with steel and kindness he said softly, "Tell me, Lissa, please tell me what's going on. What are you afraid of? I promise I can help you, doesn't matter what it is."

Another sob escaped. "Nico, donnae ask me again." She laid her head on his shoulder. "I cannae tell you."

114

Turning her head to rest her face back against his shoulder, sniffing back the end of the tears, she sighed, "Don't worry. I won't try tae jump again," her body nestled in his strong embrace. "We're probably too far away now." Her eyes drifted closed.

Jace rocked slowly, disappointed that she would not trust him enough to confide her secrets. He reminded himself again, he had abducted her, cursed her, molested her, threatened to beat her and rape her. His face cringed in shame, *damn*, he wouldn't trust him either.

His long thick fingers caressed her cheek until he felt the tension completely leave her body. Sagging against him, she had fallen asleep. Cradling her head against his muscled broad chest, he smiled drolly, at least she felt safe enough to sleep in his arms.

Jace held her curled against him and rocked, pondering what on earth could upset a woman to the degree that she would take the chance of leaping to her death to get away from it.

She felt so good in his arms, relaxed against his body, he was in no hurry to move. He rocked until he grew sleepy.

Getting up slowly to not wake her, holding her in his arms Jace glanced at her bed, then went to his and laid her down.

Untying her sneakers, he tugged them off, dropping them on the floor, then pulled the covers back, slid her in and covered her.

Slipping off his own shoes, he climbed in the other side. Jace thought about keeping a space between them, but knew it would be only a matter of time when either asleep or awake, he would be rubbing up against her.

Last thing he wanted was for her to think he was taking advantage of the situation so he stayed fully clothed.

Thrusting control of his lust for her under an iron will, he squirmed over, curled his body around hers, dropped an arm over her and after a long while, went to sleep.

Chapter Thirteen

As soon as she stirred, Jace woke.

He could tell the split second she became aware that they were together in his bed, that he was snuggled up against her, holding her close with his arm wrapped around her waist. He pretended he was asleep hoping it would keep her fear meter down.

Lissa instantly scooted away from him, letting his arm that had been wrapped around her slide down on the mattress.

Even though his eyes were shut, Jace knew she was taking in the fact that they were both fully clothed, buttons buttoned, belts buckled, even socks still on. It would be pretty apparent that nothing had happened between them.

Jace suppressed a smile when she pulled the blanket over him, tucking it in.

The mattress moved slightly when she slipped off.

When he heard the shower, Jace got up, put his shoes on and left the room, locking the door behind him.

He trod down the hall deciding it would give her some breathing room if he took his shower in Ker's cabin. He had put a spare toothbrush in there the day after he had taken Lissa.

A donut in one hand, a mug of coffee in the other, still damp from his shower, Jace strode into the study.

Cad, Victor, Ker and Julio were already there, computers up, they were intensely studying them, only talking when they had something important to say. Donnie was up top deck manning the bridge.

Setting his coffee down, Jace took a huge bite of his chocolate cream donut, chewed, swallowed, said, "Julio, could you-"

"Yeah. I can go bring her some breakfast." Julio grinned, it was becoming a habit.

The men took one look at Jace's face and could tell whether things were good or bad between him and Lissa, right now he just looked perplexed and disturbed.

His grin sobered slightly, with concern Julio asked, "Is she all right?"

Finishing his donut, Jace scratched at the day old dark scruff he hadn't taken the time to shave. Gulping some coffee, his expression was somber and confused. His head slightly lowered, a hand tucked in a pocket, Jace looked up at each man.

They cared. They cared about Jace, and in the short time she's been aboard, Lissa had wormed her way into their hearts too. Even hardcore Ker who liked very few people except his core friends, had gentled towards her.

"Ah, well, physically she's fine," Jace said gravely. "But something has the fear of God lodged in her brain and she is scared out of her mind about something, and that something appears to be in Scotland. She won't damned tell me what the hell it is."

"Maybe she's wanted?" Julio offered weakly with little belief in his statement. To him, the girl seemed too gentle, too sweet to have committed any kind of major crime.

Jace shook his head. "No. She says she isn't and I believe her." He raised his eyes to Victor, said, "Vic."

Listening to the conversation, Victor regarded his laptop with the fingers of one hand paused on the keyboard. Looking up, he stroked his trimmed mustache. "Yeah?"

"Run a search on her," Jace said. "The U.S., and Scotland. I think she's originally from Scotland."

Julio's head turned. Climbing to his feet, he said, "Oh, yeah, *that's* the accent. Could not place it, she tries so hard to hide it, now I hear it. Didn't you already do a preliminary search on her to see if anyone claimed her as missing, or to see if she was involved with Warrington?"

Shrugging one shoulder, Victor replied, "I did, nothing pinged." He said to Jace, "Thinking anything in particular about her? How deep you want to go?"

Jace rubbed his thumb and fingers on his chin, pulling at it. "Everything. Family, criminal history, education, jobs, financials," he hesitated, "relationships."

This was the first time Jace had considered Lissa might be involved with someone. As gorgeous as she was it was doubtful she didn't at least have a boyfriend. She might even be married. She was young, but certainly old enough to be hitched.

She'd never mentioned family being worried about her missing. She had never threatened she was going to have her man come after Jace.

His shoulders twitched, he didn't like the thought of Lissa calling any other guy than Jace her man. And that was a ridiculous thought considering what he's done to her.

"Everything," he repeated. He thought about how secretive she was, never discussed herself, and definitely kept a wall up between her and others, especially against him. He had thought that was because he took her, but maybe there was something more to it. Was it just him or all men, he wondered.

"You got it. I've got spider trackers searching more on Warrington, there's nothing else really I can do about him right now. I'm hitting blocks because of the disposable hard drives, but I believe I've found the main one. It's only a matter of time before we have everything on him. I'll get started right now on her." Victor sent him a short concerned smile and turned to his laptop.

Finishing his coffee, Jace set the mug down. Drifting a hand over his hair, he headed for the door. "I'm gonna go work out, I'll catch you later." A T-shirt that had seen better days covered his thick chest and worn jeans encased his lean hips.

Ker stood up. "I'll come with you, One, we can spar, do some MMA practice. You can get some gym clothes from my room." He clapped a hand on Jace's back as they went out the door.

A couple hours later, in sweats and sweating, Jace returned to his room. Expecting to find Lissa rolled in a fetal ball in a corner, he was surprised when he entered the room and she was standing there with her hands parked on her slender but curvaceous hips.

The mouth a straight slash, brows down hard, she bit into him, "You locked me in. I refuse tae be treated as a prisoner. I am leavin' and I will go where I please and stay where I please!"

Taken aback, Jace set his clothes that were balled up in his hand on the desk. Surprised at her fierce attack he almost wished back for the soft, weak bundle curled up snug in his arms of last night.

His frown came automatically. "Well you can't," he snapped and started for the bathroom.

"Oh!"

Her gasp did nothing to stop him. He heard her come up behind him and whirled catching the hand that held a plate left back from breakfast that she was about to bring down on his head.

Clinching her wrist with one hand he took the plate from her with the other and tossed it over on the bed. "Lissa, really? A plate? A *plastic* plate no less? It wouldn't have hurt me anyway but you should have put more strength, effort and speed behind the swing."

Yanking her hand away she stalked to the window in disgust. Slamming her hands on the windowsill she glared out through the streaked glass, muttered sourly, "I will not be treated as a criminal kept under lock and key."

"Huh. More like a princess in a tower."

Her eyes narrowed fiercely as she glanced around the room looking for something to throw at him. "I am not a stupid princess, how dare you condescend-"

"Trying to beat me senseless, even if you had been serious about it, so you can escape this ship is futile."

Following her to the window, he said, "Remind me, honey," his tone facetious and serious at the same time, "that when we get to *Scotland*," he pronounced it hard on purpose to provoke her into maybe spilling something in a burst of anger, "and when we get to a steady location, number one on the list is I will teach you how to swim, and two, I will give you some self-defense lessons."

Angrily she kept her rigid back to him.

Aggravated at her not responding to him, he snorted, "You couldn't hurt a fly the way you fight. There was no steam, no power behind your attempt to beam me. It was half-hearted at best. Admit it, honey, you don't have it in you to deliberately harm another person.

He continued on to the bathroom, deliberately antagonizing, "So, why don't you have a nice cup of tea," his patronizing nod aimed at the hotplate on the small dresser, "and calm your little self down. Okay?" He closed the door to her response.

"Grrr, that supercilious chauvinist," Lissa clenched her teeth and fists. "How dare he keep me caged up like an animal! I won't have it!" Stamping her foot her eye caught his clothes he'd dropped on the desk. Hurrying over to them, she saw his keys sitting on top of the pile.

"Yippee." Snatching them up she said, "I'll show you, Mr. Jace Nico. You can't push me around." Unlocking the door, deliberately leaving the key in the lock to mock him, she shot off down the hall smiling at her cleverness.

Leaving the bathroom with a towel slung around his hips, it was on his lips to give a peace offering. While in the shower, Jace considered ways to appease her, make her more malleable. Catch more flies with sugar and all that shit.

His eyes popped when he saw she was not in the room and the door was wide open. "*Damn her*," he spat, didn't she understand he kept her locked up for her own good?

First that asshole Rawley assaulting her, she needed to be protected from fiends like him, and from herself, climbing up on that rail like a bird about to take flight.

Shaking his head to dispel the sight of her about to leap to her death, Jace dragged his hands down his face, it twisted his insides to think about her crashing into the ocean and disappearing in a heartbeat.

Yanking on a clean pair of jeans, muttering, "Wait 'til I get my hands on her, she'll beg me for just a spanking."

Wincing at that backfired memory, he pulled on a T-shirt shaking his head at her audacity leaving the keys in the door to mock him.

Pulling them out, he shoved them in his pocket and took off to go find her, again.

Chapter Fourteen

*H*e looked everywhere. Galley, great room, kitchen, study, makeshift gym, bridge, he had to check individual rooms now.

Fear started climbing up his chest. Praying she hadn't jumped, he pushed the fear down. Donnie and Julio were on the bridge and there were a bunch of people on the deck, someone would have seen her.

The last room he looked in was the one Donnie and Julio shared. Knowing the room should be empty, he checked it anyway.

There she was, as if waiting for him.

"Nico," Lissa said archly with a smug touch of humor. Her blouse tucked into her jeans had an embroidered collar, the top two buttons were open. Her rich shiny hair was pushed back behind her ears to flow around and down her back.

Jace's eyes were drawn to the gun she held aimed directly at his heart. Taking a few steps towards her, he said calmly, "What's this about, Lissa?"

Her nerves jangling at his proximity, waving the gun she ordered, "Don't come any closer."

Digging up her mettle, she said matter-of-factly, "You laughed at my ability tae defend myself. Although you are the one that has put me in any danger by bringin' me on this boat, you keep blatherin' about the need tae protect me," her mouth pulled in wryly at the corner, "from *other* men. Well, now I've solved that problem, and my other one too."

His brow furrowed, eyes going from the gun to her. Thinking how hard she was trying to act tough, Jace saw her hand shake slightly, the green eyes wavered around the room coming back anxiously to him. "Your other problem?" he asked.

Nodding at his not understanding her situation. "Yes, gettin' off this boat before it gets tae...there."

"What are you talking about, Lissa?" His expression hardened, he moved closer to her. "You are *not* jumping off this fucking ship."

Even being raised on basically an island, Lissa had lived in the city. Never being near water as a child, still naïvely thinking although unable to swim she would be safe floating on the cushion of ocean water, she laughed. "No, I think we are too far for the current tae carry me safely tae shore and Glennie says there are sharks." Her body gave a little shiver.

"No," she pointed the gun at him, "you are goin' tae take this ship, right now, tae the nearest port and let me off."

Both brows pointed up mildly, "Really? Why would I?"

"Be- because I will, you know, shoot you if you don't bring me tae shore. Immediately." She waved the gun at him conjuring a determined, ruthless look on her dainty face.

Jace couldn't help smiling, he repeated, "Really? You would shoot me in cold blood, baby?" Taking a step closer, he kept his eyes connected to hers.

"Stop right there, Nico, or I'll- I'll shoot!" She held the gun rigidly at his chest.

Self-confidence oozing from him, Jace's stance was relaxed. His arms slack, flint of militant in the blue eyes directed at the gun. "Where did you get it?" His eyes flipped up to hers, he was angrier about some idiot giving her gun than he was that she was threatening him with it.

She could barely hold up the heavy gun with both small hands. It wouldn't take long for her to tire and have to lower it. The shaking pistol wouldn't likely stay aimed at him in the meantime.

"Doesn't matter, now, get going." She waved the gun towards the door.

"It does matter!" He thundered so harshly she jumped. He took a step closer. "You tell me what stupid, irresponsible, fucking moron gave an inexperienced woman a goddamned gun."

Her face firmed, lips pressed mulishly. "I won't tell you. I'm not inexperienced, he showed me how tae work it." She held the gun right at his chest. "Enough, come no nearer or I will shoot. I mean it!"

Glaring the acrimony he felt for the nameless gun loaner at her, almost too quietly, he said, "I'll find out, and I will break both his arms." Acutely lethal, resolute and sincere like a bold underline to his words, his shoulders rounded and arms bowed in fierce perturbation.

Pointing his finger at her, he fumed, "Anyone teaches you how to use a gun," he thumped his chest with his fist, "it will be me."

Rocking his shoulders to loosen them, Jace held a hand out to Lissa, letting his smile take over again with another step. "Lissa, baby," he cajoled sweetly, "give me the gun."

"Nico, stop, I mean it. Don't come any closer, we need tae go tae the bridge." She waved the gun to the door again, "Now. Right now."

Surprisingly, Jace chuckled. "You would shoot me, my sweet little Lissa?"

"Yes," she nodded, her mouth in a determined line. "If you make another move, I will. I have defeated you, just admit it. I won this time. Put your manly pride aside and let's go."

Jace started talking, "Whoever got you that gun, believe me, I will take care of later. In the meantime, he should have at least showed you how to *properly* use it, you know, releasing the safety and all, apparently he was remiss in instructing you how to-" his hand whipped out grabbing the gun.

He winged her around, strapped her so fast and hard with her back flat against his chest, the air jolted out of her lungs. Holding the gun to her head he said with dry chauvinism, "This is why women shouldn't have guns."

"Let me go!" Lissa demanded, fury suffusing her sudden terror.

His heavily muscled arm a steel harness across the front of her, gun at her temple, his voice husky against her ear, Jace said, "Just so you know whom you're dealing with my pet, I could have taken this gun anytime I wanted. I could have taken it from you the second I opened the door. They only reason why I didn't was because I wanted answers."

His shallow sigh from behind blew pieces of hair across her face. "Unfortunately, you did not provide any answers." He tightened his arm like a band over her, impeding her futile struggles.

"I could have taken the gun anytime I wanted," he repeated, "just like I could take you anytime I want. I've proven that already." Spreading his legs he pulled her in as close to his body as possible.

He should know by now what a mistake that is; her butt pressed against his hips equaled instant arousal. Too late. Desire for her spread like wildfire through his loins and up his belly firing into his brain.

Upset that he turned the tables on her, and burning fear building at what he would do now, accent thickening, she said angrily, "Enough of this, you cannae do anythin' tae me. Let go of me, give me back my gun."

"Nay, pet, must I show you everything? You trying to act the tough girl is a joke. I'm going to show you why you aren't ever going to try something insanely dangerous as this again."

In one move he suddenly kicked her legs out and laid her on the ground then dropped on top of her.

Setting the gun on the floor out of her reach, he braced on one elbow and grasped her hands holding them between them at chest level with one of his huge fists. "Now, Lissa, it is you who must accept defeat and swear to me you will never do anything this foolish again. Say it."

She stayed stubbornly mute.

"Lissa, do you accept defeat? Do you swear you will never do this again to me or anyone else? Tell me and I will let you go."

"No, never, get off of me." She puffed out her refusal, her bucking and squirming only amused, and excited him more. His weight alone held her down, one of his legs covered one of hers making her chances of getting out from under him without his cooperation impossible.

Shifting some of his weight to the side so she could draw a deep breath, he held her wrists manacled by his strong fingers. Jace slowly stroked a finger up the side of her face in a gentle taunt, a lock of blond hair fell over one dark blue eye. "Last chance, Lissa, admit defeat, admit I beat you. Swear to me that this is your last foolish escape attempt and I will let you up."

"No. You sound like a child, get off of me."

Jace's sigh was long and loud. Still holding her hands, he pulled them over her head then tugged her shirt out of her jeans and shoved his hand up her blouse, to her breast.

She gasped at the sudden intrusion and tried to jerk from his touch. He cupped her breast loosely over the sheer silk bra, not squeezing or fondling, just showing her he could do it. "See how you fill my hand, Lissa? Overfill, I need both hands to hold your fullness, alas, my other hand is busy."

She didn't move a muscle, didn't draw a breath.

"You're always accusing me of behaving badly towards you, so I might as well get the pleasure out of really doing it. Now, Lissa, admit defeat. You cannot fight me, I have the brawn, you have the beauty but it won't help you now. From now on you will do everything I say without protest.

"You will not go out on your own, and seeing the consequences now that could happen, you will never do another stupid stunt like this one again. No more escape attempts. Tell me you understand."

She resumed squirming and struggling but didn't open her mouth.

"Okay," exhaling his exasperation, Jace said, "if I must, I will prove to you what will happen when you pull this shit on a man.

We will take your gun and we will take you. I already have your gun, so..."

He released her breast, she released her held breath, then he moved his hand down to her jeans and unbuckled her belt,

She wriggled and bucked silently fighting him, her breaths short violent gasps. He unbuttoned the button, lowered the zipper on her jeans, then, he very slowly slipped his fingertips under the waistband, on her warm skin then down to the top of her wispy silk panties.

"Stop! Stop!" Lissa cried. "All right! I admit... it..." her panicked breathing accelerating. "I admit defeat."

"Ah, say I beat you," he insisted, moving his leg between hers pushing them apart.

Shuddering in alarm, she said quickly, "You beat me."

His hand stopped moving but stayed there. His voice laden with sensuality, the husky timber like rough velvet, Jace said, "I bet if I were to go lower, beneath your sweet bud, Lissa, that you would be hot and wet, ready for me."

Shaking her head vehemently, Lissa cried, "Never! You use your brute strength against me, you're a beast."

Half his weight still holding her down and her hands in his iron grip, he murmured, "I think you want me, as much as I want you. Shall we find out, my sweet Lissa? Open your legs for me, you just need some nudging."

She tried to clamp her legs together but it was impossible with his weight and strong leg keeping hers apart. She looked at him with wide frightened eyes.

As he hoped, Jace could see arousal pulsing in them too. The green was glazed, her lids limpid, but still she denied, exclaiming, "You are delusional, I do not want you, I will never want you!"

"Ah." His voice heavy with seduction, Jace said, "Never say never, baby. Now, how about you and I seal this deal," he slid his hand down.

"No! Stop!"

His silky voice mocked her, "Hmmm, say the magic word, Lissa." While she hiccupped back angry sobs, he lowered his hand.

"Okay, all right, please stop."

Shaking his head, he pushed his knee between her legs spreading them apart further and lowered his hand a fraction, watching her eyes blanch, then flicker when she felt the huge, hard throbbing length of him pressed against her thigh.

"Yes, my Lissa, you are petite but I'm pretty sure you can take all of me in. We would just have to move very, very slowly at first, let you have time to adapt to me." Smiling at her crimson face, he watched her thoughts and emotions trickle across.

Seeing her brows draw down hard, that she was fighting the desire brewing in her was clear in her expanding pupils and damp lips, Jace whispered, "I can prepare you with my fingers, my mouth, make you so hot and wet you'll be begging me."

"No!" She writhed under his hand.

His mouth only inches from hers, Jace said, "If I were you, Lissa, I'd stop squirming. I mean I'm trying to make a point here, but I am, as you can see, as you can feel, a man. And as a very turned on man I have only so much control over my... actions, and your movements are kind of sending me over the edge of being able to stop, or not."

She froze. In a frantic whisper, she pleaded, "Please, would you please stop..."

Shaking his head again in reproof, he mocked, "That's not the magic word, Lissa."

He still held her hands stretched over her head, not tight but enough she couldn't get them loose, and his hand down her pants, fingers splayed over her abdomen.

His arousal swelling bigger, stiffer by the second pressing on her thigh, she looked at him utterly bewildered. "I- I don't understand..."

His smile hardened. "Say my name, not Nico, say my given name."

Brows shooting up like arched wings, she repeated, "I don't understand,"

"Yes, you do. Say my given name, say it now." He pushed her legs as wide as they could go, his fingers wriggled just above her womanhood. He could feel her hips bucking, pelvis jerking up and down with both panicked breaths and sensual ache.

Taking a deep breath and letting it out, she said tremulously, "Jace, please stop."

"One last thing." He smiled at her frustration. "Now say that I am the boss and that you will obey my orders without argument, or else," he wiggled his fingers again.

"No! I will not!"

Jace pushed his hand down so far he was a hair from an intimate touch. He could feel her abdomen twitching under his hand, her hips trying to move away from his thick fingers, but she was against the hard floor there was nowhere for her to go.

Her breath gushed out. "All right, all right."

"Say it, Lissa, say it," he demanded.

Mumbling weakly, "You are the boss."

"Say Jace, you are the boss."

Her breath spurted out, Lissa snapped angrily, "Oh for the love of-" she jumped as he cupped her mound. Her voice high, she cried rapidly, "Okay, okay, Jace you are in charge. Please stop, please."

His hot hand cupping her but not moving, he could feel her heat and wetness against his fingers.

Lissa's body betrayed her. Her neck arched, her head tilted up, tongue licking her suddenly dry lips.

Jace lowered his mouth to cover hers. Her lips moved sensuously with his. Feeling her respond, his hungry moan surged into her mouth.

Her lips opened further allowing him to thrust his tongue in and around, until he felt her stiffen. Her brain shut her body down and she withdrew from his kiss.

Reluctantly, he moved his head back and pulled his hand out of her jeans, so slowly his fingers burned a trail up her abdomen the feeling so intense they both quivered.

His voice gruff with desire, he said softly, "I was hoping you would stick to your guns. I would have made beautiful love to you, Lissa, all night. Alas, you gave in." Jace kissed her lightly then rolled off her, sprang to his feet and pulled her up.

She swayed from the abrupt ascent to her feet, he swept his arm around her to keep her from stumbling.

His nose in her hair, Jace sniffed deeply of her thinking, *what a sweet bundle of creamy silk, all slender arms and legs, tight round ass, toned but soft where she should be, she's killing me, I am dying to make love to her.*

"Lissa," his voice heavy with passion, Jace said, "if you would only stop fighting yourself. Let go, you'll see, you want this too. You're just too used to keeping the impenetrable door shut on your feelings, your body. I wish you would trust me to take care of you, your needs. I can make you feel so good."

Seeing the wall come down and close off the desire that had flamed in her only moments ago, shaking his head he released her.

He said coolly, "Remember, you agreed I was in charge. I don't want any fights about it, no back tracking, you gave me your word. You will call me by my given name, and no more of these foolish dangerous acts. I have to have some way of controlling you."

She showed him a rare scowl and lunged for the gun on the ground.

Jace easily lassoed an arm around her waist lifting her off her feet and up against his chest while he bent and scooped up the gun, tucking it in the back of his belt.

He set her down with her back pressed against his chest, and held her with one arm like a steel cable, and with the other cupped her womanhood over her unzipped jeans.

A hard edge to his voice, he said against her ear, "You already backing out on our deal, Lissa? You need me to show you the full consequences that can happen when you do dangerous things? What another more amoral ruthless man would do?"

She wordlessly shook her head.

Grinning, removing his hand he said cheerfully, "Now, that wasn't so hard was it?"

Her face blended back into a scowl. "Usin' your strength against me is wrong. I'll make you pay for this Jace Nico, you will pay!"

He hauled her around, kissed her soundly then abruptly let her go.

Watching her do up her jeans, her face bright red, fix her blouse, when done Jace held his hand out to her to take. Her eyes went to it, she didn't move.

He cleared his throat.

With a frown, she slipped her hand in his. Jace walked her to their room, opened the door, gave her a little push inside then still standing in the hall he closed the door and locked it.

Making sure he stuck his keys in his pocket, he pictured her affronted expression. On the other hand, her face might have exhibited relief that he was leaving her alone, for a while.

He needed a really cold, freezing cold shower, then he was off to find the son of a bitch that gave that vulnerable woman a lethal weapon.

Cracking the gun open, the corner of his mouth hitched. It wasn't loaded. And she had to have been aware it wasn't loaded, the person who gave her the gun would have told her he had no bullets. No wonder she waved it around so recklessly. It could have easily been loaded though, thankfully it was Jace who unarmed her.

He shuddered to think what would have happened if she'd pulled it on the wrong person. Totally lacking in experience handling guns, if it was loaded, another man would have just as easily taken it from her as he had, and might have used it on her.

That infuriated him so much he might not need the cold shower after all. Except, he could still feel her body writhing under his, his hands on her burning skin, her wetness on his fingers, her heady response to his kiss.

Jace knew damned well she wanted him as much as he wanted her, at least her body did. He needed to help her get her mind caught up.

Stopping at Ker's room, he decided he still needed that frigid shower.

Chapter Fifteen

After his second shower of the day, Jace headed for the study. Everyone except Donnie was inside.

Seeing his wet hair, Ker's brow quirked. "Do I have any clean towels left?" The quick tugging at the edge of his mouth showed his amusement at his friend's plight.

Victor glanced at Jace, pretending to be confused. "Is it my imagination, One, or is every time I see you your hair is damp? Is it a new look?"

Jace just grunted at him and found a place at the table they were all sitting around.

"Women, eh One?" Cad sent him a sympathetic smile. "You want to live with them but they make it so fucking difficult."

Julio quipped, "I think the way that's said is 'women, you can't live with them, you can't live without them."

"Okay, let it go." Jace roughly pushed open his laptop.

Julio eyed his treatment of his computer. "Uh huh, remember you always hurt the one you love, be gentle with her." He motioned to Jace's laptop that Ker had brought with him and powered up.

That brought a small curve to Jace's stiff mouth. At that moment it beeped indicating he had an email. Peering at it, his eyebrows rose then scrunched.

Ker asked, "What is it?"

Jace's lashes dropped covering his expression. He said briefly, "It's nothing." He turned to Julio. "I need to go back and stop at a port in NY. How long will that be at the slow knots we're going?"

All the men looked in question at Jace but he said nothing else.

"Uh, two days," Julio answered him.

"All right. Set for it. Let me know when we're near." Jace tapped a tab deleting the message.

"Anyway," Victor said, breaking the silence of the inquisitive men. "You asked me to do a search on Lissa." His tone warned Jace something wasn't going to be good.

"Yeah. What'd you get?" Deleting a bunch of other messages, Jace's shoulders tensed.

At Victor's hesitation, Jace swung his chair to face him. Setting a forearm on the table, he waited. The other men stopped what they were doing.

Victor cupped his mouth, rubbed it. Keeping two fingers over his parted lips, he stared steadily at his friend, then dropped his hand on the table. "Lissa Mallory is not her real name. She didn't exist until little less than 2 years ago."

All the sound sucked out of the room like a vacuum.

Jace studied Victor's face looking to see if he was joking.

Dark eyes intent, Victor scratched his fingertips over his moustache down the sides of his mouth then dropped his hand so a few fingers rested on the keys of his laptop.

Every eye beaded at Jace, waiting.

Feeling a rush like needles running up the back of his neck, Jace asked calmly, "Anything else?"

"No. Not yet. That was the easy part," Victor replied.

"Maybe she's undercover or something like that," Julio suggested.

Naw," Cad shook his big head. "That little girl is too young to have the law enforcement background that would entail."

Victor said, "Dude, she can't be but half a dozen, ten years tops younger than us, you sound like her father."

A huge shoulder pumped, Cad replied, "Yeah, well, compared to us, she is a little girl."

"Apparently we actually don't really know how old she is," Victor pointed out.

His lips pursed, Cad nodded. "True that, KM, but you can tell, she's still fresh and sweet. Sure, there's a ton of fear in that girl, but she's not been around life that much. She's naïve enough to think she can hop in the ocean and float safely ashore.

"It sounds like she's been very sheltered. The little honey certainly needs someone strong and mature to watch out for her while she finds her way." He glanced at Jace who was staring expressionless at his computer.

Victor nodded his agreement. "Yeah."

Man of few words, Ker suggested, "Maybe she's in witness protection?"

His eyes fixated on his computer, Jace didn't comment.

Victor mused, considered the remark. "It's possible. To get any deeper I need to meet one of my connections face to face. I need a fingerprint. Jace?" He waited a beat, when Jace didn't look up, he said again, "Jace?"

"Maybe she is with Warrington after all," Julio suggested disregarding the looks each man sent him. "I mean, he would have given her a secret identity so we couldn't track her back to him. Maybe she's his spy, his girlfriend," he clicked his fingers, "ya know, his bed bitch."

"Shut your face, Julio, cripes," Cad growled, his eyes skewed to Jace.

Dragging his hand from the top of his head over his face, down his jaw, Jace blinked hard a few times. Shaking his head out of his revelry, he cut a glance at Victor then back to the table. "Okay. I'll get something she's touched, hairbrush, glass, whatever."

His gaze volleyed around the table. "Needless to say, not a word of this to anyone, especially to Lissa, or," he looked directly at Cad, "to any of the other women, not mentioning any names, Ivy." They all laughed.

"Oh yeah, I almost forgot, another thing." Jace drew the gun he took from Lissa out of his belt and laid it on the table. "Ker, I need to know who the owner of this is. Can you check it out?"

Ker's fathomless eyes dropped to the weapon then up to Jace. Ker would find out later what was going on. No doubt it involved Lissa. But that soft little woman and a huge gun, his harsh lips pursed. Seriously contrary, he said, "Sure." Using a pen, Ker pulled the gun in front of him.

They hung around trading information gleaned about their mission, interspersed with jokes about previous ventures. As time moved, Julio, then Cad left.

Victor closed up his computer. "I'm going on top deck to work on this, get some sun." He left.

Jace got up. "You staying?" he asked Ker.

"No. I'm leaving in a minute."

"Later." Jace said turning off his computer and leaving it there for Ker to take and keep secured.

Jace thought maybe Lissa would be hungry, he'd take her to lunch. For now, he wouldn't be asking her about her hidden past. He wanted more information first.

But, he agreed with Cad, he didn't believe she had a nefarious past, yet she was terrified of something. It must be tied in with the fake ID. He refused to believe she was connected to Warrington, her emotions were just too readable on her innocent face to be fake.

Besides, a woman conniving enough to have been sent in to spy would never have tried to jump off the ship.

When he opened the door to their cabin, she was standing a few feet away.

"Hey," he greeted her.

The shirt she was wearing was fairly low cut with a scalloped collar, the top buttons were undone. It wasn't tucked in. Jace's attention drew down. The blouse made her miniscule waist appear unusually bulky like she had something on under the back of it.

His eyes dropped to the tiny skirt she was wearing. It was red plaid with pleats, sort of schoolgirl uniform looking, and very, very short. Although petite, her legs looked miles long in it.

Lissa smiled slightly, bringing his blue beamers back to those beautiful lips. She asked, "Where were you?"

"Um, just in the study with the guys."

"They all still there?"

Her mood undeterminable, Jace started walking towards her. As expected, she stepped backward until her back pressed against the wall. "No. Everyone split." He set his hands, then his forearms on the wall on either side of her, fencing her in.

Bending very slowly, Jace faintly touched his lips to hers, keeping his eyes opened slightly to look at her.

Her lids and her lips were closed, lashes lacey fans across her cheeks growing rosy from the kiss. When he teased her lips apart and slid his tongue inside, she opened her mouth, accepting his tongue, even meeting it, tangling hers with his.

Jace pulled back. He said softly, "I wanted to see, Lissa, if you would kiss me of your own free will, without me forcing you to, without me holding your head still and your hands away from hitting or pushing at me."

A slow smug, seductive smile curved his chiseled lips. "You did," he said with satisfaction.

Her hands pressed against the wall behind her, Lissa responded, "You find this," she glanced at his arms bracketed beside her head, "not forceful? You came at me, I didn't know what you were going tae do. I backed away from you, you dominated me by usin' your intimidatin' body, your powerful presence, to force me back until I had nowhere else tae go."

She brought her hands around putting them between her and Jace. "You should think about what you're sayin', about forcin' me tae kiss you. You don't think there's somethin' wrong with that?"

His smile still sensuous, Jace replied, "I'm not holding you now, Lissa. I didn't touch you, except with my lips, which I must say you took to with no force."

A slight nick to her pretty lips, she said quietly, "You don't consider this force, you have me trapped, I can't go anywhere."

"You haven't tried to push my arms aside to leave."

"Really, Jace. How many times have you held me like this and when I've tried tae get away you've held me back. Tis kind of like learned helplessness." She looked from his hugely muscular arms to his intense blue gaze. "I could not budge you if I tried, and you know that."

Jace thought about it, then nodded in agreement. "Okay. I see your point. But tell me this, if you don't want me, why are your fingers clinging to my pecs? You're holding onto me, babe, not pushing me away." He deliberately looked down at her small hands that were indeed clutching his buffed chest.

Appalled, she snatched her hands away like he was a burning flame. She turned her reddening face aside.

He gently put a finger under her chin turning her face forward, tilting her head to look up at him. "Lissa, you could come towards me when I'm coming towards you instead of backing away from me. Kiss me back when I kiss you.

"Freely offer me those beautiful lips," his gaze travelled down her body, "your soft curves. Touch me, baby. I yearn for your wanting touch, like you just did, not pushing me away."

Moving from his forearms back to his palms bracing the wall, he dropped one to lean away to give her space. With humble regret that he really didn't feel, he said, "I know I snatched you off the street, I've explained why I had to do that. Can't we make peace with it?"

When she remained still, he said, "You know, any other man in this situation, having you sleeping every night in his room, well, it's obvious what would happen whether or not you were willing. I can force you, but I haven't, I won't. Why will you not freely give what we both want? All I'm asking for is a real kiss. A real damned kiss."

He tried to smooth away his scowl. "We can work on other things down the road."

"You're sayin' I should just forget you're holdin' me captive, that you are forcin' me tae sleep in your room." Her mouth pursed wryly. "That since you haven't raped me, I should just be reasonable and let you...screw me." She saw his blue eyes fall, then raise to boldly stare levelly at her.

His lips pushed out in a frown. "I didn't say that. What I'm saying is, honey, I believe that you are as attracted to me as I am to you, though you deny it. If I didn't believe it deep in my... soul," he touched his heart, "I wouldn't persist so much, so strongly."

She half smiled with her disbelief. "Really?" Her arms crossed, "I don't believe you. I think you tell yourself that, but actually, for some reason you think of me as yours, and regardless of my desires, you intend on havin' me, keepin' me, workin' on me till you wear me down and I give in."

His mouth opened, closed, opened, brows lowered in reluctant concession, "I, uh, perhaps you're right. In any matter, if you would only give me a chance, I believe I can-"

"Seduce me?"

Jace laughed, pushed from the wall and dropped his other hand. "Yes. But truly, Lissa, what I want is a willing closeness with you. Your full and complete willingness to be in my arms, receiving my kisses, and giving yours with an equal desire."

"Hmmm. But if I dropped to the floor right now and opened my legs you would not hesitate to...you know, wouldn't you?"

His jaw clenched, vein pumped at his temple, he tugged the ends of his sleeves down, one arm then the other. "We're grown adults, Lissa for Pete's sake. Sex is a totally natural act."

Lissa's gaze drifted to the floor. She murmured, "You don't have tae make me sleep in your room, Jace, why don't you remove the temptation?"

Jace bowed his head, then rested his forehead on the top of her glossy hair. With an irritated sigh he muttered, "No."

She suddenly straightened up. "You know what?" She actually sounded cheerful. "How about I show you somethin', somethin' I think you'll like."

"Oh yeah?" A big smile broke across Jace's handsome face. "What is it?"

"I can't tell you, I have tae show you." Shuffling away from him in her bare feet with her hands behind her back, she tilted her head to her shoulder at him in an unpracticed coy manner. The action pulled the blouse to cling more to her curves, drawing his gaze instantly. Under the little pleated skirt, one knee bent into the other making her appear coquettish.

She pivoted and went to the door, opened it, stepped out, "Come on," she beckoned.

Loving this flirtatious Lissa, Jace felt like a cartoon character with his eyes bulging, pulling the rest of his body after her. Right at her heels, not really caring as long as she stayed in this awesome mood, he asked, "Where're we going?"

"You said the study is empty?"

"Should be. Why?" His curiosity rising he walked beside her down the hall. She didn't answer him, just smiled mischievously, which was fine by him. The fact that she offered to spend time with him of her own free will was good enough for him.

When they reached the room it was empty. Jace grinned at Lissa, "So," even though his focus skated down her body in high hopes, he figured if she had physical plans for them they'd have stayed in their room. He asked anyway with a leer, "What do you want to show me?"

Lissa hummed cheerfully, "You'll see." She moved to a big and sturdy chair that was bolted to the ground with steel legs. "Here," she pointed, "sit here."

Puzzled but interested in what she was up to, Jace complied, happily sitting down in the chair.

"Hmmm," a finger to her pursed lips, her brow furrowed like she was trying to figure something out. "Let's see," like she thought of something, she snapped her fingers. "Okay, don't move," she climbed up on his lap facing him. He about died. His grin froze. But he didn't move a muscle.

Straddling one of his legs in her little skirt, as if still trying to figure something out, she said pensively, "Put your hands behind your back, I need tae see if your arms are long enough."

With her in that skirt straddling his leg, his brain started sizzling, his voice came out jerky and jagged. "Long enough...for...what?"

"You'll see," she said gaily, then admonished, "now, do you want tae see this or not?"

Jace licked his lips, with her kneeling in front of him her breasts were eye level. It wasn't as if he could think or speak anymore with this sudden brain fog or lift an arm or anything so he just nodded.

"All right. This is tricky so do not move until I say, got it?" She instructed him with a bit of a bounce in her voice, her brows down in serious thought like she was trying to figure out a problem.

"Baby," Jace whispered trying to calm his racing heart and the hardening bulge that had arrived in his jeans as soon as she'd climbed up on him. "As long as you're willing to sit on my lap I'll do anything you say."

"Thank you, Jace. Now put your arms back behind the chair."

He obliged. Scooting up a little, she leaned into him looking over his shoulder, peering off the back of the chair, wedging her breasts against his chest. Ignoring his moan, she suddenly slid off and moved behind the chair.

"Hey," he complained.

"Don't move, I'll be right back, I promise." As she crouched behind the chair she pulled something out of the back of her skirt that her blouse had been hiding.

A tick of suspicion tightened the skin on the back of his neck, he turned his head but couldn't see her. Then he heard 'click-click'. "What-" before he could exclaim, she came around and climbed back on his lap, straddling his knee.

"Lissa, what the hell are you-" he went to move his hands but he couldn't. Bewildered, he looked at her, her face was a half a foot away, "What are you doing? Did you handcuff me?"

He jerked his arms, but they were restrained, he felt the metal circles around his wrists and the clang of the chains. "Lissa, what the hell?"

Chapter Sixteen

She leaned in as if to kiss him. Like a dog getting a treat, forgetting his manacled hands, Jace opened his mouth to receive the kiss. But she turned her head keeping her mouth just out of reach.

He could reach her neck though and did; he kissed her neck, sucked and nipped from her ear to her collarbone.

Still keeping her lips out of reach she moved closer to him. The top buttons on her shirt were undone. Without stopping, Jace slid his mouth down licking and nibbling her skin, groaning when he reached the top of her breasts.

Sucking and licking downward, with the force of his mouth, his lusty kisses on the full rounded mounds pushed several more buttons open. The thick blond hair brushed under her chin then the top of her breastbone.

She leaned back.

His eyes closed, handsome mouth wet and open, he raised his thickened lids and looked at her with daze filming his eyes.

"What?" shaking his head, Jace tried to blink back the haze. "Lissa," he went to reach for her but his hands were restrained.

He jerked at one arm then the other. Frowning, still in a lust haze, he asked, "Why did you cuff me? Undo them. I want to touch you." He stretched his neck to try to reach her again with his mouth.

Her back arched away from him, his gaze drew straight down to her breasts. The blouse stretched open and her breasts mounded, spilling out of a black lacey bra.

The blue eyes gleaming, he stared like he had lasers attached to them making it impossible for him to look away. Seeing her breasts damp and red blotched from his mouth, his pupils expanded making his eyes shining onyx.

She remarked dryly, "You act like you've never seen breasts before."

Smirking through a dry mouth, his gaze glued to her bosom, licking his lips, Jace said, "Oh, I've seen plenty my love, but none as fine as yours," his eyes scrunched closed. "Actually at the moment I can't even remember any others, don't want to remember any."

Quickly opening his eyes in case she suddenly vanished as if in a dream, staring back at her full soft flesh, he said, "I have no desire to touch any others, just yours." He looked up at her, his voice husky and low-pitched, eyes brimming with desire, he murmured, "Kiss me, baby."

Glossy hair billowing full around her shoulders, she flipped it back, her smile humorous. "You think if I kiss you that you can seduce me and I will give in completely."

Jace replied with all seriousness, "Yes, I do." He waited for her to say something but she didn't. His throat dry and hoarse, he said, "Let me kiss you, Lissa."

She didn't answer him. He didn't move a muscle watching her undo all of the buttons on his shirt, she pushed the sides open, set her hands on her thighs. He looked up and saw her eyes were on his very manly massive chest, the muscular pecs partially covered with dark hair.

"Baby," begging through his tightened throat, he rasped, "touch me, touch me, Lissa."

"Wait, let me check the cuffs." Lissa leaned in pretending to look over his shoulder to check the restraints. As she neared, Jace tried to catch her lips with his, again she stayed just out of reach.

His sigh ragged and hitching, he started to speak but she leaned in real close pressing her chest against his.

His groan a shattering rumble, Jace begged harshly, closing his eyes, "Release me, Lissa," he growled, "I need to fucking touch you,"

She didn't say anything, then she rubbed her breasts on his chest, "How's that feel, Jace?"

"Baby, it's heaven, now let me go so I can feel you with my hands. I can't take more of this. I need you." His head tilted back, eyes closed, she rubbed some more then bent away.

His head fell forward. A lock of blond hair flopped over one eye, he opened and narrowed both of them at her. "Lissa, what the hell is going on, let me go."

He jerked hard at the chains, his biceps pumping, swelling huge with the strain, sweat beaded across his hairline. He tried to move the chair with his body but it was bolted to the floor.

Sitting back on his leg, she said with a cheeky superior tone, "I told you I would pay you back for that episode with the gun. Lettin' you see what it feels like bein' restrained and pawed against your will."

"God, Lissa, baby, you can touch me all you want, it wouldn't be against my will."

Still straddling his one leg, she shifted so her knee was against his bulging erection. His tight throat strangled his voice, "Lissa, *God*."

Wriggling a little, smiling at his unstoppable groans, she said, "What would you say, Jace if I just, you know, slip off my panties, lift my skirt just a little, you know, like the night you tried tae spank me,"

"Come on Lissa, I didn't-"

"So," she slid her hands under her skirt, "what if I just push these little silky things down," she moved back up to her knees off his thigh, her fingers on the hem of the short skirt. "And lift up this skirt, open your pants and just sit, slide down until you are inside me, do only that, nothin' else."

Jace was staring hungrily at her crotch, when she stopped moving and talking he looked up at her. He shifted his thighs, his jeans were so tight they were starting to constrict.

Breathing fast and hard, confused, he huffed, "What are you saying? You would take my dick inside you but no touching and no kissing?"

She nodded, her fingers on the hem of her skirt she lifted it exposing the black silk. "Yes, that's what I'm askin' you, what would you say?"

His eyes dropped from hers to the tiny silk panties that just barely covered her private parts. The black silk like a slash of magic marker against the pure white of her skin, her thighs, her pelvis. He remembered lying atop her with his hand over her sex feeling her heat and wetness on his fingers.

His tongue rolled around wetting his lips, he looked up at her and shook his head, "No. That would just be fucking."

"Isn't that what you want?"

He peered at her through a thatch of thick, sweat-darkened blond hair, blue eyes narrowed. "No, I want to make love to you, that means both of us touching and kissing."

"I'm surprised, that's not what Brett had said."

"What the hell are you talking about?"

Shifting back down to straddle his thigh, her knee against the bulge in his jeans, she smiled at his wince. "When he was tyin' my wrists together, still stunned from his punch, I told him you would come and get me. But Brett said you just look at women as a hole tae put your – uh, penis in, and that's it, all you care about is gettin' your rocks off and you walk away."

Pissed off, Jace said crossly, "Rawley's a prick. It's not true." He blinked, "Well not entirely. What else did he tell you?"

"He said you screw anythin' that walks in front of you."

Jace rolled his head and then his eyes. "He said that shit to put a wedge between us."

"Well, Dona said that you're a serial, um, banger, you know, like a male slut."

His head dropped, he was quiet for a second. Raising his head to look her in the eye, he said grimly, "Not that I'm saying what Brett or Dona said was true, but I'm telling you that what I've done before I met you is none of your business. It doesn't affect us. I am not going to play you, Lissa.

"I haven't been with, or even desired to be with any other woman since I took…met you. I have feelings for you that I haven't ever had before, for any other woman. Baby, if you would just let me," he jerked angrily at the restraints.

"Uh huh." She squirmed on his leg earning another wince from him. "So, you think that I am a whore that just hops into bed with the man that has abducted me?"

"Lissa," growing impatient with the conversation, "we just talked about this. I told you I had to do what I did, I thought we were going to make peace." He watched her sitting on his leg with the skirt draped over his thigh, the blouse almost completely unbuttoned, beautiful breasts begging him to caress them.

Face creased in confusion, he said, "I don't understand. You just said you would fuck me, but I can't touch or kiss you, now you're denying that you would do that? What the hell are you playing at?"

"I am provin' a point. Basically, I have not touched you other than leanin' against you and sittin' on your leg. But I had tae do that, I needed somewhere tae sit," she wiggled. His erection swelled so thick and hard it was impossible to miss. She started sliding back and forth ever so slightly on his thigh until his eyes closed tightly with a groan.

He croaked through gritted teeth, "Lissa, what are you doing?"

"I told you, I'm lettin' you know what it feels like tae be held against your will and mauled."

Dark red submerged livid and hot into his face, his voice louder, harsh, he said viciously, "Let me go Lissa, by God when I get my hands on you I will-" his chest pumped and biceps ballooned with his efforts, jerking and straining at the cuffs that held him.

"See? Frustratin' and humiliatin', isn't it?" Putting both palms on his thighs to hold her up, she slid, slowly, down his leg and off to stand up. She moved back in, to stand between his legs. Setting her hands on the chair next to his head to brace herself she bent towards him, close enough for him to put his face deep in her cleavage.

He couldn't help it, her plush chest was soon red and wet again from his kisses and licks and sucking the soft mounds. Jace buried his face in her breasts, chewing on her satiny flesh, moaning with intoxication, he mumbled, "Take these cuffs off, baby, let me go, I *need* to feel you."

Laughing, she stood back again out of his reach, then stepped a few feet from him.

"Goddammit, Lissa, let me the fuck go!" Struggling against the chains, his skin dark from his exertions, Jace glared furiously at her through slits, his eyes almost closed he was so mad, "You're a goddamned cock-teaser Lissa."

She laughed again. "I don't care, there's no law against it. You didn't care how you treated me." Looking bleak for a second she said, "I can't, won't, ever have sex with you, or anyone else." Pretending to glance at a watch that she didn't have on her wrist she said cheerfully, "I have tae go now."

Spouting angrily, he raged, "I should have called your bluff, hell I should have just fucked you that very first night regardless of your unwillingness, and every dammed day since!"

Spinning on her toes, she turned from him and left the room.

"Lissa!" Shouting the house down he jerked and pulled at the manacles, yelling, "Lissa! Get back here!"

Skipping down the hall, Lissa stopped at Ker's door and knocked. Less than a second and the door whipped open.

His face impassive, not expressing a flicker of surprise at finding her at his door, Ker's cool gaze passed from the blouse still open exposing the silky black bra and a lot of rounded skin, down to the tiny plaid skirt to her bare feet, and back up to the green eyes that were brilliant with mischief.

"Ah, what can I do for you, Lissa?"

147

Her grin was dazzling. "Um, Jace is in the study, he's askin' for you."

Black brows in points were the only indication of Ker's curiosity. Usually she referred to Jace as Nico, something had happened to change things. "Uh huh."

"Okay then," she said gaily, "I have to go now." She hurried off down the hall with his eyes following her watching the pleated skirt flipping around her thighs.

Locking his door, Ker headed to the study.

When he got there, the stoic face finally displayed a shadow of surprise. His fingertips tucked in his pockets, he leaned a shoulder laconically against the doorframe. Matter-of-factly he asked, "So, One, what's new?"

Seeing Ker in the doorway with one side of his mouth pulled up in a grin just visible under the neat moustache, impatiently, jerking at the cuffs, Jace's surly growl scraped through locked teeth, "*Just get them off!*"

Acting like this was an everyday daily occurrence, Ker pulled his keys out of his pocket and went to crouch behind the chair Jace was in. He had the cuffs off in a flash and came back around.

Jace was rubbing his wrists, his face such a mask of blazing fury the blue eyes were almost invisible burning through pinched slits of eyelids.

Amusement lightening Ker's normal impassive blank expression he handed the cuffs to Jace. "Bro, you have to at least tell me, where'd she get the cuffs?"

Hanging the handcuffs over the back of his belt, Jace glared at his friend, embarrassment now crowding out the anger. "She took them off my desk." He buttoned his shirt and stuffed it back in his jeans.

"You know, I have to say, One, if a beautiful sexy woman handcuffed me, wearing what she was wearing, dude, I'd be smiling. You on the other hand, look about to spit nails." A grin tugged at the corner of Ker's mouth again.

His head down, Jace wiped his face with his hand, looked up at his amused friend. "Yeah, well, she was punishing me."

Rare shock throwing his brows up, Ker repeated, "Punishing you? What did you do to deserve that hot-" he broke off, "better yet, *how* was she punishing you?"

Jace's mouth twitched. "Yeah, well…" he rocked on his heels obviously uncomfortable, and growing more embarrassed. "She was…damn Ker, she was straddling my leg in that tiny skirt, rubbing her…damned pussy up and down on me, had her almost bare tits literally in my face, in my mouth."

"Oh yeah? Help me out here, and how was that bad?" This was getting interesting.

Sliding an angry shot at his friend out of the corner of his eye, Jace said, "Dude, I was restrained. I couldn't fucking touch her. She was only teasing me."

"I can see how that would be frustrating. Was she naked under the skirt?" Ker asked.

Shaking his head, the blood rushed to his groin picturing when Lissa lifted her skirt up to show him her panties. "No, had on this miniscule swath of black satin, didn't cover much."

"Did they match the bra with the tiny red bow between her tits?" Ker asked needling his friend.

Jace's head snapped to Ker. "Okay, you need to forget seeing what she was wearing, and forget what the hell I just told you."

Ker shrugged one shoulder. "Sure, I'll just wipe out the entire picture of her in that tiny plaid skirt, blouse open, tits bouncing while humping your-"

"Shut up, Ker," Jace barked, heading for the door, Ker's image already filling his head, totally not what he needed right now. "Drop it."

"That's okay, bro. It's bad enough she has you all tied up in knots, uh, cuffs," slight grin, "I don't need to be on that train too. Believe me, I don't want that image in my head when I'm trying to sleep tonight. At least you know there'll never be a dull moment with that saucy little thing around. And, if she were my wife, I sure as hell wouldn't let her out the door wearing that shit she had on."

As he left, Jace mumbled, "Yeah sure, you try stopping her from doing whatever the fuck she wants." He shot over his shoulder, "She's not my wife." The thought kind of clung to the back of his mind. *Sure, she already couldn't stand to be in one room with him, much less being his wife...*

His hands on his hips, Ker remonstrated at Jace's back, "Just remember while you have your hands around her slender throat, or on that fine ass trying the spanking thing again, that you've imprisoned her, and she didn't do anything to you that you haven't done to her first."

Ker's rare laughter ringing in his ears, Jace stalked off to go find her and, well, he'd figure out what he was going to do to her when he got his hands on her.

Chapter Seventeen

*T*romping down the hall, Jace continued to fume while considering where to find her. No way she would go back to their room where he could catch her alone, what the hell, he'd try there first, sometimes people go where you're sure they won't.

He checked the room, it was empty as he expected. Heading back out, he thought she might go to the kitchen. Starting towards there it came to him that she was probably hiding out where there would be the largest number of people, witnesses.

Changing direction, he went to the women's quarters, his rage building back up again as he kept thinking about her sitting on him, eyes all green sultry…his mouth marking, branding her neck, sucking her breasts, her denying him, damn- he needed to do what he told Ker, stop thinking about it.

Just as he figured, usually the door was open except at night, now it was closed. Jace could hear women inside talking and laughing. He tried the knob. It was locked. He rapped on the door with his knuckles.

The talking immediately stopped. The door did not open.

Knocking harder with his fist, he demanded, "Glennie, open the door."

Waiting again, the door still was not opening. Standing close to it, Jace did not shout but said loudly, "Glennie, open the door or I will take it down." Hearing some murmuring and shuffling he waited.

When the door still didn't open, he said in a normal speaking voice, "Okay, everyone step away from the door-"

It swung open, Glennie stood with her hand on the knob and a weak smile. "Hey, Jace, what's up?"

Looking past her, he searched the room. Spotting Lissa standing in the back, the other girls were circled around her. Jace said, "Get out of my way, Glennie," he moved into the room elbowing past the thin platinum blonde.

"Wait, Jace!" Glennie ran after him.

He stopped a few feet inside, eyes bridged across the room at Lissa. She was still wearing the skirt and blouse but the buttons were all done up, she was not cowering, but she had lost the smug look from earlier.

"Lissa, come here," he commanded. She shrunk back into the crowd.

"Listen, Jace, maybe-"

"Butt out, Glennie." Jace contracted his gaze at Lissa like no one else was in the room.

Her hair was back off her shoulders, he could see his hickeys on her neck. Darkness deepened his blue eyes, his voice rumbling rough thunder, he said again, "Come here, Lissa. Now." The rest of the women tightened the circle around her.

Her voice soft and assured, beside him, Glennie said calmly, "Jace, we don't know what happened between you two, but maybe you should leave her here for now. It would be best if you would go chill for a while. Don't do something rash that you'll regret later."

She looked up at the compressed jaw. Brows slashed down over fierce eyes, dark, furious face, hands fisted, big arms bowed. "Let her stay with us, just for tonight. All right?"

Jace didn't move or take his eyes off Lissa. Her green eyes huge and frightened wrapped around his heart, then his gaze dropped to the tiny skirt, down those beautiful legs. Feeling himself grow hard at the thought of her straddling him pissed him off all over again.

Glennie carefully patted his hard bicep strained with his anger, trying to diffuse him.

His powerful chest rounded from the angry breath he held, he let it out slowly. If he stalked across the room and grabbed Lissa and hauled her out, not only would he look like an abusive bully, but one of the women could get hurt if she tried to get in his way.

In an amazingly clingy dress that showed everything she owned, Dona sashayed over to Jace and wove her arm around his. He didn't move. Somehow she managed to get his arm down between her uber-large breasts, her siren's voice bawdy and inviting she said, "I'll go with you, Jacey."

About to dismiss her, Jace glanced at Lissa then at Dona and said, "Sure, let's go." He took one more look at Lissa through lowered lids. He couldn't read her expression, couldn't tell if she was relieved, or…he'd like to believe that was an unhappy, better yet, jealous look on her face.

As soon as they were out the door, Jace roughly dragged his arm from Dona's licentious grasp. He muttered as he moved quickly from her, "I have to go, catch you later."

"Hey, are you kidding me?" Dona cried. "Come on, take me with you-" he was gone.

Jace skipped dinner and headed straight to the bar area. One of the guys was hanging behind the bar, not one of Jace's team. Throwing a leg over a stool, Jace slumped down and said, "Harry, how 'bout pouring me a bourbon?"

The tall, skinny guy with the cheerful grin and long nose said, "Sure." Harry took a glass off the shelf behind him and set it on the counter in front of Jace. Then he picked up a bottle of bourbon and started to pour, when he was going to stop at the normal shot, Jace waved his hand up indicating for the guy to keep pouring.

Harry shrugged, whatever, he poured a healthy drink. As he turned to put the bottle back Jace said, "Leave it."

"Oo-kay," Harry obliged setting the bottle down. "You at least want some cubes?" At the snarled lip, and the look like he wanted

153

to snap an iron bar in half with his teeth, Harry decided he had some place he needed to be and left.

A couple hours later Ker found him still there, his head almost flat on the counter. Ker slipped an arm under Jace and pulled him off the stool.

Jace slurred, "Nnn-not done yet, go'way."

"You're done." Ker slung Jace's arm over his shoulder and half walked half dragged him back to his room. When he got there, Ker was surprised the door wasn't locked. Jace normally locked Lissa inside when she wasn't with him.

He pushed the door open and dragged Jace in and hauled him over then let him drop to sit on his bed. Ker looked over at the other bed Lissa normally slept in, it was empty and still made up from the morning.

"Uh oh, more trouble in paradise...that explains the bender," he gave Jace a little push so he fell down with his head on the pillow, took his boots off him then he left.

A few hours later, Jace groaned, tried to open his pained eyes. Took a moment, the pounding headache didn't help. Moving very slowly he slung his legs over the side and sat up.

When his head stopped spinning, he looked over at Lissa. Then blinked hard, her bed was empty. "Where the fu-" then it all came slamming back to him. Lissa's lap dance, her running to the other women for protection. He'd been forced to leave her there.

When he went to shake his head the room started spinning again, *should not have left her there.*

One positive thing he thought about her punishing lap dance, was that she'd let him suck and kiss her tits. She did it to fuck with him, but there's no way she'd let just any guy do that no matter what her motive.

Pushing to his feet, he stumbled past her bed to the bathroom, got some aspirin and water, brushed his teeth.

When he came back and plopped down on his bed, he laid on his side facing her bed. This was the first night they hadn't slept together, well, slept in the same room, since the day he took her. He didn't like it.

Closing his pained eyes, he rolled and thrashed back and forth all the rest of the night. Every time he opened his eyes and saw her empty bed it gave him a little stab in the heart. He was not about to let a precedence start.

In the morning, Jace grabbed a cup of coffee and a donut and stood in the galley chatting with Benny as he scrambled a bowl of eggs.

Darting a glance at Jace, seeing the unshaven face, bloodshot eyes, the blond hair over the dark was barely combed, Benny said cheerfully, "You look like hell, what's going on?"

Wearing a blue sweatshirt with a hoodie, and holey, weathered jeans, Jace leaned his shoulder against the wall, one foot crossed over an ankle.

Stuffing half the donut in his mouth, Jace said, "Nothing. How's the kid doing?" He asked about Colby to change the subject.

Benny took the hint and babbled for a few minutes about his apprentice's good points and his foibles. When he heard a group of girlish chatter and laughing, Benny looked to the front of the dining room.

The women piled in, giggling and talking. Seeing amongst them the petite woman with the burnished gleaming hair, Benny clipped a knowing look at Jace. "Ahh…"

"Shut up, Benny."

The cook laughed. "Well now you've confirmed it."

"Don't you have some bacon to fry?" Jace said crossly, finishing the donut, he licked his fingers then drank his coffee.

"You used to be a lot more relaxed and carefree, son, could get a female with barely a glance in their direction. Maybe you need to change whatever tactics you're using."

"Benny," he warned the cook.

"Okay, okay, just trying to help." Wiping his hands on his apron, a grin on his plump face the big-hearted cook toddled off to get some more butter to put in the hot skillet.

Jace stood where he was waiting for the women to finish eating. He was off to the side so he wasn't easily seen, he did not want to look like some crazy stalker-guy.

When he noticed the girls getting up, dropping off their trays on the stand and dumping their trash, he sauntered leisurely towards Lissa with his hands in the pockets of the sweatshirt.

Ivy saw him first, she tried to discreetly get Lissa's attention but she was facing the other way.

"Hey." Jace greeted them, inquiring courteously, "How is everyone doing today?"

Glennie's smile was wary; Ivy gave him a broad, cautious smile. After seeing him so scary enraged like a mad bull all threatening last night, Vicki, Eve and Tori's smiles were nervous.

Lissa stiffened hearing his voice right behind her. Jace smiled pleasantly at all the women as Lissa carefully turned around.

Vicki started babbling about what they planned on doing today, Jace nodded politely at her and at the same time slipped his hand in Lissa's. Her fingers were icy, her arm rigid but she didn't pull away.

She was wearing more borrowed clothes, jeans that were too long for her and a black short-sleeved sweater that softly outlined her curves.

Cutting off Vicki, Jace said, "Well, isn't that nice, so we'll see you around we have somewhere we need to be, don't we honey?" He tilted his head and smiled innocuously at Lissa.

She wordlessly fluttered her long lashes over distrustful, anxious, green eyes.

"But, Jace, we girls were gonna do makeup and stuff," Vicki called out but Jace was already parading Lissa to the door.

They didn't speak all the way back to their room.

Jace opened the door letting her go in first then he closed and locked the door in her face. Pocketing the keys, he made his way to the study where the other men were already working.

They glanced up when he entered. Ker's head lowered, he peered up at Jace. Seeing the slight smile curving on Jace's face he said, "You look almost better than you did yesterday. But you still look like shit warmed over."

That elicited a grunted chuckle from Jace as he slid onto a chair. Ker had brought Jace's laptop as usual, it was already on.

Slicking his dark straight hair back off his forehead with broad fingers, Julio said, "We'll be docked around four."

Jace nodded, his attention on his monitor. Julio asked him, "So, why are we docking here, One, it's not in the itinerary."

All eyes turned to Jace who was tapping nonchalantly at his computer. He shrugged, still typing. "Just a little something I need to look into. I'll fill you all in later."

"One, you-" Ker started,

"It's okay, Ker. It's nothing. Don't follow me. I will lose you, so don't waste your time."

Ker glared through tapered eyelids at his friend. He was up to something and Ker didn't like it. But he knew better than to fight him on it. Jace was stubborn as hell, never gave in, or up. That poor girl locked in his room didn't know what she was in for.

"Oh yeah, Julio," still typing Jace didn't move from the monitor.

"I know, I know, just lunch or dinner too?" The men chuckled at Julio knowing Jace wanted him to take Lissa to lunch and dinner and otherwise keep her locked in his room.

Cringing slightly at his friends knowing more of his woman trouble than he'd like, Jace said casually without emphasis like he was discussing the weather, "Both. Thanks."

This earned another darting displeased look from Ker that Jace was going to leave the ship for what sounded like hours, alone, with no backup. Jace ignored him. "Julio."

Julio turned his light olive skinned face to Jace. His dark brows rose up in question over his round brown eyes.

"We're docked. I don't want a repeat of what happened last time. Do not let her out of your sight. Do not take her near the deck. Hold onto her at all times, ignore her if she complains, and keep her locked up. No mistakes."

They all knew Lissa had tried to jump into the ocean last time they docked, foolishly thinking she could get to shore without actually swimming, and seemed to accept dying if she didn't make it.

Scratching his jaw with his fingers, Julio's expression turned very serious. "I got it, Jace."

Jace stayed at his computer several hours, the others came and went, he didn't move. Then without a word, he left the study. Grabbing a quick sandwich for later, he trod back to his room and went inside.

Seeing Lissa sitting calmly sewing, back where she belonged, he let out a silent sigh of relief. He felt her eyes on his back as he went to his desk and unlocked a drawer.

Taking out a gun, he stuffed it in the back of his jeans and pulled his sweatshirt over it, then grabbed a few extra magazines and shoved them in his pocket. He knelt, pulled up one leg of his jeans and took a very small gun out of a holster there. Although he knew it was, he checked that it was loaded then put it back and pushed down the pant leg to cover it.

Next he picked up a pair of sunglasses, and dropped a ball cap on his head. He went over to Lissa where she was sitting in the rocking chair, pretending he didn't see her stiffen and imperceptibly move back at his approach.

He crouched in front of her. She had a pair of his jeans on her lap and was sewing up a long tear. Stifling the feeling it gave him seeing her with his clothes in her hands and repairing them for him, he said, "I have to leave the boat for a few hours." He almost smiled at her swift intake of breath, she actually looked concerned.

"The guns," she said, sounding anxious that he seemed to be going to need them.

Not responding to her concern about his weapons, he said, "It's all right, Julio's going to take care of you while I'm gone. But," he slid to his knees. "I'm asking you, please, Lissa, please don't do anything reckless while I'm gone. Please just stay in this room."

He took a deep breath and said it again, "I'm *asking* you, please do this for me."

The big green eyes regarded him solemnly.

Jace emphasized the asking part, but he knew she would know he was really *telling* her. Her complaint was that he was always telling her to do things, not asking her, so he was trying to be diplomatic, give her some feeling of control of her life. Even though he was still going to keep her locked up, for her own good, he told himself.

"Okay, Nico." When he frowned, she said sweetly, "Jace." That earned her a smile.

"I will behave myself, just for tonight." It was enough for her that he hadn't come barging in still all mad and ready to punish her in some way for what she'd done to him.

Getting to his feet, he said, "Thank you." Bending over her he cupped her chin, kissed her lightly on the lips then was out the door.

Chapter Eighteen

*J*ace had a car waiting at the dock. He hopped in and entered the address he was given from the email in the GPS. It was quite a distance away, by the time he reached the destination the sun had almost set.

It was a blue-collar redneck kind of bar a few miles outside the rural village of Helensport. The bar was a small wooden structure with neon liquor signs blinking in the windows.

Parking the car in the gravel and dirt lot, he hoofed inside the bar. Leaving the ball cap on he removed the sunglasses, hung them on the front of his sweatshirt and looked around.

It was just a regular bar, no frills. It was about a quarter full with people sitting at square tables in the middle, and others lined the barstools along the straight bar counter that took over one wall.

There were pictures of New York City in the 1800's on the wall. The floor was dark green tile, the walls a light paint, and typical amber lighting made it seeable but slightly dim.

Not seeing anyone that met the description of who he was supposed to meet, he trod over and lounged halfway on a bar stool with one foot on the floor the other on the bar railing. Wanting to keep his faculties sharp he ordered a beer and nursed it. Periodically he checked his watch.

"Hey there," a pretty woman with long blonde hair smiled up at him. "I haven't seen you around before, do you live around here or just visiting?" Slightly exotic brown eyes feathered on his broad chest and slid down his denims. Leaning in closer to him, her nicely shaped lips turned up, she twirled a lock of hair.

"Uh, yeah, I'm just visiting. Here on business." Jace picked up his beer holding it in his hand between them. He saw a table of young women grinning in their direction. He assumed they were her friends.

"I'm Kristina," she announced with a purr moving closer to Jace. Looking up at him, her shoulder shifted forward flirtatiously. With a kittenish slant of her eyes, she set long narrow fingers on his sleeve. "You are?" Her chest brushed his arm.

Jace didn't check out her legs in the short black skirt or her breasts pouring out the top of the yellow low cut blouse. "I'm married, and I'm here on business. Sorry honey," he gave her a polite smile wondering if her eyes would be quite as exotic when all that makeup was washed off.

The only eyes he was interested in were crystal green and attached to a curvy, rosy-brunette currently locked in his cabin on the ship.

Pouting at him, Kristina glanced at his fingers then up to his dark blue eyes. "I don't see a ring, how married are you?"

Using the arm she was touching, Jace put the beer bottle to his lips and took a healthy slug. After swallowing, he replied, "Very." He smiled politely at her again then half turned from her.

She got the hint. Kristina shrugged her shoulders, the yellow blouse moved up then dipped down. She grinned over at her friends, and shaking her head she went back to join them.

After two hours Jace decided he'd been stood up. He had no way of reaching his contact. She had sent the email asking him to meet with her, and other than describing herself as a tall thin redhead and she would be wearing a lime green jacket; that was it.

Paying his bill, he stood up, stretched, it was already late and he had a long drive back to the boat.

Disappointed, he hit the bathroom before leaving. It had been a long shot anyway, taking one last look around, he headed out the door fishing his keys out of his pocket. Halfway across the lot, he halted when he heard a scream. Then another, a woman screaming.

It sounded like it was coming from behind the bar. Jace dashed towards the back of the building. It could be an ambush, he would be careful when he got to the back-

Bang!

A shot rang out- Jace felt something slam into his rib. Dropping to his knees, he put his hand on his sweatshirt then looked at it, blood covered his palm.

His vision funneled into darkness, he fell forward on the ground and was out.

"Uhhh," groaning, Jace forced himself to sit up. Having no idea how long he was out, or how much blood he'd lost, he struggled to his hands and knees then pushed to his feet.

Yanking the sweatshirt off over his head, he rolled it up and placed it on his wound. "*Aghh*," it hurt like hell. Stumbling to the rented car, he managed to get it open and get in.

The engine wheezed once then turned over. He couldn't believe someone shot him, assumed he was dead and split without checking.

Spinning out of the parking lot, he drove well over the speed limit, considering how he was weaving it was shocking he didn't get stopped by the police.

His vision blurred, he almost passed out, his head bounced on the steering wheel waking him back up.

Lissa was sound asleep when something woke her. She sat up, something was making noise at the door. She looked over at Jace's bed, it was empty. Not sure what to do, she got up and was almost to the door when it opened.

A screamed peeled out of her when Jace tumbled in falling to the floor.

"Jace?" Was he playing a trick on her? She inched over. He was on his stomach, something was pooling on the carpet.

Kneeling down, she almost fainted, it was blood. "Jace!" Lissa yelled trying to roll him over. Finally getting him on his back she saw the sweatshirt he'd dropped was soaking red, his black T-shirt was soaked, so were his jeans.

Her hands shaking, she lifted his shirt to see what was causing the blood. There was too much blood to see the wound. Nausea roiled in her stomach, she had to fight the dizziness threatening to make her pass out.

Jumping up, she ran to the bathroom, grabbed as many towels as she could, hurried back and dropped them on him. Slipping to her knees she pressed on the towels.

Crying, "Jace, Jace, can you hear me?" She had no idea what to do, hearing him moan, she leaned over, whispered, "Jace,"

"Dre…" his voice so weak she could barely make out what he was saying. "Dre," the word came out in a shudder then his head rolled to the side.

"What are you tryin' to say, draw?" Frantically she tried to understand what he was saying. Then, "Oh, Drew, the doctor!"

Leaping to her feet, she ran barefoot down the hall in her T-shirt and shorts heading straight for Ker's room. When she got there she banged on the door with both fists.

The door flew open. "Lissa? What the fuck are you-" The girl pounding on his door half dressed, in the middle of the night did not bode well.

She gushed in one breath, "Jace- it's Jace, go tae him," then she kept running down the hall. Ker didn't go after her, he raced to Jace's room.

When he got there, he found Jace sprawled on his back, a pile of towels turning red bunched on his stomach.

"Jesus, One," Ker muttered. He knelt to put pressure on the towels. Jace was so white the white towels were darker than his drained complexion. While he debated to leave him to go for the doctor, Ker heard pounding feet coming down the hall.

Drew Manor burst into the room with his medical bag in his hand. He plunked the bag on the floor and crouched down beside Ker. "What happened?"

Ker shook his head grimly, his long black hair swept across his broad shoulders, "No idea. The girl came and got me." His head swiveled, "Where is she?"

Lifting up the towels, Drew said, "She's behind me, can't run as fast as me."

Ker asked, "She didn't tell you what happened?"

Prodding with his fingers, Doc grabbed his bag. Opening it, he said, "It's a damned bullet wound."

Shocked, his face growing wickedly dark, ebony eyes narrowed. "Where did you say she was?" Ker asked, his voice dangerously quiet.

Then he remembered how distressed she looked at his door. If she'd shot Jace she wouldn't have come for Ker. He looked up when he heard her small running steps.

Lissa rushed through the doorway breathing heavily, her face white as a sheet. Ker took his cell out and mumbled some words into it then dumped it in his pocket.

"Doctor, will he be okay?" she cried breathlessly. Covering her mouth with her hands, she stared down at Jace pale as a ghost, his eyes closed.

Manor didn't answer her, he was pouring antibiotic into Jace's wound. "Ker," he said, "hold this towel on him, while I," he looked up at Lissa. "Honey, can you find me some more towels? Clean ones?"

Nodding, she ran off to the linen closet. By the time she came back the room was filling up with the other team members.

"What the fuck happened?" Victor barked at Ker, his face was outraged and frightened.

"All we know is that he was shot." Ker said quietly. All eyes turned to Lissa as she came back laden with towels, sheets and pillowcases.

Donnie made a move to go after her, his furious roar making her jump, "What did you do to One?"

Ker snapped, "Victor-"

Bewildered, scared and angry himself, Victor caught a hold of Donnie keeping him from attacking Lissa.

Ker said calmly, "She didn't do it." He'd had time to visually search the room. It wasn't disturbed at all, there had been no fight here, she looked like she'd climbed straight out of bed and gone directly to his door.

There was no gun in sight and no other blood except on and around Jace in the room. There was no blood on the walls and there was no blood on the girl except her hands.

Lissa stood appalled that they thought she had shot Jace, her jaw dropped, eyes reflecting fear and worry.

Two big steps and Cad was beside her. He took the towels and sheets from her, handed them to Victor then took Lissa's arm and brought her over to sit down on the bed.

His voice gentle, he said, "We can help more by staying out of the way."

She smiled weakly at him through the tears that were streaming down her face. He patted her hand, "He's survived worse, honey, a lot worse, he'll be okay." Her attention turned riveting to Jace lying so still and pallid.

Doc told Victor which blood type of plasma to retrieve from a locked fridge in his room.

When Victor returned with the plasma, Drew hung it over a lamp and hooked it up to Jace so the fresh blood flowed while he worked for an hour, digging out the bullet.

With many anxious pairs of eyes watching his every move, after what seemed an eternity, sweat dripping from his temples, Doc poured in more sanitizer, stitched up the hole, then taped a bandage around Jace's entire lower ribcage to keep it tight over the wound.

Wiping his forehead with his sleeve, Drew took a deep breath, rolled back on his heels. "All right guys, let's get him on his bed." The men picked Jace up and placed him carefully on his bed.

They all stood back and stared down at their chief and friend. It was strange seeing the vital, strapping man lying there, skin colorless, eyes closed, not moving a muscle. His brawny chest rose and fell only slightly with shallow breaths.

Ker said, "Drew?" Strong and stoic as always, yet there was a trace of worry in his dark eyes.

The doctor pulled out a handkerchief and wiped his face with it. Peeling off his surgical gloves he climbed to his feet and threw the gloves in the trash.

He replied, "Like Cad said, he's had worse. He lost a tremendous amount of blood. He must have been far away or passed out for a while when it happened. Where was he?"

Ker shook his head. "We don't know, he wouldn't tell us where he was going. We'll have to wait until he wakes to fill us in." Twisting his head, he looked around the room settling on the rocking chair as it was the biggest chair in the room.

"I'll stay the night." His gaze flickered to Lissa who was standing by the bed wringing her hands, staring wide-eyed down at Jace.

"Good. Well, that's all I can do. Any changes, get me right away," Drew instructed Ker. "All right," his arms out like he was shooing sheep, "everyone out. You know he needs as much rest as possible."

The men murmured while quietly leaving the room. Drew trod over to Lissa. "You okay honey? Do you want me to give you something to help you calm, to sleep?"

She looked at him, weary and surprised, shook her head vehemently, her eyes back on Jace. "No, certainly not. What can I do for him, Doc?"

Drew smiled kindly at her. He could see Ker gazing at her in interest then at Drew. Then the two men shared a smile. She may deny it until the cows came home, but she cared about Jace.

"There's nothing more to do right now. We'll see how he is after a few hours rest. All right," the doctor turned, nodded to Ker. "I'm outta here, call me if anything changes. I'll be back in the AM."

Ker walked him out, closed the door, wasn't sure whether to lock it or not. Glancing at Lissa, her eyes glued to Jace, he concluded she wasn't going anywhere, and no one would dare bother her with Ker in the room, if they wanted to live.

166

But then again, whomever shot Jace was still out there. He went over, took Jace's key out of the door and locked it.

Then he picked up an extra pillow off Jace's bed and a sheet off the floor and trod to the rocking chair where he dropped the pillow. He sat down, kicked his boots off, put his feet up on a hassock and pulled the sheet over him.

Lissa looked over, her fretful eyes blinked, trying to keep her composure. She hopped up and walked over to Ker. "Ker, please, take my bed, I can fit in that chair better than you, or even the floor."

When he didn't respond, she insisted. "I will be fine, you're too big to be comfortable sleeping there, please, take my bed."

When he didn't open his eyes, after a couple of minutes she gave up and turned away.

Peering through almost closed lids he watched her go to Jace where she stood for a moment looking at him. She bent, brushed the blond hair back off his face then laid her hand on his cheek.

Dashing at a tear that slipped out, she went to her bed and dropped down on the thin mattress. Shifting onto her side, she watched Jace sleep.

Smiling for the second time that day, *this smiling thing was getting to be a damned habit, it's her fault*, Ker thought, settling on the rocker and closing his eyes. The little wench cared about Jace, and the big lummox didn't even know.

And Ker wasn't about to tell him. Nope. He was gonna sit back and watch the fun evolve.

Chapter Nineteen

Lissa's lids fluttered, she opened them slowly. Still lying on her side, remembering, she peered through her lashes across to the other bed. "Oh!" Her lids sprung up.

Jace was lying on his side too, with his head propped on his hand and his lively blue eyes staring keenly straight at her, a lazy smile on his face.

"Good morning, beautiful," he said with a crooked grin.

Sitting right up, Lissa pushed back a sheet that someone must have covered her with last night, swung her legs around to sit on the edge of the mattress. "How are you feeling? Are you all right?"

Worriment harrowing her face, she pushed her heavy hair back off her shoulders. A mug of steaming coffee sitting next to him on the nightstand caught her eye, "Where did that come from?"

"There's one for you too," Jace said pointing at the table next to her bed. A mug was there with faint vapor drifting from it.

He moved to sit up, a gasp of pain urged out of him. He leaned back on his elbows, his neck arched. Draping his head back, his eyes crunched closed with a groan, "Uhh…"

Lissa jumped up and hurried over to him. "Just lay back, Jace, stop movin'." She pressed at his shoulders trying to push him back down on the mattress.

Groaning, he nudged her hands away and wriggled up, braced now on his hands, elbows bent.

"Here," Lissa gathered up his pillows and stuffed them behind him. She held his arms, helping him to sit back against them. Glancing around, she saw the sheet and pillow were on the rocking chair, but Ker was gone.

"Where did Ker go?" she asked, handing him his coffee.

He sipped the dark brew. Groaning now with delight, "Ahh, that is so good," he drank some more. Licking his lips, he said, "Well, if you weren't such a sleepy head, you would have woken up when we did, you know, at a reasonable hour," his gaze cut to the clock on the nightstand, it read 7 AM.

"You would have seen Ker check on me, saw that I was fine, chucked out and got us some coffee, then took off."

Lissa picked up the other coffee, took a tiny sip then set it on the nightstand. "I can't believe you are all right," Lissa said, her voice and expression incredulous.

"I mean, you were shot for heaven's sake!" She wrapped her arms around her body shivering at the thought and the picture of Doc pulling a bullet out of Jace's bloody body.

Setting his mug on the table, he snaked his hand out grasping her wrist. He tugged her to the bed, looped his arm halfway around her waist and drew her down on the mattress. "As they told you last night, I've had worse. It was no big deal, it's over and done with, no need to worry about it."

Sitting on the bed facing him, her gaze fell to the bandage wrapped around his ribs, her mouth dropped open. "No big deal? Are you kiddin' me? You could have died, you-"

He scooted over, pulling her next to him to sit back on the pillows. Draping his arm around her shoulders, he retorted easily, "But I didn't, and it's done. A couple of days and there will only be a tiny scar, another one to join the many others," he said ruefully looking down at his body which had its share of bullet and knife wounds.

"But Jace," she shifted to get up.

"Shhh," he held her, "just sit with me. Doc said I needed peace and quiet to heal." He slid down on the pillow a fraction, pulling her with him.

169

Lissa muttered, "No big deal my butt." Not pushing away from him as she normally would have, Lissa settled against his side. A trace of a smile spread over his face as he closed his eyes.

"Jace?"

"Hmmm?"

"What happened? Where did you go?" She was met with several moments of silence. About to give up on him answering her, she thought he had fallen asleep, then he spoke.

"We...my team and I...are involved in clearing up a...matter. I received an email from the wife, or at least she said she was his wife, of a man possibly involved in the matter. She said she wanted me to meet with her. That she had some information for me, heavy, important information."

"You went on a date?"

He frowned. "No, don't be ridiculous. She had info for a...job we're doing."

Detecting something in his tone, she asked, "A...perilous job?"

She might find out later what he'd done and not wanting her to know he lied to her, he mumbled noncommittally, "Hmmm."

"So, you just went blindly alone, without your other men into unknown danger?" Her tone implied her feelings about his lack of judgment.

A wry smile tugged at the corner of his mouth. "You can skip the lecture, I already got an earful from Ker. The woman said I had to come alone, she would be watching, she said she feared for her life and wasn't sure she could trust even me.

"It was a bar out in the open in the middle of nowhere, there would have been nowhere for my guys to stash and hide. I had to take the chance." His voice dropped, turning defensive then he stopped talking.

Lissa fidgeted anxiously with her hands. It was so scary, it had turned out to be horribly dangerous for him, almost deadly. "So what happened?"

Jace reached over and stilled her fidgeting laying his big hand over both of hers. "I waited for her, she didn't show. As I was almost to the car I heard a woman screaming from behind the bar."

"You didn't," she cocked her head to look at him, saw his nod.

"I did. What was I supposed to do? Hear a woman screaming for her life and say, 'oh well' hop in the car and drive back to the boat without another thought?" He snorted his indignation.

"Sure, I thought it could be an ambush, but I had to go. I assumed the danger, if there was any, would be when I got behind the bar. Then I would be on the alert and cautious. As it turned out, I wasn't even near the back when I was…" he didn't like to say it, he'd seen the terror in her eyes when he had fallen into the room last night.

"Shot," she said it for him, sounding nauseous when she did.

"Yeah, well," he hugged her to him. "Like I said, it's over and done, I don't want to talk about it again." Smiling down at her he kissed the tip of her nose. That was all he'd dared to do, it was difficult enough having her cuddled up against him, in his bed.

He wasn't going to do anything to ruin this moment like rolling her under him and removing both their clothes. His eyes drifted closed, then, his face relaxed into sleep.

Lissa watched him sleep. His lids down over the twinkling blue eyes hiding the mischief inside. A lock of blond hair flopped over one dark brow, his full masculine lips closed peacefully.

She gently lifted the lock of thick hair and set it back off his forehead, then laid her hand on the dark stubble covering his rough handsome face.

Sighing, Lissa slid down, rested her head on his chest, her palm on his uninjured ribs, she didn't move when his other arm rolled over her snuggling her to his chest.

True to his word, in only a few days Jace was almost completely healed.

They spent his recovering days quietly. One of the team would come and get Lissa and wait for her while she baked cakes, cookies, pies, donuts, that were gobbled up before the day was out.

Another man would take her to the dining room where she would get meals for her and Jace that she would bring back and eat with him.

But Lissa had to run and fetch Doc Drew the first morning. Jace had gotten up too quickly and passed out in his weakness, crumpling to the floor.

When he came to, he had to suffer through a scolding from Doc Drew. Then Drew went on to lecture him, instructing he was only to get up to go to the bathroom, slowly, and that was it.

He had turned to Lissa and admonished her for being in Jace's bed with him, even clothed. It was obvious by the other neat bed that Lissa had not slept in it.

"The man needs his complete rest," he had chastised, "there is no way that will happen with you in his bed, in his arms." He had smiled at the pink staining her cheeks, glancing over he grinned at the annoyed look on Jace's face. "If you don't do as I say, it will take longer to heal, and you could cause internal damage, so, cool it."

As he was leaving, he said, "Jace is only to have soft food for now, soup, eggs, liquids, lots of liquids, no alcohol at all, tea would be good for him."

"Don't you have somewhere you need to be, Drew? Birthing babies or yanking out kidney stones?" Jace grumbled irritably. "I hate tea. I want a steak, medium rare and I need a beer, actually bourbon would be-"

Doc had burst out laughing. "Too bad. You are a terrible patient, One." To Lissa, he said, "Don't mind him, and don't let him browbeat you. Remember, soft food and tea. Oh," he said at the doorway, "his *entire* body needs complete rest, it would help if you put on more clothes."

His gaze slid down the cropped, white T-shirt her nipples were poking through, to the tiny shorts she slept in and back up to her mortified face. He closed the door chuckling at Jace's curses he hurled after him.

Two days later, dressed in jeans and a blouse, Lissa brought a tray with eggs, grits and several biscuits with a teapot and cups and set it down on the desk.

At the groan, she looked over at Jace sitting up against the pillows with a scowl on his face. Having not shaved for three days, he rubbed his fingertips over the dense stubble.

"I'm tired of eggs," he groused. "I want meat, french fries, a beer..." he grumbled watching her pour him a cup of tea.

She added a drop of cream, a cube of sugar, which she had censored him on, soapboxing how bad sugar was for a person, but he refused to drink the tea without it. He drank his coffee black but he didn't like tea so he wanted as many other ingredients as possible added to it. Especially anything sweet.

Sticking a spoon in the cup, she stirred it and handed it to him smiling at his frown. She said mildly, "You are such a crybaby."

He took the cup glaring at it. She went back to the desk, sprinkled salt and pepper on the eggs, she'd given him a discourse on that too, about the evils of salt, which he also ignored.

She put a pat of butter on his grits and the biscuits, she let the danger of butter go. At least she could control the amount of salt, sugar and butter he had when she put it on his food instead of letting him do it.

His nose wrinkled in distaste when she brought the tray and set it on his lap. "I want real food," he whined picking up a fork.

"Doctor Drew said tomorrow. Now, stop bellyaching and eat up." She laid a napkin on his chest, picked up a knife and spread blueberry jam on his biscuit.

Actually, Jace was grinning like an idiot on the inside, he loved his little Nurse Lissa. She was being sweet to him, treating him kindly with patience and care. Soothing his brow with her cool fingertips when he winced in pain. Hell if he'd only known, he'd gone out and gotten shot a lot sooner. He sassily slapped her on the butt when she got up.

"Hey!" she exclaimed, shaking a finger at his cheeky impudence. But a tiny smile arced as she walked away from him.

173

The bullet hadn't killed him, she had told him when she had gone and gotten Doc, because he was too ornery to die by one little bullet. Rubbing her butt, she sighed, he was getting better.

"Where's your breakfast?" Jace asked through a mouthful of biscuit, staring at her ass. He had been pissed when Drew had ordered Lissa to stay out of his bed and to wear more clothes.

"I ate with Victor in the dinin' room." She picked up her sewing basket.

His brows stiffened, he set the biscuit down. "Why?"

Oblivious to his cross tone, she told him, "He said he thought I could use a change of scenery. Wasn't that nice of him?" Lissa picked up a flannel shirt then sat down and opened the sewing basket.

Snatching up his fork, Jace stabbed his eggs and shoveled them in his mouth. "Yeah, damned bloody nice of him." Scooping up a pile of grits he shoved them in with the eggs. Chewing his irritation, his eyes slanted at the shirt she was sewing a button on. "Whose shirt is that?"

She smiled down at the needle she was threading. "Oh, it's Victor's."

His expression seething resentment, Jace kept shoveling in his food, chewing fast, swallowing hard. Scowling at his squishy eggs he tossed the fork down, picked up the tray and set it on the bottom of the bed, pushed back the covers and got to his feet.

Stomping into the bathroom, he slammed the door behind him. The shower turned on almost immediately.

Lissa was putting the thread and needle back in the basket when he came out, his hair wet, dripping around his smooth-shaven face, towel slung around his neck, and another wrapped around his lean hips exposing hard as stone abs.

He went straight to his dresser, yanked open one of the drawers, took out a shirt, opened a lower drawer, got a pair of jeans, underwear and socks.

When Lissa got up to put the basket away, Jace dropped the towel and jerked up the underwear then the jeans, pulled the shirt on and was hooking his belt when she turned around.

"What are you doing now?" he asked, trying to tamper the growl, Victor was deliberately goading him, and it was working.

"I'm foldin' his shirt, I can't hand it back wadded up in a ball, you know." She laid the shirt on the bed and folded the sleeves over then the rest. Lissa looked at Jace, frowning at him, watching him button his shirt then comb his wet hair.

"You sound kind of grouchy, are you in pain?" When he sat down and pulled on his socks and then his boots, she asked in dismay, "Where are you goin'? Doc said one more day in bed-"

"I don't need any more rest. You done with that?" He nodded to the shirt she was neatly smoothing with her hands.

"Yes, when Victor comes back for-"

Jace snatched the shirt up. "I'll save him the trouble." The flannel crushed in his hand, he strode out the door.

Chapter Twenty

Stalking down the hall, feeling a hitch in his rib, Jace pressed his hand over it.

When he reached the study, the team was already there, all except Donnie who was manning the bridge. They looked up as Jace entered.

His laptop was on the table. As he went to the chair in front of it, Jace hurled the shirt in Victor's smirking face.

Laughing at Jace, Victor picked up his shirt up and set it on the table. He lifted a lapel and said grinning, "Yeah, easy on the eyes, great seamstress, and that little lady can bake up a storm. I wonder what else that honey is good at."

Thumping down in his seat Jace glowered at Victor. "You aren't gonna find out because she's done sewing your shit for you." He thrust the computer open with a testy shove and stared peevishly at the blank screen.

Victor chortled from across the table, "Ahh, it seems someone has the little green monster roiling around in his head." He grinned at Jace. "She made a batch of cookies just for me, my favorite, cinnamon spice. Did she tell you?" He held up a plate filled with cookies topped with white icing. "Want one?"

"Screw you, Victor," Jace snarled, glowering at his computer that was now powered on.

"Okay boys, pull 'em in." Ker rebuked the two men. "We have work to do. We'll be docking briefly at one of the islands in a few days and then the next day we should reach Scotland."

Jace glared at his laptop. Victor was laughing across the table at him, taunting him.

Watching them spar, they were good friends, everyone knew Victor was only playing with Jace, he'd never go after his woman.

Ker said, "Leave off, Victor, tell us what you've learned."

"Yeah," Cad chuckled from his chair, "leave lover boy alone."

"Cad, you can suck my-"

Ker cut Jace off, "Knock it off guys, Victor," he nodded at the tawny skinned man who was always skimming his palms over his slicked back hair.

Snickering, Victor pointed at his own computer. "I don't have positive evidence yet, but I think Warrington scammed his venders saying the tax break in Scotland would be huge, hundreds of millions even, for them to close down their manufacturing plants in the US and build them in Scotland.

"If he's clever enough to sell out after he's paid off, it could be a long time before anyone realizes they've been conned. Chances would be they probably would never figure it out. It'll be years before they find their losses, and by then they'll forget about Warrington and blame the trouble on other things."

Jace nodded, agreeing with Victor's conclusions. "Yes, as we thought, he talked the giant chain store conglomerate into pulling up stakes and going to Scotland where the tax differential is extreme, costing them half as much to produce merchandise as it would in the states.

That's in addition to the regions contributing up to billions of dollars towards the taxes owed to get the manufacturing business." He tapped the keys. "We just need to prove it, and-"

"Find out who murdered the general manager and the accountant in America, and the foreman in Scotland," Julio said.

"I think they were killed because they figured it out too." Jace stood up, reached across the table and grabbed up a handful of cookies. Ignoring Victor's obnoxious grin, he said, "We ask around at the construction site, see if we can discover the killers, then hit the weakest link and turn him against Warrington." He stuffed a whole cookie in his mouth. Wiping his chin, he looked down and brushed the crumbs off his shirt.

Setting his arms on the table, Jace angled forward in his chair, his eyes on the plate still containing cookies, he asked Victor, "How did you get into Warrington's hard drive?"

Victor wrapped an arm around the plate pulling it in front of him. Inclining his head to his laptop, he replied, "There were a few duplicate sites to hide the primary documents. Julio whittled them down until he found the primary." He nodded towards Julio who was busy at his own computer. "When we located the main one I used a Trojan horse to get in."

Ker asked, "Wouldn't they be able to detect they were being hacked?"

"Sure," Victor affirmed, "normally. But I piggy-backed it on their spyware, the main software, as well as I tagged some on their ads for the spyware."

"Clever," Jace commended him. Eating his last cookie, he settled his back comfortably against his chair and crossed an ankle over a knee. He pushed up his sleeves and clasped his hands behind his head. "I assume Warrington had at least two stat books, one for the real numbers and one of course for the fake. What's our next step?"

Victor set his elbows on the table, and put his hands together in a steeple. With a canny grin, he said, "That was also my conclusion. That's normal scamming procedure. I think though, the important documents, the ones that can hang him are probably on a drive. So it can't be hacked and he can physically secure it."

Cad added, "Where he could keep it close by him for quick access."

Jace yawned, closed his eyes and said, "Warrington would have given his doctored stats to the GM or the accountants for them to verify his financial findings. The accountant was undoubtedly killed because he might have worked up his own numbers and came out with vastly different results. He may have contacted the wrong person and told them." He yawned again. "I wish we'd gotten to our informant before they did. Dead guys can't talk, dammit."

"We need to find that drive," Victor muttered.

"Well," Ker said, "we can't do any of those things until we get off this ship." He turned to Cad. "You get the house and vehicles all set up?"

Snagging a few cookies, incurring a frown from Victor, Cad nodded, "Yes, done deal." He popped a cookie in his mouth. Crumbs flying as he spoke, "Jace, bro, you need to bring that little girl with us to the house. I can't live without her baking. She-" he broke off mid-word, everyone stopped moving. Cad's eyes twirled around, the men shot warning looks at him, Jace's head was down, he was staring unblinking at his laptop.

"Uh," Victor broke the awkward silence, "so, the day after we arrive, Jace meets with Warrington at his office to get the lay of the land, and we hit the site."

"Yeah, that's the plan. Well," Jace stood up, closed his computer. "I think I need a nap. I'll be back later."

Ker stood up too. "I'll walk with you."

"You don't need to," Jace protested.

"Yeah, I do. I know where you're really going." Ker walked beside his friend.

His hands stuffed deep in his pockets, Jace shot him a begrudging smile. "You've always been able to read my mind." They headed straight to the makeshift bar.

Jace looked askance at Ker's usual uniform of starched long-sleeved shirt tucked into sharply pressed black pants, his more lightweight, black cowboy styled boots made a lighter sound tacking across the planked flooring than Jace's steel-toed boots. "You going to wear that pretty white shirt to the construction site?"

Ker's raised shoulder was his only response. As they strode with strong confidence down the hall and through the great room, many a female eye followed the two tall, powerfully built men. Jace, with his strong jaw, a few scars, the furtively lethal glint tampered with looming mischief in his dark blue eyes made him roughly handsome.

The women found both men to have a hard, mysterious edge, but Ker was always blankly unreadable. Women had told Jace what they thought about his friend. That although Ker was extremely good looking in a fierce brigand kind of way, with his dark glittering eyes in a sharp diamond shaped face and neat, sort of triangular beard, long hair, he scared off the less aggressive females.

The ones looking for a...different...more dangerous...sort of experience pursued him. But Jace knew the black-haired male had no interest getting involved with any of the women on the ship. He was a very private man, and very particular with whom he spent his intimate moments with.

At the bar, Ker said, "I'll get 'em, you really should take a break, Jace, take a load off." He went around the bar to get their drinks. "What do you want?"

Sitting down on an iron barstool with seat and back cushions, Jace twined his fingers and set them on the faux wood counter. Mulling it over for a second, he said, "I'm in the mood for whiskey."

Ker raised a brow over one eye with a frown. Jace sighed. "Okay, give me a beer."

Ker got two bottles, twisted the tops off, set them on the counter then came around and sat down beside Jace. "Lissa finds out you're drinking after Drew said none for a week she's going to give you hell." Ker put the bottle to his lips and slugged half of the cold brew down.

Jace shrugged his shoulder. "It's beer, not hard alcohol." He took a hefty few gulps. "Ahh, that's good," he sighed, enjoying the cold tartness of the drink rolling down his throat plunging into his gullet where it warmed.

"Uh huh. I dare you to try that one with her, or with Drew for that matter. He'll ream you a new asshole if he sees you drinking. You're supposed to be taking it easy, quietly mending."

"Bro, where's my frosty mug and cocktail napkin?" Jace asked to change the subject.

Finishing his bottle, Ker got up and retrieved two more beers. "This ain't the Ritz, son." He twisted the top off one of the bottles and set it in front of Jace.

Jace's forehead furrowed. He said slightly churlish, "Ker, I'm not an invalid, I can open my own beer. I've been shot plenty of times before and healed just fine without a medic or a nagging woman watching everything I eat and drink, and sleep."

His bottle to his lips, Ker said, "Sure. I'm thinking you're enjoying the nagging part way too much." He chugged some, wiped his mouth, set the bottle down and wrapped his hands around it. "Well? We're almost there, what have you decided to do about her?"

Not even pretending to not understand, Jace rolled his bottle between his palms. "She...uh...is coming with us."

"One, how can you rationalize that? It's clear as day she doesn't want to be in Scotland."

"She is still not safe. Just because we'll be in Scotland doesn't mean she won't tell on us to the police, or the guys that killed our informant in the alley the day I took her may have travelled here as well." Jace took a drink. "It's actually quite likely they did come here if they were Warrington's hired killers."

"Come on, One, there isn't-"

"Besides," Jace interrupted him, "whatever has the fear of God in her is in Scotland. She doesn't have a false identity for no reason. Hell, Ker, she was so afraid of something she was literally trying to jump ship."

Shaking his head, Jace went on thoughtfully, "I'm not taking her there and cutting her loose to face alone whatever has her scared to death. Besides, she has no passport to be able to get back to the US. She'll be stuck with no visa to live and work in Scotland, and no way to return to the States."

Ker lined his two beer bottles next to each other contemplating a third. Lissa would kill him if he brought the injured Jace back to their room drunk. "Bro, you need to admit it to yourself. You think you can keep her until she falls for you. She obviously *cares* about you, but any more than that is unknown. You're afraid if you set her free she'll leave you in a heartbeat."

He turned to face Jace. "How long can you really keep her against her will? A week, a month, a year?"

Jace silently drank his beer until it was empty, he set it down. "I need another."

"You probably shouldn't."

"Okay," Jace mumbled, he slanted his head at Ker. "You know, you gave me an idea."

"About what?"

"How to keep her."

"Cripes One, you are not listening to me. She is not a stray puppy you can *keep*. I agree with you, the girl is extraordinary, if it were me I'd have a hard time letting her go too. And yeah, I'm getting used to having her around just like the other guys, and you know there're not many females I can tolerate on a regular basis. But," he clunked his two bottles together, "you've heard the old saying, if you set it free and it doesn't return, it wasn't meant to be. If you set it free and it returns, then…"

Jace arched a brow at him, "Then what?"

Ker bunched his shoulders. "Dunno, that's all I remember."

"I need another beer," Jace said.

Ker got up. "Okay, a third can't hurt."

Chapter Twenty-One

*T*hey would be docking on an island in two days. Lissa did not speak to Jace or Ker for those two days after Ker dragged Jace back to the room after they'd been drinking all day.

Madder than a wet hen, Lissa followed Ker to Jace's bed.

"What were you thinkin'? He's sick, Ker, he's nae supposed to be drinkin' alcohol! Doctor Drew said-"

Ker tuned her out, all he heard was "Jace, blah blah blah, Doc, blah, you blah," he dropped Jace face first on his bed, saluted Lissa with an intoxicated half assed salute and lopsided grin, and then staggered out the door to go crash in his own room.

When Jace woke with a pounding hangover headache, first thing he noticed was the room was empty. Popping aspirin and getting a soda from the small fridge, he guzzled it down and felt better.

He washed his face and brushed his teeth then wandered around looking for his phone. He looked everywhere, couldn't find it, until he realized he was still in his jeans and shirt. He felt his pockets, found his phone. He didn't need to push any buttons, Ker had left a text message.

"She is baking, pissed at U and me. Hide."

Chuckling, talking to himself, "You think she's mad now, just wait," Jace went to take a shower and go meet the guys to plan for when they disembark.

When he told them his plan regarding Lissa, they did not hold back their opinions or shock.

"Are you insane?" Julio spat his shock.

Donnie looked at him like he had three eyes. "But Jace, you don't know her, I know she's hot piece of tail but-"

"Watch it, Donnie," Jace's warning frown shut the younger man's mouth. He only told them his plan because he needed their help, from some of them anyway.

Ker and Victor glanced at each other, they didn't argue or voice their concerns. They trusted Jace to know what he was doing, even if it was a crocked crazy idea.

As they neared the island, Jace was getting mad that Lissa was not speaking to him. After all, it was his body to do with what he wanted. He did admit though, that it was nice she cared.

Jace retrieved her from the galley where she was baking as usual and brought her back to their cabin so she could change and clean up.

They walked in silence back to the dining room jogging briefly across the open deck under a light rain shower on the way.

They sat with his team, joking and telling stories while eating. Lissa talked to everyone but Jace, even Ker now, who had the audacity to smirk at Jace.

Trying to break the ice, Jace said to her, "Babe, your hair is so pretty all curly from the rain and diamond drops on your lashes."

"Victor, please pass the pepper," Lissa said with a bright smile to Victor, who returned that bright smile with one of his own.

Victor didn't have to look at Jace to know it aggravated him when he flirted with Lissa, it only made him do it more.

Handing her the peppershaker, making sure his hand brushed hers, he said, "Here you go honey, anything else I can get, or do for you?" The girl was so sweet and beautiful it went against his grain not to flirt with her. Provoking Jace was just icing on the cake.

"Ow!" Victor glared at Jace who was innocently cutting his steak pretending he wasn't the one who kicked him in the shin. The kick hurt but still brought a furtive grin to Victor's handsome face, it was hilarious getting Jace stirred up.

This was the first time the team had ever seen Jace lose his peace of mind over a woman and it wasn't likely to happen again, soon anyway. So, being practically brothers for more years than they could remember, Victor was milking Jace's pain for all its worth.

When they finished dinner, they all played a resounding game of pickle ball. After only one game, Lissa mumbled that she was tired and was going to their room. She immediately started walking out of the rec room and towards the hall leading to the cabins.

Jace stared after her, still holding his paddle and a ball, he and Ker had just tried like hell to beat each other and had to call it even.

Ker held his hands out, a satirical lift to the corner of his mouth raised the moustache slightly. "Give them to me, I'll put them up."

"Thanks, bro." Jace didn't hear the quiet chuckle as Ker watched him chase after Lissa. This was the most amusement the guys had enjoyed in a while, watching Jace become pussy-whipped.

"Hey," Jace jogged to catch up with Lissa. He moved alongside her, shortening his strides to match hers. His mouth pulled in, he asked, "Why didn't you wait for me?"

She kept walking.

"Lissa," he moved to stand in front of her without holding her so she couldn't complain he was dragging and pushing her around.

"When are you going to get over it? I'm a grown man; I can take care of myself. It's my decision what I put in my body and how much rest I need...you don't-"

"You are absolutely right." Her nose in the air, Lissa sidestepped him and kept going. "You don't need me tellin' you what tae do. You want tae go out and get your stupid self killed and then don't take care of yourself properly, it's nothin' tae do with me, not my concern. Why should I care?"

Smaller than Jace, the angrier she got the longer more furious strides she took to keep ahead of him. "I don't care, go ahead and die, see if I care," she choked as tears gathered in her throat.

"Baby," now Jace did stop her. Grasping her shoulders, "Hey," he tipped her chin up with a few fingers and saw the tears swelling in the green eyes. "I'm sorry. Really. I thought it was great the way you cared for and took care of me."

She tried to tug away. "Sure you did, I was just an annoyance tae you, a naggin' bug."

Jace stopped her again. "No. I mean it. I loved the way you hovered over me, feeding me, it's just," he raised a shoulder. "I don't like feeling weak, like an invalid. Creeps me out. I'm used to just crawling in a hole alone for a while until I recover then move on."

He brushed his hands down her arms and took her hands. "It's nothing to do with you, it's me, you're wonderful. I just wasn't prepared for you to be so caring of me."

A single tear rolled down her cheek, he pressed his thumb over it. "Why are you crying?"

She half turned to start walking again, he slid his hand along the side of her jaw, splaying his fingers behind her neck to gently hold her still and carefully edged her near the wall so people could pass them by.

He waited for a couple of people to go by, then moved his hand cradling her head. Bending slightly so he could see into her eyes and other people couldn't hear him, his deep voice soft, mouth inches from hers, he said, "Tell me, what is upsetting you?"

Lissa didn't fight him when he slipped his other hand around her waist holding her lightly. She wasn't even aware she'd lifted her hand and set it on his chest, but he was. She looked embarrassed to be in an intimate position in the hallway.

"I...I..." she gulped, tried to look away from him but he held her with a gentle firm grasp.

"Tell me, baby," he coaxed softly. His skin under his shirt where she laid her hand was burning. Whenever he was this close to her he got aroused. Thinking about it now, he should have let them continue on to their room in privacy, but he had this feeling if he didn't grab the moment she would close up and that would be it.

It looked like she was feeling emotion for him, and as far as he was concerned it didn't matter what emotion it was, the main thing she was feeling something for him.

"Jace…" She said nothing else.

Watching her lips when she said his name, he felt a tingle run the length of his body. Encouraging her to continue, he softly rubbed his palm on her the side of her waist and prodded, "What, honey?"

Their eyes connected. With a hitch in her voice, she said "You almost died. You were shot. That you didn't die was a miracle in itself, but when you flaunted Doctor Drew's orders. I mean, it could have led tae…"

Jace stroked his hand up to press on her back and pull her close in an embrace. When she let him tug her against him, a slim smile edged up his mouth.

He tilted her head up and moving his lips towards hers, he whispered, "Baby, I think it's wonderful that you-"

"Jacey!"

They both stiffened at the shriek.

Dona was tripping towards them, carrying her high heels in one hand and a drink in the other, hair a messy blonde cloud around her head.

Jace turned into Lissa as if shielding her from Dona. "Baby, don't pay any attention to her."

"Jacey!" Dona shrieked again and stumbled right into Jace's side knocking him and Lissa into the wall. She giggled drunkenly, "Oops, me a bit tipsy, solly…"

Still holding Lissa, Jace regained his balance and tucked her in the cradle of his arm and chest. "Listen, Dona, we were having a private conversation."

"Oh I know, sugar, I remember, you told me you needed to let her down gently. I unnerstand." She pushed a finger into his shoulder. "You said that you were dumping your little foreign felon trash and then...you and me...would..."

Much taller and heftier than Lissa, she insinuated her body, literally pushing between the couple like she had done the day Lissa climbed on the railing.

She thrust her drink into Lissa's hands and sniffed, "Here, hon, be a dear and hold this," then still holding her shoes, she threw her arms around Jace's neck and slapped her lips on his. She did it so quickly Jace and Lissa were both stunned.

"Goddammit, Dona." Jace grabbed her wrists, dragging them apart and off his neck. Angry red rolled up his neck, his voice ground coarsely, "What the hell are you playing at? I never said that shit." He pushed her to the side to catch Lissa.

Knowing Lissa, she was so walled up and fragile, he didn't need her thinking he said what Dona was claiming. "Baby," he stuck his hand out as soon as he muscled Dona out of the way, but she was gone.

He snarled at the buxom blonde, "Thanks a lot, Dona. Just stay clear of me, okay? And Lissa too." He stalked past her not seeing the sneaky demi-smile she showed his back.

When Jace reached the room and went inside, Lissa was in the bathroom. He slumped down on his bed and waited for her. When she came out she was dressed in the T-shirt and shorts she slept in, her wet hair in braids.

Except for her curves, with the big eyes she could have passed for 12. She went straight to her bed without looking at or speaking to Jace. Climbing in, she turned her body to face away from him.

"Geez, Lissa, come on, you know that woman lives to cause trouble." He got up, went over and stood by her bed.

There was no response from her.

Feeling his phone vibrate in his pocket, he pulled it out, read the text. It was Ker reminding him it was his turn the next four hours on the bridge. Cursing, he shoved the phone in his pocket.

His voice hard, he said, "Lissa, you and I have some things to talk about. You're obviously not too receptive right now and I have to go cover the bridge. But tomorrow, we have to discuss something. Something important."

He glanced at his watch, cursed again. Leaning over he kissed the top of her head then said, "Just remember Dona for who she is. I did not say what she just said I did. Don't let her make trouble between us."

His derisive snort a gentle laugh. "We do that just fine on our own. I'll see you in the morning. Sweet dreams." He didn't like leaving things open like this but he had to go.

He locked the door when he got outside and hurried to the bridge.

Chapter Twenty-Two

When Jace woke the next morning, yawning and stretching, he shifted his head slightly to look over at Lissa in the other bed.

"Dammit," he cursed a few vulgar words. She was gone. When would he learn to keep his keys with him?

After showering and dressing, he passed by the galley to grab a coffee and a donut and started looking for her.

It took him twenty minutes to find her, which it shouldn't have, they were on an island of a ship.

She was out on the open deck leaning against the side of the bridge with her knees tucked up and her arms around them. She appeared to be daydreaming while staring out over the sea. His shadow fell over her.

Tearing her gaze away, she put a hand over her eyes to block the sun and looked up at him.

"Hey," Jace greeted casually. "We, ah, remember I said we need to talk? Come with me." He bent and held a hand down to her to help her up.

Her mouth pulled to the side in wry sarcasm. "Not that I've never mentioned this before but, have you ever considered *askin'* me tae do somethin' instead of *tellin'* me?"

He bumped a shoulder up indicating what was the problem? "You aren't doing anything, what's the difference?"

Jace's hand was still out, she ignored it. "What you're sayin' is you don't need tae waste time on being kind and polite tae me."

Seeing she was going to make things difficult as usual, sighing, Jace bent over, snatched her arm and pulled her to her feet.

"You see? This is what happens. You want to debate everything. It's easier and quicker for me to just tell you and take you." With that, he pulled her across the deck to a small salon behind the bridge.

He opened the door, drew her in and closed it. All of the caring that had developed between them had vanished when Dona had played her last hand.

Both wearing jeans, she had on a white cropped T, he a long sleeved, dark blue shirt that was tight enough to reveal every bit of his heavily muscled masculine chest and thick biceps.

Lissa slammed her hands on her small curvy hips. Pique showed in the color that stained her cheeks, and narrowed her green eyes. "Please stop draggin' me around like I'm a dog on a leash with no rights."

He braced his long legs, crossed his arms over the powerful chest and stood in front of the door indicating she wasn't leaving until he let her. The wind had pushed his blond hair slightly awry, he ran the fingers of one hand through the locks once then crossed his arms again.

Ignoring her complaint, he blurted out, "We're getting married."

"What?" Thinking he was kidding she joked, "I did not get you pregnant, that must have been some other girl. You need tae check with Dona." She waited for him to laugh or spout an annoyed retort about Dona, but he didn't, his face was set and serious. His eyes were like blue headlights and she was caught in them like a trapped deer.

Casually, like it was no big bombshell he dropped on her, Jace stated, "I need a wife for this job that I am going to. When I heard the Director only hires married men in his top level," he looked sheepish, "I told him I was married, or actually about to be."

The room they were in was small containing a sofa, two chairs and several tables, some had magazines and paperback books scattered on them. A window overlooked the deck.

Jace moved closer to her, she backed away until they now stood in the center of the room.

Lissa moved a few more feet away from him. Tossing off matter-of-factly but with tension, she said, "So, why is that my problem?"

"Because you are going to be the wife that I need."

Doing a double-take, she blinked rapidly like he was out of his mind. Her mouth dropped open, she exclaimed, "Oh no I'm not, you're crazy. What kind of stupid joke are you playin' at?" She eyed him warily waiting for the grin she was sure was coming when he admitted he was just messing with her, trying to push her buttons.

The planes of his face tightened; there was no twinkle of mischief in the blue eyes. "I am serious, Lissa. Like I just said, I can't get to where I need to be without toting along a wife. That wife will be you." On the outside he impassively watched her digesting his pronouncement. On the inside he prepared for the fight she was about to launch.

She took another step away from him studying him closely.

The set of his jaw, line of his brow, eyes wide and non-deceptive, he was not kidding.

"You're out of your mind if you think I would," her head shook back and forth emphatically, the wavy hair swept across her back. "There is no way on this earth that I would- donnae even entertain it."

Jace covered more ground moving closer to her in one step than she had in three moving away. "Don't make it into a big deal, Lissa. We'll get it annulled right after the mission... uh, I mean like right after the job is done."

"Donnae make it a big deal?" she squeaked, moving back again. She had gone as far as she could, next she'd have to sit on the couch and she wasn't letting herself be that vulnerable to him. "Are you kiddin' me? It's marriage, it's holy!" Her fair complexion darkened, green eyes gleamed frightfully. Shaking her head harder, she choked in despair, "I am not gettin' tricked into marriage again."

His head jerked up. "What are you talking about? Are you married now?"

She quickly looked away. "No."

"Then what are you talking about already getting tricked into marriage?"

"I'm not discussin' it. It's none of your concern." She turned her body slightly so she was not facing him, her gaze steady on the door. "Why don't you just lie tae the boss and say you left the wife at home?"

"I can't. I have to produce her and a notarized certificate. Warrington said he had been duped so many times that everyone he hires he makes them submit SS info, DL records, deeds to houses, leases to cars, everything. So it has to be real. He says he has more trust in hiring a married man, that they're more responsible and reliable."

His brow jumped at the sarcastic huff sound she made. He watched her steadily, seeing the color draining from her fair skin taking the roses from her cheeks, the look in her eyes turned stark, and anxious.

Biting her lower lip like she was trying to keep control of her emotions, Jace could see her trying to hide her secrets from him, it only made him more determined than ever to find out what her demons were.

"Anyway," he drawled, "I told him I've been engaged for a year and am doing the romantic thing, getting married at sea." He reached for her arm but she swung out of his grasp.

Becoming irritated at her resistance, he pounded out his words without inflection, "I am not asking you, Lissa, I'm telling you." Closing the space between them again, he muttered in exasperation, "Stop moving away from me."

Growing warm from the heated argument, he rolled the long sleeves of his dark blue shirt up over his forearms.

Her eyes on his rocky forearms, having seen the damage he was capable of inflicting on another person who made him mad, she looked fearful and angry at the same time. Her head lowered in disbelief, then she brought it back up.

Stuffing the fear, she sputtered furiously, "How dare you, I am not marryin' you. Go get one of your plastic dolls, any of them would love tae get hitched tae you." She enunciated carefully, "I do not."

She flounced towards the door, he went right after her and grabbed her arm. Lissa immediately tried to shake off his grip.

Trying to come up with a plausible explanation, Jace thought quickly. "You're right, they'd be willing. But I have to keep you close to me and I can't have a wife and a…a…another woman too. So, you're it."

Keeping his expression blank, he watched her trying to decipher how much she believed, waiting to see if he needed to add something to his preposterous explanation. Getting married had seldom ever entered his mind except peripherally in the back of his brain he figured someday he'd settle down and have a family.

But he never pursued the vague thoughts too deeply. So far in his life he hadn't met anyone he wanted to see the next morning much less every morning for the rest of his life. Until now.

And Jace knew she was so utterly terrified of something, the second he let her loose she'd be gone into hiding. He'd never see her again.

The color seeped back in her face and deepened as she grew more upset. She rattled off furiously, "You can't make me." Sunlight filtering its way through the water spotted window lit up the highlights in her dark wavy hair, pulled the green hue of her eyes brighter with her agitation.

Yanking her arm from his hold, she tensely pushed the thick locks behind her shoulders. A sliver of bare skin showed between her short T and jeans from the movements.

His eyes immediately dropped to her midriff, his pupils flamed. He glanced at the sofa then back at her. His thoughts were clearly indicated with the lowering of his lids as he rested his sight on her.

Seeing her shoulders stiffen, eyes turned wary, her arms crossed tightly over her chest, he tore his gaze away from her creamy skin and swallowed down his arousal.

Keeping his mind on track, he said coldly, "First of all, Lissa, I can make you do anything I want. Even marry me."

Her mouth parted in disbelief and his words so disturbed her that they might be true. "You can't," she insisted.

Jace said evenly, "Let me put it this way, you're going onto foreign land with no passport, no visa. If you're with me it'll be no problem, I have connections. But if not, how do you think the police will believe your wild story of being abducted? They'll toss you in prison so fast you'll never see the light of day again."

His stomach twisted guiltily seeing her face blanch. But he had to follow through, it was a means to an end, he hoped.

Her eyes narrowed so tightly the green almost disappeared. Compressed lips barely seethed out the question, "Why is it necessary for you tae have tae keep me close tae you?"

Catching her glancing at the door, he moved slightly to stand between her and escape. "Because someone could have seen you with us that night in the alley, it could, would put your life in-" he broke off, *damn, shot off his big mouth without thinking.*

Aghast, she unconsciously backed away from him again, "Danger? Are you sayin' my life could be in danger?"

"If you must know the truth, yes." Annoyance at her continual shirking from him was plainly written across his face. He stuffed his feelings, she wasn't at fault, it was his statements that kept her in a continual state of fear of him and her situation.

"What do you mean *if I must know the truth*?" Sarcasm and the sudden gripping in her stomach made her voice strident, she could hear it but couldn't help it. "What the heck is the truth? Tell me why I am in danger, you owe me that after abductin' me."

His brow puckered, shaking his head, he crossed his arms and stared hard at her. "Can't."

"Or won't?"

"Doesn't matter. You will do as I say, you have no choice."

Her gaze was drawn to his biceps that bulged from the way his arms were crossed.

Piqued at herself for even looking at them she snapped, "You need to stop tellin' me what tae do. You are not my parent, or a policeman, or a – a husband. Not that I would do as you *ordered* anyway if you were, this is the 21st Century for heaven's sake. You always act like it's the medieval times and you have rights over me."

Her brows drew down in a frown, she was getting confused. Wrapping her arms around herself, Lissa said firmly, "Like I said, you owe me answers, you took me against my will, and you won't let me go." Her lips bunched, she stared just as hard back at him as he was glaring at her.

He shifted his hands to set them squarely on his hips. "Honey, you were in the wrong place at the wrong time, I can't help those circumstances. Maybe if you had simply quietly slipped away that day in the alley and not taken Donnie's wallet," he shrugged.

"But you still might have been seen and tracked down, by…others." He frowned. "I don't owe you anything. And, because I did capture you, I own you, for now, and there's nothing you can do about it." Scratching his chest he watched her face morph in furious wrath as he knew she would at his words.

To Lissa, he looked like a caveman. All brawn, scratching his chest, next he'll be beating on it and roaring.

Frustrated with his sexist attitude, she said, "You can't *own* me, how dare you!" Her sputtering broke off at the sly grin teasing his mouth up. Still she persevered, repeated, "You can't make me do anything."

He bent, leaning in closer to her, invading her personal space. "You, honey, need to stop telling me that I can't do something. You are utterly under my control, stop trying to kick about it all the time. Life would be smoother, simpler, and a ton less noisy if you would just shut up and give in gracefully."

Her mouth dropped as twin red spots scored her cheeks, "You bastard-"

"Tut, tut, no need for that kind of language," he taunted, the mild smirk on his face at her outrage set her off even more.

She opened her mouth, but he said, "The conversation is over, Lissa." His voice dropped, his mirth at her annoyance disappeared. "You will do as I say and that's it." He crossed his arms again like some big warrior after winning the battle and was about to carry off his prize.

Seeing his unarguable resolve, the anger fled replaced by burgeoning fear that he could actually make her do this. Panic underlying her words, trying to strike a bargain, she said quickly, "If you marry one of the other *plastiques* I promise I will stay by you, do whatever you say, I swear."

"No. I told you, I can't have two women."

She almost laughed out loud chasing away some of her fear. Snorting in derision, she said sarcastically, "Really? I've heard you've had plenty more at the same time."

An angry flush rolled up his face. "I told you to stop listening to gossip. Besides, what I've done before being with you is none of your business, you will do as I say."

Stamping her foot, she insisted, "I will not marry you!" Seeing his implacable face, she changed tactics. Deliberately speaking more sweetly, she wheedled, "You won't need me by you, I promise if you put me in a room, a closet, whatever, I will stay there. I won't run, I'll do whatever you say, I swear. Please."

He couldn't believe that all these damned women dying to marry him and he has to choose the only one that refuses. As far as her claiming she would do whatever he says, he knew that was bullshit, she hadn't yet.

"Why don't you ask Dona, she would leap at the-"

"Don't go there, Lissa, I'm warning you." It pissed him off that he thought Lissa was jealous over Dona when it appeared it was only wishful thinking on his part.

He said coldly, "You will do as I say. You can't stay on the ship when we dock, and you can't enter foreign land without a passport, or me. You have no choice. As soon as the need for it is over, we will get the marriage annulled. No problem."

Her hands crunched into fists at her side, she stamped her foot again, shouting, "No problem? This is my life! How the heck can you spout such idiotic words?"

This was getting too taxing, Jace held up a hand. "Enough. Victor will order the license today. I can pick it up on the island we will be docking at tomorrow that doesn't require advance registration, and Ivan Jax on board is a notary, he can marry us. On Saturday."

He kept his hand up as she opened her mouth, "Case closed, it's a done deal. Live with it." He turned away heading towards the door leaving her standing flustered and furious.

Her body etched with rigidity, shoulders hardened, she flexed her fingers then rolled them back into fists. Her voice hard as iron she said flatly, "I will not ever sleep with you or any other man. You would have tae force me."

Lissa watched Jace hesitate in the doorway but he didn't turn around. Biting her lip, she knew he was quite capable of forcing her, especially if he felt he had a legal right to her body. She said meanly, "You can go consummate the marriage with one of your...other women."

Stepping back in the room, pretending he didn't see her cringe when he faced her, Jace stared hard down at Lissa. Then, his face smoothed to bland acceptance as if they were making a simple business deal. "If those are your terms I will abide by them, as long as you give me no trouble about this. I expect your full cooperation."

He couldn't believe she'd bought his story, she was giving in. His eyes softened a shade. "There will be no other women for me while we're married, Lissa. Don't dirty this by saying things like that." His face hardened again. "And there will be no other men for you."

She stood like a statue in utter disbelief that he truly planned on carrying through with this farce of an idea.

His smile sincere, he said quietly, "I promise you, Lissa, I will honor you. This will be a true marriage, you will be my wife. I will not do anything to disrespect you or our...union. I will agree that we shall have a sexless marriage, since those are your terms," his lids shifted down letting only a trace of blue out, "until you say otherwise."

On his way out the door he called Julio to come and stay with Lissa. There had been no trouble from Brett since Jace had beaten him. Brett was seldom seen out of his room, but Jace wanted to err on the safe side and he knew Lissa had enough of his company for the day.

He kept moving even as his shoulders rose to his ears when he heard her scream of frustration echoing down the hallway.

The next few days Jace spent on the bridge, in the study or bunking in Ker's cabin. He felt it was best to stay away from Lissa, she would only try to grind him down with arguments and he was not going to change his mind.

He had Julio and Victor keeping an eye on her. She'd already given Julio the slip several times. Julio said he would leave her in the kitchen then would find her later sitting out on the deck staring off over the water.

Hearing that Lissa was hovering near the railings contemplating the ocean beyond, fearing another jumping attempt, Jace now kept her locked in the cabin, he didn't even let her out to go bake in the kitchen.

He couldn't take the chance of her hurdling overboard again. Although he felt enormous guilt at treating her the way he was, he also believed she would see down the road that it was 100% the best thing to do. For her. And him. Maybe. Hopefully.

Chapter Twenty-Three

Saturday, Jace went to retrieve Lissa.

She had managed to slip out again and was hiding, but he knew where she liked to go now.

He found her on the top deck sitting with her back against the wood wall at the tip of the bow.

Her arms wrapped around her knees, the wind blowing her hair, she felt him before she saw his shadow crawl over her. She refused to look up at him.

"Come on, Lissa. Don't make me pick you up and carry you there. This is going to happen, I told you that. Don't make it harder than it is. You said you would cooperate."

She looked up at him, the sun was glinting off his blond hair like a halo. She snorted at the angelic thought, *sure, he's anything but an angel…*

"Jace, you don't want this any more than I do. You're not the kind of guy that wants to be tied down to one woman even temporarily. I'm sure if you speak with the guy, the boss, and tell him, tell him you got a divorce, or the engagement got broken, whatever, he won't-"

Scowling at her words, he demanded coldly, "Get up, Lissa. Now."

When she didn't move, he bent and took her hand, pulled her to her feet. Holding her arm just above the elbow he led her back downstairs to their room. Neither said a word.

Opening the door, he ushered her inside, closed the door then turned her to face him holding both her upper arms so she had to look at him.

The green eyes swarming with glimmering tears, she was chewing on that bottom lip like crazy to keep them from falling. *God, she looked so afraid, so apprehensive*, he took a deep breath, swallowed it down tight.

His voice forceful, commanding, yet with a gentle undercurrent, Jace said, "We talked about this. You agreed. Ker and Drew, our witnesses, and Ivan Jax the notary will be waiting up in the great room."

Seeing her eyes dart anxiously to the side and her cheeks pale, he asked, "What?" She didn't answer.

He followed her tense gaze, to his bed. Taking her hand he brought her over to her bed and said, "Sit down, honey." When she did he sat down beside her, still holding her hand.

Looking like if he made a move towards her she would flee in a heartbeat, she stared at the floor, her mouth a grave, anxious line.

"Look at me, Lissa," Jace said sternly yet kindly. He waited until she raised her wavering gaze to him.

"I told you this marriage would be in name only. You don't have to worry that I will claim my…husbandly rights. Things will stay as they are, except for the name change. You'll still sleep in your bed. Unless," he wiggled his brows at her, "you want to join me, my bed is open any time you want to share it with me."

Her panicked glance twisted his heart. He was pretty sure at this point that it wasn't him she was rejecting, it was a deep dastardly secret that reared its fearsome head every time he tried to be intimate with her.

She's told him several times she won't have sex with him or any other man. Clearly someone has scared the living daylights out of her, and it must have involved sex. He didn't want to think it, but it was likely rape or some sort of other horrific brutal act.

Keeping his smile, Jace thought, *you can tame and gentle a wild horse, how is a frightened woman any different*? He bit back a chuckle. She'd definitely kick him in the balls if he shared that thought out loud!

Wanting to caress her face, instead he wiped his hand down the side of his own face and over his mouth.

Leaning slightly away from him, her wild gaze followed his movements as if she expected him to suddenly put both large hands around her slim neck and throttle the life out of her.

"Dammit, Lissa. It's a simple wedding, not a funeral, you're killing me here with your apprehension. I swear to you, I won't force myself on you. Really, you should know that by now, I haven't yet have I?"

She said in a small voice, "We weren't married before. You might think you have rights."

"Come on, I just damned told you, I won't. How can you still be so afraid of me after all this time? Have I ever hurt you? Maybe I have touched you improperly, but I haven't raped you and I darn well could have, and you wouldn't have been able to go to the police about it.

"With my connections they never would have believed you. So stop already with this shit." He shook his head slightly embarrassed. "I don't see what the problem is anyway, why you don't want to, I mean, am I that horrible? I've explained it was necessary for me to take you with us, you could have been in danger if I'd left you there."

Not that he had ever told her *why* she would have been in danger. He couldn't tell her that, not yet. He also could not explain why he couldn't leave her there as a witness against them.

Not answering his question, her voice meek and pained, Lissa asked, "What about other women? Where shall I go when you want tae bring, you know, someone…here?" Her gaze travelled over his broad shoulders, the handsome yet harsh face, his big strong hands spread on his knees.

Jace's dark blue eyes never wavered from her face, they were bright and clear and vital but they suddenly narrowed in anger.

His skin swiftly darkened. Fury in his voice he ground out, "God, Lissa, you always manage to make me sound like an amoral monster. I already told you there will be no other women for me. Have I even done that before? We may not have a…sexual relationship in this marriage, for now, but everything else will be for real. I will not disrespect you, I swear to God."

Then a thought occurred to him, he blinked, suspicious. "Are you asking me because you want to see other men? Because if that's the case, there's no way in fucking hell that you will be with another man, you hear me? I'll tear anyone apart who dares touch you." His face blew up red, not meaning to, he was crushing her hand.

His anger actually helped lessen her anxiety. "Oh my gosh, Jace, calm down. I never said that. I was just askin' about you." She glanced at their hands. He looked down, her fingers were white, he loosened his grip.

Her face bleak, she said softly, "I've told you, I will not be with a man, any man. Ever."

Trying to clear the sudden blast of jealous temper, he ran his fingers through the top of his hair. With a whoosh of tension blowing out with a heavy breath, Jace said, "Yeah, well, you get some kind of an itch, you come to me. That's final. Clear?"

She nodded.

Letting go of her hand, he stood up. "Okay. Look," he walked over to the closet, opened it and took out a dress on a hanger.

Her eyes widened. "That's beautiful, Jace, who is it for?"

His eyes rolled heavenward. "It's for you, silly. I sent Cad to pick it up when he went on a business meeting on the island. It's for your, *our*, wedding. There're shoes and a bow thing for your hair too. I wanted to make this at least a little special for you, baby."

Watching her face travel through emotions of tense anxiety to perplexity, he said softly, "Now, take a shower, do your hair. Ker will come down and bring you up when you're ready. Okay?"

She should have an escort anyway, but he also didn't tell her he wanted to make sure now they were docked near the island that she didn't try to leave the ship and think she could swim, or float as it were, to the island.

Getting to her feet, Lissa moved close to him, gazing at the dress in awe. "Oh, Jace, that was so thoughtful of you." Tears threatened as she gingerly touched the dress.

It was a floor-length, antique white satin shift with spaghetti straps like a bride would wear if she was getting married on a tropical beach, simple yet elegant.

Hanging the dress on the doorframe, Jace said with a measure of embarrassment, "Okay, don't cry, honey, you don't want your eyes all red and puffy." He bent and cupped her chin, tilted it, kissed her hard, lustfully but short so she wouldn't freak, then strode to the door.

Still looking at the dress, the back of her hand pressed to her mouth, the kiss was unexpected and so quick before she could object. She asked him, "Where are you goin'?"

Seeing that she seemed to finally be acquiescing to the wedding with no further blowups, Jace's mouth melted into a warm smile. "I'm going to Ker's room to get ready. You okay now?"

She clasped her hands behind her back, a stab of shyness gripping her. Words sticking in her throat she could only nod.

Wanting badly to touch her, yet knowing she was already feeling brittle enough to splinter into tiny little pieces, he resisted, keeping his hands at his side.

"Lissa, I swear, on my honor, it will be all right. I will never hurt you or abuse you in any way." His voice dropping deeply solemn, he said with sincere forthrightness, "My duty is to take care of you and to protect you, and I promise I will. You have nothing to fear from me. Okay?"

Lissa's gaze moved over his earnest face. His features sometimes so hard it made her legs tremble, then so opposite like now when he smiled kindly at her. She let his words tumble inside, she'd chew on them later when she could think. Right now she felt as if in a strange fantastical haze. "Sure, other than being forced into a marriage, I'm okay."

An hour later, there was a knock at the door.

Lissa stood awkwardly waiting. She was locked in as usual.

Ker opened the door and stood there with a goofy smile on his normally austere hard to read face. His hair was neatly tied back and his short pirate's beard was trimmed. And, she couldn't believe her eyes, he was wearing a suit.

He still had a ruthless brigand look about him, but he looked so handsome, scary still, but gracefully handsome.

"Ker, you look beautiful." Surprised, she admired him with an amazed smile.

A cough cracked out then he laughed. "No, Lissa, men don't look beautiful. Women do. And honey, you top the cake of beautifulness." He swept his approving gaze from the top of her shiny burnished waves tied back on one side with the bow, down the body hugging shift that outlined perfectly every curve and hollow of her body to the tips of the high heeled sandals that peeked out of the bottom of the dress.

He smiled warmly, a rarity for him, "Really, you look stunning, ethereally elegant. Kind of like you always do, just more so." His smile widened at her blush. "Are you ready?"

The blush instantly drained from her face leaving her pale with worry tightening her mouth and eyes.

Ker stepped forward quickly to calm her. "Honey, it'll be okay. There's not a better man than Jace Nico. He will take care of you. You don't know him, I do, he would lay down his life for you.

"Hell, he ran to help a woman he thought was in trouble and got shot for his efforts. Mind you, he knew it would be a possibility considering why he was there in the first place, yet, he still went to her aid. And she was a total stranger."

Even though they were many more words than Lissa had ever heard from the implacable male, she still looked so shaken Ker took her elbow and helped her to sit on the bed.

She ran a finger under each eye to wipe away tears that threatened to ruin her makeup.

He went to the nightstand, plucked some tissues and handed them to her. Dabbing at her eyes, she murmured, "Thank you."

Brows knit with nervous fear, she said to him, "Ker, you know he's forcin' me tae do this, right?"

He stood with his legs apart, hands clasped behind his back, nodded slightly. "Yes. He told us his intentions."

Her forehead wrinkled in confusion. "But why? He has this ridiculous story about his boss needin' him tae be married, that's the most ridiculous thing I have ever heard. And he says I am trapped, that if I leave the ship I could be arrested because I am here illegally, under a false name. He says the police would never believe my claims that I was abducted and brought here against my will. Is any of this true?"

His mouth tightened, this was not a conversation for him and her to have, this was between her and Jace. Taking a deep, nerve settling breath he said, "He has his reasons. Those he didn't share with us."

The men did have their suspicions though which they had voiced to him when he told them about the forced marriage. Jace had admitted nothing so they were almost in the same dark as her.

Ker knew why he was doing it, Jace was scared to death if he let her go, there was something or someone terrifying her that she was hiding from. That she'd run and he'd never see her again, but Jace refused to discuss it with him.

Sounding calm and convincing, Ker held out his arm for her to take. "Whatever his reasons, he would never do anything to hurt you."

"Ker, he said that when this…thing…is over, your job, that we would get the marriage annulled. Do you think he'll do that?"

Striving to keep the chagrin off his face, Ker stammered, "Uh, he…I can't…uh," he leaned over further, indicating for her to come along with him, now. "Lissa, this is all between you two. I can't speak for him. Just try to trust him. So," he swallowed, "are you, ready?"

It wasn't her intent to put her troubles onto this dangerous but very kind man. Gulping down a sigh, she stood up and wound her arm under his, time to go face the music.

They walked in silence. Ker was pissed that Jace was harming this young woman, not physically but definitely mentally by forcing her into a marriage she did not want.

He could see, feel her wrapped up in nerves. Her palpable fear of the unknown, about to be tied to basically a stranger in a sham of a marriage. She was so tense clearly she couldn't speak now if she wanted to.

They reached the great room. Ker opened the door, Lissa's mouth dropped.

Someone had gone to the trouble of decorating the room with paper flowers and almost everyone on board was present and grinning at her.

At the front of the room, Jace was standing with Ivan Jax and Doc Drew.

Wearing a dark suit and tie, Jace's hair combed so hard the top was a saffron sheen, the rest of it was almost as dark as his suit. His eyes burned a blue streak across the crowd straight at her.

Someone had hooked up music to the stereos, a lovely hymn was playing softly.

Jace could see his beautiful bride's face wrought with incredulity and stark apprehension. It was slamming into her that this was really happening.

One day she was walking down the street minding her own business and the next she was standing here on a ship about to be wedded to a total, almost total stranger who had literally snatched her off the street and was holding her prisoner. The green eyes huge and uncertain, she looked about to dash away like a startled fawn.

He saw her legs balking, he figured she had to be thinking as she looked at him that she did not know this man and she was getting married to him.

Even though he was doing this thing on purpose, Jace still couldn't help feeling a little nervous himself. After, all, a man doesn't get married every day. At least he didn't, and he didn't plan on doing it again. This will be the one and only time. He'd have to find a way to deal with Lissa's fury when she finds out he has zero plans to get an annulment or divorce.

For now, he drank her in.

She was so incredibly gorgeous in that satin dress it made his knees weak. Her brilliant tresses in fat curls held back with the bow waved around one shoulder and down her back.

The only thing ruining this moment, actually two things, one was that she was not here of her own free will, and two, she had said they would not be consummating the marriage. He rolled his shoulders, good thing he loves a challenge. He smiled tenderly at her, willing her to relax.

Apparently it worked, because her eyes were streamed at him, like she saw no one else in the room but him. His handsome smile soothing the rigidness out of her shoulders.

When Ker had tried to walk with her down the aisle, her feet had frozen to the ground. Her head barely reaching the Asian's broad shoulder, he glanced down at her with a calm smile and patted her hand that clung to his arm, then he nudged her slightly and they started down the aisle.

Jace's burning blue lights drew her like magnets, never breaking contact with her. This time she went with Ker without balking.

When they reached Jace, Ker tugged her frigid hand out of his arm, which she was now clutching with a death grip, and positioned her to stand beside Jace then he moved to stand on the other side of him.

Jace took her hand, threading their fingers together. He wished he could pull her in his arms and assure and comfort her.

Standing beside Lissa, Dr. Drew touched her shoulder, leaned in and gently kissed her on the cheek, which instantly caused both her cheeks to blossom into a pearly pink. She gave the doctor a watery, tremulous smile.

Jace chose Drew and Ker as witnesses. He'd thought about having one of the girls, Glennie maybe, to stand with Lissa, but they hadn't know any of the women that long and Jace decided to stick with what he knew, and he did know Lissa was comfortable with Drew.

Nudging Lissa to face Ivan Jax, Jace whispered in her ear, "You are so stunning, Lissa, you take my breath away." He squeezed her hand gently, trying to get her to look at him, but her attention was concentrated on Ivan, her shoulders had turned rigid again.

Grinning ear to ear now that the woman had finally made it there on her own without Jace carrying her in like he had told his men he would if he had to, Ivan Jax held the Bible open in his hand and said, "Everyone, please be seated."

Most of the crowd sat, a few people had to stand in the fringes.

Ivan read a few words from the Bible, a bit of Solomon's Song, 'I am my beloved and my beloved is mine,' he added some poetic phrases he'd gotten off the web about love and honor.

Lissa's eyes dropped at the word love, she felt like such a fraud in front of Ivan and all the others present. When Ivan got to the part of the 'wife will obey the husband,' Lissa frowned at him shaking her head.

He glanced at Jace. Jace nodded subtly, firmly. Ivan sighed and said, "And obey." Hearing Lissa's swift intake like she was about to say something, he quickly prattled on frowning at Jace's smug smile.

Ivan half turned to Ker and asked, "I believe you have the rings?"

Ker nodded, took a step forward and held out his hand.

Lissa's mouth dropped seeing two gold bands sitting in Ker's large palm. She swung her head to Jace. "I don't think I-" she broke off at Jace's brows drawing down at her objection.

He picked up the smaller band and nodded to Ivan.

Ker pressed the other ring into Lissa's trembling hand.

Jace had full intentions of branding Lissa as his, she would wear his ring if he had to glue it to her finger. There will be no repeat of the Brett Rawley episode. Everyone would know she was his and be warned of his wrath if anyone ever did anything untoward to her again.

Watching the interplay between the couple, Ivan coughed back a sigh. He continued with the oath, "Repeat after me, 'With this ring I do wed.' "

Jace went first to give Lissa a moment to compose herself.

When it was her turn, her fingers were shaking so hard Jace had to help her push the ring on his finger. He held both her hands as she repeated her vows, people strained to hear her hushed voice.

Jace could have fallen in and drowned in her crystal green eyes the way she was looking up at him when she said the words *I do*.

He'd sworn it to himself before, but it burned in his heart at that moment that he would lay down his life for her and it would be his quest to find whoever or whatever had put the fear of God into her and destroy, terminate, or dispose of it. Whatever it took.

He couldn't help her if she kept running and hiding. Whatever he had to do to make it go away so the terror in her eyes would disappear, and the tremble in her lips would be only for him, while he was bringing her to soaring heights when he finally makes love to her. Hearing her oath to be his wife filled his heart so full he thought it would burst.

Looking pleased with himself, Ivan held the Bible to his chest and announced loudly, "I now pronounce you husband and wife. Jace, you may kiss your bride."

Lissa was staring down at the ring on her finger when Jace swept his hands around her face and lowered his head praying she would let him kiss her and not resist in front of all these people.

His mouth covered hers for a brief second not moving, then he lightly sucked her upper lip pulling it up, when her lips parted he pushed them open further and gently sunk his tongue inside.

He prodded her shy tongue with his until both ribbons of flesh were mating. Slanting his head to seal his mouth more tightly on hers, his tongue plunged in and out teasing her to rival him.

When she did, fire started building in his loins. His hand slid down her back to pull her in closer to him. Her fingers clutched at his shoulders, their chests pressed together so hard the friction of her soft breasts against his-

"Ahem." Ivan coughed politely. The audience twittered. "I said kiss her, Jace, not devour her." The audience broke out in loud laughter.

Reluctantly Jace pulled away from Lissa and heatedly gazed at her. Her eyes glowed vibrantly albeit a shade unfocused. Lips red and plumped, her cheeks were tinged pink with embarrassment. Jace didn't care as long as she kept clinging to him like she was.

"Uh, okay, Jace, Lissa, turn around," Ivan said quietly with a humorous grin seeing Lissa's red face and Jace's obvious desire to pick her up and run off with her to be alone.

Jace held her hand pulling her gently to turn and face the crowd.

Ivan proclaimed with cheerful rigor, "May I introduce, Mr. and Mrs. Jace Nico!" He leaned over to Jace and told him, "Now, you can walk her down the aisle to where we have the food set up in the rec area."

Jace smiled at his friend. "Thanks Ivan, you did great."

Grinning, Ivan put his hands on their backs and gave them a little push.

The new couple strode slowly down the pink petal-strewn aisle to whoops and cheers and well wishes. Like Ivan said, Jace ushered her out of the room and down the hall to where they had played pickle ball.

When they reached the room, Lissa smiled. It was decorated too with paper flowers and streamers. Food was lined up buffet style along a big table and someone had hooked their phone to speakers so it could play music.

The crowd trailed in behind them. One of the men, not one of Jace's team, turned on a slow song and said, "All right, Nico, first dance to the bride and groom."

Laughing, Jace obliged. He settled his arm around Lissa's waist and held her hand with his pressing it against his chest. Her face was still pink. He leaned in, asked quietly in her ear, "You okay, honey?"

Lissa didn't answer. He let go of her hand and slid his fingers to hold her jaw and raise her head. "Lissa?"

She smiled briefly. "I...Jace...they're all so nice tae do this for us. I feel like a cheat. Our weddin' isn't real and it doesn't seem right."

Moving his feet slowly, rhythmically to the music, Jace covered her mouth with his, pulling her into a deep, gentle kiss. Caressing her back, he leaned away slightly and whispered, "It is real, Lissa. You are my wife, this is all very real, very legal."

"But- but Jace it's not for the right reasons, it's-"

He kissed her again. "The reasons are mute, Wife," he smiled, he couldn't help it. "All that matters is that we are legally, lawfully wed. We can just move forward from here and take one day, one minute, at a time. Okay?"

His arm still around her as they danced, he stroked and caressed her back, watching her visibly accept his words and calm down until he finally felt her relax in his arms.

"Okay," she sighed.

"You have to say husband," he told her seriously.

Lissa smiled up at him. "Okay...Husband." She felt the shiver travel his body at her words. She appeared stunned at how happy he seemed to be about marrying her.

Before she could ponder further, he gentled her face to rest against his shoulder and led her into a dance around the floor.

Everyone danced and ate and toasted the new couple. Jace's friends sat around them when their dance ended and they joined the group at the table.

The men were vastly surprised at Jace's actions. They knew he was crazy about Lissa, but his marrying her like this, in an instant, the couple didn't really even know each other. But Jace had always known what he was doing when he led them on missions and they figured he knew what he was doing now, so, they toasted them and gave the couple their blessings.

Each member of his team stood up and when they toasted them, they each swore to Lissa their fealty, honor, devotion, and protection.

Late into the night, Jace quietly led Lissa out of the reception making sure no one noticed them leave. He didn't want her further embarrassed if people called out crude things about their first night as husband and wife in bed.

In their cabin, they took turns getting ready for bed. When Lissa went to climb into her bed wearing a t-shirt and shorts, Jace coughed and cleared his throat. "Uh," he went over and stood in front of her. "Listen, this is our wedding night. I would really, Lissa, really like for you to sleep with me."

He quickly held up a hand at her expression and opened mouth, "I swear on my life I just want to be close with you. I won't try a thing, I swear. We did it when I was recovering from the gunshot."

He'd said that deliberately to stir back how scared she'd been for him, how she had taken care of him, that they'd slept together without any trouble before Drew had put the kibosh on it. Actually, it would be tough on him, sleeping with her, but he wanted it so much he'd live with the discomfort of an all night hard-on.

"Please Lissa, it doesn't have to be but this one night," of course he had hoped to start a habit. "I won't pressure you," *not much*, "to do it every night. Just tonight." He tried to give her his most sincere, earnest, boyish smile encouraging her to agree.

She saw right through him. The corners of her mouth tugged up. "All right. Don't make me regret it, Mr. Nico," she teased.

His grin ear-to-ear he took her hand and pulled her to his bed. "Okay. Mrs. Nico." He drew back the blanket for her to climb in. When she did, also wearing a t and boxers, he slid in next to her and pulled the blanket over them.

Nestling behind her, Jace slipped his hand around her waist and pulled her in. Curving his knees under hers, he tried to keep a space between her tush and his erection. He went for the spoon thinking that would make her feel more comfortable not facing him.

At first she was completely rigid. After a few minutes, Jace felt her relax inch by inch. When she felt boneless, he pulled her in closer, nuzzling his chin in her hair.

"Baby," he murmured against the soft tendrils.

"Hmmm?"

"When we get settled I can take you into town and buy you a ring of your choice. You don't have to keep the one you have. We didn't have much time to get one. You need a diamond engagement ring too." She stiffened slightly, he cuddled her closer.

"Jace, it's not a real marriage, we don't need rings. I don't need a different one. There's no reason for me tae wear this one except maybe if I see your boss and I don't see that happenin'. I'll keep it safe in a box."

His heart dropped a bit at her words, but he still had faith he could woo her. "Lissa, like I said before, it is a real marriage and I want rings. I want my ring on your finger. In fact I insist on it. This is really important to me, please don't fight me on this one thing." He wanted the whole world, at least the male part of it, to know she was taken. "All right?"

Let him have just this one thing? Huh. The man had gotten everything he wanted. He just pushed and persevered like a darn turtle until she caved. Seriously? Were they not married when she was adamant it was the last thing she'd ever do?

She was quiet so long he thought she was either going to refuse to wear it or she was asleep. Her "Okay," was a soft sigh.

Now he relaxed. The tension oozed out of his shoulders. Jace pulled her as hard against him as he could and curled his knees tighter up behind hers, whispered, "Thank you, baby."

Now he could feel her smile, that was so much better. Through her wavy hair he watched her hold her hand up and stare at the ring on her finger. For a long time.

He wished he could read her mind, what was she thinking about looking at the circle of gold on her finger? Was she thinking it was just a manacle of imprisonment albeit a symbolic one, or a sign of Jace's protection?

Eventually her hand lowered as she fell asleep.

Now that she wasn't aware, he could press his hips more comfortably against her and settle in for the night with a throbbing, rock-hard erection.

Chapter Twenty-Four

A day later they pulled into the dock at Dynshire Scotland.

Jace was almost done packing his personal items he would need while staying on land. Lissa sat on a chair watching him silently. She only had a few things and they were all borrowed so she was already packed.

Putting his duffle bag and suitcase that contained his computer and paperwork by the front door, he turned, perusing her mellow expression. "You okay, Lissa?"

Her diminutive brief smile and half shrug revealed nothing of the turmoil he could see vibrating in her eyes. "I'm fine, Jace." Her gaze drifted to the window. "I just...don't know what tae expect, now that we're...here."

She took a breath, exhaled it cautiously. "At least on the ship I knew what tae expect, sort of, but now, I..." a small shiver shook her, the green in her eyes dimmed.

Jace picked up a chair, set it in front of her and sat down. "Listen, Lissa, uh," he wondered how much to tell her. "We, everyone on board, we're staying at a complex, kind of like a big lodge. Some people will still share rooms, some have their own.

"Everyone already has their job assignments, like Glennie is doing inventory for the company, and Vicki will be doing interior research, some of the others are telemarketers or receptionists. The men are mostly all scheduled for construction."

"Uh huh."

Jace picked her hand up, held it on her lap. "What? Tell me what you're thinking about, worried about." He waited, watching her eyes flick to the window, to his bags, to him.

"What, I mean, am I stayin' at the lodge, or will I be taken tae the police, or, uh," her brows knit with anxiety.

"Oh baby, I didn't realize you didn't understand," he squeezed her hand and smiled gently at her. "Why would you think that? We didn't go through getting married so I could turn you over to the police."

His thumb rubbed absently over her hand. "You will be staying with us at the lodge. Like I said, you have no passport or visa."

"But- but what about work? What am I expected tae do?"

"Honey, you won't be going to work. You will stay at the lodge. If you want you can still help Benny, or whatever you want to do." Jace patted her hand.

Her expression brightly slightly. "How about online college classes?"

His lips pursed. He didn't want her to have internet access until he was assured she wouldn't try to leave him. "Uh, we'll…talk about that later."

She looked up at him through her fringe of heavy lashes. "What about…sleep, um, where will I…"

Jace frowned. He'd given this a lot of thought. He had a room to himself but it only had one bed. There was no way he could have her sleeping in his bed every night, he would eventually give into his desire for her, and he couldn't do that until he defeated whatever had its claws in her, until then he knew she would not allow intimacy between them.

It wasn't his thing to force himself on a woman, but…at this point, he was too hungry for her, it would be too dangerous for him to have her in his bed until she was willing to have sex.

"Well, let me ask first," he watched her eyes swing warily to his, he cleared his throat. "Do you, want to you know, sleep with me?" Before she could misunderstand he said quickly, "I mean, sex. Do you want to have sex with me?" The swift anguish that struck her pretty face answered that for him. He let out a labored sigh.

"Jace, I..."

"It's all right." He tried to sound matter-of-fact, not like his dick and his heart were having a big fight over her. "I will stick with our wedding terms."

He patted her hand again. "Lissa, if you," he leaned in real close to her, put his fingers under her chin so she was looking at him, "swear, give me your honorable promise that if I let you have your own room," he hesitated with a painful pang at her surprised and happy look, "ah, that, you will not run. You will not leave the lodge, ever, without me with you. You have to swear to me, Lissa."

His earnest stare at her was severe and adamant. He watched her considering what he was saying.

She pulled her hand from his and twined her fingers. Staring down at them, her mouth drew down. "Jace, I...will I be safe at the complex?"

He leaned over quickly and scooped up both her hands. "Baby, I've already had people checking the security. There are cameras and codes and we're having a couple of guards patrol at night." He didn't tell her that was also for the security of the workers. Since the employees were murdered the business was taking extra precautions.

His brows lowered seriously. "You won't tell me what else you are afraid of, but no one will get into the lodge and especially where you and I and my team are staying, we have our own wing. We chose it specifically for the steel door that locks us off from the rest of the complex.

"The windows in the entire lodge are up high enough a person could not climb through them without a ladder or something else that would attract attention. The building sits on a hill, plus, there deliberately are no hedges or trees or bushes near the facility for someone to hide in or approach unseen."

Jace watched her eyes flit around the room and her face firm as she contemplated his words. While she thought, he picked up a long dark curly end of her hair and rubbed it between his big fingers letting it coil around his hand, reveling in the shiny brilliant softness of it.

His gaze lifted from the curl to her. "It'll be just like on the ship, Benny will cook dinner with the assistance of Colby and the others. Breakfast and lunch will be pretty much laid out buffet like for us to take care of ourselves."

Lissa's chest lowered from her expelled breath, her shoulders relaxed. "So, uh, then, what about our marriage? Once you prove it tae your boss will we be, gettin' the annulment?"

"Goddammit Lissa," he snapped crossly. "No, we are not getting it annulled." At her sudden widening eyes he said more quietly, "Not yet, we're not getting it annulled yet. You and I are husband and wife." He took her hands again, his voice calm, he told her, "We will act as the legally married couple that we are. I know people may question us not sleeping in the same room."

He frowned, he'd hoped they would be together in the biblical way by now. "But most outside my team won't know." He was surprised that she didn't look that unhappy about not getting an annulment, she actually seemed almost relieved.

"Okay." Lissa stood up and to his dismay, moved between his legs. She set her small hands on his bulked shoulders. She smiled at his uneasiness at her actually touching him, he was so used to her rejecting him.

"Thank you, for trustin' me. I promise, Jace, on my honor, I will not run from the house. I will not run from…you." She leaned in and pressed her lips to his, his body was stiff at the unexpectedness of her making the first move.

She kissed him sweetly and with some passion then pulled back and away from him before he caught his wits and could grasp her for more.

He sat stunned watching her twirl and catch up her small bag and trot out the door.

"Hey, Lissa wait up!" Jumping up quickly, Jace grabbed his gear and hurried after her.

A couple of days later, wearing a dark suit and dark blue tie, Jace went to the room Julio shared with Donnie.

Cad, Ker and Victor's rooms were on the other side sandwiching Jace's room and Lissa's room between the five men. Jace wanted as much cushioned protection around Lissa as possible, he also liked to have his men handy to keep any eye on her.

He knocked then walked right in. Julio was tucking his shirt into his jeans and then buckled his belt. He nodded at Jace, "Hey One, you ready?"

"Yeah." Jace strode over to Julio. "I'm about to leave. So…"

"I know, Jace," Julio grinned. Pulling a comb out of his pocket he drew it through his dark hair. "Don't let her out of my sight. You told me ten times yesterday, I wasn't drinking so I remember what you said." Amusement layered his slight Spanish accent.

A few inches shorter than Jace he was nearly as strongly built as him. All of Jace's team members were tough bruisers.

Jace smiled at him. "I keep repeating it, bro, because she can be guilelessly lured. She looks out the window and sees a bird or a flower or whatever catches her eye and she goes out the door without a second thought to get a closer look."

Julio's dark eyes sparkled in humor. "I've got news for you, bro, all women can be lured. They're sneaky. It's part of their nature. They can't control us with brawn so they use their talents."

At Jace's arched brow, he said, "You know, sex, illogic, crying, all that stuff, it's their arsenal."

"Uh huh. All right." Jace said, "Donnie, Cad, you guys ready? Where's Victor?"

His wiggly brown hair hanging half over his eyes, Donnie was sitting on a chair bent over his long legs tying his boots. The youngest of the crew, he was muscular but in a tall, lean almost sloppy way.

His jeans were worn thin with holes, the bottoms ragged, shirt half tucked in. The other men teased him that he wore his messy clothes like a uniform, never changing up. He jerked his head to the side and said, "Victor's in our bathroom getting pretty."

That brought a snicker from Cad. Holding a construction helmet in his huge hands, the mountain of a man said, "Primping, he's primping." The men laughed.

At that moment the bathroom door opened and Victor emerged. His black hair still wet combed straight back, dark brows bumped over defensive dark eyes at their staring. "What?"

"Hey pretty boy," Cad trilled, the men laughed again.

"What?" Victor repeated. "What's so funny?"

Jace opened the door. "Nothing, come on, let's go."

"Phew-wee." Donnie held his nose, smirking at Victor. "You got enough cologne on to sink a damned ship, bro. We're going to a construction site, not on a date."

Victor threw a swat at Donnie's head, the younger man ducked in time to miss it. He snapped out a big hand with long narrow fingers trying to smack Victor back. They slapped at each other all the way out the door.

Cad walked beside Jace shaking his head at the guys' antics, muttering affectionately, "Some kids never grow up."

The men headed for the side door, Julio went in search of his task, guarding Lissa.

Outside, the other four men continued to the truck where Ker joined them. They climbed inside, Jace and Ker in the front, the other three crammed in the back. It was a big truck, but the men were all so huge they sat shoulder to shoulder. Jace and Ker had a little space between them with the center console.

The complex they were staying at was a one-story cement and stone building that sat on a hill surrounded by a vast green lawn then encompassed by a dense forest that went on for several miles.

Jace drove down the winding driveway to the two-lane road and headed west towards the closest town.

Passing soft rolling green hills, a few sheep grazed on one, fuzzy dots of white against the lush green. Edging the paved road, the flowing grass rippled in the breeze. Following the GPS, it took 45 minutes for them to reach their first destination.

Jace pulled up and parked in front of a plaza under construction.

Dozens of trucks, cars, bulldozers, cranes littered the half-dozen acres. Men and a few women in helmets, gloves, work boots moved in all directions like ants. Most had something in their hands; hammers, wood, drills.

Piles of dirt alongside deep holes were scattered around with stacks of hardwood. Barrels of tar were being poured into smaller more manageable buckets. A buzz of drills and pounding of hammers mixed with talking filled the early morning. Partial plaster walls, cement, exposed wiring were the beginnings of the new plaza.

"Okay, here you go. I'll be back at 1600 to pick you up," Jace said. The doors on the truck opened up and the men piled out. "Have fun," he told them cheerily.

With a snide grin, Cad replied, "Sure, we will, working in the dirt and heat, lifting and digging and nailing. Yeah, don't worry about us while you're sitting all comfy inside an air conditioned building on a soft chair enjoying a latte and pastries."

Jace shrugged with a corner smile. "Hey, someone has to do the hard stuff, I'm the one that has to sacrifice. I'll be thinking of you boys while my feet are up and I'm sipping that tasty creamy brew and stuffing my face, eh? Later." He drove off with a wave.

Following the GPS again, it was another thirty minutes before he reached his destination.

The fifteen-story building was all silver and shining black glass that reflected the town around it. It was a big building for a relatively small town.

Driving into the parking garage where he had been given instructions to park, Jace found an open spot and pulled into it.

The elevator was right there, it opened as soon as he pushed the button. Stepping inside, Jace pushed number 15, the doors closed and he was whisked silently to the fifteenth floor.

The doors opened with a quiet ding to a large, plush carpeted lobby decorated in soft beiges and satiny white.

Jace could see numerous offices lined down halls on both sides of the front desk. Expensive, comfortable lounge furniture was grouped in clusters around the room with tables scattered amid them. Paintings hung all over ivory walls, and vases blooming with colorful flowers were set on a few glass tables. Light music played softly in the background.

A young blonde woman beckoned him with a smile from the glass and marble desk.

Jace made his way to her, his eyes flitting in all directions, taking in the series of offices.

When he reached her, he gave her his businesslike, slightly flirtatious smile. "Hello, I am Jace Nico. Mr. Warrington is expecting me." He was dazzled by her overly bright, unnaturally white smile.

The woman wore a deep V cut, skintight emerald green dress that revealed every nook and cranny of her figure. She leaned forward so her breasts could be more appreciated.

Red shiny lips purred, "Oh yes, Mr. Nico, Mr. Warrington said to send you right in." Her blatant lusty gaze appraised him head to foot and back. Her smile widened, it appeared she liked what she saw.

Jace's suit fitted perfectly defining the strapping shoulders and muscled arms. The white of his shirt contrasted nicely with his tan, along with the solid jaw and strong chiseled features. His look was low-key yet polished, and purely masculine.

Honey brown eyes twinkled at him through a fringe of thick false lashes. "Would you care for something to drink, Mr. Nico? Coffee? Tea? Soda?" She leaned over further trying to draw his attention down the front of her dress.

"No, thanks." Jace said politely, deleting the flirtatious tone making it strictly business. He kept his eyes on her face.

It looked like she'd plastered the makeup on with a spatula covering all sorts of complexion problems, until she looked like a distorted mannequin with a face made out of cotton wool.

Lissa's creamy skin and vibrant health emanating from her crystal eyes, a purer more beautiful green than the receptionist's dress jumped into his mind. His mouth curled in a slight smile.

The woman didn't move. He wasn't sure what he should do next. Then slowly swiveling in her chair she stood up. The six-inch heels brought her head higher than his shoulder.

The dress was impossibly short and tight. She had to literally tug it back down to cover her ass. Jace was somewhat surprised, the office had such a high-class business atmosphere, she looked a touch above a stripper.

She approached Jace moving with a practiced sensuous sway, her head tilted coyly. "I'm Suzy Grant. You have unusual colored hair, so light blond on top and so dark..." her eyes swept down his chest then deliberately lower before they slid back up, "everywhere else?" He stood stiff but relaxed under her bold perusal.

She asked sweetly, "Do you mind if I ask if the blond top part is natural?"

The side of his mouth pulled in at the personal question. He never explained to anyone how the sun just lit up the top of his head only with light yellow, especially to crude strangers. "Miss, uh..."

"Suzy," she said it with a drawl on the S making it sound like a hiss. Inching with sinuous hip sways until she was close enough to touch him, she set a few fingertips on his arm. "How about you and I meet up later and-"

"I'm married. Sorry." Moving from her groping clutch, he held his left hand up wriggling his ring finger. He'd gotten the rings mainly to brand Lissa as his, he never thought he'd be relieved that he'd gotten one for himself as well.

"So, which way is Mr. Warrington's office?" He started walking towards one of the offices.

"Honey, wait, we don't have to let a little thing like a wife get in the way of us getting to know each other!"

She skittered after him in the sky-high heels and dress so short and tight her thighs practically didn't move at all, just her lower legs flicked back and forth.

Chapter Twenty-Five

A man came out of one of the offices and strode purposefully towards Jace with his hand out. "Jace Nico?" he asked with one brow raised pleasantly.

Relieved he didn't have to stalk up and down the hallway searching for the man, Jace moved his long legs quickly to greet him. "Yes. Mr. Warrington?" He infused his deep voice with a blend of friendliness and slightly cool professionalism.

They shook hands briefly. "Yes, I am Foster Warrington, please follow me." His disapproving glare aimed at Suzy didn't faze her one bit.

Ordering coolly, "Miss Grant, please bring coffee," Warrington headed down the hall, Jace alongside. When he reached his office he held his arm out to Jace indicating for him to go in.

"Have a seat, Mr. Nico." He gestured to a beige divan with faint gold striping, and waited until Jace sat down then he sat kitty-corner on a wide, gold wing-backed chair. A twin chair was to the right.

A huge corner window displayed the still rising sun lighting the entire panoramic city spreading out and around the fifteen story building.

Warrington eased his trousers up slightly at the knees and unbuttoned the top of the line designer suit coat he wore. The white cuffs appearing under the jacket sleeves were buttoned with diamond and gold cufflinks. Settling back, he elegantly crossed his legs.

Jace sat back against the divan. The cushions were a bit hard but not enough to be uncomfortable. He unbuttoned his own suit coat and smoothed the tie that he noticed with amusement matched the dark blue threading in the French linen tweed drapes.

A quick glance around the office exhibited an enormous room containing a massive mahogany desk with a huge leather chair behind it.

Besides the divan and golden winged chairs, there were several glass-topped end tables and a matching coffee table in front of the divan with golden-clawed legs. Paintings of European cities in gilt frames decorated the walls.

Setting his arm along the back of the seat, Jace studied the man who would temporarily be his boss.

Mid-forties, precisely cut, short dark hair starting to thin with grey at the temples, Warrington had sharp aquiline features. His eyes bothered Jace. The dark brown irises were common, but it was the look in them, Jace felt a chill in his gut.

Although Warrington smiled that deepened the creases around his mouth and eyes, the smile didn't warm the dark brown any. Jace figured the man was handsome enough the ladies would be after him, even without the great wealth, but to Jace, his calculating eyes were creepy.

Suzy swished in with a tray containing a small decanter of coffee, steam roiled up out of it. The tray held two coffee cups, sugar, cream pitcher and spoons. She turned her back to Jace, and bent over to set the tray down on the coffee table that was in front of the two men.

Jerking his eyes away, Jace was pretty sure she was commando under the dress. A less confident inexperienced man would be blushing to the roots of his hair.

Peripherally, he noticed Warrington's cold eyes staring at Suzy, his hooded lids levered up and down like a reptile's. He had a slightly different view than Jace of Suzy, his was of the front of her. The décolletage of the dress now dropped almost to her navel.

Suzy filled both cups with coffee. Straightening, she turned her full wattage smile at Jace, but said to Warrington, "Anything else I can do for you, sir?"

"No," Warrington replied flatly, his eyes still on her chest. "You can leave."

Her face crumpling in disappointment, she pivoted moving closer to Warrington with a pout. "Can I-"

"There are my earlier notes you need to spellcheck and print out." His tone hollow, he dismissed her as he reached for his cup. Spooning sugar into the cup, he said to Jace, "Please, help yourself."

Sniffing with a "Humph," Suzy sashayed as hard as she could out the door.

Jace picked up his cup, leaving it black. He took a small sip peering discreetly over the rim at the man beside him.

"She's the sister of our regular receptionist who is on maternity leave," Warrington explained with a sigh.

"I see." Jace figured as blatantly sexually inviting that girl was there's no way Warrington wasn't currently, or hadn't done her.

"So," Warrington drank some of his coffee and settled back again in the winged chair. "Have you been to the site?" he asked Jace.

Nodding, Jace set his cup down on the table. "I stopped there before coming here this morning."

An almost genuine smile lit Warrington's face. "And? What did you think? Damned colossal project, eh?"

"Yes. It was quite impressive. How many stores are planning to be in the plaza?"

Warrington added more sugar to his cup. Crossing his legs again, he answered, "There are already 101 applications."

Although Jace already knew everything about the plaza, its dimensions, cost, blueprints, plans, he had diligently studied everything long before leaving the States, he pushed his brows up in feigned astonishment. "Wow, that's quite a lot. It sounds like a mega-mall."

"Yes, yes, quite." A bit of color tinted Warrington's sallow complexion, greediness widened his smile. "It will generate income beyond our wildest dreams, son."

"Just out of curiosity," Jace said casually, "how come you've hired mostly from America and not Scotland?"

Dark brows rose with an indifferent shrug. "We had some union issues, so we decided to hire from the States and bring you all over on the ship. The sail over was uneventful?" A brief smile, Warrington sipped his coffee, his eyes scrutinizing Jace from head to toe.

Jace nodded. "No problems." Appearing thoughtful, he sipped his coffee then cleared his throat. "There's word sifting through the pipes that there's been some trouble. Can you fill me in?" Again he already knew but acted like this was all new information.

The smile vanished, a dour grey pushed out the pink tint from Warrington's cheeks. Stalling his answer, he poured himself some more coffee.

Jace could see the thoughts flitting in irritation across the sharply hewn face. Warrington's chest rose then fell in an exhale of sullenness. "Oh, it's nothing really, just some competitors, agitators pissed about losing kicking up dust." He perused Jace obviously considering how much to tell him.

Settling back with his coffee cup on his knee, Jace threaded slight curiosity through his question, "What's their beef?"

Warrington sucked in another deep breath, let it out slowly. With clear reluctance, he replied, "I'm sure you've heard that some people in the States were pretty angry that a few of the big companies were pulling up stakes and moving all their manufacturing here where they are producing things at nearly half the cost. It makes sense for crying out loud." He glared at his coffee cup.

"Mmm." Jace pondered this information. Raising his head, his face puckered in question, he said, "I've heard there's been," he leaned in speaking hushed like it was a secret, "that there have been…" He glanced around as if to see if anyone was listening. "*Murders*," he finished sounding a tad nervous.

227

Shaking his head with an annoyed frown, Warrington said, "No, no, nothing like that." He set his cup on the table with a clank then plunked his arms down in irritation on the arms of the chair. Drumming his fingers on the ends of the chair arms, he levelled the frown to a more bland expression. With a smoothness to his response, he said innocuously, "Well, there have been...some...accidents."

"Yes?" Jace prompted him.

His exasperation came out in a heavy sigh as he admitted, "All right. Three of the upper level administrators, two in the U.S. and one here, were...uh...murdered."

"Murdered?" Jace exclaimed, adding a touch of tension to his voice.

"Yes, yes," Warrington nodded tetchy, his face clouding with annoyance like three dead men was a ridiculous problem for him to have to deal with.

His eyes narrowing at Jace, he said, "You're a big, strong looking fellow, you're not going to let this foolish murder business run you off like a scared rabbit are you? There haven't been any attacks on the very top-level managers such as yourself, or the lower-mid, or line foremen, or the laborers, so you will be safe." He rubbed at the sides of his face trying to soften the pinched features.

Jace appeared to be contemplating this fearsome information. Clasping his hands together, he bent and set them on his knees like he was thinking really hard about it. Then he sat back with a smile. "I guess everything will be all right. Shouldn't affect me any." He took a breath, "So, why were those men murdered?"

Warrington looked annoyed again. "Like I said, there is big money at stake here. America will be losing a lot of income; even the taxes that these huge companies paid will put a hurting on the states that are involved. People kill for less than hundreds of millions of dollars."

Jace's eyes popped at the money Warrington dropped so casually like it was pennies instead of dollars. "Do the police have any idea who the killer or killers are?"

His head shaking crossly, Warrington grumbled irascibly, "Scotland Yard has their heads up their asses. They don't know if they're coming or going. Listen, as soon as the plaza is done and the shops start moving in, and the factories are up and running, all this trouble with just disappear. Mark my words."

Warrington picked up his cup, drained it and set it down on the coffee table placed between them. "So you're set to start as one of my lead managers tomorrow?"

"Yes." Jace replied. He allowed his expression to maneuver between fear then confusion, then mindless acceptance as if he decided he didn't believe any harm would actually come to him. "How many top-level managers do you have for this project?"

"Five, and each of you have several assistants to direct your orders to the lower level foremen. Mike Mills, one of your assistants, will meet with you at the site first thing in the morning, he'll show you around and where all the paperwork is, there's an office on the site."

"Sounds good." Jace moved to stand up. He said with a small polite grin, "If that's all…"

Warrington stood as well. "Yes, yes. I believe that's it. I just wanted to meet you and touch base." He walked Jace to the door where they hesitated.

"Oh, I almost forgot. There's a party for staff on the 21st. I hear congratulations are in order on your wedding. I almost didn't accept your application in the beginning because it indicated that you were single and I really didn't want to have unmarried staff at the upper level. My experience has shown me that family men are much more responsible and reliable. Our follow up from HR advised me of your engagement. The wedding must have been an impulsive event?"

"Uh, yes." Jace let his face color slightly with faux embarrassment. "The little woman wouldn't let me come here without her so we decided to get hitched on the way."

"Must have been romantic doing it onboard, eh?" At Jace's nod, he said, "Please bring the wife, we'll all want to meet her. You'll attend the party then?"

"I need to check with…my wife to make sure we don't have any plans, but since we just got here that would be doubtful. But you know how the women are," he smiled in conspiracy to his new boss. "They insist on being asked to do things, not be told. Am I right?"

A short burst of laughter belted from Warrington's thin lips. He nodded emphatically. "Oh yes, you are so right. My wife, Lindy, she thinks she wears the pants in the family. Every so often I have to…" his eyes darkened, "shake her up and get her back on track. You know what I mean?"

Jace grinned in camaraderie while his insides lurched at the implication that Warrington knocks his wife around. "I know what you mean."

"Anyway," Warrington said, "everything will be fine, you'll see. Any problems and you give me a buzz. Just drop off your paperwork, W2's, etc. at HR on the 4th floor. I will contact you to set up our next meeting. All right, son?" He patted Jace on the back.

"Sure. Thanks. Pleasure to meet you, sir." Jace shook his hand and left the office walking briskly down the hall.

"Hey handsome."

Jace's shoulders bunched up in a cringe, he'd hoped to get past Stripper Suzy without attention. He kept walking while tossing a smile over his shoulder, "Nice to meet you, miss, uh, Suzy."

He heard her heels clicking and shuffling across the plush carpet after him. He reached the elevator and quickly pushed the button.

But she was there before the door opened. "Mr. Nico, Jace," she mewed, petting his sleeve. Her lips near his ear, she nuzzled hard against his chest letting him feel what she tried to show him earlier with her low cleavage.

"I get off in like fifteen minutes, how 'bout you and me going across the street, there's a dandy little bar there where we can have a few drinks and get to know each other." She slid her fingers down his tie until they slipped off and down onto his abdomen.

"Oh, baby," she crowed huskily, "what a fucking six pack!" She set both hands on him, rubbing his taut stomach, and moving lower to cup his package.

Jace grabbed her wrists. Resisting the urge to shove her violently away, he gently pushed her back as, *thank God*, the elevator door dinged open.

Stepping in quickly, he said, "Sorry, gotta go, wife is expecting me. See ya." He wiggled his ring finger as the doors closed on her furious face.

As the elevator moved, Jace leaned back wearily against the wall. He felt ill, loosening his tie helped. Then he remembered he had to stop off at HR, and had a series of other errands and meetings to get to before he could go home.

What he needed was a cold beer, and a cuddle with his wife, if she'd let him. He'd grab her in a bear hug the second he sees her before she has time to hold him off.

Shaking his head, Jace couldn't believe he was saying the word wife in relevance to himself. It felt alien, and, last thing in the world he would have expected was that he liked the sound of it. *Wife. My wife. Mine. And I am her husband.*

His challenge was getting Lissa to accept the word husband, related to him of course, and in a permanent way, and along with the physical part. He needed to up his seduction skills. Feeling a lot better, a pleased grin brightened his face as he strode swiftly to his truck.

Hours later he picked up his men at the construction site. They piled in dirty and dusty from head to toe.

"Watch the carpet, boys," Jace needled as they settled in.

"Screw your carpet, Jace you son of a bitch in your fancy suit and silk tie you asshole," Donnie grumbled sourly, trying to rub dried tar off his hands. The other guys laughed at him.

"Donnie isn't used to working so hard, are ya honey?" Cad joked slapping the young man in the head flinging his light brown mop of hair. "Jace will get his tomorrow, beanpole, don't you worry your sissy little heart."

231

"Asshole," Donnie growled trying to jab his elbow in the big man's side. But they were crammed in too tightly he couldn't hit him hard. He jerked his head back tossing some of his scraggily hair out of his eyes.

"So," Ker said, up front next to Jace. "How'd it go?"

Jace glanced at him.

Ker looked odd not in is normal black and white. His flannel shirt and light blue jeans with worn holes in them were filthy and his boots were caked with mud. Yet, the sleek black hair was perfect as always, the entire mass pulled back in a low ponytail trailed past his collar, the beard precise and neat. Plus his hands and face were spotless. Jace would love to know how he did that but Ker never gives up his secrets.

"I met the big boss, of course, Foster Warrington as we planned. I didn't learn anything that we didn't already know. He's being very closed-mouth about the murders, acts like they are just trifling nuisances. Plus, he lied. He said none of the upper level managers have been attacked, when we know full well that's how I got this position. I'm replacing the murdered Jason Bligh."

From the back, Victor said, "Maybe he just wants to keep the fear factor down. If he acts frightened or upset it will only stir up the masses, people could get scared and up and quit leaving him short to complete the enterprise."

Saying, "No," right hand curled over the wheel, resting his left forearm on the door handle, Jace shook his head. "The man was as easy to read as a book. Greed drowns out his slick businessman persona. Other than a malignant evil aura that gave me the creeps, there was zero emotion in his cunning eyes. I had to stop afterwards and wash the smarm from the guy off my hands."

Cad chuckled from the back. "Tell us how you really feel, bro." The others joined in laughing.

"Whatever. Plus, he's doing the receptionist, I can tell by the way they look at each other. But then again I think every other guy in the building is likely doing her too." He swung the wheel turning off the main highway leaving the city.

Now they plowed through small clustered suburbs before they reached a more rural area where the sprawling buildings were big but few and far between. Acres of fields and woods separated the structures.

"How do you know that?" Donnie asked with avid interest.

One shoulder rolled, Jace responded mildly, "I can just tell. If the dress she wore was any tighter or shorter she might as well have been naked. The bitch was all over me like cheap perfume, and she was doused in that too."

He lifted his arm and sniffed his jacket sleeve and made a face. "Shit, she got that crap all over me."

"Oh?" Ker quirked a brow at him. "Was she cheap or wore cheap perfume?" His lip twitched at the scowl on Jace's face.

"Both." His brow hard and mouth grim, Jace glared straight ahead thinking about what trouble the woman could cause him with Lissa.

"She was all over you, dude?" Donnie gushed. "She hot?"

"What's the diff to you, horndog, if it's female she's met your criteria." Cad mocked the younger man next to him.

"Whatever," Donnie sniped at Cad. "Tell us, Jace, was she really all over you?"

"Geeze, Don, keep it in your pants will ya? What are you, like 13?" Victor sneered with contempt. Donnie was sitting between him and Cad, Victor didn't want to know Jace's private business.

"Shut up," Donnie snarled at him, "he brought it up."

Ker murmured quietly to Jace, "Good way to start the wedded bliss. Coming home from your first day on the job with some other woman's perfume pouring off you like a stinking fog." He playfully pinched his nose, then reached over and flicked Jace's collar. "And her lipstick branding you."

"What? Are you kidding?" Jace stretched his neck to see in the rear view mirror. Scowling at the red spot on his white collar he tried to rub it off, but he knew would be futile. "Damn bitch," he muttered.

"Oo, worried the little woman will hit you in the head with a frying pan?" Cad teased.

"Knock it off, guys," Jace growled. He would rather Lissa hit him with a pan than freeze him out like she's more apt to do.

"He is worried, dudes." Donnie giggled. "He's worried his new wife is going to be pee-issed-off, especially since they haven't-oof-"

Cad socked him in the side, grunting, "*Shut up, stupid.*"

Grimacing, Donnie rubbed his stomach. "What'd you do that for? Not my fault One Shot is pussy whipped, he's too damned nice to her. If it were me, I'd bend that smokin' bitch over the closest chair yank those panties down and- ugh-"

Cad hit him again, harder. His coarse voice grit low in Donnie's ear, "Shut the fuck up right now, you're talking about the man's wife. Keep it up and Jace will show you why he's called One Shot. Now shut your pie-hole."

Seeing the rigid set of Jace's shoulders, Donnie decided to clam it.

Driving faster, knuckles clamped on the wheel, Jace's ears burned. It was all he could do to keep driving and not pull over and whip Donnie's bigmouthed ass.

A brief shake of Jace's head stopped Ker from reaching back and slapping the shit out of Donnie. The kid was young, 22, a nickel younger than Jace, Donnie was thinking with his dick instead of his head.

Understanding it, Jace himself couldn't believe his own restraint and patience with Lissa considering how fiercely he wanted her.

Life was so much easier when he just took what willing women offered and moved on. He tersely pushed his hair back off his forehead. But he had no desire for any other woman, he had forever feelings for Lissa. He wanted her to be his wife for the long term, for life.

But, he *has* to wait until she comes to him. If he forced himself on her, as soon as she could she'd run, she'd leave him. It wasn't only the fact that he held her prisoner, there was whatever that other thing was that made her so damned gun shy. So far his attempts at seducing his own wife had gotten him nil.

Back at the complex, Jace parked and they all heaved out. Inside, they each headed in a different direction to clean up. Ker elbowed Donnie and gestured with his head to follow him. Obliging, Donnie's face paled, his head hanging nervously, he followed Ker. Clearly Ker was going to give the younger man a lesson in not talking trash about another man's wife. Especially his friend and boss.

Chapter Twenty-Six

*O*n his way to his room, Jace was about to pull his tie off when he almost ran square into Lissa.

"Hey," he said smiling reaching out to brace her so they didn't crash. "Where are you going in such a hurry?" His heart skipped a beat, he'd missed those beautiful flashing eyes and that sexy mouth today.

"Hey, Jace," she murmured. Seeming distracted and surprised to see him, she nudged her tousled hair off her face with the back of her wrist. "I was just goin' tae the room tae get the sewin' kit, a button popped off Julio's shirt."

Her smile amiable, she said, "You look nice," admiring the suit and tie he seldom wore. "How was your first day at work?"

"Thanks." It pleased him that she noticed what he was wearing. Reluctantly letting go of her, he tucked his hands in his trouser pockets and leaned back against the wall. "It was all right. Just did meetings and stuff. Tomorrow I go to the construction site."

He looked down the hall, his mouth flattened. "Speaking of Julio, where is he?" Jace could feel irritation pricking at the back of his neck. Julio had strict orders to stay with Lissa, keep her in his sight at all times.

"He's in the great hall waitin' for me tae come back. He was on his hands and knees tryin' tae get the button out from under the couch." A merry grin tickled her mouth, eyes like green stars sparkled gaily at Jace. She twisted a lock of hair between her fingers.

She smiled so rarely at him, and it always enchanted him, made him hard. Like now. *Down boy.* He wished it were his fingers playing with her hair. Not wanting to say anything to chase away her merriment, he let his anger at Julio not following his orders go, for the moment. He and Julio would talk later.

Pushing off the wall he closed the space between them. "Say, Lissa, I need to shower. How about you wait and we can go to supper together then-" he broke off, her smile was suddenly gone, her eyes narrowed. *Oh crap.*

Declaring, "Jace, you reek of perfume," her glare pinpointed, latching onto the red stain on his collar. "There's..." she looked closer, then stepped back. "Lipstick on your shirt." Her lips pulled down, she said with an angry sneer, "I'd say your first day at work was not just okay, more like dynamic."

"Lissa, listen-"

She huffed and twirled away. Reaching her room, she yanked the door open and stalked in slamming it behind her.

Muttering, "Aw fuck," exactly what Jace figured would happen. Women were so predictable. They smell a little perfume, see a spot of lipstick and they immediately surmise the worse. Rankled, his chest filled with vexatious air. Exhaling it out of his lungs, he followed her and opened the door.

She was across the room, her face a veil of gall. She sniffed back tears he knew she didn't want him to see. Snatching up her sewing kit, she held it against her chest and made to storm past him.

He snagged her arm. "Lissa, this is not going to fucking happen. You are going to stay right here and hear me out."

Sniffing back the tears, she jerked her arm trying to shake off his grip. Her chin up, she announced, "Please do not curse at me. I do not have tae, nor do I want tae hear your cheatin' lies." Glaring outrage at him she snarled, "You promised, you said you would respect our marriage."

He couldn't help it, he shook her in his aggravation. "I meant what I said, I do respect our marriage. What there is of it." His tone relayed his feelings about the nonphysical aspect of their in name only union.

Refusing to look at him, she jerked her arm again. "Let go of me, Julio is waitin' for me."

"Fuck Julio." Already pissed at his teammate, Jace was reminded that she was on her way to sew his shirt for him, kind of an intimate act in Jace's mind, limited to a husband's right, not another man's.

He didn't care if that sounded stupid and petty, it was how he felt. It was bad enough when she'd done it for Victor. Julio had also failed in his task of staying with Lissa every second, he was on his shit list.

"Sorry," Jace apologized for the curse. He pulled her over to a chair, took the sewing kit from her, set it on the bed then made her sit down. He grabbed another chair, set it in front of her and sat down.

Shrugging out of the suit jacket, he tossed it on the desk chair and unbuttoned the top few buttons of the starched shirt. The tie still hung around his neck. "Listen-"

Her voice shaking with anger, Lissa cut him off, "I resent you pushin' and pullin' me, movin' me around against my will. You are a big bully usin' your strength tae make me do what you want." Her lower lip pouted out. "It's not fair, it's not right."

"I'm sorry." Jace sighed, this was going to be his day of apology. He dragged his hands through the sides of his hair then dropped them on his thighs.

"If I didn't force you, you would constantly flee from me and we would never resolve things. It's bad enough you refuse to allow me even the minutest of touch, a brief hug, or a harmless kiss." The urge to suck on that pouty lip tugged fiercely at him.

She crossed her arms. "You forced me tae marry you, you agreed tae no…sex."

"Dammit Lissa, I agreed to your terms to make you feel more comfortable getting married to me. If I didn't care for or respect you I would rip your clothes off right now, hurl you on that bed and shove my dick inside you so fast and so deep-"

"Jace!" She jumped up, her face red as a beet she started for the door.

He grabbed her arm and without getting up forced her back in her chair, fair or right be dammed. Scooting his chair closer so his knees bracketed hers, he caged her without touching her. "Okay, calm down. I'm sorry, it's just that you try me." He ground his fingers in frustration through his hair making it stand up.

Lissa sat back, her face a placid mask. She said calmly, "After some thought, I have come tae the conclusion that I have been such an idiot."

Jace looked surprised, then smiled nodding, relieved that she was coming around, that she believed him.

But then unfortunately she continued in an empty, aloof voice, "I now realize that you forced me tae marry you so I could not testify against you." Although she tried to keep up a wall over her feelings, anguish crept across, clouding her brilliant eyes.

Her pained look cut him to the core. Exclaiming in shock, "What?" he jumped up, she quailed from him.

Dragging his hands through his hair again he paced a few steps back and forth then came back and sat down. "That is not true, honey, that is not why I married you. The law is that a wife can't be compelled to testify against her husband. I promised you an annulment. You would be free to do what you felt…was right…at that time."

Leaning forward, Jace took one of her hands. Quietly with earnest strong in his voice, he said, "Lissa, I swear on my mother's life, and she is still alive, that I did not marry you so you couldn't testify against me."

She kept her head down, not looking at him, long curls covering half her face.

Jace stood up. His voice harsh with bruised pride, he said, "You still don't believe that we've done nothing wrong. Not I, and none of my team killed that man in the alley. Eventually you will see the truth in that."

Raising her eyes, she saw the sincerity blazing in his dark blues, and the hurt that she didn't believe him. She crossed her arms, the look on her face said she wanted to believe him, but didn't.

"Anyway, back to today, the point is, Lissa," his voice softened, "I do respect you, obviously, or I would have already done to you, you know, what I said." Jace trailed off, he didn't want her to freak out again. He sat back down in his chair.

Her gaze settled on the lipstick on his collar, one brow arched sarcastically. "Really? You respect me after you spent the day in another woman's arms? Why on earth would I ever want tae hug you or…or kiss you when I know the player that you are, that this is what you'll do again and again without compunction?" She slapped furiously at the tears that slipped out.

Sitting back, Jace pulled the tie down and off tossing it over the jacket. He would really be pissed that she kept accusing him of being a man whore if at the moment she didn't have every reason to believe he was.

"Lissa, I did not do anything with another woman today." Seeing her eyes strike like an arrow at the lipstick smudge, he furiously grabbed his shirt with both hands, ripped it open, shrugged out of it, balled it up and threw it at the door.

Working to take a calming breath, constraining his growing aggravation, he un-grit his teeth and spoke evenly. "When I went to meet with my boss this morning, there was this receptionist," he glared at Lissa, she was nodding like she knew it.

"No, cut it out. This woman, I swear, she just threw herself at me, literally. The only time I touched her was to grab her wrists and fling her off of me. I swear to God, Lissa. I know it sounds like a story, and not a good one, but it's the truth."

His mouth pursed gravely as he hoped she would believe him. Worse comes to worse he would drag her to Warrington's office and make that bitch tell Lissa the truth. Her slutty behavior was pushing his and Lissa's relationship back to the beginning, worse because she now thought he'd cheated on her.

"Oh come on, Jace, are you really expectin' me tae believe that some random woman you've never met, a receptionist right smack in the middle of the office of the man you will be workin' for just happened for no reason, no provocation tae throw herself at you?" The disbelief screamed out of her pores. "Just admit it," she said bitterly, wearily, "you slept with her."

Jace leaned forward. Propping his hands on his knees he looked her square in the eye. "Lissa, I told you exactly what happened. I did not sleep with her or do anything else with her. Foster Warrington said she was temporary. It was obvious he, and probably every other man in the building has been with her. She's like some kind of nympho or something."

He leaned closer dying to take her hand again, connect with her, but knew it would upset her more.

"I told the guys about it on the way home. Ask them, they will tell you how pissed and disgusted I was. Donnie couldn't believe I'd shut down the brazen slut. I even told her I was married. Showed her my ring, she didn't care. Baby," Jace did it anyway, pushed his chair closer, picked up her hand, twined their fingers and set them on her leg.

"All I could think about while she was clutching at me was you. Her face was all gunked up with makeup, she was dressed like a cheap tramp. And, you smelled her perfume," his nose wrinkled. "The woman was a total turn off. She couldn't hold a candle to you."

He lifted her hand and kissed the back of it, "She was disgusting trash. Only made me want you more, if that was even possible."

Lissa's enigmatic gaze spanned his bare chest. She stared at every cut, every virile mound of rippling muscle, every dip and curve, the matting of dark hair. A slow blush burned up her fair skin, her eyes dropped, she sat silently looking down at their twined hands.

She could see both their gold wedding bands. Her gaze was drawn back up to his carved chest then down to his taut abs, the blush deepened.

His groin burned watching her canvassing his torso. The blush told him she wasn't immune to his body. Keeping his smile stuffed under his pressed lips, he said with serious slow diction, "Think about it, Lissa."

She cut a look up to his face. Desire shone clearly in Jace's eyes, but there was a significant solemnity there as well.

He said, "The facts are, I don't have to lie to you. I don't have to be faithful to you. I don't have to bother trying to convince you I was not with another woman. I don't have to wear this ring." He shifted his fingers to bump the ring to catch her attention on it.

The anguish that spread across her face, tightening the corners of her eyes, tortured him. His head dropped, then he looked unwavering at her. A hunk of blond hair hung over one brow, he impatiently pushed it back.

"I am truly sorry to say, because it's not right and I know it," he took a deep breath, his voice chewed out husky. "But you have no choice, in any of this. You can't leave and you can't divorce me. The fact is, I can fuck you anytime I want without your acquiescence, we both know it. But I haven't."

She gasped, he kept talking, "So, honey, please, think about it. I have no reason to lie to you. I don't *have* to give you the space and time waiting for you to finally come to the realization that you want me as much as I want you, but I have and I will."

Jace rose to his feet, looked down at her pretty face tilted confused up at him. "I am not going to apologize for saying fuck because if I raped you it would be fucking. If," he said more forcefully, "*when* you finally accept me, we will not be fucking," he softened, "we will be making love."

He set his fingers under her chin, shifted to a caress then he dropped his arm. "Now, we're done with this conversation. We're not talking about it again. I told you the truth and that's it. I am going to take a shower, then you and I are going to dinner." Without another word he left her room to go to his leaving her to stew on his words.

He was hopeful but not surprised when he came out and she wasn't there. Pulling on his jeans, he zipped them but hadn't buttoned the top or put his belt on yet. Disappointment grating in his gut, he yanked open a drawer and reached in to take out a shirt. Hearing the door open he turned around.

"Oh. You're not dressed yet." Lissa came in with a slight smile. She had a shirt in her hands, she moved to the bed and set it down next to her sewing kit. Her gaze flit back and forth over his chest. She lowered her eyes, then peeked again. Pink seeping into her cheeks she lowered them again.

Pleased that she was there, he knocked down the jealousy at seeing Julio's shirt. It pissed him off that it was on the bed. As soon as she turned her back Jace was moving it. He didn't want Julio and bed being synonymous in her mind.

In the meantime, a thrill rippled through his body again when she gawked at his bare chest. Seeing her eyes dropping to the open top of his jeans that hung low on his tapered hips, his body automatically hardened.

Her gaze lowered to the growing bulge in his pants. The darker color flooding her face told him she was aware of his physical reaction to her scrutiny.

"Uh, so…" her lips parted, she licked them as if they were suddenly dry. Her eyes moved back up to his magnificent chest then dropped back down to his lean hips to probe his tight denim.

Jace moved to her, she backed away until she was against the wall.

Exploring the movement of her eyes, her glowing pupils enlarging, he dissected the fear from the desire that kindled ever so slightly. He set his large hands on the wall on either side of her and lowered his head.

"Jace," an uncertain objection.

His biceps flexing next to her head, he drew his mouth down on hers. Against her lips, he murmured, "Yes, say my name, baby, say it again." He could feel her suck in a tremulous breath, then the sighing warmth of it leaving, misting his mouth with her fresh scent.

"*Jace…*"

The throaty whisper steamed through him. Little shock waves rode up his legs making him so hard he thought his jeans would burst.

A hoarse growl deep in the cavern of his chest spread rumbling through his torso. He pressed his mouth over her parted lips bringing her with him in a seething, soaring kiss.

Lissa splayed her fingers on his chest sliding them up, sifting the hair through each slender finger. She pressed her palms stroking over every hard contour. Then her hands stole up his shoulders to his head where her fingers tangled in his hair, tugging the soft locks so hard in her rapture his brain burned.

Jace flattened his forearms on the wall to get closer, tighter to her. He moved his hands across the plaster to cradle her head, his mouth searing hers. He bit at her lips, licked across and spread kisses along her jaw, sucked the smooth skin down her neck and back up.

He moved his hands from the wall to encircle her tiny waist. The keening moans in her throat vibrated softly against his lips.

His heart beating a racing drum, Jace slid his hands around her back pulling her in tight, feeling her soft breasts spread against the sheer hardness of his chest made his skin quiver.

Sweeping his hands up the sides of her ribs he brushed his thumbs against the sides of her breasts, ready to capture their suppleness in his hands and relish their fullness.

Lissa's body melted into his. Her quick shallow breaths feathering his face, her knees weakened, slightly buckling causing her to lean harder against him. His hands rolled around her back to hold her fiercely against him as his mouth besieged hers.

Her forearms fell along his. She raised her hands trying to span his huge biceps but her hands were too small, she gripped them, digging her fingers into the thick muscles.

A double rap knock on the door didn't stop him, Jace barely heard it with the blood pounding in his ears. But her hands came between them, her palms pressed against his chest, pushing, blocking him from getting closer.

Lissa turned her head from his, murmured, "Jace, the door."

"*Shit*," his agonized groan burred in his throat. He whispered, "Ignore it." Pinning her against the wall with his hips, he bent his knees and pushed between her legs, spreading them so he could press his erection up and against her core, smiling tightly at her wriggling hips and open-mouthed moan.

Her surprising tentative rubbing his shaft with her sex almost sent him over the moon. He cradled her face bringing it back up and kissed her so scorching the green in her eyes sizzled.

Lissa stroked her hands up his strapping chest to his shoulders where she clung to the iron mass. Digging her fingers into his sinuous muscles her whimpers brushed against his mouth.

His throbbing erection strained so hard at his jeans the zipper was sliding down. Jace stroked his palm up her body covering her breast with his big hand. Hot with aroused fever he crushed it in his long fingers. Kneading her plump flesh, he felt her nipple pebble hard in his fingers.

Jace moved his other hand to her bottom pulling her to grind hard against him, his fogged brain trying to decide whether to pick her up and carry her to the bed or just sink to the floor before her brain kicked in and shut down her body,

The knock was louder, insistent.

Cupping her chin, he growled hoarsely, "Don't move." He stomped to the door, kicked his shirt out of the way and threw the door open. "Goddammit this better be important," he barked.

Victor was standing there, amusement pulling up the edges of his mouth. His gaze went from Jace's mussed hair to his bare heaving chest, dropped to the very evident bulge in his unbuttoned jeans and up to his furious face.

He glanced inside at Lissa standing a few feet away, embarrassment coloring her face, but the obvious glaze of passion still clouded her eyes. Smirking, Victor said, "Gee, I'm not interrupting anything, am I?"

"What the fu- uh, hell do you want, KM?" Jace jammed a hand on the doorframe blocking Victor's view inside the room.

Victor tried to mush the smirk off his face, Lissa was a startling babe, Jace had every right to be mad if they had been in the middle of something. Especially when the team knew she rebuffed all his advances. "Sorry, One, uh, I mean Jace. I was successful with the hacking, I," his eyes flicked to the room.

Jace scrubbed a hand over his face scraping over the bristles then started to close the door. Grumbling, "I'll meet you and the others in the study," he shut the door in Victor's face. "Baby," he turned. *Damn*, she had disappeared into the bathroom.

He cursed knowing it was going to take work and time to get back to where they just were.

A smile stole curving his mouth, he brushed the back of his hand across it, but hot damn, that was the hottest kiss, hottest make-out session he'd ever had. That was the practice one, it will only get better.

As he trod to the bathroom, remembering the feel of her lush breast in one hand, her fine ass in the other, the thought of her responding to him the way she rubbed on his erection when he ground their hips together, blew his mind and heated him right back up.

The faster he had his meet the sooner he could be back with her and take up where they had left off.

Calling through the door, "Lissa, I have to go meet with the guys for a while. I'll come back to take you to the dining room. Okay?" He heard an indistinguishable mumble.

Buttoning his jeans, he pushed a belt through the loops then pulled on his shirt. Quickly dragging a comb through his hair, he strode out the door buttoning his shirt on his way down the hall.

Chapter Twenty-Seven

*J*ace joined Ker, Victor, Cad, Julio, Donnie, and Doc Drew in the study. Flopping in a cushioned chair like the rest of them, he draped a leg over the stuffed arm of his chair and waited for Victor to spill what he'd found.

Victor got up and stood next to his laptop on the center table. "I was able to hack deeper into more of Warrington's files. The stores are paying him a fortune up front to rent warehouse and manufacturing space once they're built if he doesn't sell. He's well on his way to becoming a billionaire."

Jace folded his hands behind his head. "That's pretty obvious without hacking into his financials, Vic."

Victor slid his hands into the pockets of his slacks and shrugged. "Yeah, I know, I'm just telling you what I found. Anyway," he glanced around the room at all the men and back to Jace.

"On two occasions in Illinois and then once here, an exact amount of money, 75 grand in total, of which 25 thousand was deposited into three men's accounts that are on Warrington's payroll, the day after each murder. I haven't traced it back to Warrington yet, he uses so many shells, but I will."

Now he had their attention. Jace dropped his leg and leaned forward, folded his hands and laid his elbows on his knees. "Okay, good work, Vic, payoff for the hits. What are their names?"

Victor edged over to his computer and pushed a button, the screen lit right up. He bent to read the names. "Uh, they are Sam Leeds, Bruce Kinder and Earl Bandman."

"No info in our cells, boys," Jace reminded them, "use paper."

"Say it again, KM," Julio said writing the names in a notebook.

"*Victor*," Jace frowned at Julio, "we all need to remember that at the site. Our military monikers will make us look suspicious."

Julio peered up with a nod. "Sorry, habit." He wrote down the names and handed the notebook to Cad who did the same and onto Ker until they all copied the names, tore them off and stuck them in their pockets to be destroyed later.

Long scraggly hair in his eyes, Donnie rubbed his chin and then his nose. He asked, "What's your theory, Jace, why the murders?" His lanky thin legs stretched out in front of him, pointy elbows on the chair arms.

Jace loosely tapped his thumbs together, took a breath then sat back crossing his legs. "We talked about that, Victor, did you find any evidence of what I thought?" All eyes turned to Victor.

A slow easy smile crossed the bit of beard shadow Victor always had. Black hair, dark intelligent eyes, narrow, elegant jaw lined with the Fu Manchu moustache, the ladies swarmed around the dark, dangerous looking man.

Like Ker and Jace, he had a sinister aura about him. With their tough hard exteriors matching their actions and their words, for some reason women liked the scary bad-boy image.

Victor replied, "Yeah, I tracked letters scanned in his computers from some people. There was a governor, a few landowners and people who rented the stores and factories that were closing in the States to open in Scotland.

"The letters indicated that they threatened, bribed, begged, sweet-talked to try to get the factories to stay in the U.S. They were losing millions of dollars from the factories pulling up roots and planting them in Scotland."

He leaned forward, his dark eyes intense. "I came across an email from the murdered accountant. The guy sent a vague notice that he might contact the authorities. Maybe he was hinting at blackmail."

Jace pondered Victor's info. He set his hands on the chair arms and drummed his fingers on them. "It's still a good theory that one of the people losing their manufacturing to Scotland could be mad enough to commit murder…"

"There's the other side of the coin too," Cad offered. "They're digging up a lot of rural forest and are going to build a megalopolis of stores and plants and warehouses. There might be an angry person or two that doesn't want it in their rustic little town."

Jace nodded, still drumming his hands. "Sure, yeah." He dropped his leg and sat up straighter. "But I think it really leads back to Warrington. I think he's killed to keep the people quiet that disseminated the stats."

He stood up, stuck his arms straight up, stretched and yawned. "I think I'll go take a little siesta before-"

"Uh uh," Ker shook his head. "We aren't done. We have more work to do. Sit down, she can wait."

Jace flipped him the bird then flopped back down on his chair.

The next morning Jace drove to the construction site with a smile warming his face. Last night after the team meeting, he had managed to get Lissa alone for a very late dinner.

She asked about his family and listened with engaging interest at his funny stories of his and his sibling's childhood antics. He didn't tell her he hadn't yet informed his family of their marriage.

He wanted them to have a firmer foundation before he dropped the news. His mother was going to kill him when she found out he basically eloped and didn't tell them.

Lissa told him a few details about her earlier life, but when she got to her college time a wall came down and she awkwardly changed the subject.

In time, he'd break through her roadblocks and find out what was scaring her so much. At least while she was with him whatever she was afraid of couldn't get to her. They had a pleasant, relaxing evening and he felt they were maybe making some headway with their relationship.

He parked amongst the jumble of vehicles, and strode across the dirt and litter of tools and junk, moving through the crowd of workers looking for the guy Warrington had told him to meet with.

Mike Miller greeted Jace with a friendly smile and handshake. A little over average height, he had a good build but not as beefed as Jace, with sandy blond hair and brown eyes.

He said to Jace, "Let me show you the place, introduce you around before we go review the paperwork."

Carrying a clipboard crammed with papers under his arm, Mike spent the next hour taking Jace around to meet the foremen and laborers.

The area was packed with carpenters, engineers, heat and AC specialists, roofers, plasterers, the list went on and on. The main uniform seemed to be jeans or khakis, boots and flannel or T-shirts.

Now loaded with a solid knowledge of the lay of the land, Jace had met most everyone, including the few women sprinkled in amongst the workers, but Mike said more new men came every day.

He brought Jace to the trailer they used as an office. The trailer was large and designed to be an office not a residence. The main room contained a big table in the middle, filing cabinets along one wall, a desk piled with two laptops, papers and numerous chairs scattered around.

A small kitchen and bathroom were to one side and on the other end were three rooms, one for supplies, one to lock the blueprints and permits in at night, and one as a second office with a couch that often had someone napping on.

On the walls were photos of the plaza in progress and an artist's rendition of what the completed structure will look like.

Teeming with stores, the walkways around the buildings were wide. Green grass and several small ponds were painted in, voluminous parking lots were generously spread around the entire perimeter. Pictures of the factories under partial construction were tacked to a bulletin board.

A set of blueprints lay open on the center table.

"Okay, let me show you where we're at." Mike went to the table and set a palm down, leaning over the blueprint. Jace came up beside him to view it. They studied and discussed it for a long while, Mike answering Jace's questions.

After some time, swiping his hand over his head with a long exhale, Mike said, "How about a soda break?"

"Sounds great," Jace replied.

Mike trod to the kitchen, removed two cans of soda from the fridge and handed one to Jace. They plopped down on a couple of beat up cushioned chairs, dropped their feet on a low table crossing their ankles and drank thirstily.

Jace waited a few minutes then said casually, "So, there's word on the street that there's been some murders here and in the U.S. What's that all about, do you know?"

Swallowing a mouthful of soda, Mike wiped his sleeve across his mouth. "Not really. Two high ups in two of the companies bought it in the States, then a month back Jason Bligh, one of the managers was taken out here." The can at his mouth he motioned his head at Jace. "Actually, you are Bligh's replacement. Did you know that?"

Not answering his question, Jace asked, "Did the cops tell you guys how it happened?"

Mike drained his soda then crushed the can in his hand. "It was in the papers, everyone knows. The first guy arriving on this site one morning, Lee Campbell found the body. Like they say, execution style, two shots to the back of the head. Bang, bang," he made a shooting gesture with his fingers.

"Huh." Jace asked, "Does anyone have any idea who might have done it?"

Mike's gaze dropped suddenly to the can in his hand. He licked his lips, wiped his mouth again with his sleeve. "Uh, that's a negative. Probably all just random robberies or whatever. Warrington told us it had nothing to do with these projects." His words were firm but his posture changed. His shoulders stooped, his eyes flit back and forth across the floor in front of him.

He abruptly stood up and tossed his can into the trashcan. "Let's go check on the plumbing problem they're working on." He didn't wait for Jace's reply, just strode right out the door.

Standing up slowly, Jace finished his drink, tossed the can and followed him out.

At lunchtime Jace tracked down his team. They bought lunch from a lunch truck and found some stacks of wood well away from the others to sit on.

Munching on a loaded hotdog, Jace asked, "Anyone find any of the guys we're looking for?"

Cad said, "I asked around, got nothing. No one knows them." He bit a huge chunk of his hamburger and almost at the same time shoved in several chips.

"Same here, nada," Victor said.

Jace looked at Donnie. Donnie shook his head his mouth full of ham and cheese. He burbled out through his food, "Nope."

Ker shook his head.

Getting to his feet, Jace started to pace in one direction then revolved to stalk in the other. "We need to keep asking. They might not be construction workers, but someone might still know one of them."

He dusted his hands together then wiped them on his pants to get off the relish that had seeped on them. "Okay, let's go back out."

"One, I mean Jace," Donnie said quickly, "don't you think people will be suspicious seeing us together?"

A corner of his mouth pulled in. Jace replied, "No. We were hired and brought over together on the ship, it would only seem natural that we after housing together we would hang together. Just be cool about asking questions, anyone catches on and blabs to Warrington, we'll be out on our ears if he finds out who we really are. Let's go."

Chapter Twenty-Eight

A week and a half passed. Every day, the team left early, worked hard, asked questions, came home late, ate a quick meal, debriefed after and then dropped into bed to do it all again the next day.

Lissa had given her word that if he left her free to roam the house without a guard that she would not try to leave. Jace had Julio stay with her the first two days then let it go and brought him to the site with the rest of the guys.

Jace and Lissa had not spent but a few minutes together the past week due to the work. Missing her like crazy, after returning from work and taking a quick shower, Jace went searching for her.

He looked for his bride everywhere. Finally determining she was not in the building, he headed outside. He searched the near grounds to no avail.

His stomach churning, Jace came over the small hill the structure was built on. As he breached the top, he saw Lissa about a quarter of a mile away sauntering along the road.

Deep woods braced the east side of street for miles. On the west side where other houses were, fields and open expanses of grass made it easy to see someone coming near the house. The next closest buildings were separated on either side by acres of lumpy meadows and tall grass.

A car was parked down the side of the road. Making a sudden U turn Jace ran back inside, grabbed a shotgun then sprinted back out and raced tearing down the hill barking into his cell.

Lissa picked a daisy, then a few more. Holding the bouquet and humming, she strolled along looking for patches of other wildflowers to pick. A hand tucked in her jean's pocket, the top half of her hair was held back with barrette the rest flowed in shimmering waves over her shoulders and down her white shirt.

Her nose in the bouquet, she was nearing a parked car when a man stepped from the woods startling her. "Oh!" She exclaimed in surprise and stopped.

The man's smile was friendly, he said cheerfully, "Hi there. My car broke down, do you by chance have a phone I can borrow to call a tow truck?" His shoulder rose slightly sheepish. "The battery died in mine."

"No, I'm sorry..." She couldn't explain she wasn't allowed to have one.

Tall with strong broad shoulders, he had chestnut hair, blue eyes. The man was mildly good looking but something shifted in his eyes causing her to take a half step backwards.

Smiling more broadly, he held his hands up. "Please don't be afraid, I won't hurt you. Is there maybe a house or something nearby? Perhaps I could use their phone?" He tilted his head slightly, almost shyly, peering up at her benignly through his lashes.

Eased by his shy manner, Lissa smiled back. "Sure, over the hill there's-"

The man reached out, snagged her arm and started running, dragging her with him.

Astonished, she let him pull her for a second then she tried to stop, struggled to pull away. When he didn't let go she fought him. Punching at him with her free hand, Lissa twisted her body trying to wrench her arm out of his grasp.

He slapped her then backhanded her hard enough she dropped stunned to her knees. Quickly, while she was dazed, he stuck his hand in her hair. Gabbing a fistful, he jerked her to her feet and hauled her with him, forcing her to run down the inclined road towards the car.

Bellowing, "Let her go!" Jace was racing down the hill with the shotgun in his hand. Seeing the man slap her, he exploded in fury and bolted faster.

Lissa looked up at Jace, her eyes widened at the weapon he held.

The man stopped, threw his arm around her neck. Holding her tightly against his torso, a gun materialized in his hand. He yelled, "Back off, Nico, we just want to talk!"

The cocking of the Jace's shotgun could be heard even at that distance. "Let her go shithead!" he demanded. "Get the fuck away from her!" He kept coming, closing in; the shotgun in both hands raised up and aimed at the man.

The man jerked Lissa back into his body and pressed his gun to her head. "No, you back up or her beautiful brains will be splattered all over the road."

When Jace kept coming, the man pushed the gun so hard against her temple her head was forced sideways. "Stop right now, Nico or she's dead!" The menacing threat rang over the blacktop to the grass, Jace slowed but didn't stop. He slightly lowered the shotgun.

"That's better," the cocky man said, a nasty sneer creasing his face, then his mouth turned hard. "Now stop moving completely, drop the fucking gun or I swear she buys it." Tightening his arm over her throat until Lissa could barely draw a breath, he pulled the hammer back on his gun.

Jace still didn't stop but moved very slowly, his muscular legs gliding like a stalking tiger's down the hill. He said calmly, "Listen, bro, let's talk. You don't want her, you want me. Let her go and I will come with you, peacefully."

The man shook his head smirking. "Sure, you'll really do that." He laughed harshly. "I'm not stupid. You ask too many questions, my friend wants to see you. She's leverage, both of you are getting in the car and- uhhh-"

Behind him, Ker leashed one arm across his neck, the other hand snatched the wrist holding the gun and shoved it straight up in the air, the gun fired with an earsplitting explosion.

The man still held Lissa reflexively jerked back. She screamed at the gunshot.

Cracking the man's head back, Ker twisted his wrist until he yelped and dropped the gun that clattered on the asphalt. Still gripping his wrist, his forearm like a steel bat over the man's throat, Ker wrenched the guy's neck backwards half crushing his windpipe.

The thug let go of Lissa to scrabble at Ker's hands trying to pull them off him. Ker abruptly released him. Lissa promptly stumbled away from both men, her hands grasping her throat where the man had half-strangled her.

The man staggered a step then went for the gun on the ground.

Jace raced over, pushed Lissa aside, dropped his shotgun and charged at the man. Tackling him roughly, he took him down hard on the pavement.

As the man hit the ground, Jace straddled him then went wild on him beating him with his fists. Blood gushed everywhere, the man's screams bombarded the street.

Jace couldn't stop, red fury blinded him, all he could see was the man striking Lissa, he wailed insanely at him.

"All right, enough, One." Ker stood calmly over the two men, his voice deeply quiet. A camouflaged colored canvass bag was slung over his shoulder.

Although quiet, his voice fought through the raging haze blinding Jace as he viciously punched and punched, pounding the man who had since stopped screaming and struggling. "Jace, bro," Ker repeated softly.

His bloody fists held up in front of his chest, Jace sat back on his heels, panting. Sweat poured down his face splattering with the thug's blood. It even dripped from his blond hair. Out of the corner of his eye he saw Lissa's horrified expression.

Glancing down at the prone man he straddled, Jace wiped his sleeves across his face clearing the blood and sweat and rage out of his eyes and climbed to his feet.

Ker said, "He'll be out for a while, we-"

A spray of gunshots rang out all around them! Bullets struck the ground shooting up pieces of tar like shrapnel. The rat-a-tat-tat noise was deafening.

Jace grabbed Lissa's hand and raced with her and Ker to the car. As they dove behind it Jace shoved Lissa down and both men crouched with guns out.

Ducking as bullets whizzed over their heads pinging in and off the metal car, the two men moved to opposite sides of the vehicle and one at a time shot back at where they saw the guns flash.

Ker dropped the canvass bag on the ground; it contained extra magazines for the shotgun and both Glocks each man carried, unfortunately the shotgun was out of reach laying near the grass where Jace had dropped it.

Suddenly, an eerie silence held. Both men slowly stood, still bent behind the shield of the car, scanning the area for the shooters.

Near Ker, a shaken Lissa struggled to her feet to see what was going on. A barrage of gunfire blasted across the yard- bullets slammed into the car.

Ker threw himself on top of Lissa, turning as they hit the ground, landing on his side he rolled on top of her. He stayed over her, covering her as Jace glanced once at them then retuned the gunfire.

Ker rose on one elbow, looking at Lissa's frightened face, he whispered, gruff and low, "You okay?" She nodded.

"Stay down," he ordered then jumped to his feet in a crouch and mirrored Jace shooting over the cover of the car.

Jace pulled his cell out and said calmly into it, "Victor, surrounded, south of hill." Gunfire lit up the surrounding area like machine guns, the hail of bullets didn't stop coming.

"Can't tell how many, I'm with Ker pinned behind car." Clicking off, he shoved the phone in his pocket then shuffling bent over, he moved to the other end of the car from Ker, stood up, fired a round of shots then ducked back down.

A volley of bullets continued spraying around the car. When Jace ducked, Ker stood up and fired.

Lissa lay on the ground curled in a ball with her hands over her ears trying not to scream.

Suddenly the hail of gunfire sounded different, it came from higher up the hill. Jace glanced at Ker, reinforcements. Gunfire burst all around from all directions.

Less than five minutes and the shooting diminished. Then it grew quieter, sporadic until no more shots sounded. Waiting, Ker and Jace moved closer together sandwiching Lissa between them. They both smiled when they heard Victor calling out.

"One? Ker? Where are you bros?"

Jace stood up and saw his men rambling down the hill. As they passed bodies lying around the grass they kicked their weapons out of reach before checking each male.

Jace helped Lissa get back up to her unsteady feet. Her arms wrapped around her trembling body, she looked from Jace to Ker and back.

Both men were curled forward in boxing style, arms bowed, guns clasped tightly in fists, their eyes unnaturally blank. Dual expressions in killer warrior mode. She stepped back, suddenly fearful of them they looked so frighteningly menacing.

Jace started to say something to Ker, when out of the corner of his eye he saw movement. He whipped around and saw the man he had pulverized about to grab an unaware Lissa. With a roar, Jace vaulted past her, slammed both hands on the man's head, and with one twist snapped it, instantly breaking his neck.

He let go, the man dropped to the ground like a broken puppet, his dead eyes wide open.

Lissa gasped. Clamping both hands over her mouth, she looked down at the man then up at Jace. She hardly recognized him. His eyes unnaturally fired with the glow of a lethal storm, mouth set grim and hard. He moved towards her, she backed away until she knocked into the car.

Clearly afraid of him, Lissa pressed her back and palms against the bullet-riddled car.

Jace stepped right in front of her. Jabbing a finger in her face, his face dark and enraged, a vein pumped at his temple. Every word ground out in an unarguable command, "You do not leave the building again without me. Ever. You shouldn't have fucking been out of the house in the first place."

He leaned closer to her, gripped her chin, his bloody fingers dug into her skin, his eyes hard and piercing, fearsomely cold.

"Jace," Ker murmured a soft warning.

Demanding, "Am I clear, Lissa? You do not go anywhere without me." He held her chin so tightly she couldn't talk, could hardly move.

Her eyes darted to Ker. He looked just as grim but cooler, not as enraged.

"Lissa," Jace's voice harsh and severe, his eyes bore furiously into hers making her look at him. She tried to drop her head in a weak nod. But Jace raised her head back up and shook her jaw. Every word a panted bark, "Out loud, tell me you understand me." Sweat dripped in his eyes, he was covered in the dead man's blood.

Through stiff trembling lips, she mumbled barely audible, "I understand you." She looked at him, he was not the man she had come to know.

His dark blue eyes turned black as icy midnight, they glared right through her. His mouth pressed in a rigid line. The broad shoulders relentless, his bicep muscles pumped huge from his fight.

Abruptly releasing her, he moved back slightly, bent and scooped up the dead man's gun, tucking it in the back of his jeans.

Lissa slipped from the car and moved over to Ker. She stood slightly behind him.

Smiling down at her, the Asian drew a strong arm across the front of Lissa and pulled her around and pressed her safely with her back against his chest. He stared blankly at the furious glare Jace shot him.

Jace's shoulders rose in a deep breath, he lowered them pushing out some of the toxic tension still held there. "Take her back inside, lock her in her room. I'll meet with everyone in the study when we're done out here."

His eyes emptied of the fury and danger, the black cleared from the blue, but there was no warmth in them.

A twitch pulled up a corner of Ker's mouth. "Come on, honey." His arm around her shoulders, he walked her up the drive, holding her head against his chest so she couldn't see the grisly bodies littering the grounds.

When they neared the house, Ker dropped his hand to her back. He said, "Jace was just scared, Lissa. He was terrified for you and he doesn't know how to handle the fear. It's like a kid that runs out in front of a car and the mother is mad at him because she was so afraid he could have been killed. Jace would never hurt you, but as you can see, he will kill anyone who does."

Lissa stopped walking. Ker waited.

"Ker, I...I'm not used tae this- this violence. He changed, his eyes, they were deadly, cold and empty as ice." She shivered. "He scares me."

Ker set a hand on her shoulder keeping an eye out for Jace knowing his friend hated seeing anyone with their hands on Lissa.

"It's just a mode we all go into when we have to fight. We shut down parts of our brains to funnel what we need to the forefront. You should know by now in regards to you his bark is worse than his bite. Come on, let's go before he sees us lingering outside and I have to listen to his whining and nagging about keeping you safe."

She giggled at him as they went inside.

Two hours later, Jace made his way to her room. Unlocking the door he went inside, closed and locked it behind him. Lissa was sitting on the edge of her bed. She didn't look up when he came in. A shirt and sewing material lay untouched on her lap.

Stuffing his keys in his pocket, Jace crouched in front of her and put his big hands on her knees. The fierce ruthless warrior cloak was gone, his tone gentle, he said, "Honey, I'm sorry you had to experience that. But," her head was down, he cupped her chin lifting it.

Tears in her eyes glimmered like green lights in a mist. "You're okay now. I promise, baby, it won't happen again. You'll stay by my side-"

She jerked from his hands and abruptly jumped to her feet. Her face blanched at the blood covering his shirt and his cut and bloody knuckles.

Uncomfortable at her accusing gaze, he curled his hands turning them under so she couldn't see them. It was his fault she was in the position she was in today, he forced her to be here. It was obvious seeing him kill that man with his bare hands had freaked her out, which was dreadfully unfortunate. He wished to hell it had been Ker and not him who had killed the thug in front of her.

But Jace knew the second he saw the guy going for her again he would take him out for good. He sighed, back to square one trying to gain her trust. He watched her move away and head to the bathroom.

Her feet stumbling slightly, she mumbled, "I need tae wash my face."

Jace stood up. "Uh, okay. I'll leave you in um…peace to…" She was almost to the bathroom. "I'll have Cad come and get you for dinner. All right?" He was talking to the closed door.

He waited a few minutes, heard the water running then left to go clean up in his room.

Chapter Twenty-Nine

After dealing with the local authorities, the team had returned to the lodge looking roughed up but triumphant.

Most of the other occupants of the building had gathered at the sounds of gunshots, and stared in awe at Jace covered in blood when he returned.

Now he was cleaned up, the blond hair darker still wet and combed neatly. Doc had worked on his bruised and cut hands, he wanted to completely bandage them but Jace had shaken him off.

How would it look for him to walk around with his itty-bitty sore knuckles all bandaged up? For sure his men would tease him unmercifully. His fists have been in worse condition before.

Thirty minutes later, Jace was sitting with Ker and Victor in the dining room. They had their heads together in quiet discussion.

The other people in the room surreptitiously watched them. Nervous and excited they whispered about the gunfight they couldn't help but hear. They were making up stories what it was all about, later they hoped to find out what really happened.

It was Jace's face, a hard brutal mask that radiated his dark mood cutting through the room like a black sword that drew attention. Whenever he looked up all that attention nervously skittered away leaving nothing but the clattering of dishes and cutlery.

Victor had a glass of milk and a tuna fish sandwich with chips in front of him. He tossed several chips into his mouth. Speaking through the crunches, he asked, "How's my girl?"

Ker slid a sidelong glance at Jace, amusement twinkling in his dark eyes.

His shoulders hunched, Jace had both hands wrapped around a coffee mug. Lifting the mug he muttered into it, "My wife," he reminded him, "is fine."

Ker sat back against his chair. Setting one ankle over a knee he leaned forward quickly snatching a few Victor's chips. He said slyly, "I don't think she was too happy watching *her husband* kill a man. A big man, breaking his neck with his bare hands with one move." He and Victor shared a smirk.

Red tinged the tips of Jace's ears. "Whatever. She'll get over it," he growled into his mug.

Victor gobbled half his tuna sandwich, chewed, gulped it down and popped the other half in. Chewing with vigor, he said cheerfully, "Don't count on it, Jace. Women are odd creatures when it comes to coldblooded killing. Actually seeing us do it, they find it uneasy lying beside us in bed at night. Don't forget she doesn't have the harsh battle experience we have."

The three men grew quiet, recalling their tough times in combat. Victor spoke again, "That pretty little package of femininity wouldn't last a second in our world."

"Don't cut her short, Vic, she's a lot tougher than she looks," Ker drawled urbanely, sneaking a glimpse at the rest of Victor's chips.

Seeing him, Victor rolled a protective arm around his plate and pulled it closer to him.

Crossing his arms, Jace rested them on the table and grumbled, "It wasn't in cold blood, the fucker was going after her again."

"Not like a man to get up after getting a beat down from you, Jace, you're slipping," Ker informed him.

Picking up a few chips, Victor waved them at Ker while saying to Jace, "Yeah, something making you grow soft?"

Ker grunted. "Uh, maybe it's the other way around. Something growing hard." He and Victor snickered like schoolboys.

Jace's forehead grooved, brows crossed in a heavy frown, he started, "Listen, assholes-"

Victor interrupted, "Speaking of that lovely package," the other two men looked at him. He motioned with his head to the front of the room.

Cad Munro was entering with Lissa on his arm. Jace's eyes narrowed at the pair.

"Wow," Victor muttered. Ker sent him a sideways warning. Ignoring him, Victor gushed in fascination under his breath, "What the hell is she wearing?"

Sliding into a seat next to him, seeing the annoyed look on Jace's face, Donnie snickered. "Dude, they call that a camisole. Looks satin or silk with miniscule straps, it clings quite damn nicely. The skimpy low front shows off her very fine tits-" he could hear Jace's growl from across the table, but kept grinning watching Lissa and Cad approach them. "I think it's supposed to be worn like lingerie under a blouse or suit jacket. Man, look at those babies jiggle-"

"Shut the fuck up, Donnie. You're talking about my wife," Jace barked softly enough but was heard at their table. The dark tone would have sent terrified shivers through anyone who didn't know him.

Ker leaned across the table and said quietly to Donnie, "After dinner you and I are having another talk. Out back." He ignored Donnie's suddenly pale face digging into his food.

All the men stood up as Cad pulled out a chair for Lissa to sit. Jace sat back down, his face a blur of warring emotions.

Glaring at her under his low-bridged forehead, Jace snapped, "What the hell are you wearing?"

Donnie laughed out loud. "Bro, I was just explaining it to you, it's a-" he stamped his lips together at the killer look Jace shot him before turning his attention back to Lissa.

Confused, Lissa looked down at her blouse, or lack thereof. A pink hue crept across her cheeks. "I, uh, Cad came. I didn't think, I just left, my blouse is on the chair. I didn't realize-"

"Apparently."

She went to get back up. "I'll go get-"

"No. Sit down." Aware everyone was staring at them, his eyes spitting blue ire, Jace sent a swift sarcastic glare at the huge, heavily buffed black man with arms the size and steely strength of cranes. "You want to go get her a real shirt, Cad?"

Toying with a gold earring, Cad had the nerve to smirk at Jace. "Sorry. We started talking as soon as I got there and left right away, I didn't really notice what she had on."

His gaze slid over to Lissa, lowered to her breasts that mounded over the satin bodice of the short, tight, camisole. A scant inch of fair skin showed between the blouse and her jeans.

"Like hell you didn't." Jace's brows crossed in a scowl, "Well?"

Grinning, Cad nodded his closely shaved head then turned and strode in no hurry out of the room.

Jace shot his black scowl around the room until everyone turned back to their own tables. "Here," he pushed his glass of water to Lissa. "You probably need this."

She looked down at it, then raised her eyes to his. She leaned back, away from the intense inscrutable emotion looming behind the dark blues. Their eyes crashed together, held, then hers dropped and she picked up the water and sipped it.

Cad returned, striding his thick muscled legs through the room, the lights glinting off his dark shaved head. Reaching the table and winking at Jace, he ceremoniously dropped a long sleeved blouse over Lissa's shoulders then helped her on with it enjoying the black looks Jace sent him from the other side of the table.

He moved to take a seat when he caught Ivy Innes a few tables away wiggle her fingers at him. Grinning at his friends, he said, "I'll catch you all later." Smoothing his huge sausage fingers over his bald pate he swaggered his way over to Ivy.

"Well, that was a hell of a Sunday, hey boys?" Julio asked joining the group with a burger and fries.

After dinner Jace walked a silent Lissa to her room. He left her there to go back and meet with the team to discuss who and why they thought the men had been sent to their house.

Victor said, "We checked all the bodies, not a piece of ID on any of them. The car was stolen. We'll have to wait for prints to find out who they are before we can track them back to who sent them."

"It had to have been Warrington," Jace said.

Shaking his head, Cad offered, "Not necessarily. It probably was one of the assassins trying to find out why we're asking about them."

"The guy had said his friend wanted to ask me some questions, but he could have been here for any of us." Jace pushed his hair back off his forehead, crossed his arms and sat back. "We all live here and we were all asking questions."

"Uh huh," Victor agreed. "The good news is, we have to be on the right track, we're shaking them up."

Jace frowned. "I don't want them shaken up. We need to tie Warrington's false statistics to him and find evidence on the killers and tie them to Warrington. If they're suspicious of us they may clam up and get rid of us, fire us. They tried to take Lissa as collateral to make me talk. That's bullshit I won't fucking let go."

Julio said quietly, "Maybe you should send her back to the States for her safety-" Jace's black look withered the rest of his words until Julio put his full attention on his laptop.

The team talked for a few hours. Jace left them and went straight to Lissa's room.

Using his key, he silently entered and tip-toed to her bed. She was sound asleep. He carefully scooped her out from her bed and took her next door to his room and gently laid her down on his bed.

Quietly removing his clothes and putting on a T and shorts like she was wearing, he slipped under the sheets and squirmed over to her. Throwing the blankets over them both, he wrapped his arms around her and settled her head and a hand on his chest.

When she snuggled against him, a smile softened the harshness off his face from the grueling day. It was torture on his dick, but after the fright she gave him today, he was sleeping with her tucked safe in his arms tonight.

Chapter Thirty

*T*he next day Jace got a phone call telling him that due to the inexplicable shootout, Warrington wanted to move them to a different complex. In the meantime, he said to have the entire staff re-board the ship and stay there for a couple days before the next place would be available.

Jace and his team had managed to twist the tale that some members of a street gang or such had tried to rob them which resulted in the firefight.

Warrington had questioned that Jace and his friends were armed. Jace easily explained some of them had previously lived in less than safe areas therefore armed themselves for their security. Many of the male workers transported on the ship to Scotland carried concealed weapons, even Lissa had managed to get her hands on a gun from one of them.

"Great," Victor grumbled when he heard. "We have to move, not once again but twice while fucking working, what a bitch."

Nodding his head, Cad said, "The local gendarmes are investigating the firefight but, as we know, they won't come up with anything. The thugs were just hired guns, they won't trace back to anyone concrete."

Everyone in the house moved back to the ship. Jace was relieved he had Lissa back in his room.

The next couple days passed the same as before, the men got up before dawn, drove the longer ride into the city, worked until after dusk, ate a late dinner, debriefed in the study then crashed into bed.

The other men working at the site usually hung around a few hours after dinner drinking and watching videos.

One night the girls were sitting around the living room talking. Getting herself another drink, Dona Southerland saw the men leave the study and head wearily to bed. Watching them, she poured scotch into a glass, added a splash of water and some cubes. She stirred it and turned her attention to the girls in the room.

Lissa was playing cards with Glennie, Vicki and Ivy. Ivy slept every night with Cad and right now she was yawning and looking at her watch. She had been complaining earlier that the men, all of them, worked so hard and long they all came home bushed and went straight to sleep. She whined it was ruining her sex life.

An hour later, Dona eavesdropped hearing Lissa say she was playing a last hand and then was going to bed. As soon as Dona heard they were on the last play, she got up and without a word discreetly left the room.

She hurried to Jace and Lissa's room. Back on the boat Jace and Lissa were again sleeping in the same room but separate beds.

The door was unlocked. Dona slipped in and closed it behind her. She tiptoed over to the bed and peered down.

Jace was sound asleep; one arm flung outside the sheets and hung over the side of the bed. He wore boxers but his chest was bare.

Tiptoeing to where he'd laid his clothes, she picked them up and tossed them in the closet then stripped off her own clothes and dropped them beside the bed.

Very slowly with as little movement as possible, Dona slid naked into the bed. She carefully pushed the sheets down off both her and Jace exposing their bare torsos and listened for sounds at the door.

269

When she saw the door open and Lissa step inside, Dona sat up and squealed.

"What the?" Lissa flipped on the light switch. Her mouth dropped wide open.

Dona, naked as a jailbird was sitting in Jace's bed, her big naked breasts glistening in the light. Her hair tousled, she had a hand to her mouth like she was in shock at getting caught in bed with Jace.

Hearing the commotion, Jace moved to sit up. Squinting at Lissa in the doorway, he asked slightly befuddled at being woken from a sound sleep, "What's going on, honey?"

Then he realized nude Dona was beside him in the bed looking smug. His baffled gaze went from her to Lissa's shocked white face. "What the hell is going on?"

Lissa made a strangled sound then turned and fled.

"Lissa! Wait!" Jace yelled. Next to him, Dona giggled.

He turned to her and it clicked what she'd done. "You fucking did that deliberately, what the hell- why?" Not waiting for her response, he rolled to the side of the bed to get out, Dona reached and grabbed him with both hands.

"No, stay with me Jacey, let the whore con go back to jail or wherever she came from. You know you want me, you want this, me." Grinning slyly she cupped her huge breasts and pushed them against Jace's bare chest.

Jace shook her off with a curse and stumbled out of bed. Glancing around, he barked, "Where the fuck are my clothes?"

Ignoring Dona's giggles and calls for him to come back to her, he ran to his dresser. Yanking out jeans and a shirt, he pulled the jeans on then stepped into his boots. Grabbing his cell, he dragged the shirt on as he ran out the door.

Running down the hall he saw one of the other men they worked with at the site. "Did you see Lissa?" Jace asked in a hurry.

The man said, "Yeah, she just left."

"You mean the boat? She left the boat?" His hair stood on end.

"Yeah. She looked kinda upset. Ran right down the gangway pretty quickly. Probably shouldn't," the guy said, "a woman alone, it's dark. I don't think-"

Jace raced past him pulling out his cell. Clicking it, when Ker answered. Jace said, "Go to my room, right now. Give Dona money for a taxi, hotel room and a plane ticket and see that she is gone today. She snuck in my bed when I was asleep and waited until Lissa showed up- Lissa freaked and ran off the damned boat."

He took a breath then said, "Just get that bitch the hell off the ship and out of here." Shoving the cell into his pocket, he ran down the gangplank to the parking lot and straight to the young man at the gate.

He quickly asked him, "Did you see a beautiful girl, long darkish reddish hair and green eyes go by?"

"Oh yeah." The guard grinned. "What a babe. Helluva body, nice rack."

"Which way did she go?"

"Down that first street there, Pendon Road. After that I didn't see."

"Give me the keys to your vehicle." His hand out, Jace said it with such vehemence the guy took out his keys and gave them to him, said, "Gold Impala, tan, over there." He motioned with his head.

"Thanks." Jace hurried to the car and jumped in. He drove down Pendon Road. It was a short street that spider legged into numerous others.

As he feared, there was no sign of her. He hit street after street, looping around to catch further perimeter streets.

He searched for an hour. With clouds covering the sky and few streetlights it was pitch black. The longer he looked the more his gut constricted. It was time to think instead of move. He pulled over to the side of the road and put the car in park.

Jace tried to climb inside Lissa's mind, almost chuckled at the thought. No man could read a woman's mind. "Concentrate," he told himself.

It was doubtful she would go to the police; she didn't know who to trust. She has no money for a taxi or a hotel. Where the hell could she be- an idea hit. She might have just gone back to the docks hoping to talk someone into letting her sail back on their boat. The thought struck dire panic through him.

No one was going to let her sail for free, they may say they would but no way- throwing the car in drive he sped back to the docks.

As he neared the waterfront he passed a dark narrow street more of an alley than a road that was lined with closed buildings. Just barely through the dim light shining from some windows he could see the silhouettes of people in the shadows between the buildings.

A feeling of dread pricked the back of his neck. The car wouldn't fit in the narrow corridor so he quickly parked it on the side and jogged stealthily on his toes into the dark stone lane with sprouts of weeds and grass growing through the cracked pavement.

Tall decrepit buildings bracketed the cobblestoned lane that was slick with waste. Staying behind dumpsters, he trod silently over trash strewn everywhere, never even blinked when a black cat leaped from some torn up boxes and scooted past him.

When he got close enough, his heart pounded, fury and terror ran up his spine and into his fists. Through the smelly murk he saw three men, and Lissa.

One was holding her arms behind her and had his hand over her mouth. Another man was trying to pull up her shirt, and another stood egging them on. The surrounding buildings soaked up their coarse laughter so sick and eerie in the dark.

The man to the side snarled, lewd excitement trebled up and out his throat painting his face with a gross leer. "Come on, Jed, quit playing with her and get her inside, I'm taking first turn."

They didn't look like bums to Jace. Their hair was fairly kempt, one had a neat beard, their jeans and pullovers were relatively clean.

The man with the beard called Jed was in front of Lissa. He reached out and tried to grab her blouse again and she kicked at him, her screams muffled behind a big hand. His face darkened. With a growl, he slapped her hard, her head snapped to the side. The three thought it was uproariously funny.

Jace raced up so fast they didn't see him coming. He lashed out with his boot kicking the man that was holding Lissa violently in the head, the man dropped to the ground like he'd been shot.

Jed, the bearded man that had slapped Lissa swung at her with a brutal fist sending her flying to the ground, her head slammed onto the cobblestones.

Twirling out of the kick, seeing Lissa get hit and fall, in a ferocious rampage Jace punched up at Jed's groin. When Jed doubled over, Jace bashed an upper cut to his jaw then a cross to his face. The guy dropped to the ground folding into a fetal position holding his junk and screaming that his jaw was broken.

Lifting his leg, Jace stomped his boot ruthlessly hard on the man's head smashing it on the rocks like a pumpkin. Then he turned to the third man.

Dazed, Lissa struggled to push up on her palms to sit. Her head spinning, eyes unfocused and clinging to stay conscious, she watched the fighting going on around her unable to get out of the way.

The third man threw a few punches that Jace easily dodged. As soon as Jace swung his fist and punched the man, the guy's head jerked back from the blow and he immediately turned tail and ran down the alley.

Jace watched until he was sure he was not coming back then he crouched, clutched the collar of the man he'd kicked in the head, lifted him, the man was out like a light. Jace let go and let his head clunk on the street.

A quick glance over checking the bearded guy, told him the guy's face would never look the same again and it would be quite a while before he moved again, if ever. Jace gave him a hard kick in the kidney for the punch he gave Lissa.

Then he knelt down beside her, she was leaning way back on her elbows and slowly sinking to the ground.

Jace slid his hands under her back and her knees and stood up with her. Cradling her tightly against his chest, he moved swiftly down the alley to the car.

He stepped cautiously from the alley in case the fleeing man had brought reinforcements or returned with a gun. The dingy stores and bars that lined the street were dark and empty.

Jace set Lissa on her unsteady feet keeping an arm around her and opened the car door. He helped her in then ran around and hopped in the driver's seat and tore off for the boat.

Shooting quick glances at Lissa while he navigated the way back, the pressure in Jace's shoulders released when Lissa, leaning in the corner against the door and the seat gingerly lifted her head.

She pressed the back of her hand over her eyes. Passing streetlights lit her pale face for a fleeting second then the car darkened again.

After a few moments, she wiped at her eyes then opened them slowly getting her bearings. As soon as she realized she was in a moving car with Jace at the wheel her back stiffened. Pushing her hands against the seat to sit up straighter, she crossed one arm tightly over her chest and clung to the door handle with the other.

With both hands wound tight around the wheel, seeing her dazed and confused expression, Jace said softly, "It's okay, Lissa. You left the boat, you were in a…situation and…you got…hurt. We're on the way back to the boat. Are you all right?"

She winced and set her fingertips on her forehead then closed her eyes. Her voice weak and tired, she murmured, "I don't know."

When they reached the dock, Jace parked the car and turned off the engine. Turning to face her, he set one forearm on the wheel and slid the other across the back of the seat observing her ghastly pallid complexion.

Using both hands, Lissa pushed back her wad of thick wavy hair and warily looked over at him. "I have a headache, but my vision is gettin' less blurry." His lowered brows and the line deepening between them showed his concern.

She said weakly, "I'm okay."

He waited, watching her settle until she offered him a feeble smile. Sitting in the car surrounded by the quiet night, Jace asked, "Why did you run, Lissa? You promised you wouldn't run from me."

Her eyes popped at him in surprise, then shuttered, the lids lowering halfway as she remembered. Lips pulled in, she gave him a hard glare. "Huh. You were in bed with that- that- woman. Brett was right, you are a player with the morals of a junkyard dog." She turned her head away and stared out the window blinking back tears.

Jace scrubbed his hands up and down his face, exhaling his aggravation. "Lissa, I swear to God, it so sounds like a crummy cliché, but seriously, it was not as it seemed. Dona set the whole thing in action. She waited until I was dead asleep from a long day and knew you weren't there.

"She must have snuck in the room. Someone on board had to have seen her, to know she couldn't have been in our room that long. As soon as she heard you coming she must have taken her clothes off and got in bed and pretended surprise when you came in." Jace sighed at her pained and disgusted glare at him.

At her obvious disbelief, he said cryptically, "You can ask anyone, the other girls, ask them the time they last saw Dona and you came to our room. It could only have been minutes. Dona has been all over me since she got on the boat in the beginning.

"I did not have any interest in her then and I sure as hell don't now. If I wanted her I would have married her. I married *you* for Pete's sake." His hand curled tightly around the steering wheel, he fisted the one on the back of the seat.

He hated this, he had to defend himself again, it was like sleazy Suzy all over again. This is why he stayed out of relationships, he shouldn't have to explain himself, and he sure as hell wasn't used to doing it.

Her brows nettled across her forehead. Angrily she spouted at him, "You left with her that day, the day I handcuffed you and…uh, you know, then again when you almost kicked the girls' door in."

Remembering that day, his pants instantly tightened. Recalling Lissa restraining him, rubbing her half naked tits all over his face, him sucking and licking them. Her in that tiny plaid skirt straddling his leg– he pushed aside the picture, this wasn't the time to reminisce.

He gripped the knees of his jeans, tugging them down to loosen them and scowled. "I did that because I was so mad at you, you teased the hell out of me then ran off like it was nothing. Then you wouldn't leave with me, I, uh, wanted to hurt you." His voice dipped in a stump of a sheepish tone, he admitted, "I was trying to make you jealous."

The words out, his eyes dropped slightly embarrassed before rising back up to meet her surprised, confused gaze.

He reminded her, "How soon did Dona return that night? Five minutes? Where was I first thing the next morning? I was in the galley waiting for you." He inched a hair closer to her, she stayed tucked tight in the corner.

They ever get around to making love, he was going to insist she wear that little plaid outfit, without the handcuffs, well, maybe they could use them at first...but on her this time. He had been furious and frustrated at her antics, but incredibly turned on. When his Lissa played sultry she was fucking hot.

Ignoring the heat brewing in his body, the timber of his voice still deep rose slightly. He said fiercely, "But, back to today, you can ask anyone, check the damned sheets for semen, the trash for a condom. I swear to you she set it up deliberately to run you off, and it worked."

Lissa studied his earnest expression, his fingers still white-knuckling the wheel. Shaking her head in disbelief, she asked, "Why would she do that? It makes no sense."

His mouth quirked, it was time they had this conversation. "She wants...me. She knows I want you. Even though we're married, she doesn't care, so she tried to get rid of you."

Lissa shook her head bleakly. "Dona's your type, Jace, not me. I find it hard tae believe what you're sayin'. You're tryin' tae trick me." She pulled her hair around to her front and combed it with her fingers.

His head cocked with curiosity. "My type? Please explain that to me."

Peering sideways at him, Lissa let out a breath. "Uh, yeah, all right. One day while Brett was tryin' tae talk me into goin' down tae the study again where he could lock the door and um, visit."

His face instantly turned livid, Jace barked, "What the hell? Where was I during this? When was this, how come you didn't tell me?" He threw out a hand to grasp her arm but she flinched away from him.

Her nose in the air she sniffed. "It was a while ago, weeks after he... attacked me. I don't want tae talk about it. I told him if he didn't let go of me I was going tae go complain tae you. That's when he said you wouldn't care, that you wouldn't give a plain Jane like me the time of day for very long."

"Really?" Jace said sarcasm dripping. "If you're such a plain Jane then why was *he* all over you?" She started to respond, he said, "Anyway, go on about my type, I'd love to hear this."

Jace was willing to talk about anything as long as she stayed. The longer she stayed the better the chance of her believing him about that scheming bitch Dona. Really, she had to only see that he had chased after her, was sitting here with her, not Dona.

Releasing her hair, she flipped it behind her back then twined her fingers and folded them gracefully in her lap. "Okay, fine. Brett had said that your type is," her uncomfortable gaze dropped from him to her clasped hands.

"That you only like women that are tall because you're so tall, and with meat on them so you have somethin' tae... hang onto. That I am too petite and, uh, delicate for your tastes." Seeing him roll his eyes, she hesitated.

"Go on," he grunted.

"Well, Brett told me that you prefer blondes who wear a lot of makeup like models do and are really aggressive, brazen he said. And most of their body parts are plastic, lips, breasts, doesn't matter. And I'm," she looked down at her body ruefully.

"I'm hardly tall, blonde, plastic. I donnae, uh, don't even wear makeup," her mouth twisted thoughtfully. A lopsided smile pushed her lips up dolefully. "He said you don't do relationships that you do the old one and done, that-"

Jace held up both hands palms out. "Okay, okay I get it." Dark color surged in his cheeks, his lips pulled in wryly. He didn't look so pleased with himself. At least not as much as usual. "Later we will discuss what that asshole said to you."

"It doesn't matter anymore, Jace. After you...beat him, other than that one other time he hasn't even looked in my direction. I understand afterwards, when he was healin' with Doctor Drew, that Ker, Cad and Victor went and visited him. I don't think he's a worry anymore."

She smiled uneasily. Regardless that he had attacked her, that a man had been hurt because of her was something she couldn't come to terms with, and Jace was well aware of it.

"Anyway, back to my type," he turned more to face her. "Yeah sure, it's true I go for that type, not because it's my taste but because I know they're easy. I don't have to chase them, unlike you," his grin was more of a grimace, "they come to me. I can get what I want and move on quickly without getting involved, no strings. If they want more from me I buy them a designer purse or expensive earrings or something and they go away happy."

Seeing her glum nod, he decided it was time to bear his soul, tell her the truth. Some of it, anyway. "But, Lissa, as soon as I saw you, baby, you're so goddamned rich. I don't mean financially, not that I would know since you keep everything a big dark secret."

"Jace, this isn't helpin' anythin'," she admonished sighing, tucking runaway hairs behind her ears.

"No, sorry, I'm not used to talking like this." He sucked in a deep breath. "Like I just said, I don't actually converse with the women I-" he broke off at her raised chin and her hand suddenly on the door handle.

He spoke quickly, "What I'm saying is that you're rich with sweetness and vibrancy. You're brave, funny, you make me laugh even when you don't mean to. You fit in my arms like you were made for them. You're intelligent, real, everything those other girls aren't. I even dig those crazy freckles like little sprinkles of cinnamon on your cheeks and nose."

He eyed her hand still on the door handle like she was about to flee, her face awash with skepticism.

Jace hurried on, "Even though you have that secret that is terrifying you and keeping you from being intimate with me, you are still kind and caring and sweet, with everyone, even those that treat you badly."

His eyes skimmed her expression. Her cheeks stained pink as usual whenever she was given a compliment, and the green eyes were lowered apparently in surprise at his words about her.

"Honey," he kept going, "you have energy to live life. Those other women only have interest in shopping, partying, manicures." Feeling only slightly foolish for his diatribe Jace grinned, amused that her skepticism turned to reflection of his statements.

He declared, "I *married you* for God's sake. You don't see how so out of my stratosphere that is?"

Holding up a hand to stop him, she looked at him like he had two heads. "Oh my gosh, stop it. I'm so less than those sophisticated women, so less interestin'. What are you sayin', are you drunk?"

Smiling at her consternation Jace shook his head. "I'm just telling it like it is, Lissa, getting it out there while I have the nerve. It tickled me that you were so enchanted with the stars in the night sky when there were no other lights to diminish them. You gushed over the first sunset on the open sea, none of those girls even look up when on deck. They're only there to sunbathe or be seen in their bikinis.

"If you'd take the time to notice me, you would see that I don't even look at them. They're all the same, cookie cutter. You're the real deal. You're the only one that has ever made this ol' heart go flip-flop. The only one I want to see in a bikini is you. And so far, that hasn't happened." His grin widened at the color brushing her cheeks. "But I am ever hopeful."

"Please, Jace, don't say anythin' else. Anyway, you said you had tae marry me because you needed tae…because your boss said…uh, and you said you couldn't have two women…"

At the time, his excuse almost made sense, now it sounded…lame. She eyed him with suspicion again. He'd seemed so adamant at the time…she believed his reasons why they should- needed to wed. Her perplexed gaze went from him to out the side window.

"Baby," he murmured and leaned in closer to her. He had no intentions of letting her run from him. "Since you fell into my lap, well, actually, after I did my caveman thing, capturing you and dragging you off to my lair, you've been stuck in my mind like glue.

"So hot, if we'd had sex that first day, it would have been utterly fantastic, and instead of diminishing my desire for you I think it would only have led to more mind blowing sex. Besides that you are so hot, now that I factor in you, the whole package, I think if the more I had you the more I'd want you. The other women were a means to only one specific end, and they knew that. To me, you are my entire end. Did I mention how sexy you are?"

Her face burned with mortification. She put her hands over her cheeks but she couldn't hide the color his words produced, she palmed her closed eyes.

"We should just do it, have the damned sex, it's all you're interested in. And then you can get over it and move on, and," she looked wearily at him, "let me go."

The planes of his face stiffened, jaw tightened, the blue eyes narrowed. Ignoring her comment about letting her go, he said harshly, "You aren't listening to me. I said I find you sexy as hell, and yes, I've made no secret of wanting to make love to- with you. Please recall the handcuff episode where you offered to sit on my cock, and I said no because I wanted all of you, I didn't want just a quick unemotional fuck. I wanted to make love to you."

Jace took a breath to calm down and lighten his tone, if he yelled at her she would leave.

"Jace, I wasn't going tae really-"

He shook his head. "Your intent doesn't matter right now to prove my point, mine does." Carefully, he said, "I want you, Lissa, all of you. I want to get to know you better, spend real time together." His eyes drifted to the side, a shade of guilt in his voice, he said, "I can't let you go and you know why."

Then he directed his gaze back to her and said with sincere determination, "But hear what I'm saying, Lissa, I want you. If you don't want to make love with me, I can wait until you're ready. Just," he took a breath, "spend some time with me, let's learn about each other. I want to know your favorite color, song, food, whatever, everything. I want a real relationship with you."

Jace was silent for a moment, letting his words sink in. He knew it would be an uphill battle convincing her of his sincere intent; it had been since they met.

She still hadn't told him what was going on in her life that was making her hide, it would still take time for her to trust him enough to tell him. His lips pursed, brows dropped, and that damned Dona pushed everything right back to the beginning, again.

Seeing Lissa's body language become less coiled and tight, his chest eased, he let out his held breath. Taking a chance, he touched her shoulder, she flinched but didn't move away.

"The marriage is only temporary, Jace. Why do you go through all of this? There are a million women out there you can satisfy your lust on." The green eyes were huge and luminous and sad in the dimly lit parking lot.

He had already explained all that to her, she was just going to continue to argue about it. She refused to believe he genuinely cared for her. Sliding an inch closer to her he reached for her hand, picked it up and loosely threaded their fingers together.

He twiddled her ring with his thumb, turning it back and forth. Dipping his head so they could see each other clearly, he cleared his throat and said, "Lissa, you had a pretty extreme reaction to...to me being in bed with another woman. Which I wasn't, technically, but nonetheless, that tells me you actually really do care, about me."

Her eyes closed, he inched closer. "Be honest with me, baby, be honest with yourself." His voice grew very soft, husky. He stroked her hand with his thumb, slowly bringing her hand to his face, he pressed her palm lightly against his skin.

Lissa's eyes opened, they drifted down to the seat between them. She was mute, but he could see her thinking. Lifting her hand to his lips, he kissed it gently, on top at first, then her fingers, then he trickled small kisses on her palm. She watched him, her gaze uncertain, still suspicious of his intentions.

With little imperceptible movements he pulled her closer to him. When she didn't fight him, he gently cupped her chin turning her to face him.

Her eyes were still focused down. Jace kept holding her chin forcing her to face him and moved his head closer, so close he could feel the warmth of her skin, her breath soft on his chin.

Against her mouth, he whispered, "Since I laid eyes on you, Lissa, there have been no other women. Even though you deny me, I have no interest in any other." He brushed his lips softly across hers.

"You can't refute that you want me too, I can see it in the way you look at me, Lissa. The way you responded to me that day Victor interrupted us."

Pressing his forehead against hers, he looked her in the eye. She raised her green orbs nervously, peered at him then quickly lowered them.

That she didn't pull away lit a pleasant warm feeling in the pit of his stomach. Encouraged, Jace brushed her lips again, then kissed the corner of her mouth. She turned slowly into the kiss.

Pulling back, Jace watched her, waiting for her reaction to show on her face. His body electrified seeing that he had been right. She raised limpid lids halfway so he couldn't see her eyes, but he could see a hint of the fire blazing bright green she tried to hide.

A new flush of pink sheen flooded her face and her lips parted, she looked up at him. Jace lowered his mouth, descending slowly on hers, giving her the opportunity to pull away, object, slap him even. She didn't.

She allowed him to push her mouth open with his. She let him taste her, let his tongue swirl inside her mouth, thrusting in and out until she responded, which she did, with heat.

The kiss intensified. Feeling her melt like a boneless kitten in his arms, Jace moved his hands to cradle her head. He stroked his hand around her shoulder, pulling her in tighter, sealing their lips as closely as possible for the kiss to deepen.

Lissa shuddered when he slid a hand down her back feeling each bump of her vertebrae as he stroked over it then drew her tightly against him until her breasts crushed against his chest. His groan rumbled deep in his throat as he devoured her.

She responded with suffusing passion, her hands roamed up his powerful chest over the muscled broad shoulders and into his hair. Her fingers gripping his thick locks fired him to slide his hot hands all over her back, up to her shoulders then down the sides of the curve of her waist.

With difficulty, Lissa pulled back to catch her breath, get an understanding of what they were doing, what would it mean. Trepidation dug into her passion laced husky voice she murmured shyly, "Jace, thank you for, for rescuin' me…"

"Uh huh." Feeling her withdrawing, her body stiffening, he slid his hands back up to cradle her face, holding her from moving away from him. Opening his lust saturated eyes to peer hungrily at her, he said, "I really like kissing you, Lissa, and now that you're finally letting me, I really want more."

He drew her back to him, murmuring against her lips, "Kiss me, Wife, before one of us says something to mess it up." He fused their mouths together quickly before she could speak.

Her stiffness subsided. Letting his held breath out slowly, Jace wrapped his arms around her, crushing their lips and their bodies together. Her hands stole around his neck; he slid his palms under her shirt, splaying his fingers over her warm flat belly. She didn't resist his touch, only pulled him tighter as they kissed.

He stroked his hands up her stomach, over her ribs to her breasts cupped in a silk bra. Filling his strong hands with her soft fullness, encouraged at her fiery moan, he caressed and kneaded her warm flesh, groaning at the luxuriant feel of her. She arched her back curving into his skilled hands with a tiny mew.

He slid one hand out and around her shoulders to lean her against the back of the seat so she could relax more- a cry of distress broke against his mouth.

His eyes flashed open. Still holding her, he pulled back. A shock of extreme pain slashed across her face. The creases around her scrunched eyes cut in, her lips parted as she gasped for breath.

"Shit, Lissa, honey, are you okay?" Bracing her head and neck with one hand, the other still supporting her back, Jace scanned her to perceive her distress.

"*Jace*," his name a frightened cry, she put a hand to her head wincing. Her mouth twisted, lips parted in agony, she clutched at his shirt.

"What honey? Tell me what's wrong!" His normally calm voice sparked stridently in concern and rising panic.

Lissa grabbed at her head with both hands and cried out, she lowered her head then raised it. Her eyes burst wide and scared beseeching him to help her, then she fell limp in his arms. A gash over her eye split wide running blood down her face. A bruise had formed on her cheek since they'd gotten in the car.

"*Shit.*" Pulling her into his arms, Jace said urgently, "*Lissa!*" Pushing her hair off her face, he shouted again, "Lissa!"

She didn't respond.

Carefully, Jace leaned her back against the seat. Hurrying out of the car, he pulled out his cell, pushed a button, when it was answered, he said, "Victor, find Drew, tell him to meet me in my room, *right now.*"

Slipping the cell into his pocket, he ran around, opened Lissa's door and scooped her out and up in his arms. Moving briskly, he strode past the guy at the gate tossing him his keys and carried her up the walk to the boat.

Jace brought her straight to their room and laid her down on his bed. He was taking her shoes off when the doctor bustled in.

Chapter Thirty-One

Doc Drew moved quickly to the bedside. Seeing Lissa pale as the moon lying still as death with her eyes closed, a streak of red spilling down the side of her face, he asked, his voice low and steady, "What's going on Jace?"

"She got punched, fell and hit her head."

Doc shot him a look growing in fury. "Jace," he growled tightly.

"Come on Drew, it wasn't me." Affronted, Jace ran his hands through his hair again and again. "I don't know what's wrong. She, uh, she got punched like I said then she fell. She seemed all right in the car. I drove back and we were," he trailed off, didn't want to blab their business, "um, talking, when she suddenly cried out in pain, grabbed her head then passed out."

He kept raking his fingers like daggers through his hair, until realizing what he was doing and shoved them in his pockets. Hovering like a shadow, he leaned over the other side of the bed as Drew examined Lissa. The mattress sagged slightly under the weight of his palm.

Sitting on the edge of the bed, Doc glanced in annoyance at him and ordered, "Get back, Jace, give her some space." He set his bag down on the bed, opened it, took out a stethoscope, a blood pressure monitor and a small flashlight.

He gently pressed open each of her eyes and shined the light in. Then he checked her blood pressure then used the stethoscope.

Shoving them all back in the medical bag, he shifted his hands under her head feeling for lumps. He rolled her head lightly back and forth then gently laid her back down.

He frowned again at Jace. "I can hear you breathing like a bear, you're making me nervous, can you chill a bit? Go take a walk, I'll let you know when I'm done."

Jace stood motionless staring at his friend. Bristling, he stalked to a chair and flopped down. "I'm not leaving," he said redundantly.

Doc shrugged one shoulder then turned back to his patient. He ran his hands up and down her arms then legs, then checked her back.

Jace crossed an ankle over his knee, elbows on the chair arms he clasped his hands together and set his mouth on his knuckles. He didn't move or say anything again.

Nimbly feeling around the cut on her head, Doc took out a box of bandages and antibiotic ointment, and patched up the cut.

Jace stood up impatiently and came back to the bed. He looked down at Lissa; she looked so fragile and pale. Not big to begin with her slender frame had lost weight since he'd brought her on board.

He needed to do something about that. He shoved back a wad of blond hair off his forehead then stuffed his hands back in his pockets. "Well?" he asked Doc.

Doc stood up, pulled the covers over Lissa. "I think she has a slight concussion. She should be all right." He looked long and hard at his friend.

"What are you doing, Jace, keeping her here against her will? She's had nothing but trouble. The unscrupulous men on this boat are constantly trying to get in her pants, including you I might add. My God, you forced her to marry you for fuck's sake, who does that? And now you say she's been beaten?"

Jace wilted somewhat under his accusing glare. Drew went on, "I've never seen a woman get more abused, dammit. She's thin as a bone. According to you, she implied that she's in trouble and wants to stay hidden. What's going on? Why won't you let her go?"

His face hardened, jaw clenched, Jace crossed his arms. "Why she is here is my concern, Drew. Not yours. Just tell me what to do for her."

Doc's lids lowered, he watched Jace for a minute. Jace was standing stoically, his worried eyes on the girl.

Letting out a sigh, Doc said, "All right, whatever. Just let her rest, I'll be back in the morning. If she does anything, well, odd, like moans or gets sick, has deep confusion, unsteadiness on her feet or stops breathing, call me, immediately." He turned to leave.

Jace walked with him to the door. "Drew, I'm trying to protect her, I just can't seem to protect her from herself." Opening it, he asked very quietly, "This concussion, will she remember, everything... that happened tonight?"

Contemplating the question, Drew's shoulders drew up slowly then down. He said, "I think so. It doesn't seem to be a serious injury. Why?" He eyed Jace suspiciously. "You do something you don't want her to remember?"

Jace's lip quirked up. "Actually, the opposite. Thanks Drew." Seeing the doctor out, he locked the door, trod back to the bed and pulled the covers back off Lissa. Lifting her slightly, he took off her jeans but left everything else on.

Holding the covers to put back over her, his attention dropped to the wisp of panties she was wearing. Feeling his body tighten, he probably should have left her jeans on.

Quickly pulling the covers over her, he turned off the lights, took off his shirt, changed from his jeans to shorts and climbed in beside her.

Gently he pulled her against him and dropped his arm protectively over her.

Hours later, a drop of morning sunlight filtered through the window, light edged the bottom of the curtains. Feeling her stir next to him, Jace levered up on a forearm and watched her.

Her eyes fluttered for a second then slit slightly. Seeing him staring at her inches away, her eyes opened completely and she struggled to sit up, to get away from him.

"Wait, Lissa, hold on." He rolled towards her and put his hand on her shoulder pressing her back against the pillow.

"Jace, what are you doin' then? Let me go this minute." Suddenly a thought crossed her face, she looked down at her clothes. Her face whitened.

At her obviously disturbed expression, his irritated sigh filled with chagrin. "Don't worry, Lissa, nothing happened." He hesitated, his words stumbled, "At least nothing sexual. Uh, I mean not really sexual."

Furiously she turned to him, rattling off her words like angry bullets, "What are you sayin'? Why am I in your bed? Who took off my clothes?"

"All right, calm down, honey. You fled from the boat last night. You got injured, I brought you back. Doc came and checked you out. He said you have a slight concussion. I took off your jeans," he held up a hand when she opened her mouth.

"Only your shoes and your jeans so that you would be comfortable. Look," he pulled back the blanket. "See, I have my shorts on." Shirtless, he still held her shoulder pressed on the mattress. "Doc said you need to take it easy, move slowly."

Feeling the heat of his bare chest inches from her, Lissa's eyes narrowed at him. She asked calmly with slight sarcasm, "Did he say I couldn't sit up?"

Thoughts rumbled around inside his head, it would have been nice if Drew had said for her to lie flat on her back...*that was a mistake to think about*, he scolded himself, picturing her lying down and him over her. He gazed at her for a moment, then released her, and only slightly rolled away.

Without him holding her down now, she tried to sit up. Her hand flew to her head. Wincing, she felt the butterfly bandage on her forehead. "What-"

"Okay, wait Lissa, take it slow for crying out loud, let me help you." Jace pushed a pillow against the headboard then slid his arm around behind her back and helped to her sit up.

Seeing her eyeballs twitching as she tried to focus on anything in the room, except him of course, he waited for her to get her bearings. It looked to him like her head was spinning.

Her eyelids flipped rapidly open and closed. She pressed at her eyes with the tips of her fingers then finally looked at him, at his mouth.

Jace saw the sudden bright color flood her face. He said quietly, "You remember."

Her lips pressing in a tight thin line, her gaze dropped to her hands. She raised them and covered her mouth.

Jace pushed her hands away, cupped the side of her head turning it to face him. He said gently, "Do not deny, to yourself, or me, what happened in the car last night. It was real, it's written all over your face. Do not even think about claiming you don't remember."

His voice firmed staking home his assertion, "And that you were a fully willing participant." He watched her gaze lower to his lips again, she turned redder. He nodded in triumph. "Yeah, you remember. We kissed and you liked it. A lot."

Angry, embarrassed, she yanked her jaw out of his grasp. Turning her head away, her brows slashed down between the confused eyes. She lowered them so he couldn't see into them. "Please let go of me. I'd like tae get up, I'm hungry."

"Lissa, we need to talk about-"

Her lids shuttered to hide her feelings. She said flatly, "No, we don't. I've told you, I don't want to have sex with anyone. "

Growing annoyed that they were sliding back to square one again, still holding her so she wouldn't get up and run away from him, he reminded her, "Come on, why are you acting this way? You wanted those kisses as much as I did. What's so wrong about it? Dammit, Lissa, we're husband and wife, there is nothing wrong with us making out."

She pierced him with a cold, direct stare. "I made it clear when you forced me tae marry you that I had no intentions of havin' sex with you. You agreed tae my terms. Besides, what makes you think I didn't give in tae, uh, *to* thank you for savin' me?"

Taken aback, he frowned unconvinced of her words. "Are you saying you only kissed me as gratitude?" He scowled as he considered her words.

Getting a little angry, he said, "A simple verbal thank you would have sufficed, Lissa." He watched her as she very carefully did not look in his direction. Sounding a little sulky, he said, "I never asked you to offer yourself as a…a reward. I would never accept," he looked at her, the pink kept flooding her face.

His pique slid into a thin smile. "Oh no, you're not getting off on that, honey. You liked it, you wanted it. I can tell when a woman is kissing me with passion and when it's remote, robotic.

"You, my sweet," he grasped her chin to face him, said cheerfully, "you kissed me for real. Accept it. We need to finish what we started yesterday and that day when Victor interrupted us. Think about it for once instead of shutting down."

She refused to look at him, closed her lids and sat silently.

He waited a second. Then sighing heavily, he released her and got out of the bed then went around to her side. He grasped her shoulders helping her off the bed to stand up.

Inches away, she was staring nervously at his bare chest.

Seeing her consternation, and remembering the feeling last night of her hands stroking his chest and passionately pulling his hair and moaning with desire, his tone soft he murmured, "Even with cuts and bruises, your hair a tousled mess, you're still striking, baby."

Catching her chin, he kissed her before she could object. A deep, long, hard kiss. He forced her lips apart with his mouth, groaning at the sweet petal softness. Thrusting his tongue in, he slid it across her teeth, then prodded, coaxing her tongue to meet his. The second he felt her respond he pulled away.

291

She blinked rapidly in confusion, trying to catch her breath. More shiny color flushed her cheeks. Her lips plumped and the green eyes torched with heat.

His own eyes reflected intense fire. His erection visibly straining at his shorts, he let her go carefully, said tonelessly, "Go clean up and get back into bed, I'll get you some breakfast," and pivoted away to put on some clean clothes.

She waited for a few hesitant beats, then went into the bathroom.

Chapter Thirty-Two

Warrington's assistant called Jace and advised the police said it was okay that they could return to the same complex they were originally at.

Jace brought Lissa back to her room where she slept for most of the day and the next.

Doc came in, checked her out and declared that except for her mild headache she was fine. Jace paced behind Drew until he packed up his med bag and left.

Jace sat on the bed beside her and took her hand. He asked her gently, "How are you feeling, honey?"

She smiled softly at him. He had been waiting on her hand and foot like she had when he had been shot. Doc Drew had told her that Dona had been kicked off the boat and sent home.

"I'm fine, Jace, you don't need tae hover. You work hard all day, you rushed home today at lunchtime tae take care of me, you're goin' tae wear yourself out."

"I'm pretty tough. Here," he had picked up some spaghetti and meatballs from the galley and she had been eating it before Doc came in to check on her. Now, Jace was trying to stuff her with more of the meatballs.

"Take another bite," he was determined to get that frail look of hers plumped up.

"No Jace," she shook her head, "I've had enough."

"Just one more bite of meatball and I'll back off." He smiled, swooping the fork right at her mouth making her laugh when she opened it to accept the food.

Seeing she couldn't be talked into another bite, Jace set the plate to the side. He drew his fingers through her hair combing it, then let it fluff off her shoulders. "Lissa," he said as she lay back against her pillows propped up against the headboard.

"Hmmm?" She smiled at him.

"There's a party tomorrow night. Warrington is throwing it. Do you want to go? Do you feel well enough to go?"

Her face settled with a serious expression.

"What?" Jace asked. "What's wrong?"

"Um," her lips softened. He always was so concerned about her wellbeing, how could she not trust him? "We, well, we will be meetin' people we don't know, as…well, being married…"

His brow furrowed. "So? Is there something wrong with that?" He picked up her hand and held it, pushing her ring around her finger with his thumb.

Her eyes dropped to his fidgeting, then back up to his earnest expression. "I…don't you think we're not bein'…uh, honest?"

He frowned still pushing at her ring. Sighing deeply, Jace said with a trace of frustration, "We are legally married, Lissa, doesn't matter how or why, we are legally married. We are not faking anything. Maybe if we have sex you will see it as being more real." His frown moved to a grin at his suggestion.

She couldn't help but smile back at him. "Okay." She said swiftly at his leer, "I mean okay tae the party."

Jace stood up with a big smile. "Great. I need to go meet with the guys, I'll see you in a few, all right?" He bent and pressed his mouth against hers. Urging her lips apart, he kissed her hungry and hard until they were both panting.

Obviously pleased with her response going by his broad smile, separating their mouths, he stood up and headed to the door. "You might want to think about the sex too," he proposed. Grinning at her flushed cheeks, he left.

Friday evening, almost everyone from the boat was going to the party.

Jace drove his rented truck with Lissa belted in on the passenger side of the bench seat staring pensively out the side window. He had treated her with kid gloves since her concussion and didn't push himself on her. He knew that last kiss had rocked her and decided to let it fester.

An absolute gentleman, he was aloof, almost impersonal around her. He surreptitiously saw her watching him, perplexed at his coolness. He thought she looked like she couldn't figure out why he had kissed her so passionately, had given her that impassioned speech in the car, then suddenly was barely speaking to her, and not touching her. Hardly.

They entered an affluent section of the city. The further into the city, the bigger the houses were. Finally reaching the street that he'd put into the GPS, Jace drove the truck up the winding driveway that led to a mansion perched on a slight hill of neatly trimmed grass.

Some of the guests had parked down along the street. Jace had been told there was a large parking area down the side of the hill from the mansion, but Warrington had advised him to go ahead and park right up in front. So he settled the truck alongside a dozen or more vehicles in the driveway.

Shutting off the engine, he climbed out and went around to get Lissa. Opening her door, he could tell right away she was nervous. She sat rigidly clutching her hands together in her lap, staring unblinking straight out the window.

Saying, "Come on, baby, there's nothing to be afraid of," he touched her arm very lightly. She dropped her head to look at his hand.

He gently insisted, "What's the matter, honey. Talk to me." Jace waited.

Then she turned a tremulous smile to him and said, "Nothin', nothin' at all. I'm fine."

Patting her arm, he smiled back at her then helped her out. Watching her swing those beautiful gams out of the truck, Jace set her hand on his shoulder to brace herself as she climbed down from the high running-board.

Closing the door and locking it, Jace slid his admiring gaze down her figure and back up. "You look amazing, my gorgeous wife, totally amazing."

She was wearing a short white skirt and a shimmery pink ribbon of a top with a draped décolletage. The blouse was form fitting but the draping loose. Loose and low enough to show off a good bit of her soft rounded cleavage.

On her feet were strappy, high-heeled sandals. He was dying to climb down the valley between her breasts, stick his face against her warm-

"Ahem. Eyes up here," Lissa scolded him with a giggle.

Grinning at her, he held out his arm for her to take. He was thinking it would be a good idea to keep her by his side this night. She looked way too good to be let loose amongst the wolves. Who knew Glennie's little sister had such sexy outfits?

Slipping her hand in the crook of his arm, Lissa smiled shyly, "Thank you for the compliment."

He patted her hand, teased, "Thank you- what?"

Knowing he was teasing her, her smile up at him widened. She replied, "Thank you, *Husband*."

"That's my girl." Jace grinned broadly moving them up the long walk to the big double front doors.

Made of huge stones, the mansion had three levels with five chimneys and windows shuttered in white. The endless green yard was studded with maples and oaks. Fat red robins jumped around the yard looking for worms scattering butterflies like fluttering flecks of confetti.

"You look really nice too, Jace." Her approving smile took in the brown jacket and tan shirt. His shoulders so broad filled out the jacket nicely, the black slacks hung sexy on his lean hips.

His voice warm and full, he whispered, "You keep looking at me like that baby, and we're getting back in that truck and going home."

"Hush, Jace, be good," she giggled, hugging his arm.

Jace's grin expressed he was pretty pleased at the moment. His beautiful wife was on his arm on the way to a party, and she was being touchable and flirty. Life was good.

The doors were propped open; a woman in a black server uniform greeted them.

"How do you do. Welcome." She smiled politely. "Please come in. Follow the tile," she gestured to the gold flecked white marble floor. "Down the hall you'll come to the great room. Guests are there as well as outside at the back by the pool. Enjoy yourselves." Nodding to them, she turned to greet more guests coming behind them.

"House big enough for you?" Jace quipped, leading Lissa down the cavernous hall. They could hear music and conversation before they reached the room.

It was a huge, wide-open, opulent space. Plush furniture lined the room, cream and pale blush colored walls were warm and rich.

Most of the people were standing and mingling. Several were sitting on the low slate bench on the sides of the immense stone fireplace that anchored one wall.

Jace looked around, nodded at a few of the people he recognized. "Come on," he took her to the bar. "I'll have a Heineken, the lady will have a coke," he said to the bartender.

"Jace, I want a real drink."

He looked down at her. "Um, I don't think that's a good idea with your recent head injury."

She pouted so damned prettily he couldn't say no. "Fine, just one." He told the bartender to get her a rum and coke, make it light on the rum. The bartender brought their drinks, Jace handed the rum and coke to her.

"Drink it slow, okay?" He chugged some of his beer.

"Yes, Daddy," she replied sarcastically.

"You don't have to be fresh, Lissa, I'm just looking out for you, you know. Glennie told me you girls drank that one night I left you there, and that you stumbled and almost fell, that it didn't take much liquor to knock you out."

Her lips pursed in a frown, remembering the bad headache she'd woken up with the next morning after a glass and a half of wine. "Isn't Glennie the little blabbermouth. I can handle it." She took a sip of the rum and coke and her nose wrinkled in distaste.

Jace burst out laughing. "Just as I thought. You're not used to hard liquor. So," he cocked his head at her, "take it slow."

She stuck her tongue out at him and took a big swallow, and was stunned at the burn that scoured her throat. Her mouth gaped opened, eyes watered. Coughing, she glared at the drink in her hand with Jace's laughter in her ears.

"Let's mingle, come on." Jace brought her over to three of the men he was working with on the site.

After greetings and introductions, the men drifted into work conversation. Jace set an arm around Lissa's waist holding her right against him.

Their conversation drifted pleasantly around Lissa although she wasn't involved in it. She was actually content to stay like that all evening. But it was a party and they were expected to circulate and socialize.

They moved around speaking with other people here and there. All the men Jace introduced Lissa to, didn't hide their admiration of her looks. Jace kept his hand on her waist, squeezing it occasionally to remind her who she was with, sometimes caressing her side with his thumb or stroking her back.

They were hanging with a group of men and women. As before, Lissa was content to let the conversation flow around her without getting involved in it unless she was directly spoken to.

Several people held plates with finger food and their drinks. One man gestured while talking with a plump shrimp between his fingers.

A woman appearing to be in her mid-forties with short curly hair and tired brown eyes, came over to the group. She tried to get one of men's attention.

"David," she tapped his arm. The burly redneck ignored her, he was in the middle of a story of how he fell off a ladder and landed arms first into a hot barrel of tar when he was roofing.

Wolfing down a pigs-in-a-blanket, he was in the middle of describing the agony when his wife was trying to interrupt him.

"David, I need help with the-" he brushed her off again continuing with his tale. Wearing summer white capris and a blue peasant blouse, the woman's face compressed in perturbation at his ignoring her.

"May I help?" Lissa offered.

The woman turned from her husband to Lissa. The wrinkles around her eyes softened, "Sure, I would really appreciate that. I need some really easy help in the kitchen, would you mind?"

Lissa smiled at the frumpy woman. "Of course not, I'd love to help." She tried to tug away from Jace but he held her tighter. She tugged harder, frowning.

He glanced at her then back to David who was still telling his gory story.

Lissa stood on her toes and said quietly in Jace's ear, "I'm goin' tae help in the kitchen, I'll be right back." She tried to pull away but he still held her.

"No, I think you should stay with me," Jace replied quietly, firmly.

"Oh, you newlyweds, can't let each other out of each other's sight!" One of the other men chortled. "Go on, Jace, let the little woman go. She'll be in the kitchen, she can't get in any trouble there."

The other men teased, "Come on husband, let the little wifey go."

The tips of Jace's ears turned red. Still frowning, he looked down at Lissa. Her smile up at him was all capable and confident. Between being in an unfamiliar place, having to beat off men like Brett Rawley, and Lissa's propensity for running off, Jace was not comfortable letting her out of his sight.

But she looked so eager to please and help out. Against his gut feeling, he released her. Before she left, knowing she wouldn't make a fuss in front of other people, he slid his big hand around the back of her head and gave her a long kiss.

When he let her go, her face was red, but she didn't look unhappy.

Feeling Jace's eyes on her back, more likely her butt, Lissa followed the woman down a hall to a commercial kitchen.

A big open space with two islands, two commercial ovens side-by-side and a giant fridge. Everything was stainless steel except all of the small appliances were blue.

The islands were covered with mostly empty food containers. There were caterers hired to work the party, none were currently in the kitchen, they had removed and set up the food already and were now around the house and outside on the patio serving.

The woman bustled in. Pausing with a cheery grin, she turned quickly and said, "I'm Gail. I can't tell you how much I appreciate this. Foster, you know Mr. Warrington, his temporary receptionist, Suzy was supposed to help me because we're using new caterers and so far they have not been up to par.

But Suzy has disappeared. She is probably off with someone's husband in one of the bedrooms or closets or bathroom, whatever." Her shrug and twisted lips revealed her feelings about the young woman.

"Anyway," Gail hurried over to one of the islands, then spun quickly. "I'm sorry dear, what's your name?"

Smiling brightly, Lissa told her, "My name is Lissa, nice tae meet you. What can I do tae help?"

Gail scurried to the long counter next to the first oven and picked up a peach cheesecake with brandied fruit on it and a propane gas torch. "I need to take this outside and flambé it and cut it up. I have a baked Alaska in the oven. It's almost done. I just need for you to keep an eye on it, that's all I need. Can you do that?"

"Of course. You go do what you need tae and I will guard the Alaska," Lissa said with a competent smile and right away walked over to the oven to check on her charge.

"You are a dear. Thank you so much. Don't worry about anyone coming in and annoying you, I've pretty much been the only one in here after the caterers took off with the food." Holding the cheesecake and the torch, she rushed out the back door to where people were mingling on the patio surrounding the big turquoise pool.

In less than five minutes the Alaska looked done. The peaks all around the white were nicely browned.

Lissa turned the oven off. She thought she should hang around and wait until Gail returned. Maneuvering around a white-tiled island with two sinks and a set of burners, she stood near the glass doors to view the outside scene.

The shimmering pool lit from the bottom, was a bright blue basin soft and wavering in the dark evening. Aquamarine pavers encircled the figure-eight pool. People holding drinks were scattered all over the glossy pavers as well as the vast green lawn.

Chapter Thirty-Three

*G*uests mingled and wandered, carrying a plate or drink, some sat at round tables covered with white cloths. Music blared from speakers in the trees strung with colored paper lanterns.

Even from inside, Lissa could hear people talking loudly over the music, the occasional spurt of raucous laughter breaking through.

Lissa was wondering if maybe she and Jace could take a stroll around the beautiful pool. She pulled a tall stool with a blue padded cushion over near the window and was about to sit on it when a man in his forties, GQ from head to toe in a perfectly tailored Armani suit entered the kitchen.

Not sure what to do, she asked, "Can I help you with somethin', sir?" She thought he was overdressed for the party. People weren't in shorts but they weren't in cocktail dresses either, more like chic-casual.

His skill of assessing a woman was so highly incised, without appearing to, the man could discern a woman's entire being even if she was dressed in a sack, in one pulse of his pupils. The wide avid smile indicated he liked what he saw.

"Hello, dear, now whom do we have here?" Grey touched his temples but the rest of the finely coifed hair was brown. "I am Foster Warrington, the host of this party."

Lissa returned his smile but something about him chilled her, gave her the willies.

The brown eyes lanced through her like a dissecting scalpel. His sharp but handsome, aquiline features made her think of one of those evil cartoon characters in a suit, rubbing his hands together with a sly avarice smile while he planned your demise, your dreadful tortured demise. She shook her head with a tinkle of a laugh at her silly fantasy.

Holding out a hand, Lissa said genially, "How do you do? I'm Lissa..." oh this certainly felt strange. "Lissa Nico. Jace Nico is my...husband." Aware the word husband rolled stunted out of her mouth, it was all weird. Weird but not entirely unpleasant.

Her lips curled up softly. For once she felt there was someone really on her side, and it was a husband. Husband. The smile drifted away when she remembered it was a totally temporary situation and one done out of necessity. And, not the first.

Casting away her random thoughts, she said, "You just hired my...husband. I believe he is one of your new staff."

"Yes of course, my new lead manager." Quite tall with an average build, his cultured voice, perfect pitch, perfect tone, not too high, not too low, perfectly modulated, sounded created, developed, not natural.

He was suddenly right next to her when she hadn't even noticed him moving. Lissa automatically took a step back to maintain her personal space, but she hadn't been aware she had been only inches from the wall.

"Um, so, Mr. Warrin-ton is it? I must check on the baked Alaska for Mrs., um, Gail, you know the-"

"Yes, of course I know Gail. However, I don't know you, and I'd like to remedy that." The full veneered smile drew his ears up and sharpened his features even more.

Lissa stepped back again but this time she was flush against the wall. Warrington set a hand beside her head on the wallpaper penning her near the corner wall. It reminded her of when Jace had done the same thing. But Jace didn't give her a creepy feeling.

"Mr. Warrinton," she stiffened.

"Foster, please call me Foster. I must say dear, you are an absolute heavenly delight." His bottom lip pulled in, he sucked on it. "I thought Nico was either gay, or he had to have something extraordinary going on at home to push off Suzy Grant. That girl is so wanton, Nico's the only man I've seen turn her down that she's gone after. He practically peeled her off him like she was the shed skin of a snake sliming on him. First guy I've ever seen wave his wedding ring at a woman to try to run them off."

He studied her, leering. "Now I can see why he did. You are definitely extraordinary. So young and fresh, with an innocent sweetness. 100% class, you've got it going on sweetheart."

Not moving his head, the brown eyes slid down her figure, heavy lids lowered cloaking his thoughts. "You are a true beauty, dazzling eyes, sweet-cream skin." He stuck his finger in a roll of her hair, twirled the finger around, like he was imitating a sex act.

Murmuring, "Seriously radiant hair," his eyes dropped down to the swells rounding over the draped material. "And girl, those are the prettiest tits I've ever had the pleasure of viewing. I bet Nico wears them out, eh?"

The cream skin blanched then her cheeks reddened. Lissa pulled her hair from his finger. Trying to bury her anger and sound blasé, steadying her voice, Lissa said firmly, "Uh, I need tae go, Jace will be wonderin' what's takin' me so long."

His hand still like a bumper keeping her from leaving, he set his other hand on her waist. His fingers stroked her side wickedly.

"Mr. Warrinton, please, get your hand off of me, I have tae go." Lissa shoved his hand off her waist and tried to pass by his arm but he lowered it blocking her way.

The sharpness of Warrington's face whittled even sharper like knife blades, his displeasure clear. "Let me tell you, Mrs. Nico, my employees make a lot of money. Sometimes they can earn a little extra, maybe a lot extra. Like most women, you must want your husband to buy you pretty things. Maybe a bigger house, maybe he'd like a nicer car."

Lissa glanced around the room to locate her best avenue of escape. Flustered, her accent thickened, "I donnae understand what yer sayin' then."

His arm moved closer to her body blocking her now like an iron gate. The friendliness in his voice withered to erotic annoyance. "But, I'm sure you do, sweetheart."

Seeing her face darken, her chin pulling up in defiance, he said quickly, "Listen, you're shy, I see that. We'll start slow. Just let me get a little feel. Trust me, what Nico doesn't know won't hurt him, or you. He'll never know and you all will get a nice pocket of change." He dipped his finger in the draping of her blouse.

"No!" Lissa hit his hand away from her.

Seeing she was about to charge at him, his voice narrowed darkly, he said ominously, "Listen to me sweetheart, I can give money, and I can fire. I can fire your husband just like that," he snapped his long piano fingers. "It's a wife's duty to help her husband climb the corporate ladder."

Lissa raised her forearm and clenched her fist as if preparing to barrage through him. She said impudently, "I think my husband would rather live dirt poor than have me be with another man. He tends tae be very possessive of things he believes are his. Now, I am leavin'."

Warrington propped his hand back on her waist holding her from fleeing. "Sweetheart, believe me, he'll get over it when he sees the green. Come on, Nico won't mind me having a little feel of those damned luscious tits." Pushing her back against the wall he slid his hand under her blouse.

"I'll scream," Lissa cried. Punching him in the chest, she kicked him in the shins. He howled under his breath but kept moving his hand up her blouse.

"Darling! There you are," Jace strolled in all smiles. Warrington spun away from Lissa. She hurried to Jace; he put his hand around her shoulder drawing her in close.

Lacing his arm around her neck, Jace pulled her head to him and kissed her on the lips, which she did not back away from. Through the screen of her hair, Jace could see pressing against the perfectly tailored slacks, Warrington's hard-on for his wife.

"Honey," he dropped his arm to her shoulders, "there are some people I want you to meet."

Her breathy, "Okay," rushed out.

"Warrington," Jace nodded at his boss as he ushered his wife to the kitchen door.

Composing himself, Warrington's skin had paled when he had seen Jace come in. Clearing his throat, he ran his finger under his collar to slacken the tie a bit. He called out, "Mrs. Nico," and waited until they both stopped, turned and gave him their attention.

"There's a party for the ladies next weekend. It's, uh, for ladies only, my um, wife, Lindy is, uh, putting it on for the wives of the foremen. I would...um, I mean she, would love for you to come." The color was returning to his complexion.

Warrington didn't indicate which day, but Jace said, "Gee, that is so nice of Mrs. Warrington, but unfortunately we have another obligation on that day that is quite unbreakable. But I'm sure your assistant, Suzy, would love to come in Lissa's place. I promised some people that I would introduce my bride so, we'll see you around." He led Lissa out the door.

Down the hall, Jace muttered under his breath, "You know that was going to be a party just for the two of you, that there wouldn't be any other women there, including his wife?"

Her bewildered eyes flashed at him. "I don't under- oh."

As they reentered the main room, Jace took Lissa's hand. He squeezed it so hard she cried out.

"Jace you're hurtin' me."

Still holding her hand but more lightly, he moved them near a wall away from the bulk of the people and coiled her into his arms.

"Baby," he said beneath his breath. "I heard that motherfucker. I can't do anything about him now, and I can't explain right now, but I will tell you why at some point. Then, I will tear that fucker limb from limb when this is done. In the meantime, you are never going to be in his sick presence again."

Pressing her head to his shoulder, he put his lips in her hair, tasting her soft natural perfume. "And, I am getting you a weapon. Pepper spray or electric shock or something. This whole thing is getting ridiculous. These men are just wild dogs around you."

Holding her upper arms, he held her out so he could look at her. "You want to go, baby, leave this party or do you want to stay? We'll do whatever makes you happy."

Lissa tipped her head back to look up at him. A string of tiredness clinging to her words, she said, "I think I've had enough party, I'd like tae go home."

"Okay. We'll leave. I swear," he growled, "I've never seen this kind of shit behavior in my life. Maybe I never noticed because I just didn't care about the other women I, uh...you know." He didn't say the rest of it, that he didn't care about the women he slept with. If someone hit on them, he would shrug it off. They just weren't important enough to him to protest or give a shit about.

Her hands were on his shoulders, fingers faintly clenching and unclenching his muscles. It felt wonderfully incredible to Jace. He saw her eyes focusing on his mouth. His gaze dropped from her eyes to her lips. Jace wanted badly to kiss her.

But the image of Warrington's hands on her hit him like ice water. He said with an incensed sigh, "I just can't have you helpless, defenseless. I am so sorry I've put you in this wretched position."

Lissa murmured, "Then let me go." Watching his jaw grow hard, his skin tighten, she said, "You forget, it's not just other men pawin' me, you know."

"Uh huh. But I'm the only man that is your husband." Jace set his hands on her waist, he had no intentions of moving, not when she was holding onto him with her own free will, she just wasn't aware of it.

His brain was streaming between murderous rage against Warrington, with frustration that at least for now he couldn't go beat him out of existence, and the thrill of hearing Lissa's words about him when she had been talking to Warrington.

Jace struggled to keep the grin off his face. She called him her husband, and she obviously was not any kind of a gold-digger turning down Warrington's offer of money for sex.

He could still hear her sweet voice referring to him as her husband, or hoosband with her sexy little accent. *Damn.* Even now, as her words about him pawing her niggled, he told himself he knows she cares for him. There's just something that has its fear talons hooked in her and she was not going to give herself to Jace as long as it did.

Jace had discussed this with his team. They were all of the same mind to help him find out what frightened her so badly that she had taken on a new identity to hide herself.

For now, her fingers were unconsciously stroking across his shoulders and down his arms. His hands were still on her waist, he set his forehead against hers and looked at her.

She was making no attempts to move away from him. He lifted his head, his eyes dropped and warmed. She actually looked like she was waiting to be kissed. Her head was tilted up, her lids had lowered, lips parted.

This was his opportunity to get her more comfortable with him. Become more comfortable being in his arms, touching him, letting him touch her. A chance to…he moved his hands up to cup her face, lowered his head to kiss her-

"Hey, Jace, dude, what's going on?" Tyrell McClan clapped Jace on the back.

Trying to hide his irritation at the man's bad timing, Jace smiled weakly, said, "Hey, Ty." He slipped his arm around Lissa's shoulders again. "Honey, this is Tyrell, he works with me. Ty, my wife, Lissa." Jace beamed when he said the word *wife.*

"Mrs. Nico, Lissa, a real pleasure to meet you." Ty grinned at Jace. "I can see why you keep her hidden away from the other men."

Jace just ducked his head and squeezed Lissa's shoulders. She actually leaned into him.

"Anyway," Ty said, "I came to bother you because they need to move some big tables on the patio to make room for dancing. You know, the drunker they're getting the more wanton and crazy they behave. The caterers are all crying bad backs, can you come and give a hand?" Ty talked to Jace but his eyes were all over Lissa. She modestly kept hers down and shuttered.

"Uh, we were just leaving," Jace started. Ty glanced at him with the expectation that Jace wouldn't say no.

He sighed, "Okay, all right." They were still in the main room near a wall by a curving staircase that flowed to a second floor. Sighing deeply, he said to Lissa, "I will be right back. Do not go anywhere, don't move from this spot, okay?"

"Okay." She smiled rolling her eyes at his fear that something would happen to her if she was out of his sight. She had pushed the time with the smarmy Warrington out of her mind.

Bending, Jace kissed her on the lips then followed Tyrell out of the room to go through the house and out the back.

Feeling awkward, Lissa tried to discreetly melt into the woodwork hoping no one would notice her and that Jace would be back quickly and they could leave. She glanced around, maybe there was a chair she could sit down out of the main thoroughfare on and wait for him.

No such luck. Before she could move, a pudgy young woman with red hair cautiously approached Lissa with an odd look on her face.

"Hey," she greeted, squinting strangely at Lissa. Then she shook her head, and still eyeing Lissa puzzlingly, she said, "I have to tell you, it's so weird. I know this guy, Doug. He showed me a picture of his wife, and it is so bizarre but you are the spitting image of her. You look so much like her you could be twins. It's not like you have a common look either, those green eyes alone are unusual. And that hair," her sigh slid out covetous.

Every drop of color drained from Lissa's face. She froze, couldn't talk, couldn't move.

Oblivious to Lissa look of horror, the woman rattled on, "Let me see, her name was," a finger on her chubby chin, her eyes rolled to the ceiling as she worked through her memory. Lips covered in freckles pulled in. Her eyes fell hazy to Lissa, then they cleared.

Nodding emphatically, she said, "Yes, yes, I remember, Keira. It was Keira." Her gaze focused pinpointed at Lissa. She whipped out her phone and took Lissa's picture so fast before Lissa could react.

"No! Stop, please don't," Lissa protested, but the woman slid the phone into her purse.

Gleefully, the redhead crowed, "Doug just will not believe how much you resemble his wife. Did I mention he said she's been missing? He's been frantically searching for her." She squinted hard at Lissa, nodding vigorously. "Oh yes, you have that same unusual colored hair, burnished like it's been highly polished with a hint of rose in it, and those insane crystal-like green eyes, huge and haunting he called them." She chuckled.

"I thought he was just being poetically dramatic! Anyway," she glanced up and down Lissa's figure. "You're the same height, slender build with full, uh, anyway, I have to call him right now!"

She twirled and was gone in a shot, Lissa couldn't even holler after her, she had disappeared into the crowd.

Lissa murmured frantically, "Oh my God, oh my God, oh my God," and she ran for the door.

Chapter Thirty-Four

Done helping with the tables, Jace hurried back to get Lissa and take her home. He stood in the entrance to the big room and glanced all around. As tall as he was he could easily see everyone in the room. And Lissa was not there.

Maybe the bathroom. He dashed from room to room, but no Lissa to be found. He had been out by the pool moving the tables so he knew she wasn't there. *What the hell*, fear spiraled up his spine, did she run? *No, goddammit,* not when they were making headway.

Racing outside, he darted around the big yard looking for her. Maybe she was waiting for him by the truck. His heart pounding, shoes tapped down the driveway like a drum beating faster and faster.

Then he saw her. He almost cried in relief.

She was sitting on the ground huddled by one of the tires of his truck with her knees pulled up, her arms wrapped around them and her face down on her knees.

She looked up at his approach, made a sound like her breath caught and tried to make herself a smaller object.

Jace realized to her he was only a dark figure as the sun had set. Seeing her fear, he forced himself to slow his pace as he made his way to her.

He spoke softly, "Lissa, it's Jace." When he got near to her, he crouched down, bracketing her with his long legs, unconsciously penning her in as well as shielding her. She seemed to calm a little when she saw it was Jace.

"What is it, baby, was someone mean to you? Did someone say something to hurt you?" He knelt leaning back on his heels, his face sharpened and turned hard. He said ruthlessly, "Tell me, I'll take care of them." He didn't touch her, not sure if it would make her more distressed.

When she just stared at him wide-eyed, he grew angry. "Honey, was it," his skin darkened, "that bastard? Did that son-of-a-bitch Warrington go after you again? Tell me, if he did. I'll fucking kill him. Screw the mission, I'll-"

"No," she uttered bleakly, shock starred all over her white face. "Please, can I please get in the truck?"

Looking at her distraught face, Jace could tell she wasn't hurt or angry, she was afraid, make that petrified. "Yes, of course."

Standing up, he caught her arm and helped her up then unlocked the truck, opened the door and helped her up the high step. He asked gently, "Do you feel safer in here?"

Curling up in a ball, she wrapped her arms around her knees and nodded silently. Eyes radiating intense emotion were fixed on her knees.

"Do you want to go home?"

Nod.

"Okay, let me go tell someone we're leaving so they don't look for us." Closing then locking the door, Jace hurried into the house.

He came back out in a few moments. Chucking off his jacket, he climbed in the truck, tossed the jacket in the back, stuck the key in and fired it up.

He tugged the black slacks up, his legs so long his knees hugged the steering wheel, and half turned towards her. One arm on the wheel, his heart bled at the little dark ball on the far side of the bench seat quivering in the corner, the big green eyes glowing in the dark, so afraid they were shaking.

"Can we go, Jace, please." The tense anxiousness in her trembling voice sounded like she thought something, or someone was coming after her.

Putting the truck in gear, Jace said, "C'mere, baby." Reaching across the seat he wound his fingers around her arm. She hesitated then scooted over and leaned against him.

Heading down the driveway, before turning onto the street, Jace reached over her with one hand and belted her in the middle seat belt then settled his arm around her and drove straight home.

Shooting her quick glimpses along the way, he could feel Lissa visibly relaxing inch by inch as they drove into the complex.

Jace parked the truck, turned off the engine but didn't get out. She unbuckled her seatbelt and moved slightly away from him.

Swiveling in the seat to face her, he asked gently, "Lissa, do you feel safe here at the complex?"

Staring out the side window, she nodded weakly, mumbled, "A little safe." Her blank gaze rooted, unseeing at the window. She said tonelessly, "But you need tae let me go, you and your friends will be in danger bein' near me."

He said firmly, "Lissa," that was not happening.

Wordless, she shook her head adamantly back and forth. Not trusting herself to look at him, she struggled to clear the quaking from her voice. "No. I swear, you all will be in terrible danger if I stay." Emphasizing each word, she stated, "You *have* tae let me go tae save your lives."

Taking the keys out of the ignition, Jace exited the truck, went around and opened her door. Lissa slowly turned to him, her face was as pale as the full moon up in the night sky. She swung her legs out, the short skirt riding high up her thighs.

He grasped her around the waist and lifted her out of the truck setting her down gently on the blacktop.

Jace could literally see her legs trembling. Threading his arm around her he walked her inside.

The place was mostly empty everyone was at the party. Turning on the lights he brought her to the couch. He sat down but she stood as if frozen in fear, her hands clenched tightly together. Gingerly, he took her wrist and gently pulled her down next to him. They sat in silence.

Jace scrubbed his hands up and down his face, although he'd shaved before the party, already whiskers made a scratching sound. He rolled up the long tan sleeves to his elbows. The muscles in his forearms flexed with his movements. Running his fingers through his hair he turned to face her and draped an arm over the back of the couch.

In a voice unarguable yet quietly gentle, he said, "Lissa, honey, you have to tell me what you're afraid of, you have to let me help you." He watched her blink back tears, her teeth nibbled at her lower lip trying to keep it steady.

"Baby, it's time. We are not moving from this couch until you tell me." Reaching out he took her upper arms, pulled her over and cradled her against his chest.

Murmuring against her hair, he said, "I can't let you go for several reasons. Therefore, if you genuinely fear for me and my team's safety you must tell me what terrifies you so, why you think you and we being near to do you can be in such danger. Only by my knowing the breadth and depth of the threat can I protect us. You *must* tell me, for all our welfare."

Sobs bubbled up inside fighting to get out. Lissa fought to suppress them, but to no avail, they climbed up her throat and poured out of her mouth. Heaving and hitching she wept, her tears soaking his shirt.

Smoothing her hair back with his strong fingers, he patted her back, whispering nonsense words of comfort. His arms flowed around her, pressing her into the safety of his embrace. "Baby, even if...if you committed murder, I will help you. It doesn't matter, you will tell me, now."

Unwinding from his arms and without warning, Lissa climbed on Jace's lap, straddling him with her knees bent on the couch cushion. His mouth dropped open in surprise.

She pressed her mouth over his, kissing him tentatively at first, then her lips lavished urgent desire, conforming her feminine softness to his full masculine mouth.

He raised his hands to hold the sides of her head. Pushing her lips further apart, he thrust his tongue in. Surprisingly she matched his moves and their mouths exploded with hungry fervor.

Lips fused together, she started to unbutton his shirt. If he wasn't so hard already and his blood racing and burning through his body he would have shouted for joy, she finally wanted him.

When she had four buttons undone, something pricked at the back of his brain. *Why does she suddenly want me, and how far is she planning on going?* As intensely as he desired her, Jace fought it.

Letting go of her head, his fingers furled around her wrists stopping her, and he drew his head back. Her eyes were wide open and utterly blank.

What the hell- "Lissa, what is going on?"

Not saying a word, she tried to wriggle her wrists out of his grip and press her lips back on his. It was everything he had wanted, but the blank look in her eyes troubled him. Still holding her hands he kept his face out of her reach.

"Lissa," he growled. Then with firm gentleness, he commanded, "Stop. Tell me what is going on."

Her gaze unsteady, unsure, dropped down. Gathering herself with effort but without meeting his eyes, she said, "I want you, Jace. I'm comin' tae you like you keep askin'."

She yanked her hands free then resumed unbuttoning his shirt. Jace moaned, dying to feel her hands on his bare chest, but he grabbed her wrists again, curled her fingers and wrapped them in his hands holding them still on her thighs.

A glint of wetness blurred the green glass of her now disoriented eyes. Still straddling him, she leaned back, her gaze unfocused. "No? I don't understand, Jace, you don't want me anymore?"

Tightly holding her hands, as much to stop her as to control himself, his Adam's apple bobbed hard, Jace swallowed his insane ardor for her. But it was difficult with his throat so constricted with need.

315

Struggling to get a grip on his body and fevered brain, the cells sparking and firing all over him were fighting his internal censor.

His body screamed *who cares why, just take what's offered*, his brain screamed back, *no, something's wrong*- His dark sideburns damp with sweat, Jace's gaze hot but steady at her, he declared, "Oh, baby, there's no question I want you more than the air to breathe."

He couldn't take his frying eyes off her wet lips all swollen and pink begging for him to kiss them. Blinking rapidly, he tore his vision from her lips and brought it back to her confused, rejected expression.

Her hands still in his, he said, "But, Lissa, I want you to want me with a totally clear head, not confused, not...not thanking me for protecting you, or...any kind of payment for taking care of you."

Her cheeks rounded red with anger and...guilt. Lissa insisted, "That's ridiculous, you're sayin' that I'm showin' my gratitude for your protection by payin' you with sex?" Flabbergasted she sunk away from him. Her voice less sure, she still said firmly, "No, I want you." But she still did not look directly at him.

"No," he sighed like he had the weight of the world on his chest, "you don't. Not right now anyway, I can see it in your eyes. You say it but there's something else going on."

He squeezed her hands. "Believe me, this is the last thing I want, or ever thought I could do, push you away." Watching conflicting emotions war across her face, he figured she didn't even know what she was feeling or wanting right now. Then he realized that this play of hers right now was her way of distracting him from his question.

Jace knew if she kept sitting on his lap it wouldn't matter how much his brain told him it was wrong, he would be powerless to not push her down on her back and take her.

Releasing her, with his strong hands around her waist, he started to lift her up and set her down next to him, but her shocked and unhappy face slowed his movements. She looked so fragile and sad, his heart clenched like a fist.

Stammering, her words wobbled, "But Jace, I said I..." she reached out and set a tense hand under his shirt on his bare chest.

The heat of her hand on his pulsing chest spread like scorching spikes on a wheel in all directions.

Struggling to cool his turbulent breath, he said, "No," and moved slightly away from her so he couldn't smell the sweet fragrance of her vibrant hair. Feeling her palm burning on his chest he picked it up and set it in her lap. He only had so much control; he had an erection that could hammer nails.

The timber of his voice deep and serious and regretful, he said, "You've been on a rollercoaster since I...abducted you. I've...made relentless passes at you, you've had to fight me off and a bunch of other horndog assholes as well.

"I took you and have been holding you prisoner. I forced you into marriage, and besides being scared to death of me, you're frightened out of your mind about something that you won't freaking tell me. I'm sorry Lissa, I have been such a hurtful pig to you."

His fingers dabbed at the loose hair twirling around her face. "I want you, Lissa, badly. But I want us to be us, for...a long time, and I don't want you to do something you may regret and then hate me for it."

He tucked the tendril behind her ear. "Any other time I would not hesitate, we'd already be naked," he grinned gently. "But I need you to really want me. For me. For no other reason."

Her voice tight and small, she whispered, "You pointed a gun at my face, dragged me out of my car, carried me onto your boat. Then said you were goin' tae...tae force me that first night that you took me. Because of your...threats, and holdin' me against my will, God, Jace you tried tae- tae spank me for heaven's sake. You're right, I have been frightened of you."

Still on his lap straddling him, she dropped her hands and moved back slightly. "Honestly Jace, I'm still scared tae death of you."

Shameful heat rushed up his neck, his head hung. "I'm...sorry." He wiped the perspiration off his forehead with the back of his hand.

His eyes turned up to her. "I was wrong to do those things to you. When I caught you that night, Lissa, I, uh, well, men are designed to chase and catch, conquer, and savor the prize." His lids lowered, remembering that day, a small smile turned up one corner of his mouth.

His deep blue eyes glimmered at her. "Baby, I was so taken by how hot you were, and the courageous way you took the wallet and the wild chase. When I carried you off to the ship, my head was cloudy with the chase and capture, and your beauty and brazen boldness, I," he wiped his head, the hair around his face darkened from his perspiring.

"My body was bursting with adrenalin and- yeah, I was wildly crazy with lust, I admit it. I told myself that you were, oh, adventurous and you would be into it, having sex with me right then and there."

Taking a few deep fortifying breaths, he let them out slowly. "Anyway, I wasn't thinking about it from your point of view. As a female being abducted, ripped off the streets, tossed on a boat, taken to another country for heaven's sake, and held against your will and threatened with rape."

His lips twisted in a shameful crooked line. "If anyone had done that to my sister, or mother, or whatever, they wouldn't have survived the night."

When he saw her slight nod that he had for once really put himself, in his mind, in her position. Picturing the night, the chase, taking her at gunpoint to an unknown destination. Forcing her onto his bed and trying to take her clothes off, her not knowing if she was going to be raped and let go, or possibly killed. His face flamed with guilt and shame.

He'd been thinking like a total self-centered ass, a Neanderthal's mentality, *duh, me want, me take.* He raked his fingers down his face, the sound of sandpaper when he scratched over the stubble. He thought about the times he touched her against her will, *God*, what a dog. He hated himself right about now.

She still said not a word, just framed those big green eyes on him, her hands clasped in her lap.

"Uh, so, you know by now, Lissa, that I would never have forced you. If I was going to, I sure would have done it that night and every day since. Anyway, that night, when I realized you weren't going to be willing, I did threaten you with sexual assault, to purposely frighten you," a shameful flush ran up his neck.

"I, uh, wanted to scare you so you would do whatever I told you to without question."

His hands dropped to the couch, he pressed them on the cushions on either side of his legs. "I swear on my life, Lissa, I truly regret frightening you, especially using the threat of rape to subdue you. As much as I wanted you the second I laid eyes on you, it is also true I took you so you wouldn't endanger our mission and also to protect you." At least that's what he told his team.

Her lips curved into a rueful smile. She said, "Well, your plan was great, it worked, you scared the life out of me." She drew her knees up and wrapped her arms around them.

Smiling slightly, he said wryly, "It didn't work, you have never done what I've told you."

Lissa chuckled. Then her brow furrowed. She said seriously, "The thing is, Jace, I realized tonight," she squirmed closer to him, dropped her knees, folding them on either side of his thighs. "That I am not really afraid of you anymore. You've never hurt me, never raised a hand tae me. You didn't even spank me that night when you were so angry."

Her lip curled up cheekily. "And no, you never, well, you have taken liberties." She smiled at the guilty look that brightened his chiseled cheeks.

"However, I do feel safe with you. Safe in your truck, in this complex, but that's because they're an extension of you, and I feel safe with you." She put her hands on either side of his head and brought their lips together into a meltingly mind burning, body torching kiss.

Savoring it for as long as he could, Jace pulled back again. His fingers brushing her lips to take away the sting of rejection.

"We're stopping this now, Lissa." He slipped his hands under her butt and stood up, her legs automatically wrapped around his hips. He turned, set her down on the couch then moved away from her.

"When your emotions aren't skyrocketing and you're not being grateful, not trying to distract me, and you want me, only me, for no reason other than you just want me, then we'll…be together."

He knew he'd made the right decision when he saw relief flood the turmoil on her face. She slumped back wearily against the couch and closed her eyes.

"I think it's time we go to bed." He chuckled at her sudden look up at him. "I mean, you know, time to go to sleep. Come along, baby, while I still have myself under control."

He took her to her room, kissed her lightly at the door, told her to lock it and went to his room to look forward to a long cold, lonely night.

Her explanations of her trouble will wait for yet another day.

Chapter Thirty-Five

*J*ace had run back into the party not to tell anyone they were leaving but to find out who or what had spooked Lissa.

Fortunately, the first person he spoke with knew the woman Lissa had been talking to. The person noticed because Lissa was so pretty, yet so sad looking that she drew attention. The guest had told him that after the woman suddenly took her picture, Lissa had looked terrified and then ran right out of the house.

The woman's name was Jayne Madison. Jace asked swift, direct questions about who she was, what she looked like and then searched quickly but couldn't find the woman. Not wanting to leave Lissa alone a moment longer, he had run back out to take her home.

After denying both of their ardor that night, Jace surprisingly slept fairly well. He got up early the next day, Saturday, and after calling a few people at the job site, he was able to track the woman down.

He called Jayne Madison and asked if he could speak with her.

After her agreeing to meeting with him, Jace took off for the city to find her. It was an easy direct drive. Seeing the building where she had told him she worked, Stokes Publishing, he pulled up and parked in front of it.

A bell tinkled when he opened the door. By the time he was a few steps inside, a chunky young woman with unnatural looking red hair appeared from a back door and approached him with a friendly smile.

"Are you Jayne?" he asked.

"Yes, you must be Jace. I remember you at the party. You were with that pretty girl, the one with the shiny hair, and the..." she paused as she reflected. "The haunting green eyes." She rested a plump arm on the counter, her gaze raked Jace from head to toe.

Her approval was apparent in the way her little pug nose wrinkled with her freckled smile. Standing up a little straighter, sticking her chest out, she coyly fluffed one side of her shoulder length curly red hair.

"So," Jayne said sidling closer to Jace, batting her lashes at him. "You with that spooky girl or..." she set a few fingertips on his arm, "are you free to...see someone?"

Jace took a step back from her. "Yeah, I mean no, I am with her. I called you to ask if I could meet with you. I wanted to ask you, actually," he cleared his throat, "about her."

Disappointed but not undaunted, Jayne moved right up close to him again. Tucking her flowered blouse into the black skirt, the short woman peered up at Jace. "Are you two exclusive?" She clawed at him daintily with long manicured fingernails painted in bright blue.

Jace blinked. "What?" Then realized what she meant, he frowned. "Yes. She's my wife." He'd never get tired of saying that. Leaning away from her grasping fingers, he said casually, "Listen, you were talking with her. Someone said she was upset at something you said."

He watched her face. Her dark brown brows not matching the red hair drew down over berry brown eyes as she frowned. She looked about to deny this, then her expression cleared. Her cheeks rounded when she smiled.

"Oh yes, I remember. It was so uncanny. She is the spitting image, I mean identical to a friend of mine's wife. So unusual because both women are unbelievably stunning, their beauty not at all common. The weird thing about it, is that she's missing."

"Who is missing?"

322

"Doug's wife. Oh, he is so in love with her, you can tell. His eyes just light up when he mentions her name." Her face fell sadly. "But, he says she disappeared about two years ago and he has been searching for her since."

She wiped a teary eye. "He says he fears foul play, but he said he will never, ever give up looking for her." She sighed, "Isn't that so romantic? Just like Heathcliff in the-"

"Yeah. So, what's this guy Doug's last name?" When her brows knit in suspicion, he said quickly, "It's just that I think I know him too. You and I might have him as a friend in common."

He let his voice simper, making his stomach turn, "Wouldn't that be just, uh, fabulous?" He struck her with the Jace Nico full wattage smile that brought every woman to her knees, except of course, Lissa Mallory. Correction, Lissa Nico.

Shoving aside that thought, he let Jayne shift her chubby breasts so they pressed against his arm. How he managed not to gag he did not know. His gaze bounced around guiltily. With his luck Lissa would come strolling in right at that minute and confirm all of her previous accusations of him being a player. But this was important.

Her heavy breasts stroking his brawny arm, Jayne wound her own flabby arms tangling them around his. She cooed, "Oh, d'ya think so? I'll have to ask Dougie next time I see him, that would be so cool."

"Uh, yeah, Miss, uh…"

"Jayne," she inserted slightly miffed he already forgot her name.

"Uh, yeah, Jayne. So let me make sure this is the same Doug. It's Doug Galloway right?"

Frowning her disappointment, she said, "Oh, no, his name is Doug Calero. Darn, I-"

"Darn, I was so sure we were all friends. Can you spell that for me? Maybe I know his wife, what was her name again?"

"Oh, it was a lovely name, Keira, Keira Calero of course. C-a-l-e-r-o. Do you know her?"

Shaking his head glumly, he reflected her disappointment. "Um, no. I'm sorry. Gee, I had so hoped that we, you know, that you and I could, you know."

She stood up on tiptoes, still clutching his arm, her lips pursed to his. "Yes? We could…" she prompted him.

"Oh, wow, would you look at the time! I am so freakin' late, my boss is gonna have a fit. Gee, I'm sorry, I gotta go. Maybe I can come back tomorrow. What do you say…sorry, I have to go!" dislodging her flabby arm he rushed out the door.

"Okay honey, see you tomorrow then! I'll be here!" she called out after him.

His mind racing a mile a minute, Jace tried to sort the information out in his head as he drove back to the base. Lissa was scared to death of something, or someone she refused to tell him.

She even intimated that Jace and his friends could be in danger by being near her.

Jayne was so astounded at Lissa's resemblance to some man's missing wife that she took her picture to show to the man. Lissa freaked out and ran terrified from the party.

When Victor ran her background, Lissa didn't come into existence until approximately two years ago. The man's wife had disappeared around two years ago. When Jace told her they were getting married, Lissa said she wouldn't be forced into a false marriage again, her words were actually *like last time*.

Even Lissa's panicked attempt to jump ship knowing she couldn't swim, chancing drowning not to go to Scotland, added into the story.

He muttered out loud in consternation, "It's too crazy, too farfetched, there's no way in hell there is a connection, no damned way…" He caught his disconcerted expression in the rear view mirror, his dark brows drawn down hard, eyes flitting back and forth, jaw clenched.

The words *there's no such thing as coincidences* crossed his mind. He shook his head, *dope*, he's watched too many crime shows. He drove as fast as he could keeping an eye peeled for some ticket happy cop.

Chapter Thirty-Six

*T*he next morning, Sunday, Jace pulled on khakis and a dark blue long sleeved shirt. He left the room rolling up his sleeves while trotting down the hall to the kitchen. "Hey Benny," he greeted the cook who was busy melting butter in a big skillet.

"Jace, what's up?" The always jovial Benny smiled, cherubic cheeks red and shiny from the warm kitchen.

"I need a small favor."

"Of course, Jace, anything for you. What can I help you with?"

After speaking with Benny, Jace waited patiently for Lissa to rise and shower.

He was waiting in her room when she came out of the bathroom with wet ringlets tumbling down her back, dressed in a skirt, sandals, and a cap-sleeved blouse. She'd lost so much weight her arms already very slender were now almost frail appearing.

Combing her hair and humming, obviously thinking she was alone, Lissa jumped when she saw him sitting in a chair. A corner of her mouth pulled up, she should be used to it by now, he made himself at home whenever he wanted to see her, never gave her notice, just was there.

Setting the comb on a dresser, she said, "Jace."

He stood up, smiling. "Your hair is all wet ringlets, you look like one of those fairytale princesses."

She rolled her eyes but still smiled.

He took a step towards her. "Baby, I have a little surprise, can you come with me for a minute?"

She looked suspiciously at him. He was all blue-eyed innocence with a pleasant smile. "Uh, okay. I thought we were goin' tae church?"

"Um, yeah..." he said vaguely. Taking her hand, they went down the stairs, through the house and out the back door.

The sky was clear blue, the sun warm but not too hot, he brought her to the back patio where Benny had put coffee and orange juice on a table set for breakfast for two.

Lissa smiled, there were fresh flowers in a small vase in the center of the table. Looking up at him, she said, "This is nice, is it for us?"

He pulled out a wrought iron chair with cushions on it out for her to sit. Helping her take her seat he pulled another chair right next to her.

"What-" Lissa was cut off at Benny's cheerful arrival.

"Well good morning, kids." He swooped in wearing his traditional white pants and apron, big happy smile on his pudgy face. Carrying a tray laden with omelets, croissants, fruit and sausages, Benny held the tray in one hand and set the food down with the other.

He added jam, butter, milk and sugar then stood back grinning at the couple. It wasn't often he saw the pair sitting together with smiles on their faces. Usually there was some drama going on. "So," he looked from one to the other, "anything else I can get you?"

"Salsa?" Jace asked, his eyes on Lissa. Sharing his soft gaze, Lissa nodded. She had gotten him hooked on salsa on his eggs and now he couldn't imagine them without the spicy condiment.

Benny left and returned in seconds with the salsa setting it on the table with a flourish. Crossing his arms over his thick chest, he hovered helpfully, grinning from one to the other.

Jace slowly pulled his eyes from Lissa and said to Benny, "Thanks, Ben, we're fine. Leave us okay? Until I call for you?"

Benny's eyes narrowed at him. "Uh, I-"

"Goodbye Benny," Jace said firmly He watched the cook twaddle off before he turned back to Lissa. Smiling, he said, "Eat up, baby, you need to put some meat on those bones. Doc Drew has voiced his concerns often at your wraithlike figure."

She giggled, slightly embarrassed, slightly annoyed. She admitted she was slim to begin with, and the ordeals she encountered since being taken had stalled her appetite. But it was no one's concern but hers. Her face firmed as her eyes dropped.

"Lissa," Jace reached over and placed his hand over hers. "I only care about you and your well-being, you have to know that by now."

He lifted her hand and kissed her fingers before gently setting her hand back on the table then moved to pick up his coffee. Sipping the hot brew slowly, he regarded her over the rim of the cup. "Eat up, baby, for me. Please."

He looked so endearing in his coaxing. Blond hair combed back neatly, the dark sideburns trimmed, strong jaw freshly shaven. Dressed in khakis and a dark blue shirt that matched his eyes, with the devil in the mischievous grin alluring, she picked up her fork.

Cutting into a sausage she hesitated, "But what about church? We really don't have time to eat."

Sprinkling salt on his eggs, Jace said, "I just wanted to have a little us alone time." He slid a sideways look at her. "Is that okay?"

Lissa bit her tongue so she wouldn't comment on his salting, smiled. "Sure. We can go next week. Maybe some of the others would like tae go with us."

"Uh huh," he muttered noncommittedly. When it concerned him and Lissa, he preferred the less the merrier.

They chatted about Jace's experiences so far on the construction site. He told her mostly stories about the other men.

Benny had left a coffee carafe on the table, Jace refilled their cups while they ate and talked. Every time Lissa set her fork down he pushed her plate closer to her until she forced down another bite.

327

Half her breakfast consumed, she dropped her napkin on her plate so he would let up. With a relenting smile, Jace gave a short whistle and Benny came right out. "You can clear it up, thanks, Benny."

"It was delicious, Benny, thank you so much," Lissa complimented warmly to the big man.

"Aw, honey, anytime for you." He shot Jace a haughty look. "Him," he shrugged, "not so much." Benny and Lissa shared a laugh at Jace's expense.

"Yeah, whatever," Jace grumbled good-naturedly. He knew he had Benny's loyalty and love, even though Benny had confronted Jace several times on his treatment and captivity of Lissa. His head down, Jace peered up at the cook.

His tone turned serious, he said, "All right, Ben, we're done. Can you give us some privacy when you're done clearing?"

With respectful affection, although Benny's expression stayed cheerful, a slim seriousness firmed his lips. Jace had discussed this morning what he wanted done today.

"Sure Jace." He took everything off the table except for the flowers, the carafe and their coffee cups. Nodding with his ever present cheery grin he toddled off into the house.

Jace knew Lissa was aware of his intense speculative stare at her as his humor dissipated and was replaced by a hint of gravity.

She set her cup down, said, "What, Jace?"

His lips puffed out, then he compressed them. Reaching over, he grasped the seat of her chair and pulled her closer to face him with his knees bracketing along the outsides of her legs. His sober intensity made her lean back, drop her hands in her lap.

Jace's mouth opened, then he closed it in a tight smile. Then, "Honey, Lissa, this is it. We're talking, and we're not leaving until everything is out."

She blinked in brief confusion at him, then lowered her gaze to the table.

Clearing his throat, his voice gruff, he went on, "You," he took a breath, cleared his throat again to soften the gruffness. "You distracted me the night of the party. I had full intentions of not leaving that couch until you'd told me everything." He squinted at her.

"Not until later did I realize that your little attempted seduction of me had ulterior motives." He sat back. "I thought at the time that you were frightened, and your emotions were stacked high. That the mix of adrenalin from fear emotions, and feeling safe in my arms had made your, uh, body confused. You know, heightened your sexual-"

"Jace, really, stop," she blurted. As usual, pink blossomed across her cheeks.

A corner of his mouth pulled in. "Yeah. It's that embarrassed reaction. That's why I know it was your way of distracting me from answering my questions. The sad thing is, I know you would have put a halt before things got interesting. Because you still weren't ready."

He leaned forward, watching her face stiffen. Folding his hands together he rested his rocky forearms on his knees, and observed her eyes flit all around searching for an escape. The embarrassed blush had turned to panic.

Realizing he was upping her fear factor by pushing himself close to her, he leaned back against his chair to give her space. Her deep breath of relief at his lessened proximity made his brows twitch.

Annoyed, he said gruffly again, "Anyway, this is it. We are not, and I mean it, you can strip naked and throw yourself under me," now his face heated and hardened. "But we are not leaving here until you tell me everything." He jabbed a finger on the table in emphasis, repeating, "Everything."

She gripped the ends of the chair arms, obviously about to get up and leave. "Really Jace," she said nonchalantly. "I don't know what you're talking about."

"Who are Doug and Keira Calero?"

Her body turned as rigid as a statue. She didn't move, her mouth fell open, the pale skin of her face instantly drained of color. The green eyes so wide and afraid they made Jace ache.

She jerked and stood up, her whole body was already quaking. Shoving her chin in the air, she made to stomp off. "Really, I have no idea what you're-"

"Sit down. Please." Jace's hands were still twined lying on his lap. Legs apart, still bracing hers, he looked calm, but the harshness of his voice and the vein hammering away at his temple belied the calm.

He didn't move, but by the tone in his voice and the look in his eyes, she knew he would set her down if she didn't do it. She dropped back down in her chair.

Her hands gripping the chair arms like she needed the support, she perched on the edge of her seat with her head turned towards the side. She still looked about to flee.

Working to soften his tone, Jace said carefully, "Honey, I already have a good idea. You must know with my resources we were investigating you." He watched the emotions flicker across her white face; she kept her face turned from him.

"Tell me." He rolled some iron into his voice, forcing her to turn and face him. "Tell me, *Keira* why you are hiding from your...husband...Doug Calero."

His gut crunched when he said husband. His eyes never left her, watching the fierce thoughts and feelings, fear and dread and alarm, strike and strain her face.

Squirming back in her chair, Lissa settled against it and deliberately set her hands calmly in her lap. "Let's make a deal, Jace, *Husband*," she saw his face flinch, but she had his attention. "You tell me why you and your team are really here, and I..." her glance drifted to the side then pulled back to stare directly at him,

"I will tell you...everythin'...the truth of who I am, and why..." she couldn't finish, her throat closed up. She gulped hard, blinked rapidly to hold back the threatening tears.

It broke his heart to see her so distressed. Jace sighed deeply, but he had to know. He couldn't help her if he didn't know what was going on. He studied her, gauging her honesty, then shook his head.

Her secret, which if truth be told, she had every right to keep, she had no obligation to tell him anything. She was the victim here. Nonetheless, he wanted to make sure she wouldn't back out like she had before.

He was done with half a marriage. The only way to move them forward as a couple was to learn her secret so he could eliminate it. "I will tell you about our...mission, do you swear, Lissa, promise to tell me everything?"

Pulling her hair around to cover her shoulders like a protective shawl, her lip curled sadly, she nodded. "Yes, Jace. I do."

Her saying 'I do' reminded Jace of their wedding. His brows turned tensely inward, mouth tugged tight in angst. He hadn't thought about it before. It hit him hard- could their marriage not be legal?

Stifling a shudder, he said, "But first, I need to know," taking another deep breath he watched her face, pleaded with his eyes. "Are you still legally married to this guy?" His heart gripped like a fist waiting for her answer.

A tiny bleak smile lifted the plush lips. "No, Jace. The only good thing out of any of it is that, no, I was able to...get it annulled because," her mouth shut. Incredible pain lanced through her eyes, pulling the edges down, digging fearful grooves in her forehead.

She saw Jace let out his held breath, relief eased into his eyes. He released his clenched teeth before the compassion he felt for whatever had its hold on her radiated from the dark blue eyes. He waited but she said nothing else.

He let out his held breath. "All right. Fine. Me first." For something to break the tension, he picked up the coffee carafe and freshened their coffee.

He took a sip and set the cup down. "I...my team, Ker, Victor, Cad, Julio, Donnie, and I, we are actually FBI stealth agents." He saw her eyebrows jump in shock and bewilderment, but she didn't say anything.

"This may sound complicated, but I'll give you the gist of what brought us here to Scotland. You've heard of the Gamo-Merch chains?"

331

She nodded. They were a giant corporation.

"Okay. The states of Ohio and Illinois gave Gamo-Merch over 50 million dollars in corporate income tax credits of the past 15 years in a deal that they would create 1,000 jobs and pay for first class remodeling of shops and offices.

"Ohio also paid out hundreds of thousands in other tax incentives and other incidentals. Gamo is a pharmacy chain with several sister retail conglomerates. They are a massive organization"

Jace draped an arm over the back of his chair and crossed his legs. Lissa sat without moving, she followed Jace's words with interest, trying to understand what he was describing.

"So, the problem is, Foster Warrington mocked up some phony, complicated statistics and showed them to the owners of Gamo. He told them if they merge with Sigils Inc. in Scotland, they could lower their tax bill by around half. It's called an inversion, a tax-skirting tactic."

He saw Benny peeking out at them through the window. In a second Benny scurried out with a plate of store-bought small pastries. He set them down and quickly disappeared again.

Taking a pastry, Jace continued. "So, what happens is, companies merge with foreign rivals in countries with lower tax rates and then reincorporate in the other country while getting the benefits of doing most of their business in the U.S."

Jace's voice had turned official and emotionless. "Dynshire is a tax haven. Gamo is one of the biggest pharmaceutical chains in the States. It has other pharmaceutical chains in different titles as well as various retail chains all over the states, its headquarters is in Ohio.

"If it leaves the United States to build its factories and headquarters in Dynshire, Scotland, which it already has, America stands to lose maybe billions of dollars." He popped the pastry whole into his mouth and licked his fingers.

Lissa nodded that she was listening, but confused. "So your team is, um, I don't understand what your job is?"

Downing his coffee, Jace pushed his cup away and sat back. Stretching his long legs, he crossed his arms. Lips puckered, he considered another pastry, decided to wait. "The FBI became involved when a GM, General Manager, high up on the ladder of Gamo in the States, and an accountant were murdered in Illinois."

He talked over her shocked look, "Then in Dynshire, a site manager was murdered. We were brought in to solve the murders, bring the perpetrators to justice. Along the way we uncovered the fraud, the fake stats."

A line deepened between Lissa's brows as she struggled to keep up with his story. Then, her lashes flapped, her gaze a hard line at him, she asked, "This manager," she watched him.

He was working too hard to look casual, mumbled, "Hmm?"

"You were hired to replace him. You are...what is it...undercover?"

Uncrossing his legs, Jace tucked them under the table and poured himself another cup of coffee. "My entire team is."

He spoke quickly as she digested this information, "Anyway, we believe that Warrington falsified his financial statistics to draw in Gamo Corporations and Company, and it worked. We got ourselves hired by Warrington to build the factories and the stores. That was our in to get close to the players, especially of course, Warrington.

"The new mega-mall, Castletian, is the merger of Gamo and Sigils. We think the accountant ran his own research and numbers and figured out the false statistics, and probably told the GM, so they were murdered to keep them quiet. They may have even been resorting to blackmail."

Lissa hadn't realized Jace was playing such a dangerous game. She had figured he and his team were too confident, too dangerous looking, too powerfully built to be run-of-the-mill construction workers. But she had never imagined it was something like this.

The way he and Ker and the others had come out shooting when that man had tried to take her, they were all too expertly trained to just be average laborers. She shivered remembering Jace breaking that big man's neck with one move. The carnage Ker had calmly walked her past, it was all starting to make sense.

"The- the manager, why was he killed?" Lissa asked nervously.

He shrugged his broad shoulders. "We're not sure. I think he figured out who the assassins were. Someone might have said something he picked up on. I'm working on tracking his trail to see if I can find out the same information. That day I got shot I had been lured by a message that said they had info."

"Jace…" Lissa's worried eyes dusted across his masculine toughened face, from his strong jaw to the dark blue eyes that never lost that hint of desire for her. "You…you're replacin' the murdered man."

Her brows drew down, eyes leveled at his. Fear for his safety suddenly expanded in her green orbs. "I am not stupid, you could be in terrible danger."

"Lissa, you don't need to worry, I am-"

Her brows rose high. "That man, that's why he came tae the house that day. But why?" They lowered in consternation as she tried to work it out. "I don't understand, why did he try tae take me?"

Jace's lungs inflated, he huffed the air out. "Baby, it sounds kind of contradictory, but it's one of the reasons why I abducted you. These are dangerous men. If they had seen you that day in the alley when you took Donnie's wallet, they would have undoubtedly killed you." His lids lowered not wanting to see the fear lancing her eyes.

"And, uh," he tried to clear the guilt out of his throat with a cough. "That day at the house, apparently someone was getting suspicious at my team asking questions and they came here to grab one of us to, uh, interrogate.

"I think, the guy saw you and figured he could grab you and use you as leverage to get one of us, me, to cooperate." Jace peered up at her to see her expression. Her brows knit, she still looked confused.

"I don't…" Then the confusion cleared some. She looked hard at him. "You mean they wanted tae take me with the threat that if you didn't cooperate with them they would…kill me?" Her voice trailed off feebly.

His guilt-ridden lids reared down in the affirmative, he didn't need to say it out loud.

"So, what you're sayin', is you took me originally tae protect me, and now in doin' so you've put me in the direct line of fire?"

Jace's gaze flit around the yard before landing back on her. "Uh, you could say that. But, I took you for other reasons as well. There was the danger you could go to the police and tell them about us and the dead man in the alley.

"Who by the way," the corner of his lip turned up, "like I tried to tell you before, he was an informant who was going to give us info about Warrington. When we got to the meet those other thugs were there and they had already killed him. You telling the police could have brought the spotlight on us, expose our undercover operation. We couldn't take that chance."

Before she could respond, he said, "This is why I can't let you run around free, why I'm always so adamant someone is with you. Besides protecting you from the other asshole jerks like Brett Rawley, and you trying to jump off ships and aiming empty guns at men, you are in danger."

Ignoring that, her frown darkened, then lifted some. "You're right, I would have gone tae the police. But Jace, back tae you playin' this manager, the murdered one, who's tae say you won't be taken out the same way? Especially after they're already suspicious of you. What's tae say-"

He cut her off, his head dipped at her indicating there was nothing she could say that was going to change anything. Moving her away from the talk of both of them being in danger, he continued, "Anyway, we've been snooping around the last weeks, discretely asking questions.

"But," he sighed, "the murderer could just as likely be a disgruntled politician or business owner in the U.S. that's mad the money is leaving. Or it could be people right here in Dynshire who don't want their quaint, rustic little town to change as it certainly would with a giant conglomerate with warehouses and factories springing up in their neighborhood."

"Do you really think it could be one of those that could be the suspects?" she asked.

Jace lowered his head and shook it. The light hair on top shuffled. "No." He looked back up at her, then across the grass, squinting into the distance. "No, I think it's Warrington. Our research is coming up with different stats than he has out there, like the accountant probably discovered."

He drew his gaze back to her, his eyes narrowed, body tightened in anger. "That's why I couldn't fuck him up for touching you that day, for-"

"Okay, Jace, please don't get all stirred up, it makes me anxious." She stuck a finger in her mouth and chewed on her nail.

Gathering his self-control to clear the crimson haze clouding his vision when he pictured that bastard with his hand up her blouse-

"Jace."

He forced a smile, forced his fists to unclench, stretched his neck to relax it. "All right, baby. It is my desire, my goal in life, to help you get to the point where you are relaxed. Not just for a few minutes, but permanently. There's only one way to do that, honey, we have to destroy your demons." He leaned in and pulled her chair closer.

"Now, you will tell me why you are hiding from Doug Calero."

Chapter Thirty-Seven

Thrown off by his sudden change of subject, Lissa set her hands back on the chair arms to hide the fact that they were shaking.

Jace bent and placed his large hands over her hers, covering them completely. "Baby," his voice so hushed, so strong, "you are not alone anymore. You've seen you cannot get rid of me." His mouth twitched up, then flattened.

"Lissa, look at me." He waited for her to bring her unsteady gaze to his unflinching blue irises. "I'm fighting this with you. There's no argument, and no more refusing to tell me your secrets. Like I said, we are not leaving here until I have the whole truth."

Patting her hands, he looked her confidently straight in the eye and said, "I want a lifetime with you, Lissa. I am on your side."

With that, he settled back in his chair, making himself comfortable, preparing for her stubbornness, but there was no way he was going to let her get away with it. Not this time. Spreading his long legs keeping her fenced in, he forked his fingers through his hair then settled his big arms across his chest.

She waited, he waited. The set to his jaw, Lissa knew he meant what he said, no way around it. She tried anyway, "What about church? We're goin' tae be late…"

He didn't bother to respond, just watched and waited.

The heavy breath she let out, her deep, horrible secret bottled up inside didn't come out with it. She'd spent too long keeping her walls up. Feeling the pull of his caring supportive gaze, she allowed herself to soak in it, let it pour golden over her, comforting her, keeping her safe, loving her.

Lissa kept her hands on the chair arms, but shifted her body slightly to the side. "A few years ago," her voice shook, she gulped, took a slow breath to steady it, "I lived in Scotland."

Sucking in a deep breath, she let it out. "I had, uh have, this step-sister. Jennilee. My father's wife's daughter. Uh, one day I came tae her room tae drive her tae school. She was 17 and in her last year of high school, and, a year older I had just started college.

"When I got tae her room, I found her unconscious with an empty bottle of pills on the floor. Of course, she was rushed tae the hospital, and, thank goodness, she was saved."

Jace silently nodded with empathy for her trauma.

"So um, I visited her in the hospital, I had tae ask her why, you know?" Lissa squirmed. "Jace, I need tae stand up."

Jace warily moved a leg so she could get up.

She paced a step. "Jennilee told me she was in love with this guy, he was from another country. Not from Scotland. She said he was goin' tae be deported." Lissa stood wringing her hands.

Jace wanted to comfort her but didn't move.

"When I saw her in the hospital, so pale, so afraid, I," she was wringing her hands so hard Jace did reach out and pat them until she pulled them apart and sat back down.

"I prayed tae God, let her live and I will do anythin', anythin' in return. Well," her lips twisted wryly, "Jen told me she was so in love with this guy, and that if he was deported she would-would- kill herself. And this time ensure it was for real.

"Because, he told her if he returned tae his country, he would certainly be held prisoner and probably be executed because he had fled his country that was in the midst of political uprising. Jen couldn't bear for that tae happen."

Lissa's eyes gleamed with gathering tears. "So, uh, she said if he was married tae a citizen, Jen and I both had dual Scottish and American citizenship, that he could stay." Her shoulders rose tight against her ears then drifted down with a pained sigh.

Dashing at a falling tear, she said, "I found out later that what he said wasn't true, he wouldn't have been imprisoned upon return tae his country. It was a ruse tae play on our sympathies just tae gain citizenship. It worked."

Jace silently handed her a paper napkin. She smiled, watery and vague, took it and dabbed her eyes.

Inhaling a wobbly breath, she exhaled weakly. Her voice soft, she went on, "The thing was, she was only 17 and the folks refused to sign for her tae marry him. Needless tae say," she peered at Jace, he had already known where this was going.

"She begged, pleaded, swore she'd kill herself if I didn't do it for her. Said it was only for a year and then we could get divorced and she would be of age and she could marry him then." Lissa closed her mouth, and eyes, remembering back, Jen's frantic, relentless, heart-rending begging.

"But, something went wrong," Jace prodded.

Her lids heavy with wretched memories stilted up slowly. "Yes. Of course I married him. We all agreed it would be in name only."

Her ironic smile was not lost on him. Now he knew what she meant when she had said she wasn't getting tricked into a fake marriage again. Jace shifted uncomfortably. How could all this be so damned parallel? He asked quietly, "What happened?"

She stood up again but stayed in front of him. He instinctually tightened his knees against her legs holding her still. She didn't fight him.

"It was tae be in name only, he promised. But tae abide by the law we had tae share the residence for a year for it tae be legal. So he had me move into his house." Her face paled to practically translucence, she set a trembling hand on her heart.

"You see, I had been brought up very sheltered, very strictly. The first night," her eyes widened in horror, "he beat me almost tae death because I refused tae sleep with him and fought back. I was so- so shocked. Then he brutally, violently, raped me. I was a virgin."

Jace couldn't speak, his voice dried up in his throat. He felt he was strangling, he couldn't move, just stared helplessly at her.

"I…I…his aunt happened tae come by later. I was…on the floor, bleedin', battered. She called an ambulance. I was in the hospital for a week. When I was released, he was there tae- tae take me home.

"He said I was his wife, *his*, he owned me like chattel. I was too injured, too weak tae fight him. That night, he did it again. But he didn't beat me quite on the edge of death. The first time he told the hospital that I had been mugged. He knew it wouldn't fly again. He," her eyes flew to Jace's, "locked me in the basement so I couldn't get help."

"Baby," his voice a thread of agony, Jace reached for her. She let him pull her down on his lap. His shaking hand caressed her hair, he tried to pull her head on his shoulder but she resisted. "The police-" his voice laced with fury and pain and pity for her.

"Huh," she snorted delicately. "The police. Yes. As soon as I could I escaped and fled tae the police. When they talked tae him, he laughed, told them it was consensual sex. After all, we were married," she saw Jace's face color guiltily.

"And he told them, that I, we liked it…rough. Rough as in head tae toe bruises, lacerated spleen, broken ribs, black eyes, and so on." She blinked rapidly to push out the memories of that torturous time.

Coughing out her anguish in low spurts, she rolled her shoulders to her ears then started talking again before Jace could. He looked about to explode.

"Apparently the men all had a good old laugh about that. When the policeman came into the room they had me in and told me… that Doug was there tae take me home. He winked, he thought it was all a game."

His large hand on her back, fingers splayed covering almost all of her small back, Jace stroked her gently. "What happened then?" His voice twisted in impotent sorrow for what she'd endured. And excruciating guilt for also forcing her to marry him, threatening to rape her and locking her up too. *Oh God*, the pit of his stomach twisted, no wonder she fought him at every turn.

Lissa shrugged one shoulder then sat up rigidly. "As soon as the policeman left, I saw them escort Doug tae the restroom, I darted out, and ran. The police wouldn't help. My mother died when I was very young and my father and stepmother didn't believe me, they said I'd made my bed and all that rubbish.

"After going to the police I knew Doug would be...out of control with insane rage. I fled to a friend, a male friend. Craig. He hid me. I couldn't go back tae school. Doug had threatened when he was beatin' me that if I left him he would hunt me down and kill me." She turned blank eyes to Jace. "And anyone that helped me."

"He didn't..." But he already knew by the wall, the blank look in her eyes.

"Yes. He did. Doug asked around my friends. I had left my job in a small restaurant, he asked there too and found out one of the bartenders was a friend. When Doug questioned him, Craig's face was an open book. He lied, said he hadn't seen me, but bein' a sociopath, Doug knew when someone wasn't tellin' the truth.

"He followed Craig home. I was..." her eyes closed, she pressed her fingers against them. Lines formed around her mouth. "In a back room at Craig's house. I heard the bell- I ran tae warn Craig not tae answer it. But Craig was such a sweet, trustin'," her complexion turned ashen as her eyes welled up. Her breath coming out in sharp hitches, she twined her fingers so hard her knuckles where white.

Jace kept stroking her back that was rigid with trepidation.

"Doug beat Craig tae death with a baseball bat. While he was doing that, I was climbin' out a window. First I had started for the living room, but...Craig had already stopped screamin' so I raced tae the window and climbed out like a coward, not waiting to see if I could stop Doug, help Craig."

A sob hiccupped, she wiped at the falling tears. "I hadn't physically seen Doug beat him so I couldn't go tae the police as an eye witness. They hadn't believed me before, they sure wouldn't now. Doug could have swung it that it was me who murdered...Craig," more tears fell.

"Honey," Jace squeezed his arm around her. "You know there was nothing you could have done. Doug was too prepared. Even if you had a gun, by the time you got to them, Craig would have been dead, and you would be too. You know that." He said it so firmly, she realized after all this time it was true.

Taking deep shuddering breaths, her voice steadied. "I got out the window and ran, and have not stopped since. I went tae a shelter at one point in another city and through the women I met there, they had an attorney who helped me get the marriage annulled.

"Then they helped me get this ID, for Lissa Mallory. She was three months old when she died. I was only three months past my 18th birthday when I became her and sailed tae the States and hid." She turned to face Jace.

He cupped her jaw with both hands and pulled her in, kissed her gently. "Until I kidnapped you and brought you back here, to where he was. Is." Jace wiped at his own eyes with his sleeve. The guilt and shame were weighing him down like wet cement, his sorrow for her felt like the cement was hardening over him.

Taking a deep breath, Jace said, "The party, the woman, Jayne Madison, the one who took your picture, I tracked her down, questioned her. That's how I knew who you really were. Victor had already discovered, easily enough, that you have only existed for around two years. We've known almost from the beginning."

"Oh!" She was surprised. "Why haven't you said anythin'? They must hate me." Her face fell.

"First baby, they would never hate you. They care about you and feel as protective towards you as I do. I was hoping you'd open up to me, and tell me yourself. When you didn't, my team was going to investigate you once we were situated here. As it turned out, we didn't have to. What an insane coincidence that she would be at that party."

"Not really. Doug and the people he hung around with were from near this area and he's worked for Sigils. It was only a matter of time. That's why I was so frantic tae get away from here, from Scotland."

She climbed off his lap and sat back on her own chair. Big sad eyes looked up at him. "That's why you can't be near me. He killed…Craig. Just like he said he'd kill anyone who helped me or was with me, like a lover, or worse, a husband. You are in danger, Jace, you have tae let me go."

Before Jace could say anything, Ker rounded the corner and said, "We got a guy who is talking. We need to go, now." He glanced at Lissa then Jace then disappeared through the house to go to the truck out front.

"Shit. What lousy timing." Jace needed to comfort Lissa, tell her how he can help her, protect her. End her monster nightmare. But he had to go or more people related to the mission might die.

He cupped Lissa's face. "Do not leave the house. No matter what. We'll talk when I come back. We will handle your nightmare. Lissa, trust me, I will end it." He kissed her hard, short, heady, then released her and left.

She sat there, wondering, how soon would he take her to a ship or airplane to return to the States to get rid of her?

The thought, for once, did not offer her any comfort.

Chapter Thirty-Eight

*J*ace drove in his truck and Ker and Victor followed in a car driving through the city to where the man said to meet. They parked, got out and headed to a wide open area near a park.

The man had told them he wanted to be able to see them and anyone else coming long before they got to him. He hadn't wanted any tall buildings where a sniper could hide.

His instructions were for Donnie to go alone to the center of the area and wait. Before they neared the park, the three men stopped and took in their surroundings.

His voice hard, Ker said, "I don't like it, One. There's nothing for you to use for protection. No buildings, not even a tree or park bench. We're short-handed with Cad being sent out of town to the factory site, and, Julio and Donnie back at lodge gathering the financial evidence."

Ker repeated, "I don't like it." His hands on his hips, he scanned the area. It was wide open, all green grass for an acre or more.

There were some people wandering in the nearby park with its fountains and trees, meandering paths, people picnicked and pushed strollers. But this area was empty of people. It was rocky under the grass and not comfortable to throw down a blanket to sit on.

Shaking his head, Victor opened his mouth also to object, but Jace held up a hand. "It's the only good lead we've gotten. This guy, Merle, told Ker he heard Donnie was asking around, guess he wasn't as discreet as he thought he was. Merle said he can finger one of the killers, has evidence and will provide it, for a fee."

Ker nodded. "Yeah, extortion. I wonder if that's what happened to the murdered manager. Maybe he tried to blackmail Warrington."

Jace's brows arched considering it. "Sure, we already figured that. Anyway, we agreed, I'd play Donnie, it doesn't sound like he knows what Donnie looks like."

He glanced at his watch. "Okay, I gotta go. Vic," he turned to his dark-haired friend. "Please call Julio and remind him to stay near Lissa. He has a tendency to forget. I can't be worried about her and concentrate on this."

"Exactly why one of us should be the one to-"

Jace cut Ker off. "I'm going. I'll meet you back here." He strode off before either of the two men could protest further.

Making his way across the grassy, rocky land he continued to scan the area looking for the guy, and anyone else who could be there as an ambush. He reached the very middle of the clearing and stood as he had been instructed.

He only waited a few minutes when he saw a husky man in his forties approaching from the park side. The very top of his head was bald with thick brown hair circling the lower part. He had a large nose and was wearing a flannel shirt and jeans. Except for the long sideburns, he looked more like a farmer than a construction worker.

The man's head swiveled constantly, searching for confederates. Jace could see he was nervous long before he reached him. When he got near, Jace stared him in the eye and nodded, "Merle?"

His small brown eyes darting all around in his soft doughy face, the man licked lips, thick like a lizard's and wiped his hands on his jeans. "Yeah, you Donnie?"

Jace crossed his arms, braced his feet. "You said you have information for me."

Merle's eyes slit in suspicion. "The guy who told me about you said you sounded kind of boyish, you got a tough edge to yer voice. What's going on?"

"There would be no other reason for me to be here than to get the information I want. So, you going to give it to me, and I give you money, or are we wasting our time?" Jace stared back, half turning as if he was about to turn on his heel and walk away.

Sweat beaded across Merle's high forehead and started dribbling down the sides of his heavy face. "No, wait." He twisted his head back and forth to see if anyone was near or watching them. "All right, okay, you got the dough?"

Jace pulled an envelope out of his pocket, held it out so the guy could see the greenbacks inside but couldn't touch it. "I want the information first."

Merle's eyes lit up like greedy Christmas trees. Licking his lizard lips again, he snapped his head up and down, cheeks wobbling. "Yeah, nice, okay."

He took one more look around. Satisfied they were alone, ducking his head, he said in a very low voice, "There were three of 'em. Half the site knows. These three guys show up one day at the site wearing fancy pointed boots and brand new jeans and shirts, stood out like sore thumbs. Two days later and the manager is dead."

Jace's head was down as he listened, he looked up at Merle from under the bridge of his brow. "What kind of proof is that?"

Merle's eyes beamed at the envelope in Jace's hand. "The proof is, there was a food truck around at that time for a few weeks. The guy would leave it on site overnight but locked up.

"One day someone broke in and helped himself to a bunch of food. The owner was fucking pissed. He thought if he left the truck out again a few days later whoever the thief was would try it again." At the impatient look in Jace's eyes Merle sped his story up.

"So's anyways, the owner put up a video cam. The way it was aimed was directly at where the body was found." Merle grinned like he was the genius of the century.

"How do you know about this?" Jace asked, doubt surfaced in his voice, it was a bit too convenient.

"Yeah, well, I know you think it's a load of shit, but the owner of the truck is my brother-in-law. He told me. He showed me the tape goddammit. Clear as a bell, shows Sam Leeds, Bruce Kinder and Earl Bandman, the three funky dressed men pulling into the site.

"They must have told the manager some cock and bull story to get him there because it was late Sunday and the place was vacant. Right on the tape you can see the three guys walk up to the foreman, one of them shakes his hand, they start to walk towards the site when Sam Leeds pulls out a gun and shoots him right in the head!" Merle clapped his hands while exclaiming gleefully like he was watching a movie.

Jace was quiet. Then he said, "So why were you sitting on the tape? Why not go to the police, or Warrington?"

Merle grunted, his face settled into blobby greed. Small shameless eyes peered at Jace. "We were waiting until Warrington got most of this settled then we thought about going after him. He has deep, deep pockets."

"So?" Jace assumed he wouldn't go to the police because they wouldn't pay him blackmail. Doing a good deed like turning in the tape would have been a ridiculous notion to these thugs. "Why were you waiting?"

He shrugged one rounded shoulder. "Eh, the guy gives me the willies. I don't trust him. Can almost feel the bullet hittin' my back as soon as I split with my cash. I was hoping someone else, like you, would come along." Again he regarded Jace with suspicion. "So, why do you want to know who did the killing?"

Jace's stare back was cold and hard. "You really want to know or do you want to take your money and get lost?"

Merle's shoulders dropped, his beefy palms came up. "Hey, who cares as long as I get my dough."

"I want the tape, then you get the money. I'm not getting set up for a double-cross."

Merle's eyes were glued to the envelope. "Uh, fine. I'll call you with the information. How about just a little to tide me-"

"Tape first," Jace said, stuffing the envelope in his pocket.

"Ya know," Merle blustered, "you screw around and the price might just go up."

Jace tilted his head back. His face a chilling granite mask, pure lethality pierced from his blue eyes to the man's tiny brown ones.

The husky man withered and shrunk in alarm. "Uh, yeah, okay, fine, I gotta go. I'll, uh, call you. Later." Merle stuffed his hands in his jean's pockets and tromped back the way he came.

As soon as he was out of sight Jace strode in the opposite direction. He met Ker, Victor was already down the street waiting to tail Merle. Jace and Ker walked side by side to the truck.

"How'd it go?" Ker asked as they hopped in and went the opposite direction that Victor had gone in case Merle went that way. They already knew Merle's address, they had staked it out Friday. They didn't know the brother-in-law's.

It would be easy enough to find, but Merle may have the tape somewhere else so Jace set Victor to tail him. Chances were he'd want to at least check and make sure the tape was still where they'd put it.

After twenty minutes Victor called, "He's gone. He nearly got clipped by a train's crossing arms coming down, I would have had to blow my cover if I went through."

Jace said, "All right," and stuck his phone in his pocket. To Ker, "We're going to have to wait for his call. In the meantime, let's locate the brother-in-law." He called Julio.

When they got back to the house Julio had already found everything he could about Digger Riggs, Merle Burn's brother-in-law.

They already knew all about Merle. He was 45, in construction doing drywall his entire adult life, married to Lois with two grown kids, a dog and a small cottage-styled house in a lower middle class neighborhood. He had a few petit thefts, bar brawls and minor drug charges in his younger days, but nothing in the last 5 or 6 years. Nothing big time.

Digger Riggs owned the lunch truck. He'd done time for burglary, drugs, fraud. He lived alone in a trailer park.

Victor went back out to see if Merle's Honda accord was at the trailer park. Ker left to see if Merle had gone home. Both men lived way over on the other side of the city almost into the next town.

They came back empty. No cars at either residence. They headed home.

Back at the house, Jace was taking the stairs two at a time to see Lissa. He went to her room, she wasn't there. Damn, he needed to get her a phone. He kept putting it off because he just wasn't ready yet for her to be able to contact someone to help her get away from him.

She wasn't upstairs at all. He headed back down, thinking he was exhibiting typical domestic violence kind of behavior. He kept her phoneless, moneyless, jobless, wouldn't let her have access to a car.

He knew it was wrong, but he'd also known something abominable was out there ready to grab her, and until he neutralized it he just couldn't let her go. As it turned out, he'd been right about the abominable thing.

When he told Ker about Doug Calero and what he had done to Lissa and her friend Craig, Ker had the same enraged, sympathetic reaction Jace had. Ker had sworn evenly, "When we get this done, we'll get this Calero fuck."

"Oh, yeah," Jace had agreed emphatically, "oh yeah." But now, he looked for Lissa. His stomach always clutched whenever she was not in his sight and he didn't know where she was.

Then he saw her in the kitchen laughing with Benny, up to her elbows in flour, even on her nose. His stomach settled, and growled. She was baking something, didn't matter what it was, he was already looking forward to it. As he entered the kitchen, his phone rang.

Pulling the cell out, he went straight to Lissa and set his hand on her waist. She smiled up at him. *Good sign.* His heart soared hopefully. "Hello?" he said to the unknown caller, no name came up on the caller ID.

"Hey, Donnie, or whoever you are. I got the tape. You come to the Janger's Warehouses right now, bring the money."

"Now?" Jace asked. He wanted Ker and Victor with him, and they were clear across the opposite side of town. They'd gotten a call earlier about another guy that said he had information regarding the killings.

Ker and Victor had gone to talk with him. Jace had a funny feeling about it. Why didn't the guy meet him in the same safe location? Was it a coincidence that it was at the same time that Ker and Victor were gone too-

"Yeah, now. My brother-in-law says he's itching holding this video and wants it gone. So, now or he says he's burning it." Merle had so much more bravado on the phone than he did in person.

"All right. I'm on my way, should be there in twenty." Jace hung up.

"What?" Lissa's smile fell away at the look on his face.

He smiled, clearing his misgivings from his expression. "It's nothing, baby."

He swiped at the flour on the end of her nose with his finger. "I have to go out. When I come back, we're going to continue our...talk. Alone, in my room. What do you say?" His smile turned soft and loving, he didn't hide the flaming passion bursting in his blue eyes.

Lissa wiped her cheek with the back of her flour dusted hand depositing flour on it, smiled shyly at him. "Okay. I'd like that."

Jace felt the tension in his shoulders ease. Finally, she was finally coming around to him. His heart leaped silently.

He cupped her floury face and gave her a smoldering, blood coursing kiss, a hot promise of what the evening will bring. She returned the kiss with all the same intense fervor he pulsated against her lips.

Encouraged, he pushed her lips open and plunged his tongue inside briefly, an example for later. Sighing, he let her go with the usual admonish for her not to leave the house.

"Do not leave the house, Lissa, for any reason."

She nodded rolling her eyes at him.

Jace said to the cook, "Benny, stay close to her, all right?"

"Of course, Jace. Don't worry." Benny saluted Jace with a wooden spoon to his forehead.

One last quick kiss on the tip of her nose and a swat on her butt, Jace grinned at her faux scolding look and left to hunt up Julio and Donnie to go with him.

Chapter Thirty-Nine

Fifteen minutes later they pulled in to a block length of warehouses.

One story of plain grey and white square buildings, some connected, some stand-alones were clumped between a narrow road with a grassy hill rising along it bordering the back of the complex, and a larger road with parking areas stretching along the river.

Not a light shown from the warehouses or the few streetlamps. The moon swept a wavering ribbon of silver light across the river, blinking stars in the night's sky was a meager illumination. Jace parked and the three men got out. It was bone quiet and no one was in sight.

Jace whispered, "The guy said to come to warehouse 22." He looked up at the signs. They were at 14.

Glancing around, he said, "There are no other cars here unless they're parked inside. Julio, you go down the back of the building hillside, Donnie," he looked at the younger beanpole with the mop of squiggly hair in his eyes. Jace hesitated. Donnie was the newest member of the team with the least experience.

One arm wrapped around his ribs, Jace set his elbow on his arm and rubbed his eyes. He had a bad feeling. They'd had no time to prepare, to plan, to do even the slightest bit of reconnaissance.

Donnie waited eagerly, the adrenalin to get into action pumping through his veins, his brown eyes bright with aggression.

Pushing the squiggly mop out of his eyes, he held his fists up, he was ready to go kick ass. "Yeah, One? Should I rush the front or should-"

"Ah," Jace's stomach rolled, "no, you stay behind me, back at least five yards. I go, you count to ten before following me. You're strictly back-up."

Getting right in Donnie's face, Jace's expression was as serious as a heart attack. "Donnie, listen to me, you stay behind me, do not do anything unless I tell you to. You got that?"

Donnie regarded his team leader ruefully, he was ready to run in and pounce and Jace was holding him back. He bounced on his toes barely able to rein in his coursing energy.

"Donnie, you stay behind me. That's an order," Jace commanded, his uncompromising whisper chopping low in the dark quietness. All three men wore black jeans, black sweatshirts, black boots. Jace wore a black knit cap to hide his light hair.

Sticking his hands in his pockets, shoulders hunched, Donnie huffed a sigh, "Okay, fine."

Jace peered at him with one eye narrowed, making sure the younger guy understood to follow his directive. Donnie smiled reassuringly at him.

Shaking his head, Jace whispered, "Let's roll."

Silently, Julio darted around the other side of the warehouses, Jace held up both hands to Donnie indicating for him to start counting, then he took off running silently down the front of the warehouses.

The buildings were a mish-mash, barely following rhyme or reason to their numbered system. It was like buildings had been added in between older ones so the numbers didn't follow in a particular order. Staying close in the shadows of the structures, Jace slowed when he neared the number section he was looking for. He heard voices, then –

A shot!

Jace swung around, Donnie was nowhere in sight. He didn't know Julio's location, they had their phones on silent to not give their presence away. A man suddenly stood out from the shadows a few yards away.

"Put your weapon down," the man instructed, holding his own weapon at Jace. He was over average height but shorter than Jace with less muscle mass. He carried himself with arrogant confidence because he worked out so he had strength, and he had the gun.

Jace's first thought was to duck back behind the wall and run hoping to dodge the bullets. But he hesitated, he didn't know why that other shot had been fired.

The man said, "We have the young guy with the long hair. You run, he's dead." He watched Jace considering the information.

Without moving, Jace's gaze travelled the immediate area. Pools of light reflecting the moon's gentle beam settled on some of the blacktop. He could hear voices. He thought he heard Donnie cry out, shivers raced up his arms.

The man waved his gun at Jace. "You take one step, the boy is dead. Oh, did I mention? We have the other guy too." He allowed a nasty smile to crease his harsh face. He was wearing a long sleeved shirt and slacks, had short dark hair, slash of a moustache, olive skin.

"You have one second to set the gun down or I give the order to kill them both." The smile turned into a hard vicious line. A jagged scar ran from his temple to his mouth on one side of his face. The paler skin of the scar shone against his dark skin in the scant light.

Knowing he had no choice, Jace crouched and set his gun on the pavement.

"Ankle too." The man ordered. "Hurry up. The knife at your belt too."

Jace pulled the gun from the ankle holster inside his boot, set it down. Keeping his eyes on the man, he slid the knife out of its sheath, laid it next to his guns. He stood up slowly. "You Sam Leeds, Bruce Kinder or Earl Bandman?"

His head cocked in surprise. With a frowning smile, the man said, "They're inside." He didn't identify himself. "All right, let's go. Don't screw around, make it fast. One stupid move and we take all three of you out. Get going," he gestured with the gun.

The man made Jace walk in front of him. They passed several warehouses, it had definitely been a planned ambush.

Jace told himself, it couldn't be helped. They had been forced to move when they did or risk losing any evidence there might be for the murders.

When they reached one of the buildings, the garage door was up, light shone out, Jace heard moaning, and talking. He looked up, it was number 34, not 22.

Ordering, "Get in," the man jabbed the gun in Jace's back. He pulled off Jace's knit hat and tossed it, then shoved the gun hard into his back, said, "Move."

The garage consisted of four walls of cold cement blocks, a cement floor with parts of it painted over gray. Barrels clustered in a corner, piled around were stacks of crates, and a workbench along a wall had tools scattered on it. Oil spills and tire tracks patched the dirty floor.

Shit- Jace spat.

Inside, Julio was sitting on the floor obviously dazed. A big red gash oozed blood on his forehead, his head was bobbing, he squinted at Jace's entrance.

Worse, Jace saw Donnie's wrists in cuffs attached to chains, he was hanging from a beam in the low ceiling. Donnie's face was a rash of distress.

"One, God, I'm so sorry Jace, it's all my fault. I- I thought I saw someone slipping through some buildings, I went to follow them. They- they caught me by surprise-"

"Shut up," one of the four men inside punched him in the gut. Donnie's breath choked out in a painful explosive gasp.

"It's okay, Donnie. Don't worry, it'll be all right," Jace told him calmly, his eyes on Julio.

"Hah." The man shoved the gun harder in Jace's back. "Giving the kid false hope?" He laughed and pushed Jace further into the warehouse.

"Julio, you all ri-"

The man cracked the gun against Jace's head. "Shut up, get over there." He shoved Jace's shoulder.

His hand going to his head, Jace shook the stars out of his eyes, trying not to stumble from the hit.

Three of the other men were lifting Julio up and cuffing his wrists. They strung the cuffs through chains and pulled him up with a pulley rope so he was hanging like Donnie. Julio's grunts and faint groans as the rope cranked cut unmercifully through the building.

Donnie cried to Jace, "They got Julio 'cause of me too. Fired a shot like they were gonna hit me! Julio had to give in, they beat the crap out of him." He turned to Julio, his voice breaking. "Bro, I'm so fucking sorry,"

Julio smiled weakly at him through the blood streaming over his eyes. "It's okay, bro, not your fault."

One of the men hit Donnie in the stomach again, growled, "Shut up." Donnie gagged, almost threw up, his body swung jerking back and forth.

Jace was pushed to the center of the room. The man with the gun stood behind him, another walked over to him. Without a word he hauled off and punched Jace in the face. Jace's head snapped but he shook it out.

The man punched him again, Jace staggered slightly but kept his ground. Spitting blood, Jace asked calmly, "What is you want, asshole, why did you lure us here?"

The man said to the guy holding the gun on Jace, "Toby, don't take your eyes off this guy." He glanced at two of the other men and ordered, "String him up."

"All right, Bruce." The two men started towards Jace.

"I asked you a question, asshole, I mean Bruce. Bruce Kinder I take it?" Jace peered at the man through his eye that was swelling and turning purple.

Bruce bashed his fist into Jace's jaw, then the other two came up and started pounding on him until he fell to the cement floor. On his hands and knees, Jace's head hung, blood and saliva dripped on the floor.

"All right," Bruce said, standing back and rubbing his fist. "Get him up." The men handcuffed Jace and hung him from his wrists like they had Julio and Donnie.

His arms hanging taut over his head, Jace looked over at his team. Donnie was close to tears and looking green from the gut punches. Julio was passing in and out of consciousness.

"We'll be all right, guys, hang in," Jace said coolly. That earned him a punch to the stomach. "*Omph-*" Jace doubled in at his gut, his body hitched and swung jerking from the hit.

"I told you to shut the fuck up," Bruce snarled at Jace. "We're only keeping you alive so the boss can question you. Then it will be our pleasure to take you out." He tapped the barrel of his gun against Jace's stomach.

"Warrington? You waiting for Warrington?" Jace asked.

One of the other men, shorter, dumpier, light-haired, slammed his fist into Jace's side. "You was told to shut the fuck up."

Swinging, sweat pouring down his face, Jace said, "I bet you're Earl." That earned him another punch to the side.

"Hey Earl," Jace said through raspy heaving breaths. "I bet you don't have the balls to bring me down and fight man on man, you sissy little puke. I bet you fight like a girl- ugh-" Earl punched him again, not falling for the bait to let Jace down.

Lissa cleaned up from her baking and changed into jeans and a pale yellow blouse and hiking boots. She'd hoped when Jace came back they could go for a walk. She was tired of always being indoors.

Passing a room, she heard a voice, sounded like someone was talking on the phone. Not wanting to disturb them she tiptoed past the room. The person had his back to the door. Lissa recognized him as Dillon Boyd, he was one of Benny's kitchen help and a friend of Brett Rawley's.

Stopping after she passed the door, she heard him say, "Yeah, dude, no problem. Just like you said, Caddell Munro is at the factory, Dove and Victor went one way, and Nico went the other way with Julio and that useless Donnie."

There was silence, then Dillon, said, "No, there's no way Ker Dove could know it was a setup. If he figures it out when he gets there," silence. Then, "No, Brett, I told you, they're too far away to help them. By time they get there Warrington will be finished with them." He laughed.

Lissa could picture him nodding his head as he said, "You got that right, those bodies will never be found." He chuckled again. "Yeah, you know the ones, the warehouses on 18th by the river, only a few minutes from here." Silence.

Dillon spoke again, "I think Dove and the other two will be easier to pick off later now that they're separated from the team." Silence. "Yeah, the big guy too, Cad, big target harder to miss. We'll get him when comes in." He laughed harder.

The silence was a shade longer before he replied, "You bet, that blond asshole out of the way you'll have no problem getting to the girl." Silence. "I think she's here now. Yeah, asshole never lets her out of his sight except for right now when the whole the team is out."

Silence, then, "Sure, I got a few things to do then I'll go look for her for you. I'll lock her in a closet or something until you get here."

Sounding like he was about to hang up, Lissa sped down the hall. She ran first to her room then raced to Ivy's room she shared with some of the other girls. The door was open, she burst in.

"Thank God you're here, Ivy!" She rushed up to Ivy who was busy doing Vicki's hair.

Ivy looked at Lissa, all flushed and upset and out of breath. "What's the matter girl?"

"Ivy," Lissa spurted. "I need tae borrow your car, please, it's an emergency,"

"Uh..." Ivy was holding a curling iron, she lowered her arm with a look of uncertainty on her cinnamon face. "But Jace," everyone knew Jace kept Lissa isolated.

"Please Ivy, I hate tae say it's a matter of life or death- but God it is, please!" Lissa held her hands out.

Vicki ignored the two women, she just stared at her reflection in the mirror. Not much else ever held her attention.

"Uh, well, okay." Ivy gestured wither head to a desk. "My keys are on the desk. Do you think-"

Lissa cut her off, "Your phone, too, please,"

Ivy frowned her answer. "My car okay, it's a piece of shit, but not my phone, honey." She shook her head, wrapping a piece of Vicki's hair around the hair wand.

Lissa ran and grabbed up the keys. "All right, but Ivy," she hurried to the woman and grabbed her arm to make her look at her. "Then listen, you have tae call Cad, if you have Ker's number you have tae call him too and tell them this-"

Finished explaining to Ivy what she'd overheard and where she was going, Lissa sprinted out the door and outside.

Jumping in Ivy's little Ford Focus she tore off down the drive and out to the street. Shoving the pedal to the floor, she prayed she could find the warehouses she heard Dillon talking about.

She came upon them in less than ten minutes.

Driving in very, very slowly, after the first group of buildings she found Jace's truck, of course he wasn't in it. She parked next to it, got out and quietly closed the door.

The warehouse section was huge, where on earth was she to start? The only thing she could do was start walking, and listening. There were no lights, no sounds except traffic up on the highway a half-mile away.

She could smell the cool river and hear the slapping shallow waves against the dirt bank to her right as she moved silently. Then, she thought she detected something.

Slowing, cocking her ear, yes, she could hear voices. She followed the voices until she reached the one building deep in the back that had lights on. The big garage door was up, opening the room.

Cautiously, barely moving, almost invisible in the dark, Lissa leaned into the building slinking her head around the doorway, and just about died. She had to pull her head back or her catch of breath would draw attention. She put a hand to her frantically beating heart, her throat buckled.

Jace, Donnie and Julio were chained, hanging from the ceiling. All three were bloody. She heard voices coming near her, she ran and ducked behind the building.

She heard a man say, "Warrington ain't gettin' here for a couple hours. I want some coffee, you gonna call the wife? There's no service here, ya gotta go up the hill, why don't you come with me?" Another voice rumbled next to him.

A third male voice chimed in, "Hey I'll go get coffee with you guys. Riggs, you and Merle okay alone with these guys?" Lissa heard rumbles, couldn't make out the words.

When she heard three car doors close and a car drive off, she slipped out silently from her hiding place and moved back to the warehouse. Standing outside the door she wondered what on earth could she do?

Then she heard, "I'm not waiting for fucking Warrington."

"What are you saying Digger?" A voice asked in a nervous raised pitch. "We gotta wait for Warrington, this is his-"

"No. The more I think about it the more I think these three are cops. This will end badly. We're going to take out the cops now, it'll make Warrington more apt to cough up more money for the tapes when he sees we're serious. If we take out cops he'll be less set out to screw with us thinking we'll do the same to him."

"Geez, Dig, if ya think so." The nervous voice was gaining a whine.

"I do. Take out that Beretta of yours and make good use of it. I'll do the blond and the young guy, you take out the Hispanic. All right?"

"Yeah, okay. You first."

360

The man's anxious sigh travelled clear to Lissa and passed through the blood pounding in her ears. She was holding her breath, her body trembled with fear. She pressed herself against the outside wall of the garage to keep her legs from collapsing.

Next she heard, "Okay you asshole, you're getting yours now."

Lissa heard Jace's voice hoarse, raspy, "Fuck you, shithead."

Quickly, with shaking fingers, Lissa unbuttoned the top half of her blouse as she stepped into the doorway.

"Um, hello there," she said in her sexiest voice.

All five men gawked at her.

Jace's face radiated his horror at seeing her there.

She ignored him and stepped in further, her hands clasped behind her back. Twisting side to side coyly, she thrust her chest out as far as she could.

All five men were gawking at her breasts half exposed in the opened blouse.

Chapter Forty

"My car broke down, and there's like no lights or buildin's anywhere, and like my cell phone battery died," Lissa waved it uselessly in her hand in its pink flowered case.

"I saw your light on here, I was wonderin' if maybe you could help me," she twirled her hair, then looked up at the hanging men like she'd just seen them. "Ooh, you guys like doin' somethin' really like kinky?"

The two men standing, and Julio and Donnie just gawked at her speechless. Jace was motioning madly with his head for her to leave.

Blinking her big vacuous eyes at the two thugs, Lissa pulled her hair around the front of her and caressed it erotically, then she stroked it down over the curve of one of her breasts. The men's eyes followed her movements.

Digger Riggs was the first to get his senses. He swaggered towards her, staring stupidly at her breasts.

"Girl, I can help you, I got what you need." He watched her gather up her long curly hair and push it behind her back then sensuously drew her finger invitingly along her open blouse.

Dig's tongue rolled around his lips. Digger Riggs was big, huskier than his brother-in-law Merle, and powerfully built with thin light brown hair hanging arrow straight. Like a bee to honey, with his eyes on her breasts he moved to her.

"What about you too, sugar?" She flapped her lashes at Merle. "You in for some fun?"

Merle didn't move, he just kept his frozen gaze on her open blouse.

Lissa slid both hands under the back of her hair, lifted it in a sexy flirty pose. Watching Digger get closer, she said more passionately to Merle, her mouth parted, eyelids low, "Come on honey, I think you are so cute, come and touch me, baby."

She cupped her breasts then shook them at him. That did it. Merle gravitated towards her like a dog to a bone. She did her best to look at the two thugs and not at Jace.

The two men reached her at the same time. Dig stuck his hand out and grabbed a fistful of her hair.

Merle stood staring at her dumbstruck. His wife was fat and frumpy and missionary style always, nothing this gorgeous ever even spoke to him much less offered her body.

Holding her hair, Dig reached with his other hand for her breast- Lissa shoved her pink flowered cell phone into his chest. Sparks flew, he screamed, his body shook like a tuning fork. Then he dropped from the electric shock of her Taser to the floor where he curled up and spazed over the dirty cement.

Quickly, Lissa turned and shoved the Taser into Merle before he could even screech. His body vibrated, eyes bulged, a terrible guttural 'ah- ah- ah' came out of him before he slammed down twitching next to Digger on the floor.

"Goddammit Lissa, what the fuck are you-" Jace had grabbed the chain while she was entertaining Dig and Merle, and pulled himself up and upside down.

Holding the chain with his feet and legs wrapped around it, he held a handcuff key between his teeth and unlocked the cuffs then jumped to the ground. He ran to Julio, unlocked him and helped him to the floor then went and released Donnie.

Jace pulled his bloody shirt out of his jeans and wiped his face with it. Dragging his fingers through his hair he stood scowling across the room at Lissa.

Julio and Donnie, weak and injured, made their way to Merle and Digger, took their guns and cuffed them. As soon as the two thugs had dropped to the ground, Lissa had darted away from their reach.

His body shaking with the residual terror of seeing Lissa saunter into the garage, Jace wiped his hands on his sweaty bloody shirt and stalked slowly over to her.

Knowing he would be furious that she was there, Lissa nonetheless stood her ground.

When he reached her, a corner of his mouth quirked up. "I'm glad you were so insistent on getting the pink flowered Taser that looked like a cell phone. I thought it was too sissy for a weapon-oof-"

Lissa threw herself at him knocking the breath out of him.

Jace's arms dropped down holding her like a vice against his chest. His shaking hand stroked her hair as she wept against his shoulder. "Okay, baby, it's okay," he murmured until her sobs diminished. Then he gripped her upper arms and pulled her back.

"I am so fucking mad at you, Lissa, what the fuck were you thinking coming here like that?" Jace shook her so hard her hair flopped back and forth. "God, I was so fucking scared, if they'd gotten their hands on you-"

He hugged her to him again, his arms pressing her so hard against his torso she could hardly breathe. Then he pulled back from her again scowling furiously at her. "Wait until I get you home, this time I *will* paddle your ass! How dare you-"

"Oh, Jace," Lissa's mouth turned up in a seductive smile, her eyes flit down to his crotch and back up to his enraged eyes. "Is that a promise?" She grinned at his stunned expression. His eyes went from angry to lustful in a nano-second.

His hands slid down around her waist, thumbs rubbing on her stomach. "You serious, baby? 'cause if you are-"

"Hey, Romeo," Julio called. "Don't forget there are others out there that will be returning any second." He grinned through his cuts and bruises at Jace. At that moment he glanced at a shadow in the window. "Get down!" Julio yelled in a whisper drawing his gun.

"It's okay, Julio, it's Ker." Jace had heard Ker's low whistle. Holding Lissa's hand, he strode to the garage door and stuck his head out and said, "It's clear Ker, Vic." He waited. In seconds Ker and Victor appeared in the doorway.

"We got a crazy freakin' message from Ivy, something about you and this warehouse and danger," Ker told him. His diamond shaped face dark and intense, his black eyes flicked from Lissa's frightened face to Jace's bloody battered one.

Jace explained briefly what happened. Ker and Victor's surprised, admiring gazes at Lissa turned her cheeks pink.

Julio said, "We are grateful for the chance you took, Lissa, but we would have been all right."

Her brow arched at him. "Really? How?"

"Let it go, Julio, don't-"

Julio cut Jace off, he smiled assuredly at Lissa. "I could see Jace already preparing."

"Preparin' for what?" she asked, her eyes flitting from Jace to the others and back to Julio.

"He was already starting to swing, he would have gotten his feet around Merle who was closest, jerked him off the ground and thrown him at Digger when he came rushing to help Merle-"

Jace hugged Lissa against him. "A million things could have gone wrong. Digger could have shot me instead of going to aid Merle. Lissa saved our lives. I'm gonna kill her for it, but," he grinned down at her, "she risked her life to save us."

"Fuck yeah." Holding his stomach aching from the punches he took, Donnie's newly chipped front tooth showed with his admiring grin. "She put on a helluva show, guys, you totally missed it. She partially flashed those fucks her fine tits! Even damned held them up and shook 'em, you know like a stripper, and the men-"

"Shut up, Donnie, for cripes sake." Jace scowled at the young guy. "You need to learn to back off when you're talking about a man's wife. And you never talk about a woman like that in front of her." He squeezed Lissa's shoulders then realized her shirt was still wide open and Donnie was practically drooling over what he was seeing.

"Fuck you, Donnie." Jace moved in front of Lissa and kissed her while she buttoned her blouse.

"Dude, we're going to have another talk, and this better be the last one." Ker frowned darkly at Donnie.

Donnie's face paled. Ker's talks sometimes involved his fists.

"Geez, Ker, I didn't say nothing bad about her, what's wrong with saying she's got great tits-" his eyes shifted from Ker to Lissa to Ker. At the glittering gaze from Ker's narrowed obsidian eyes Donnie closed his mouth.

"I hear a car," Victor said. The men all jumped to attention,

Jace tucked Lissa behind a pile of crates as they prepared to take in the rest of the gang.

Chapter Forty-One

*E*verything had gone smoothly without a hitch. They arrested the other three men without incident.

Jace drove Lissa back to the house in Ivy's little car. He parked it and walked her inside and to her room. "I gotta take a shower, baby, I'll be back in a minute, okay?" He kissed her gently.

She pulled back, her brow knit with concern at his injuries. "Your face, Jace, your poor mouth, you'll hurt-"

"It looks worse than it is. Believe me, baby, it sure doesn't hurt to kiss you." He kissed her harder with bottomless hunger.

Catching his breath, Jace set her from him, his smile dopey at her glazed eyes, and lips still parted in mid-kiss. "Be right back." He cupped her butt, squeezed it, patted it then left quickly to go to his bedroom and get cleaned up.

Ten minutes later, dressed in jeans and a long-sleeved shirt the same dark blue as his eyes, Jace was just about to put his boots on when he heard the other men return. He looked up to see Lissa standing in his bedroom doorway watching him.

"Come here, baby, close the door. Lock it." He gestured to her with a seductively sly grin. Smiling back at Jace, Lissa did as he said then walked over to him.

Jace sat down on the short divan and pulled her onto his lap. Wrapping an arm around her, he set his hand alongside her face and cradled her jaw. Stroking his thumb in the hollow under her cheek, he took possession of her mouth.

Lissa wound her hands around his neck melting into his kiss. After a long delicious moment, she leaned back slightly to look him in the eye. "Jace," she started with a slight hitch in her voice. "I was so horribly scared when I saw you chained. I- I realized then how much you mean tae me. How destroyed I would be if you-"

Jace put a finger to her lips. "Shh, baby, don't dwell on it. We're all fine." He replaced his finger with his lips and pulled her in closer. Hearing her sigh out her fright from seeing him bound, trapped, and hurt, he felt her palms tremble against his chest.

Calming, Lissa brushed her hands over his pecs, stroking the hard broadness of his chest. Her fingernails lightly scraping over his nipples brought out a desperate rumbling growl deep in his throat.

She skimmed her hands up his powerful arms plying over every curving delineation, every mound of muscle then scraped her nails across his shoulders feeling the muscles flex and play under her fingers.

"Damn, Lissa." With a guttural sigh at her mouth, Jace tilted his head back to catch his breath.

Lissa pulled his head forward and whispered against his lips, "You are so strong, Jace, I love touchin' your body."

She gasped as his arm tightened around her, his hand slid from her jaw down her throat to her breastbone where his fingers spread wide like thick spokes against her blouse.

He drew his hand slowly down over her curves leaving a trail of burning goose-bumps behind it. His hand kept moving down her flat stomach to settle on her thigh, he squeezed it gently. Then he pressed his thumb against her core, watching her reaction through lowered lids heavy with desire.

Hips twitching, her neck arched back in a purling swoon. At her heady response, Jace slid his hand to cup her sex more fully. Her body shimmying at the heat of his hand lodged in the apex of her body, she lowered her head forward to take his kiss.

His mouth stroked and pulsated over hers. He bit and tugged at her plush lips while slipping his other hand between her thighs gently prodding them apart.

Jace kissed across her cheek and down the side of her face to her neck. Nipping at her neck, his hand palpating against her sex and he shuddered at the sweet convulsion of her legs and her moaning gasp.

Moving his mouth back up to her ear where he nibbled it, licking her lobe, tugged it in his mouth nibbling and sucking it. Sliding his lips behind her ear he continued to kiss her sensitized flesh, her head tilted back with soft sounds of pleasure.

He kept his hands on her thighs with his thumbs pressing and gently rubbing her sex. Wriggling against his hands, Lissa whimpered with such breathy short gasps it gave him chills.

"Baby," he growled with his lips on her skin. "You taste amazing, addicting. I want to taste every square inch of you." Licking and kissing back down her neck, he found a soft delectable spot and sucked it, marking her, savoring her humming sighs.

Lissa turned on his lap to press her breasts against his chest. He moved his mouth back to capture hers, thrusting his tongue in and around, smiling at her threaded whimpers against his lips.

Their mouths latched in lusted fire, he pulled his hands from between her thighs to unbutton her blouse. Undoing the last button he pushed it half off her shoulders.

He slipped his fingers under her bra straps gliding them knuckle side down from her shoulders feeling her skin quiver as he slid his fingers down to the curve of her breasts.

Grasping her around the waist, Jace lifted her to straddle his lap. He stroked down her arms and to her ribs then moved his fingers back up until he cupped her breasts in his big hands. Feeling their soft heat through the sheer satin bra, his groan filled his chest.

His kiss slanted hard across her mouth growing violent as his body burned. His hands roughly squeezing and caressing her breasts, Jace rubbed his thumbs over her nipples then pinched them lightly until they were hard little tips and she cried with scorching decadence into his mouth.

Panting with flaming desire, Lissa plucked awkwardly at the buttons on his shirt trying to open them. It was difficult, he was sucking her lips while her breasts swelled and throbbed in his big kneading hands. Her head buzzed with sensation making her fingers fumble.

Jace slid his hands around her back to unclasp her bra. Still nuzzling her lips so dewy he felt he could lie and float softly on them, he slid her blouse down her arms then pulled it off, dropping it on the floor. Her bra followed it. Long hard fingers cupping her breasts with relish, his mouth crushed hers, devastating both their senses.

With a small mewling rasp, Lissa arched her back and her neck, her hair draped down tickling at his knees.

Jace swept his splayed hands against her back to hold her while he looked at her. His gaze covered her face flushed with passion then lowered to her bare breasts, more beautiful than he had imagined in his fantasies.

"You're like an alabaster goddess, Lissa," his whisper gliding down his throat to a deep roiling gnarl. He moved his hands up her back, rolling her up to face him. His aching heart strummed seeing her hazed eyes green lusters of desire. Her mouth puffed and shiny from their kisses, looking like she wanted more.

"Baby," his fierce breaths huffed shallow and fast, "are you ready to-"

The corners of her mouth turned up in an enticing bow. She leaned over, dusted her lips over his and said against them, "I am ready, Husband."

Groaning a growled, "*God*," Jace shoved his hands under her butt and stood up with her legs wrapped around his waist. Lissa pushed aside his open shirt and leaned into him, pressing their chests together, skin on skin.

He moved near to the bed and set her on her feet then knelt in front of her on the soft carpet. He placed a hand on her belly feeling her silken warmth, and unbuckled her belt, undid her jeans and pushed them down. She lifted each foot and he pulled the pants off pushing them aside.

She stood in front of him nude except for her brief wisp of sheer panties. Jace could feel the sweat wetting his sideburns. He reached up and caressed her breasts then his gaze lowered to her panties.

He raked his fingers down the front of her, all the way down to her thighs. Feeling her quiver at his touch, he slid a hand between her thighs and nudged her legs apart then spread a palm on her bottom to help brace her. His touch slow and gentle, he moved his hand up to where her legs met, then with two fingers he lightly stroked up the soft slit of her sex.

"*Oh, Jace,*" Lissa cried in shuddering delight, her knees crumpled. Her hand dropped to his head, she twined his hair in her fingers.

Jace firmed his hand on her butt holding her sturdy and balanced, and nudged her legs further apart. He set his whole hand under her sex, holding her, feeling her dampness through the sheer panties, his erection throbbing at her moaning cry.

"Jace," she hushed his name like a breath. "I...I don't know much...I- I mean the only times I, uh..."

"Shh, baby." He cupped her core gently then added pressure with the heel of his palm and felt her tremble in his hand. "I'll take care of you."

Still wearing his jeans and kneeling, his open shirt showing his expanse of solid muscle, he looked up at her through a flopping blond lock.

Gripped his hair, a sheen of dampness made Lissa's face shine, her eyes glowed with heat and uncertainty at him. When he rubbed his thumb over her bud, it swelled under his touch and he watched her eyes roll back in her head. He grasped her panties and pushed them down then helped her step out of them.

Drinking in her naked beauty, Jace put his hands on her thighs with his thumbs on the insides and prodded her legs a little bit further apart then slid his hands back up. With both thumbs he chafed down between her thighs and the sides of her nether lips and smiled at her shiver.

Her legs wobbled with the unfamiliar dizzying sensations. Jace told her, "Put your hands on my shoulders, baby." He waited until her hands were setting on his shoulders before he stroked her clitoris with his fingers, her already concave belly sucked in with her moan.

"Just hold onto me," Jace said. Her legs apart, he drew the side of his hand up her sex then stroked and pressed her swelling bud, tugging on it gently. Keeping his strong thick fingers spread on her bottom to hold her steady, he teased and brushed her clit until his hand was damp with her silk, her quiet throaty pleasure strumming in his ears.

"You're wet for me, baby," he said with soaring awe, thinking he'd almost lost hope that he would ever get to this point with her. He leaned in and took her bud in his mouth at the same time he gently pressed a finger inside her.

"Jace!" Her spine arched, her head fell back. Clenching his shoulders with tense fingers, her legs instinctively tried to close but he held them apart.

Licking her tender bud, he drew his finger out, slicked it down then up her slit then slowly pushed it back inside. Her whimpers were music to his ears.

Grazing her clit with his teeth, he sucked on it and licked it moving his finger in and out, probing her until he felt her legs shaking. Her breaths were drawing shallow and rapid, little hoarse cries came from deep within her chest. Holding her tightly against his mouth, his fingers clutched and fondled her small perfectly round behind.

Her cries grew louder, she started bucking at his finger. Jace slowly inserted another one to stretch her, prepare her for him. Now he moved them in and out faster and licked and sucked and thumbed her bud faster until her entire body shook and undulated and her hoarse cry was almost a scream, *"Oh God, Jace!"*

She buckled forward, Jace caught her with one hand and draped her over his shoulders as her body shuddered through her orgasm. He kept his fingers moving, feeling her body heaving and rippling on him.

When her quaking lessened and he heard her breathing slow, he pulled his fingers out and stood up. Sweeping her limp body up in his arms he took her to the bed where he laid her down gently. Still in his jeans, his open shirt exposing his chest damp with sweat, he gazed at her.

Lissa looked up at him through lids thick with sensuous aching. Her wet lips parted and face flushed pink, her naked body lay loose and heated. Her arms were up beside her head.

It reminded him of the day he had taken her. She had lain there just like that, frightened and vulnerable, and hot and beautiful. Of course then she had her clothes on, and now she looked even more entrancing, shyly inviting rather than frightened.

"Jace," her voice weak and trembling. "I've never, I mean that's the first time…"

"I know honey. It's a husband's duty to pleasure his wife. If I felt I could hold on longer you would get more pleasuring, but I badly need you, now." He smiled at her hot glowing, *trusting* eyes.

"You ready for me, baby?" Jace whispered, already tugging at his belt. Her sultry smile struck him right in the heart, and the crotch. His smile broadened when she lifted her arms to him.

Kicking off his boots, he undid and shoved down his jeans and boxers and briefs and stepped out of them. Shrugging off his shirt, he let it fall to the floor.

The mattress sunk when he climbed on it. He settled his long form next to her. Sliding his hand under her jaw he kissed her. The kiss so deep and ravishing, when he pulled away they were both panting, pulses skyrocketing.

When he lowered his lips to hers again, he put his hand on her breast clinching his strong fingers over it. Crushing her soft mound in his kneading hand, her salacious whimpers keened half pain half pleasure. Fearing he was being too rough, he lightened his grip.

Caressing her breast, Jace dipped his head to suck on her soft plump flesh, licking and pulling her nipple, extending it, delighting in her excited wriggling under him.

She put her hands on either side his head holding him, feeling him feed on her. His hair smooth and soft as mink twining through her taut fingers, and brushing over her burning skin.

Taking turns cradling each breast, Jace kissed and sucked them until they were red and wet, enflamed and aching. He trilled his fingers lightly down her chest over her stomach, her hip, to her woman's core.

Her hips twitched when he touched her. She was crazy wet. He stroked her swollen clit with his fingertips until she was writhing and drawing in sharp strangled breaths. Then he slipped his fingers inside her trying to open her, she was so small and tight.

His mouth sucking her breasts, Jace pushed his fingers in and out, brushing over her hot spots again and again while rubbing her bud with his thumb.

When her head was rolling side-to-side, her hips moving against his fingers, her belly hitching in and out, he drew out his fingers, moved over her and positioned his body between her legs.

"Open your eyes, baby," Jace urged huskily against her lips. Kneeing her legs apart, he dipped his fingers in her wet silk and rubbed it on his engorged shaft.

Lissa struggled to open her heavy eyes. The green crystal moons in a blur of passion connected with his heated gaze then dropped to his fiercely hard erection in his fist. With a sudden quick indrawn breath she tried to move away from him.

"Jace," her voice shaky and uncertain, "it's- you are too- too much for me."

A hand on her hip to still her, his deep voice hushed and soothing, he murmured against her lips, "I won't hurt you, you know that, baby. You don't like something, it's too much, you tell me to stop and I will. Okay?" He tenderly brushed her hair off her damp cheek.

She nodded. Her soft shaky, "Okay," firmed with the fire that still kindled in her pupils. Their eyes joined, he held his shaft until it was at her opening. With his weight steady on his elbows, Jace very slowly pushed himself into her sweet channel. She was so damned tight and delicate, she whimpered.

He leaned over and kissed her, said softly against her lips, "It'll be okay, baby. I'll move slowly, let you expand to take me in. All right?"

Her eyes lighting on him with trust, she nodded.

He moved inside slowly, then pulled back slightly to let her wetness lubricate them both before pushing back in. He continued sinking into her until his entire rigid length was buried fully, deeply within her. Jace let out a contented breath.

He kissed her then leaned back to watch her as he began to rhythmically move in and out, watching her eyes flutter and roll with his thrusts. Her beautiful creamy breasts rising and falling.

As his erection swelled bigger and turned impossibly harder, he plunged in and out of her faster, his mouth hardened to a tight line, his neck strained, a vein on his neck beat.

"Lissa, baby, you tell me if I hurt you." His lips at her ear, hearing her soft, "okay, Husband," he was spurred to thrust against her rougher and deeper.

He tilted just enough to ensure he rubbed the length of him against her clits with every thrust, his chest brushing her nipples. Feeling her softness clench around his swollen manhood he knew she could feel him thrumming against her female walls.

Jace dropped his head and moved one arm around her shoulders holding her tight while the other clutched her bum lifting her to meet his plunges. He pounded into her until he felt her chest fill with breaths of low hitching screams.

Feeling the rush of burning heat curl through his own body, Jace quickly lowered his mouth on hers to swallow her screams as she came. Her body went rigid then undulated and rocked and he thundered right with her, hissing her name, *"Lissa!"*

He kept thrusting and plunging until he stopped for a second embedded deep inside her. Feeling his body burst, he erupted with a torturous growl. Gripping her body, he plunged and plunged until he finally slowed, feeling his seed surge deep inside her.

His body fell shuddering on hers. Hot and steamy, hearts beating together, his breath rushed against her face.

When their pulses slowed, he rolled onto his back, still inside her he brought her with him to lie on top of him.

Lissa's face on his shoulder, he stroked her hair. "Honey, uh, I didn't…I meant to stop at some point and put on a-"

She snuggled against him. "We're married Jace. I…I mean it's okay with me if I…you know, get pregnant. Unless," she lifted her head to look up at him. "You don't want tae be married anymore. I mean, your mission is…has pretty much ended, and I guess the need for us tae stay wedded has ended as well…"

Jace rolled over on his side and drew her beside him. Gently pulling out of her body, he brushed damp tendrils off her face and leaned in, giving her a gentle kiss.

Lissa's lips drew down in an uncertain frown. "Does that mean, you…that we will get the annulment now?"

He stroked a hand down her arm. "Hell no." He caught her chin with his fingers and shook his head. "No. I knew I couldn't protect you from your demons. If I had let you go, you would have disappeared. But even if you ran and hid from your threat, he would have found you eventually. Jayne had told me Doug had hired a private dick to find you.

"Plus the danger you were in from the people that may have seen you that day you took Donnie's wallet, so I tied you to me so I could protect you. Uh, and," he ducked his head sheepish.

She watched him, waited for him to continue, her expression curious.

Caressing her face, his gaze flickering from her eyes to her lips to her eyes, Jace said, "I've wanted you from the second I saw you looking at us in the alley. I never planned on getting an annulment. I had always hoped you would come around and realize how much I love you, and realize that you care about me too."

He moved over her, setting an elbow on either side of her. His lips tugged at hers. "Lissa, I would be ecstatic if you were pregnant. Not only would it bind you tighter to me," he kissed her, "you are the only wife I have ever and will ever want."

He kissed her again. "And I'm ready for a family, children, if you are. What do you say about that?"

Her hands came up and cupped his face, she smiled. "I fought it, Jace. You abducted me, it was outrageous that I would fall for you."

She drew her fingers through his light hair. "I was so afraid that Doug would find me and hurt you, and I knew if I let myself care for you I would grow weak and stay with you, and then you would be in danger."

"But," he prompted worried about what she was saying.

She shrugged. "I can't deny tae you or myself anymore, that I have strong feelin's for you. And I believe now that you, as you've kept tellin' me, can help me with Doug. I trust that you will protect us."

He nodded. "Yes, I will protect you until I find him and a way to," he hesitated, "never mind about that. You didn't answer me. Our marriage, Lissa, will you stay with me? Be my wife for true?" He gripped her shoulders hard causing her lips to part.

"I mean be my wife for life, forever, 'til death us do part and all that jazz?" Jace looked deep in her eyes. Her gaze back at him was just as steady and sure.

"Yes, Jace, I want tae stay married. I want tae be with you." Her lips curved into a contented happy smile.

"Yee-ha!" Jace yelled and pushed her legs apart with his knees. He palmed her breasts, caressing and stroking them. "Okay then, what do you say we keep working on having those children?"

"Jace!" She giggled and skimmed her hands down his hips. Becoming more sure of herself, Lissa reached for his shaft that was already growing hard. "I want tae feel you, Jace, I want tae taste you like you-"

A knock at the door cut her off.

Jace's head dropped back, he howled at the ceiling, "Are you fucking kidding me right now? Not again." His hands froze on her body. Gazing at Lissa, he almost cried.

Her eyes were so clouded with passion, damp lips parted, inviting him back inside her. Her small hand was wrapped around his cock and her pretty thighs were spread. He looked down at her chubby breasts rising and lowering with heavy quick breaths. He wanted to sink his face in them, kiss and suck-

More knocking.

"Deja-fucking-vu," he snarled. "Somebody damn hates us." He turned his head towards the door and bellowed, "Who the fuck is it?"

"Jace, please."

He winced at her. "Sorry, it's just-"

"Come on, Jace." It was Ker. He said through the door, "We have to take the thugs and the tapes to the police. Victor has the paperwork ready to take in to our headquarters. We have enough now to go after Warrington, to arrest him."

Jace's head dropped, a chunk of hair flopped down over his brow. Lissa put her hands around the back of his head and pulled it down to her full, rounded bosom and nuzzled her face in his hair.

"I know, you have tae go," she murmured, reaching down to grasp his manhood again.

For a second, his face buried in her bosom, Jace kissed her ripe globes. His big fingers rolled up, clutching them, stroking and kneading them while he licked and sucked her soft flesh. Groaning at Lissa's tentative strokes on his cock, he licked a nipple, drawing it in his mouth to suckle-

"Jace," Ker called from the other side of the door.

Jace pulled his head back, his hands still covering her breasts like he never wanted to let go. He smiled tenderly at Lissa. "Well, at least we've made progress. We've made love and I'm not cuffed." She smiled shyly back at him.

Grinning wickedly, he said, "Actually, we might try the cuffing thing again with some other accruements, but," he smiled at her baffled expression. Then asked quietly, soberly, "We going to continue this when I come back?"

He watched her green eyes glow, her pupils huge in them. Lips curved up in a seductive bow, she nodded. "Yes, Husband." She squeezed his shaft then rubbed her hand up and down it. "I will wait for you tae come back tae me."

His hips bucked at her touch. Gulping, Jace swallowed hard. "Shit, baby." His hands tightened on her breasts, he covered her mouth with his, sucking her lips so impatiently hard she whimpered. He moved his hips so she could stroke him more easily then slid his hands around her to pull her closer,

"Jace, bro, we need to go now," Ker sighed from the door.

"Yeah," Jace called out. He let go of Lissa, and got up on his own unsteady legs, dragged his pants on trying to loosen them around his pounding erection.

He leaned over and kissed her lightly on the lips. "Here," he left her for a minute to go to his desk, and came back with a phone.

"I got this for you. My number is already programmed in it, as is the rest of the team. I don't want to ever be out of touch with you again. Okay?"

His gaze stroked over her naked body. She had drawn her knees up and to the side modestly covering her pink tender sex, but her breasts and the curve of her bottom were there for him to enjoy, and her beautiful hair spread like a dark wave over her pillow.

Smiling broadly, Lissa took the phone from him.

"Listen," he kissed her quickly, "when I return we're going somewhere, anywhere where no one can get to us. A deserted island, whatever, with no more interruptions. A honeymoon. You'll bring that tiny plaid skirt and sit on my lap like you did the night with the cuffs, only this time I won't have pants on. And maybe you can leave the blouse off too. All right?"

Her cheeks turning pink, she nodded happily, clutching her phone. "I'd like that."

"All right, baby." Jace brushed her lips again and started for the door. "I'll be back as quickly as I can."

"I'll be here, Jace," Lissa promised.

He opened the door, took one last longing look at her lying there all pearly nude, freshly made love to, ready for more, and smiling.

Sighing, he shook his head then walked out the door closing it behind him.

Chapter Forty-Two

*J*t had taken all the rest of the day to answer questions at the local police station about the men who had held Jace, Julio and Donnie.

When they finally finished, the three men drove to a different city hours away to meet up with Ker and Victor at their own FBI satellite headquarters.

Cad was still at the factory questioning other employees.

The men produced the lunch truck tape showing the three hoods that killed the manager, and the bank records evincing the money Warrington had deposited in their accounts the day after all three murders.

Then it took another entire day to review with their FBI accountants the statistics they'd uncovered about Warrington's illegal activities.

They were forced to stay on the premises in hotel rooms while there. Jace called Lissa every three hours. Remembering the sweet promise in her big green eyes, Jace's skin prickled and his dick hardened. Both his heart and balls ached, he couldn't wait to get back to her.

The third day was the best. Jace and his team rounded up all of Warrington's cohorts including the three killers and arrested them, brought them into custody.

Merle and Digger were already singing like canaries squealing on Warrington and throwing their partners under the bus hoping for sentencing deals.

Jace had the pleasure of arresting Warrington. He was overly brutal with the clamping of the handcuffs, and the hand he wrapped around Warrington's neck digging his steel fingers into his flesh as he led him out to the waiting patrol car.

At the car, Jace said in a low ruthless voice, "Remember when you were hitting on my wife at the party?" His smile glacial and callous, Jace looked Warrington in his evil vacuous eyes.

Warrington's harsh lips pulled back in a smirking sneer. "Yes, Mr. FBI agent, if you hadn't been there what I would have done with that luscious piece of ass- ugh-" he grunted at the punch Jace hurled at his kidney.

Gasping for breath, Warrington barked, "You can't do that you fuck, you're a cop! You can't hit me-" he screamed when Jace kneed him in the balls.

Bending over gagging and huffing, Warrington cursed at Jace. He cried out to the other officers in the vicinity for help, grimacing with hate when they all looked the other way.

Jace grinned harshly, his eyes cold, hard merciless blue rocks. As soon as Warrington straightened he kneed him again in the testicles.

Warrington grunted, he had no breath left to scream. He bent over falling to his knees and puked on the ground.

Jace crouched near him, said in a low voice, "Now *you* will be the one getting hit on in prison, you dirtbag. See how you like it. Come on," he grabbed Warrington's collar, stood up and jerked Warrington to his feet.

He shoved his former boss to the patrol car, and said, "Watch your head," as he slammed Warrington's head into the roof before pushing him into the car.

Wiping his hands on his pants, Jace called over to one of the cops, "He's all yours," then he strode off to where Ker was waiting in his Ram 1500 and hopped in. The two agents took off.

On their way back to the house, Jace had tried for twenty minutes to reach Lissa. Her phone didn't even ring. He called Victor.

When Victor answered, Jace said, "Vic, locate Lissa's phone." He clicked off and sat with the phone in his hand on his thigh and waited.

"What's up?" Ker glanced over at his friend.

Squeezing the cell in his fist, Jace said, "Her phone is off. I only just gave it to her the other day, she knows I'm calling her every couple hours." He shook his head and ran his hand through the blond top of it. "I have a fucking bad feeling."

His eyes on the road, Ker said, "Why don't you try one of the girls, they should be home. The men will all be at the construction site wondering why it's shut down. Try Ivy."

"Good idea." Jace called Ivy.

"Hey handsome." Her loud cheerful voice boomed like Cad's.

Forgoing the pleasantries, Jace said, "Ivy, is Lissa around? Have you seen her?"

"Uh," Ivy could hear the concern in his deep voice. "Um, you know, gee I hate to say this,"

"What dammit, Ivy?" Jace barked at her hesitation.

"Well, uh, I know you kicked Brett out, made him go stay somewhere else. But, uh, his friend, you know, Dillon-"

"Fucking spit it out, Ivy," Jace ground his words like a saw over rough coal.

"So," Ivy's voice was shaky. "This guy showed up earlier, Dillon let him in. I think I saw Brett waiting out in the car. I heard the guy ask about Lissa. I mean, he called her something else first, Kiley or Kelly or-"

"Keira?" Jace's stomach dropped like a rock down a ravine.

"Yes." Her ear brushed static through the phone as Ivy nodded. "Yes, that was it. Anyway, I heard Dillon say she was in the kitchen waiting for Benny to come upstairs from the storage room. He saw me and told me to get lost. He uh…"

Jace's bark burst out with his aggravation, "He what, Ivy?"

"Well, Dillon is normally a quiet stay to himself kind of guy, but with that other man there, he got all cocky and bossy. I uh, was kind of afraid of them. So I did as he said, I left and went to my room."

Jace rubbed the phone against the side of his face in frustration and fear. He said into it, "You didn't think to call me, Ivy? Or even Cad?"

Hearing the censure in his question, she replied in a tiny voice, "Uh, I just didn't think. I mean, they were, I don't know, I just-"

Jace clicked off. The phone rang immediately. It was Victor. "Yeah, Vic?"

The tone of Victor's voice was not good. "The phone is off, the battery is likely pulled. I can't get her location. Is everything-"

Pressing the phone to his head, Jace took a deep breath.

Ker glanced over at him but said nothing.

Jace dragged his sleeve across his forehead. His stomach was now in knots. Through his tight throat he said into the cell, "Victor, I put a tracker chip in the phone. It doesn't matter if the battery is in or not. Go to my room, I have another cell there with the app on it to trace the chip. It's in the top left drawer on my desk. Get it."

He waited. Victor didn't respond, Jace knew he was already running to Jace's room.

Long grueling minutes passed. Jace kept wiping his forehead as sweat beaded.

"We'll get her, One, you know we will."

Jace didn't comment on Ker's encouraging words. His coarse sigh heavy and pained, Jace said quietly, "Her husband, her ex-fucking-husband has her. Him and Rawley." He could feel Ker stiffen beside him, his knuckles clenching the wheel.

Jace heard Victor's voice, he put the phone on speaker. "Yeah, Vic, go ahead."

"I got her, that is if the phone is still with her. The bad news is, she's like thirty plus miles from where you are."

"Just give me the coordinates," Jace growled into the phone.

Victor rattled off the address where the chip was.

Ker spun the wheel and changed direction racing off towards the address.

⁓

Lissa was standing in the kitchen waiting for Benny to come upstairs with the jarred tomatoes so they could get started on a sauce for the chicken cacciatore. She needed something to keep herself busy until Jace came home.

Her cheeks warmed at the memory of them making love, and his promise of more to come. Tingles of hot arousal surged all up and down her body.

She brushed her fingertips across her lips remembering how his felt on them, tugging, sucking her silky petals, her- upper lips on her face- and her lower ones between her legs.

Her cheeks reddened deeper as she thought about his hands, his mouth on her sex, then him inside her- *God*, her body heated more, she felt a flush between her legs.

She could not wait until he came home so they could do more! Since she'd finally told Jace her secret, she'd felt such relief, such a sense of freedom. She could finally allow herself to be intimate with Jace. Jace would protect her from Doug, he would-

"Keira."

Lissa froze. The hair on her neck rose one by one. She didn't dare move, turn around, blink. It must be a dream, no, a nightmare-

"Keira, turn around and greet your husband."

It wasn't a dream. It was his voice, Doug Calero's dark, ruthless, abusive voice.

As slow as an eclipse, Lissa turned. Keeping her expression blank, she said calmly, "Ex-husband. Actually not even, due tae the annulment I managed tae obtain before I fled the country."

His already mean face blackened in an angry scowl, then it slowly brightened to a crafty, depraved sneer.

Her stomach quailing inside, Lissa struggled to keep her terror from closing her throat, she was already on the brink of fainting just from the horror of seeing him standing there. Her eyes flit to his head, she almost smiled.

She remembered when Jace had first taken her, he asked why she didn't like blonds. She'd told him it was because she thought it made a man look weak.

In fact, a shiver rolled up her spine, it was because her ex was blond. Not a bright light saffron like the top of Jace's hair, no, Doug's was a dark gold blond. His arms, legs and chest were covered in the same dark golden hair.

His heartless chocolate eyes, that had seemed so warm and soft and friendly when Jennilee had introduced them, were glaring at her with hateful rage and malicious desire.

"What? No hug and kiss for your husband? It has been a long time, Keira dear, since I've held you in my arms."

Lissa could see that Doug at well over six feet tall, had gained muscle, cords of it rippled across his shoulders under the brown collared shirt. His arms in the short sleeves were bulked and hard. His hands, as big and brutal as she had remembered them, were perched on his hips. He wore dark brown slacks.

Her gaze shifted to his face. Two years ago it had been classically handsome, now the evil inside him had etched harshness across his face. His lips normally full were pulled back thin in a malignant grin.

"Ex," Lissa reminded him, watching the rage flash in his eyes at her deliberate taunt. "What are you doin' here, Doug? My husband, my *real* husband, Jace, will be home any moment and he will-"

His coarse chuckle slunk snidely down her spine as he cut her off. "Don't even try it, Keira. I know about this, man, he is not even in this town right now. Right Brett?"

He half turned to the door. His dark eyes lit with pleasure at the blanching of Lissa's fair skin and petrified eyes widen when she saw Brett Rawley's smirking face in the doorway.

"Lissa, babe," Brett said with a mean grin, nodding slyly. "We have unfinished business." He moved to lock the basement door, smiling at Benny's shout from down below.

Doug's head swiveled at him with an impatient frown. "I told you, Rawley, I might give her to you when I tire of her, or I might just kill her when I'm done as I'd promised." In three rapid long strides he was across the floor and fiercely gripping Lissa's jaw in his hand.

He held her face up to his, smiling at the pain he was already inflicting on her. "You remember, don't you Keira, what I did to your friend Craig? You remember what I told you would happen if you ever left me?"

She couldn't speak, he held her so tautly, her neck was stretched to its limits. The fear pulsating in her eyes told him she remembered his threats.

Doug smiled. "Good. Now, we are leaving, as in you and we are all leaving together. I don't want any trouble from you, Keira, I can easily break your legs and still have fun with you later. So, try and run, I will actually enjoy catching you. And so will Rawley, won't you Brett?"

He sneered over at Brett standing beside Dillon, both ignoring Benny yelling and pounding at the basement door. Brett rubbed his hands together grinning wolfishly at Lissa like he was going to cook her up for dinner.

Doug gripped Lissa's upper arm and ignoring her struggles to break free, roughly ushered her out of the kitchen and out the back door. Her legs were shaking so badly she could hardly stay upright.

When they reached their car, Doug opened the passenger door and told her to get in. She did without a fight. She knew Doug was as good as his threats, he would love acting on them if she put up any struggle at all.

Brett and Dillon climbed in the backseat while Doug strode arrogantly around the car to get in the driver's side.

"Hand over the phone, sweetheart," Doug said with his hand out to Lissa. When she hesitated, he slapped her. Stifling her cry of pain, she kept her face toward the side window, her hair covering the red imprint of his palm on her cheek.

"You want me to ask again, Keira?" he cruelly taunted her.

She reached into her back pocket and pulled out the cell Jace had given her and handed it to him. He snatched it out of her hand and immediately plucked the battery out of it then tossed both on the floor.

"Don't be expecting the cavalry, sweetheart." Doug told her caustically as he drove down the driveway. As he turned onto the street he laughed as Lissa stared bleakly out the window at the complex as it grew out of sight.

"It's funny," Doug said, but his smile was anything but humorous. "I had people looking for you in the States. They had finally located you then you suddenly disappeared. I was angry and frustrated as you can imagine. I still had feelers out here and in Ireland, Wales and England as well as some other places you could have run to.

"I'd already gotten word that you were back here in Scotland before that bitch at the party recognized you. I was pissed, actually, knowing she had given you warning of my still being around and looking for you. I figured it would put you on guard."

He turned towards her with a malicious grin. "As it turned out, none of that mattered, huh?" His tone dark, menacing, Doug said, "Because now I have you." He dropped his hand on Lissa's thigh and squeezed it harshly trying to make her cry out.

Annoyed when she didn't, he stuck his hand in her hair and dragged her across the seat to sit beside him. He slid his hand around her groping at her breast. When she pushed at him and tried to squirm away, he grabbed her hair and yanked her head back so far she couldn't close her mouth.

He pulled her head over to him, and keeping his eyes on the road, Doug said in her ear, "You keep fighting me, sugar, and I will remember every time you struggle. Then later, when I have you alone there will be paybacks for each one, before I let those other two jackals have at you. You got that?"

When she didn't answer, he jerked her head back so hard her neck cracked. "You got that, I asked?" he snarled.

"Y-yes…" Lissa cried softly, her voice scraping through her stretched throat.

"Good. Now look what Dougie has for you, sweetheart." He shoved her face down into his crotch. To her horror he was as hard as a rock. Doug rubbed her face hard and rough over his erection.

"You like that, Keira? It's all for you. If we didn't have such a short drive I'd let you taste it now, suck me dry. But, we will have to wait until we get inside, huh?"

When she made no response, he shoved her face harder on him, "Open your fucking mouth, sweetheart." He violently rubbed her face over his groin to force her lips apart.

Her tears wetting his pants, Lissa's mouth shook open. He held her down so her mouth was over his erection. "Oh yeah, I remember how sweet you were. I can't wait to fuck you again, Keira."

In the backseat, Brett and Dillon made raunchy comments while their nasty laughter flowed to the front.

A short time and Doug was pulling into a driveway leading up to a small ranch style house. It needed a fresh coat of white paint and weeds choked the yard.

Doug parked the car. Brett and Dillon got out and went right inside the house. His hand still clutching her hair, Doug jerked Lissa's head up. Staring down at her, he sighed. "Ah, even with tears in your eyes you are still one breathtaking woman, Keira."

He pulled her to him and brutally covered her mouth with his. Forcing her lips apart he violently shoved his tongue in, violating her tender softness.

When he finally let her go, glee lit his dark eyes at her bruised and swelling lips, his handprint still visible on her face from his cruel slap. He dug his fingers around her face again holding her immobile while he just stared at her.

Lissa refused to show him her fear. She glared right back into his flinty eyes that were so hard and empty of everything except his desire to hurt her, and an overwhelming lust that spiraled out and seemed to wind around her throat. She struggled to breathe evenly wishing she could slow her manic beating heart.

"I was insane with rage when you left me, Keira." The malevolence lightened slightly, his pupils shrank. His sigh angry and sad, voice regretful, he told her, "I really wanted to keep you as my wife. You would have gotten used to the beatings, all women do," he said this with all seriousness. At Lissa's brows arching, Doug began, "I would have loved you-"

Abruptly releasing her, Doug got out of the car and trod around to her side, wrenched her door open and pulled her out. Holding her arm in a vicious, tight grip, he marched her to the house.

They went up the steps and through the door the other men had left open. Inside the living room, the curtains were drawn, it was dim and shadowed, and dusty. Brett and Dillon were in the kitchen getting beer. The clanking of the bottles mingled with their raunchy joking.

Doug had moved his hand to clamp around the back of Lissa's neck when the two men returned. Brett tossed a beer to Doug who neatly caught it. He released Lissa for a second to open the beer and chug down half of it. Wiping his face, he watched Lissa's eyes flicker around the room seeking a way out.

He laughed crassly. "You are not going to leave this house alive, Keira, sweetheart. I have some games planned for you and me, and when I grow bored with you, I may give you to the others or just kill you right then instead of when they're through with you. I haven't decided yet."

Doug grinned at her spitefully. "By the way, if you think loverboy will find you, don't hold your breath. This house is leased under a friend who has no concrete connection to me. There is no way Jace Nico can find this house. So, just accept your fate with as much dignity as you can," his uproar of laughter grated in the air.

Lissa refused to let him see how terrified she was. She knew he was not making empty threats. Her heart sank deep in her soul, there was no way Jace, even if he got back in town soon, would ever be able to find her. She was so grateful she had made love with him. At least she would have that memory while Doug-

Her eyes travelled the dreary room, all hope draining from her quaking body. The living room was sparse with a beat up couch and several threadbare chairs, a couple of old tables, a television and that was it. An ashtray stuffed with cigarettes, porn and motorcycle magazines and beer bottles littered the stained coffee table in front of the couch.

Their eyes on Lissa, Brett flopped down on the couch and Dillon sprawled in a recliner. They both sucked at their beers, not bothering to hide their greedy lust blazing across at Lissa as she stood there with her hands twined so tightly together her fingers were colorless.

Doug gulped the rest of his beer and set the bottle on a table. He reached out and snatched up Lissa's hand. Heedless that he was crushing it, he pulled her roughly across the room past Brett and Dillon's lewd grinning faces.

He dragged her down a hall to one of the two bedrooms in the small house. When they reached the doorway he shoved her inside so hard she stumbled falling to her knees.

"Get up," Doug commanded harshly. He put his foot on her and shoved her out of the doorway, stepped inside, closed and locked the door behind him.

Lissa climbed to her feet, one hand clamped to her bruised side. She warily watched him approach her. He laughed when her eyes strayed to a gun visible on the dresser.

Closing her eyes, she knew better than to shrink or back away from him. She had to stand still as his hand lashed out slapping her hard on her face where he'd hit her earlier, the strength of it knocking to her knees again.

"Get up," he barked, his mouth twitched with a cruel grin.

She did, and he slapped her again and again knocking her down until she stayed on her knees, she could no longer struggle to her feet.

He moved to stand over her. "You made a fool of me, Keira, leaving me like that and disappearing." Bending over, he stabbed his hand in her hair, grabbed a handful and dragged her up to her feet. He pulled her face close to his, his teeth bright in a psychopathic grimace.

"I love that you let that uniquely beautiful hair of yours grow so long." He stuck his nose in her hair inhaling deeply. "God,

Keira, I missed you so much these past couple years. I truly have. There aren't that many true beauties like you. Perfect face." He rubbed his nose down the side of her cheek to her jaw. He put his hand on her chest, splayed his fingers and slid them all the way down the front of her.

Mumbling, "Perfect hot little body," he shoved his hand between her legs cupping and pinching her as hard and cruelly as he could.

Lissa cried out, managed to jerk out of his grasp and ran to the door. Pulling on the knob she heard his unhinged laughter behind her.

"That's my Keira, there's that fire I was looking for."

Lissa spun around, he was right there. Doug drew his hand back and back-handed her, she crashed into the door. Slumped against the door, stunned, she shook her head to clear it.

Using the door to drag herself back up to her feet, she turned her head as he grasped her blouse with both hands and tore it open, buttons flew everywhere.

Gripping the front of her neck he pulled her from the door. Dragging her to the middle of the room, he reached for her belt. She tried to run again, he caught her and threw her to the floor.

He unbuckled his own belt, snapped it out of his belt-loops and slapped it against his hand. "This is for when I get you naked." His smirking sneer crinkled his handsome face, his eyes gleamed with excited harsh promise.

Lissa leaned back on the dirty carpet propping her tormented body up on her hands, looking everywhere for a weapon. Other than the gun, the room held nothing but a bed, dresser and a nightstand.

Doug crouched beside her then pushed her down on her back. When she struggled to get up he hit her again and dropped on top of her. "You just keep fighting me, Keira," his voice a vile hushed whisper against her face. "I love it, it gives me, not that I need one, but it gives me a reason to smack you. I get so much more pleasure out of it when I have a reason."

He took her hand and forced it on his erection. "You see how hot beating you makes me?"

Doug let go of her hand and reached for her belt again. "I wanted to spend more time this first time playing with you, but I'm so fucking hot right now, I'm bursting, I can't wait to get inside you."

Lissa tried to sit up, he put his forearm against her neck forcing her back down. His arm choking her, Lissa clawed at it trying to pull it away from her throat. Her struggles only fueled him to move faster, act sadistically rougher.

He jerked at her belt with one hand until he got the buckle undone, then he yanked the button apart and pushed the zipper down. Lissa squirmed and pushed at him, trying to hit him, she wasn't giving up without a fight, but her efforts made no impression on him.

Doug needed both hands to get her pants down and off. Removing his arm from her throat, he moved to straddle her on his knees. He undid his own pants then he gripped the waistband of her jeans and pulled them down her hips.

Screaming at the top of her lungs, Lissa kicked and hit him, thrashing beneath him-

Just as something crashed through the window shattering the glass, shards exploding through the room, Doug hit her so brutally she almost blacked out.

Chapter Forty-Three

*J*ace landed on his hands, summersaulted and sprang to his feet.

Throwing off the cloths covering his hands and head from the broken glass, with a howling roar he barreled at Doug hitting him like a runaway Mack truck- so hard Doug hurtled off Lissa slamming on the floor with a grunt.

At the same time, gunshots and screams could be heard in the house.

The two men jumped to their feet and instantly punches were thrown. Jace struck such a brutal upper cut he almost knocked Doug off his feet, but Doug came back swinging. He caught Jace's jaw with a punch that snapped his head to the side.

Jace threw all of his brawny weight at Doug, catching him around the waist he took him down. Doug landed with a bang, he tried to roll away but Jace grabbed his hair to hold his head while he pummeled his face.

Doug jabbed his elbow into Jace's ribs making him release his hair, when he did Doug rolled away and crawled to the side.

Back on their feet, Doug feinted with his left and swung a powerhouse punch with his right, but Jace already had seen that he was right-handed and dodged the hit, at the same time he slammed his fist into Doug's throat.

Clutching his throat and coughing, Doug staggered backwards across the room, falling into his dresser.

"He has a gun!" Lissa screamed and lunged for the nightstand.

Doug snatched the gun off the dresser and whipped around to shoot Jace. Jace pulled out his own gun when Dough fired off a wild shot, the bullet managed to strike the gun right out of Jace's hand.

Steading the gun, aiming it at Jace, Doug's finger pressed on the trigger- Lissa yanked the lamp out of the wall and threw it at Doug hitting him in the head, the force of it knocking him backwards.

Jace vaulted at him, when he hit him the gun flew out of Doug's hand. The men fell to the floor again thrashing. Near the dresser, Doug scrambled with his hand until he reached the bat he knew was there behind it, pulled it out and swung it at Jace's head.

The hit wasn't solid but it stung him a glancing blow, enough to shake up Jace's vision.

A hand to brace his spinning head, Jace tried to lean back and get his ankle gun but Doug swung the bat again hitting him square and hard in the shoulder knocking his hand away from his ankle, and the force of the hit knocking Jace on his side.

Doug struggled to his feet. Panting and grunting, he stood over Jace with the bat up. Swinging the bat with all his might at Jace's head, Doug let out a guttural cry as the bat came around- Jace rolled-

Bang! A gun went off, bang- bang- bang- bang- Lissa stood with Doug's gun in both hands trying to empty it into her ex-husband. The gun was heavy and had a tremendous recoil causing it to shoot up and wild.

Shock, and a sick grin covered Doug's face as he looked from Lissa to the gun, then he dropped like a bag of rocks. Every bullet but one missed, the one that had gone into his heart.

On his knees, one hand still against his dizzy head, Jace crawled to Lissa and took the gun out of her shaking hands.

Bending over with his hands on the floor trying to catch his breath, panting like a horse after a race, Jace didn't take his eyes off Doug. Swiping blood off his mouth, he stuffed the gun into the

back of his jeans just as Ker came racing into the room with his weapon drawn.

Dragging his arm across his face, Jace planted both hands back on the floor. Through heavy pants, he gasped, "It's okay, Ker." His head hung, the blond hair flopping over his eyes dripped blood onto the floor.

Taking in the scene; Doug lying on his back, his lifeless eyes wide open staring blankly at the ceiling, Lissa still standing but motionless with shock, blouse torn asunder, her pants half down her hips, Jace on his hands and knees, his stomach sucking in and out with his deep huffing breaths. Ker holstered his weapon.

They could hear a car come roaring up the driveway. Ker's mouth twitched, he said to Jace, "That's our troops. I'll get them." He saluted Jace, bowed to Lissa with a grin, snagged the other gun off the floor, pivoted in one movement and left the room.

"Jace," Lissa whispered weakly.

Jace blinked, turned his head to her. His face fell like melting wax into relief, his eyes on her so filled with love he was pained by it. Climbing sorely to his feet he trod over to her.

He helped her pull her jeans back up then wound his arms around her and brought them both down, sinking to the floor. Facing her, he shuffled, moving her legs so they were wrapped around his waist and his legs around with her.

Hauling her in, he pulled her to him letting her sob into his shoulder. Sweeping his arms around her, Jace held Lissa breathlessly tight, his own tears wetting her hair.

They sat huddled like that until Victor stuck his face in the door. He was grinning ear to ear. "Hot damn, Lissa girl, you do like to make us run for our money!" He winked at her, said more seriously, "I'm glad you're okay, honey."

His dark eyes darted to Jace, "We'll be outside when you guys are ready," and disappeared from the doorway.

Lissa leaned back to look at Jace, he held onto her upper arms. Her perplexed voice shatteringly quiet, she asked, "How did you, I mean, there was no way you could find me." Her eyes warmed at the guilty grin studding his rugged face. The blue eyes twinkled with mischief.

"I uh, well, when I gave you the phone, I'd implanted a chip in it. So, ah, I could locate you if I wanted, uh, needed to." Jace lowered his head, looked up at her through his unbelievably long lashes.

She leaned back further slightly aghast. "You mean you were spyin' on me?"

His face colored with sheepish red. "Not exactly, well kind of." He lifted a lock of her curly hair, pressed it against his cheek. "You know how I worry about you running off, away, from me...into danger..."

How could she be mad at him with that little boy guilty look, his twinkling blue eyes that radiated such love for her it made her heart clench. Besides, his actions saved her life. She set a hand on his face, said softly, "I love you Jace, my husband."

Jace's skin paled, his jaw slack, he licked his dry lips. "You," his voice choked, he took her hands in his, "are you saying..."

"I did say it, Jace. I love you." She smiled at him.

Jace lightly stroked her skin, her swollen face and bruised eyes tearing at him. "You love me," he repeated in wonder. Color suffused up his neck to spread over his face. His mouth turned up in a broad smile then broke into a huge teeth-baring grin.

He grasped both sides of her head and pulled her in. Fastening his mouth over hers, sealing their lips together, he drew her with him into a splendorous dream, sailing up to the sky, just the two of them.

A few minutes of bliss then he moved his head back but didn't let go of her. "Damn, Lissa, I've loved you from the moment I saw those green eyes glowing through your car window." He brushed his lips across hers. "I just knew if I could just hold onto you long enough you would come around and love me too."

Her brows jumped, her indignant mouth dropped. "Is that really why you forced me tae marry-"

He cut her off by bussing her mouth again with his. He smiled against her lips. "I knew if I let you go I would lose you, you would run, not from me, but from your fear that I now know was Doug." He leaned back.

"You would leave me because you feared for my safety too, even though I wasn't aware of that at the time." He lifted a lock of curly hair off her shoulder and kissed where it had been. "I had to find a way to keep you until we destroyed your demon."

His joyful eyes burned into hers. "I love you, Lissa, my wife." He fused their mouths together until Julio came in to tell them they were still outside waiting.

Ignoring him, Jace's heart just twisted and broke seeing the wretched bruises and cuts all over Lissa's face and arms, fingerprints on her neck, chest. He winced at her torn jeans, and her blouse was a lost cause. He beat himself up for being too late to protect her from the pain and terror of the psychopathic evil Doug.

Jace had made his Warrington mission so important, that he neglected to foresee Doug Calero as a serious, real, imminent danger. And it almost cost Lissa her life.

His head hanging, Jace said miserably, "I don't deserve your love, Lissa. I held you prisoner just as that asshole did, to keep you and to protect you, and then I failed to protect you from him. I don't-"

Lissa threw her arms around him. "You saved me from him. If you hadn't come after me, Doug would have without a doubt killed me. I love you, Jace. Today is a new moment in our lives, let's move forward."

She kissed him, then smiled coyly, "We have a date, don't you remember? Unless," she cocked her head sideways at him, "you want tae renege, you've had second thoughts or you're not feelin' well enough tae give me more husbandly lessons?"

"You little minx," Jace slipped his hands under her and stood up with her in his arms, "I could be on death's door and I'd want you." He lowered his head to kiss her, murmured, "I love you baby."

She twined her arms around his neck as he carried her out of the house of hell to his truck.

Ker and the others were already in vehicles with Brett and Dillon trussed up like mummies looking like they'd been through a war.

Sliding Lissa into his truck, Jace climbed in the driver's side, leaned over and kissed her. Smiling into her glowing eyes, he said, "Let's go home, Wife."

Her hands twined around his neck, "Home is wherever you are, Husband, wherever you are."

Epilogue

A year passed before Warrington and the others started their trials.

Jace, Lissa and Jace's team stayed in Scotland through all the continuances. Upon conclusion of the trials and subsequent sentencings, Jace and Lissa will travel to Wyoming near Jackson Hole to build a home in the town where his family resides.

Fortunately, many of the players in Warrington's fraudulent schemes took pleas and received anywhere from 10 years to life.

The length of their sentences depended upon the extent of their participation in the fraud, the murders of the managers and the accountant, and the attempted murders of Jace, Julio and Donnie.

Diggler Riggs and Merle Burns received 50 years for their blackmail plot as well as their involvement in Jace and his friends' abductions and attempted murders.

Brett Rawley and Dillon Beck accepted plea deals of life with the possibility of parole after 25 years for aiding Douglas Calero in his kidnapping and endangerment of Lissa Mallory aka Keira Calero.

Sam Leeds, Bruce Kinder and Earl Bandman, the assassins that took out the accountant and managers, and also for kidnapping and attempted murder of Jace and his friends went to trial and all three were adjudicated guilty. Since Scotland doesn't have the death penalty, they received life without the possibility of parole.

However, in Scotland, more often than not, lifers are commonly released to relieve over-crowding.

Surprisingly, Bruce and Earl were shanked while awaiting transportation to prison after their sentencing. Neither survived. To date, the suspect(s) in their murders have never been caught and no witnesses came forward.

There were rumors at first about Ker and Victor possibly being involved, they'd been to the jail several times, but no proof of their involvement ever surfaced.

Warrington took his chance at trial. Every day he glared across the crowded room at Jace. On two occasions he was able to get word out to compatriots to take Jace out. Both times the culprits were discerned before they could do any damage. Sadly for them, none of them survived the shootouts that ensued during their aborted attacks.

After that, even with offering all the money in the universe, Warrington tried to hire more hitmen, no one took him up on his offers. Jace and his team's reputation for stealth and skilled fighting, their combat and shooting abilities surpassed any offer of riches for their deaths.

Warrington was found guilty on 67 various counts running from fraud to extortion, racketeering to kidnapping and murder. He was sentenced to life without parole.

Jace held Lissa's trembling hand. He had sat through every trial and every sentencing, but he refused to let her put herself through the trauma of all of them, especially now.

But Warrington's sentencing, he was the catalyst for their meeting each other, and now the end, the completion of the entire horrific events, Jace felt it would be closure for her. And him.

Warrington latched his hate-filled eyes onto Jace. Then the side of his lip curled up and he nodded. It was a threat. One of many he had forwarded to Jace over the last year or so.

Warrington's gaze flit to Lissa and both lips curved up in a grim, promising grin. His eyes flicked back to Jace, and his skin paled.

Jace inclined his head to Victor. With a huge grin of his own, Victor stood up from the pew and beamed at Warrington. Then he bowed to Warrington and Warrington blanched. The vile glint in the convicted man's eye withered as he realized his days were numbered.

In one lethal look it was made clear to Warrington that Jace would never allow a threat to hang over his wife's head. As the deputies grabbed each of Warrington's arms to haul him away, Warrington shot a frightened plea to Jace to spare him.

Jace stared stone-cold at him. There was not a shred of mercy in his eyes for the man.

"Nico! No!" Warrington screamed as he was dragged to the side door. "Nico don't! You can't! Please! NO! Stop! Guards help me, you don't understand! You're signing my death warrant! No! Help me!" His screams reverberated even after the door closed behind him.

Lissa was trembling terribly now, so much so Jace regretted bringing her. "Baby," he whispered cupping her chin. He lifted her face to his. "No one will ever hurt you again, I swear. Not you, not me, not," he set a large palm on her protruding belly.

"Come on, One. The curtain has come down, it's over, let's go," Ker said from the other side of Lissa. He rose to his feet and motioned for them to exit the courtroom.

The two men bracketed Lissa as stalwart sentries and ushered her out of the courtroom, down the hall, then down the elevator. It wasn't until they made it outside and the warmth of the sun stroked her face did Lissa let out a sigh and her shoulders relaxed.

Giving Jace a frown, Ker said, "Stress is not good for the bun." He had taken to calling Lissa's pregnancy The Bun as in the oven. Smiling tenderly at Lissa, he set his wide palm on her stomach. It had taken Lissa months to encourage the big cold Asian to touch her baby bump.

His grin widened with wonder. "He kicked, Jace, your brawny son kicked a mighty field goal just now!"

Jace wrapped his arm around his wife's shoulders and tugged her away from his friend, tucking her into his side. He trusted Ker with their lives, but it still rankled when any male put his hands on Lissa.

Knowing Jace's possessiveness of his bride, Ker winked impudently at Jace.

"Her," Lissa contradicted Ker. "Our daughter, not a son, boys." She smiled at the strapping males looking down at her with suddenly dour expressions.

"Bite your tongue, woman," Ker exclaimed, his eyes on her belly. "I'm not ready to fight off your daughter's suitors." He smiled at her. "She would no doubt have your beauty and boys will be falling all over their big feet to get at her."

"Over their dead bodies!" Jace swore, tugging her more tightly against him.

Sighing heavily, Lissa said, "Okay, fine. Let's have a couple of sons first and they can watch over her and save you two from jail time for assault!"

"That works for me," Ker agreed. "So," he said to Jace, "you ready to finally hit that honeymoon?"

Due to the trials, Jace and Lissa had put off their honeymoon.

"Yeah," Jace patted his pocket as Julio, Cad and Donnie approached. "Got the cruise information right here. After we meet with Lissa's dad we're on our way." He ignored Lissa's grimace.

Jace had brought Lissa home to Wyoming to meet his family. His mother was on cloud nine to greet her daughter-in-law and future grandchild.

However, she did give Jace holy hell for getting married without her and the rest of their family present. Jace indulged his mother throwing them a huge bash in honor of the union.

But, Lissa and her father were estranged since he'd refused to help her with Doug, not believing the charming man was capable of harming Lissa.

The news accounts of Doug's brutal beatings and kidnapping of Lissa and his consequent death at her hands brought her father to heel. He tried to reach out to Lissa but she balked. She was still hurt over his not believing her. Jace was working on trying to get father and daughter to reconcile.

Julio, Cad and Donnie wore beaming smiles. They were happy the trials were done and the sentencing over.

Donnie reached Lissa first, his gaze on her growing stomach. "So, you decide on names yet? You know Donald is a very revered name."

"Yo, right," Julio interjected. "A fine Hispanic name would suit the little dude. Something like Julio?" he suggested, bumping the younger man aside to get near to Lissa.

"Can't wait for my little niece or nephew to be born," Cad crowed.

"You're next, bro," Julio chuckled. "You and Ivy already have one and another on the way! I get to be an uncle all over the place between you and Jace!"

At a sudden commotion everyone's heads turned toward a restaurant on the other side of the street. In front of the red brick building decorated with hanging baskets of bright flowers, a man had his hands around a woman's neck and was shaking her.

"What the hell?" Julio barked.

The woman was young, clearly delicate and even from their distance across the street they could all see she was a beauty. She was trying to fight the man off, and scream, but he was choking the breath out of her.

At once, Julio, Cad and Donnie started towards the restaurant, all rumbling words like "Sonofabitch, putting his hands on a woman like that! I'll thump him into next week!"

"No," Ker said in a low growl, "I got this," and he stalked across the street with his hands rolled into tight fists.

The group paused and with wide-eyes watched Ker Dove pummel the man into the asphalt. When he was done, tugging his white shirt sleeves down from the black cuffs of his suit jacket, he bowed to the frightened woman with the warmest smile any of his friends had ever seen on the man.

Setting a huge hand on her slender shoulder, he leaned in and whispered in her ear. Then he held out his crooked arm.

The young woman was still for a moment. Then, she visibly pulled herself together. Firming her shoulders, she raised her head, spine straight, and tucked her small hand into Ker's brawny arm.

Ker glanced across the street to his friends, and with one of his rare yet gorgeous grins, he nodded to them. Then, after maneuvering the woman around the crumpled male lying bleeding on the street, he walked her towards the parking lot where he'd left his black Porsche.

Eyes rounded with astonishment, Lissa said to Jace, "Can you believe what we just witnessed?"

Jace glanced around at his friends. They all wore huge grins. He smiled. "Yeah." He lifted her hand and kissed it. "When we return from our cruise we can visit him and find out what happened next. You ready, my beautiful bride?"

Smiling shyly, Lissa nodded. "I'm always ready for you, my husband."

Grinning with a wink, Jace said, "I'm planning on holding you to that, baby." He bent and kissed her. "I love you, Lissa."

On her toes, kissing him back, Lissa responded, "And I love you, my hero."

They ignored the chuckles from their friends behind them.

The End

Dear Reader, thank you for purchasing or receiving a free copy of

<u>Jace's Elusive Woman!</u>

I know you could have picked any number of books to read, but you picked this book and for that I am extremely grateful.

I hope you enjoyed this novel, and if you did, **please leave a review where you purchased it***, and look for other exciting titles in my name!*

About the Author

Louise Furley loves writing romance with a huge helping of suspense. She finds it exciting to study new lands and learn everything she can about the area and the natives that call it home.

Sunny Florida is home where Louise is a graduate of St. Thomas University with a master's degree in Mental Health.

Louise is the author of numerous published novels. When not researching or writing, she is dreaming of unique plots, and discovering fresh ventures she hasn't yet experienced in the world.

Ride along with her as she travels new and thrilling journeys!